REFLECTIONS ON
A MOUNTAIN SUMMER

Reflections on
a Mountain Summer

Joanna M. Glass

ALFRED A. KNOPF   NEW YORK   1974

THIS IS A BORZOI BOOK
PUBLISHED BY ALFRED A. KNOPF, INC.

Grateful acknowledgment is made to the following for permission to reprint
previously published material:

Norma Millay Ellis: For "Scrub" and lines from "Spring," by Edna St.
Vincent Millay. Reprinted from *Collected Poems*, Harper & Row. Copyright
1921, 1948 by Edna St. Vincent Millay.

J. B. Lippincott and Company and John Murray (Publishers) Ltd.: For
lines from "The Barrel-Organ" in *Collected Poems* (in one volume), by
Alfred Noyes. Copyright 1906, renewed 1934 by Alfred Noyes.

Shapiro, Bernstein & Co., Inc.: For lines from "Oh! How I Hate Bulgarians."
Copyright 1926 by Shapiro, Bernstein & Co., Inc., New York, N.Y. Copyright Renewed and Assigned. Used by permission.

Library of Congress Cataloging in Publication Data

Glass, Joanna M
Reflections on a mountain summer.

I. Title.
PZ4.G55 [PS3557.L33] 813'.5'4 74-7221
ISBN 0-394-48919-5

Manufactured in the United States of America
FIRST EDITION

*For Austin Pendleton,
with thanks*

Part One

Somewhere in the Canadian Rockies there is a summer resort called Buena Vista. It is a magic place, or it was, and
though forty years have passed since I knew it well, I imagine
it hasn't changed all that much. I read that the Canadian
government is very fussy about its National Parks, and I know
they were concerned with matters of ecology and preservation
long before it became fashionable.

I talk a great deal about Buena Vista, especially as I grow
older, and I have been accused of exaggerating the beauty of
the place and enhancing it with qualities it doesn't have. My
friends listen to me and ask, "If it's all that great, why
haven't you ever gone back?" I have never gone back, and
never will, although I long to go. I don't know how to answer
the question, except to say that I was young in Buena Vista.
My initials are carved there in the trunks of old pines and
etched there in what was freshly poured concrete. I learned
to dance there, in a big log pavilion; I kissed my first girl in
a nearby canyon. Buena Vista is just one of those magic
places you could never return to and still keep your head together, as my daughter says.

In October of 1930, one of my father's friends returned to
Grosse Pointe with tales of glorious waterfalls, aquamarine
lakes, majestic mountains. Buena Vista was a place where
only man was vile, and not too many men had discovered it.
The friend's name was Josh Whitcomb. He was recently divorced, and was my father's age—both of them being in their
early forties. Mr. Whitcomb was invited to our house for
dinner, and I was permitted to dine with the adults while he
tried to persuade my father to build a summer place at Buena
Vista. I was very young then, twelve years old or thereabouts,
and I recall that this was the first occasion in my life when
I was given an insight into the relationship between my
father and mother. My father deferred to my mother that

evening, and I had seen him do that only once before, when there was an argument over a debt. He had bought a boat without telling her. It is amazing to me now, as I ease through my own middle years, that I could have been such an insensitive and imperceptive boy. However, when I was twelve, all I knew of my own parents was what I had overheard backstairs. At that time there was nothing about them that I had learned from direct confrontation. No, that's not entirely true. I knew them as individuals. I knew how far I could go with each of them. I knew their approximate fuse lengths and boiling points. I knew what they looked like. My mother was a tall woman, taller than all of our servants, almost as tall as my father, who was slightly over six feet. Her hair was red, a pale red mixed with a bit of gray. And she bore the bane of so many redheads: her eyelashes and eyebrows were barely visible. She would not wear make-up. She tried it once and said that it made her look like a street woman. Her hair, though it was "done" twice weekly at a salon, never looked "done." I used to think it didn't even look "begun." It always looked as if she had just come out of some sort of physical exertion, a long, windy walk, or a steep climb, or just off something—a horse or a tennis court. That was interesting because I never, ever, saw her exert herself physically. She was not at all athletic, and one of her regrets was that she never had been. She had only two regrets. First, she had never been any good at games; and second, she spent her twentieth year at a school in London, rather than in Florence, and she *kicked herself* for it because her mother had given her the *choice*. Florence had seemed just a little too daring, a little too loose and unpredictable. She had chosen London, had found it entirely predictable, and had regretted it ever since.

It did not occur to me that my mother was not pretty, although that certainly was the case. I did know, purblind as I apparently was at twelve, that my father was handsome. I knew that his clothes were "superb." My Grandmother Mac-

Allister, my mother's mother, always said, "Jimmy's clothes are simply *superb*." And, "It's an absolute *gift* to wear clothes so superbly." So I knew that my mother was awkward and timid and always looked slightly weather-worn, and I knew that my father was dashing, and striking, and always looked superb.

What is overheard backstairs is generally cruel, generally true, generally ungrammatical. My grandmother visited us one Christmas—I think I was eight then—and I knew immediately that none of the household staff liked her. She was a domineering woman. She saw to it that the staff updated their various lists of things. She was a stickler for proper lists of wine and silver and linen, and what was where, and what year it was purchased, and she wanted asterisks everywhere denoting what rooms things belonged in, and whether or not they were gifts. And if so, from whom. My mother was lax about all this, and pretty much let the help do as they wished. That Christmas Eve, while groggily sitting near a banister, hoping for a glimpse of Santa Claus, several pieces of information were inadvertently delivered to me. Our cook had brought in a cousin of hers to help with the extra Christmas entertaining. She and the cousin were sitting on a window seat two levels below me, smoking cigarettes, and rubbing each other's sore backs. I heard Cook say, "The young master's still believin' in Santa Claus, y'know. He made me leave a bottle of Coke and a piece of fruitcake in the drawing room." There was a pause and a groan as the cousin stood up and put out her cigarette. (They had brought along an old coffee can for this purpose.) "Too bad he looks like his mother," she said. "Aye," said Cook, "it's a rotten shame." The cousin then lit another cigarette. "I knew there weren't a Santa the day I came out of the womb." "Didn't we all," said Cook, "down there in Corktown?" The cousin, whom I didn't like because she had warts on her nose, snickered. "And where do you suppose Santa Claus is at this hour of the night?" Cook laughed and laughed. "Mounting a reindeer or two, no doubt!" The cousin began to howl. "Having himself a hell of a sleigh ride!"

I was not quite sure what all of this meant, but I remember feeling that I probably should not listen to any more of it. I recalled that my parents said it was necessary to take servants' talk with a grain of salt. I decided to wait as long as I could because I was sure they were wrong about Santa Claus. I rearranged my legs very quietly, and rested against a newel post. Puffs of smoke wafted up to me, turning from blue to yellow on the ascent. I tried to inhale it but it only made my eyes water. I then heard the cousin say, "The old lady's a hell of a crabapple, ain't she?" "Oh," said Cook, "she's the master puppeteer in this establishment." And then she summed up, in less than two minutes, the essential facts of my parents' marriage as she, and everyone else but me, saw them.

Because I have lived with these facts, and because they are the seed from which my story grows, I will put that conversation down here as near to verbatim as pride and memory and the passing of time will allow. And as I begin I'm aware of the brevity of the exchange, and it astounds me that the anguish of so many years could be tied up in so few sentences. Perhaps it's always that way with cold facts. (The headline this morning, for instance, is: FATHER SHOOTS FOUR CHILDREN, THEN HIMSELF.) Cook said the following, while her cousin sat behind her on a step and massaged her shoulders.

"She was left sitting pretty, y'know. Called all the shots then as now. Old MacAllister left her all that money from the lumber mills—three or four million it was. Miss Laura was twenty-six and a terrible string bean, y'know, with that carrot top and the pinched little face. They said she'd never been kissed at twenty-four. So the old lady found Jimmy Rutherford somewheres and bought him outright. Fetched him for Laura at a pretty price. They called it 'The Mac-Allister Purchase' in the clubs around town."

I fell asleep shortly after that, and nothing more was said

that is germane to my story. But for the sake of accuracy, and because the evening is so indelible in my mind, I'll report the rest of it. The cousin sat down beside Cook. "Poor Mrs. Rutherford. We're all in the same leaky boat, rich or poor." "Oh, yes," said Cook. "Still, better to be an old man's darling than a young man's slave." They both sighed and nodded. It all made sense to them.

I digress. I always digress. My wife says this habit is getting worse as I get older. According to Pat, all of my habits are getting noticeably worse as I get older. I think, in her eyes, I am the most rapidly deteriorating man in Grosse Pointe. She says that no matter what the topic, it's always a shaggy-dog story when I tell it. When I told her that I had decided to write the story of my mother and Winger Burns, she said, "Well, of course, you'll have to publish it *privately*. You can't possibly write an interesting story because you'll digress *ad nauseum*." I said, "Pat. Life, really, is only a digression between sleeps." I thought that was rather clever. She must have, too, for she said, "Who said that?" "I said it, just now," I replied. "No," she said. "Somebody said that." Off she went to Bartlett's, hellbent for leather. She looked under "Life" and "Digression" and "Sleep," and couldn't find a thing. Now, I'm the first to admit there's nothing new under the sun, but I do believe that particular wording of that particular thought is original with me. Pat is not an unpleasant woman once you learn to keep your distance.

I did, however, have an anxious moment yesterday morning when I began to write. She plunked a coffee tray down on my desk and said, "What in God's name are you going to call it?" I know very well what I'm going to call it, and I know that she will disapprove. I don't really expect her sympathy and support in this endeavor, but I won't get on with it at all if we start quibbling over the title. So I told her I hadn't decided. I told her I'd probably find the title somewhere in the writing. But I had written the letters

R.O.A.M.S. at the top of the first page, and she saw it. "For God's *sake*," she said. "I hope you're not going to call it *Roams!*" "No," I said, "I'm not going to call it *Roams.*" "Oh, Jay," she said. "I *know* you! You're going to call it *Roams!*" I said I'd see her at lunch.

I should perhaps point out that Pat's reading has always been rather narrow. She tells everyone she loves to read poetry and, indeed, she does have an affinity with Edna St. Vincent Millay. She occasionally quotes all of "Spring" rather lugubriously at parties. She and Miss Millay both attended Vassar. I believe the resemblance ends there.

I I

When Mr. Whitcomb came to extol the virtues of Buena Vista, the backstairs conversation fell into place. It was clear that my mother held the purse strings. It was also clear that she did so reluctantly. And though I've never had a very high regard for my father, the ravages of time and my own intricate arrangements in life have made me realize that he was in an impossible position. Damned if he did and damned if he didn't, no matter which way he turned. He was enthusiastic about Buena Vista. That was evident from the beginning. Because of the delicacy of his situation he tried not to be too obvious about his mounting excitement, but I saw it, and Mr. Whitcomb saw it. My father and Mr. Whitcomb resorted to an uncomfortable sort of idle chatter while they waited to see if my mother was enthusiastic. She, not wanting to appear to be twisted around my father's little finger, didn't register much of anything. After an hour or so she suggested that Mr. Whitcomb let them have a week or two to think it over. My father didn't like that tactic at all, and began to ask questions about lease arrangements, land and water. There followed a long interval in which Canadian politics was discussed and a great deal was said about prevalent attitudes in Ottawa. Most of it was boring to me, but at one point Mr. Whitcomb raved about the variety of flora and fauna at Buena Vista. Though I didn't know much about my parents, I did know that Mr. Whitcomb's vocabulary was of the meat-and-potato variety. The words "flora" and "fauna" were heavy on his tongue. We'd been studying Greek mythology at school, and to this day, when I hear the words "flora" and "fauna," my mind goes through the same chain of thoughts it did that evening. Castor and Pollux, Damon and Pythias, Flora and Fauna.

Mother said that she thought Buena Vista was a very long way to go to get away from the heat, especially since we had Lake St. Clair right across the street from us. Father said, yes, but Lake St. Clair was so damned flat. I yawned and escaped into vivid imaginings of surrealist lakes that weren't flat—lakes located lopsidedly on the hypotenuse of a mountain slope. I heard Mr. Whitcomb observe that if we lived on a mountain we'd probably vacation in the desert. "Well," said Mother, "it sounds altogether too remote for Jimmy." My father winced. "What do you mean by that?" he asked. Mr. Whitcomb jumped in and said that she just meant it might be too isolated, but the isolation, actually, was the charm of it all. Mother looked resigned. She always seemed to be on the periphery of a discussion where one person explained to another person the precise meaning of what she had just said. We do this with shy people, and it's terribly unfair. I catch myself doing it with my daughter, Deborah, who is very much like my mother. I am forever trying to explain to Pat the exact meaning of Deborah's every utterance and when I see Deborah's resigned expression I realize what my mother went through all those years.

Exactly one year before, to the month, the stock market had crashed. Though we were not affected, nearly everyone we knew was. It was fashionable to cry poor and it was most unfashionable to flaunt your riches when so many people were either ruined or at least left quaking. Mother felt there was something vaguely immoral about spending so much money when so many people were suffering. Father hadn't thought about it, but when he did, his only concern was that we would have to avoid publicizing it or every Tom, Dick and Harry would be hitting us up for a loan. Mr. Whitcomb soon showed signs of irritation. "Oh, come on, Laura! Where's your sense of adventure? Everybody's putting up those tacky lodges in Ontario. Everybody's tramping off to Charlevoix with everybody else every summer. You're *individuals*, Laura! You and Jimmy don't have to run with the pack. You don't have to be like everybody else." "No," said Mother, "we're not like everybody else." My father moved to the edge of his chair and clutched his water goblet. "What she *means*, Josh, is that all of these people tramping off to Charlevoix have something in common. They love the great outdoors. Laura just isn't comfortable out in the wild. I think she means that I can fish and hunt and fool around with boats without going halfway round the globe every summer. Right, Laura? That's what you mean."

Mr. Whitcomb would not let up easily. (We learned, years later, that he received a fifteen percent commission on the house my family built.) "Laura, you're only thirty-eight years old and you're in a helluva rut. It's fine and dandy to stay indoors and let the dust settle on you and read those strange little books nobody's ever heard of. Even bookworms need a change of scenery now and then. At Buena Vista you'd get the change of scene and none of the guff. Just think—*think* what it'd be like at Charlevoix! They all ride together and swim together and picnic together. Jesus, you can't blow your nose in Charlevoix without it being discussed up and down Woodward Avenue all winter. You wouldn't like that, Laura."

"No," said Mother. "Neither would Jimmy."

"What she *means*," said my father, "is that we've always tried to keep our affairs private." There was a silence. Mother stifled a yawn. Father's face became florid. "Josh thinks this would be the best of all possible worlds. All kinds of marvelous outdoor stuff for me and no one to organize us and make demands on you. Peace and quiet and tranquillity and anonymity." Mother was tired of the whole thing. She wilted visibly after eight in the evening, and it was well past nine. She looked so drab and pitiful at the end of the table. This was due, in part, to her clothing. She had been directed, in her youth, to steer clear of bright colors because of her hair. The two acceptable colors for redheads in those days were lavender and Nile green. I tagged along with her frequently on shopping excursions and I knew the exact moment when she would say, "Yes, that's nice, but do you have it in lavender or Nile green?" Shopping was drudgery for her. She knew she never looked well in anything, and her height was a constant embarrassment. The salesclerks said, "Oh, Mrs. Rutherford, you're so terribly *tall*, you can wear anything." She wore a pained expression at those times. I believe I was taken along purposely, for she would say, "Excuse me, I really must go before my boy tears up your shop!" I, who was quite content to stand silently by, ogling the girdles and bras, would be whisked out of the shop and onto the street among all those fully clothed women.

"I believe Laura is ready to turn in." Mr. Whitcomb had finally noticed her slumping in her chair. "Yes," she said, "it's been a long day." She wore a mauve satin dress, which was quite becoming, but it had a little lace bolero over it that looked, unfortunately, like a bed jacket replete with ribbons at the front. "And certainly," she said, "it's past Jay's bedtime." "Hey," said Mr. Whitcomb. "What do *you* think of Buena Vista, Jay?" "Oh," I said, "I think it sounds great. I think we should do it." "Do you really, Jay?" asked my mother. "Yes," I said. "It sounds terrific. I sure don't want to go to Charlevoix with all those other goons." "Well, in that case, we'll have to give it serious consideration," said Mother.

And so it was that plans were drawn up for Timberline, a

place I always described, with a nonchalant flick of my cowlick, as being somewhere in the Canadian Rockies.

III

Not a day passed between November 1930 and June 1932 when there wasn't one brouhaha or another over Timberline. The problems were legion, and I was the only one in the house who maintained any objectivity about the idea. Even in the thick of it, I knew the snags would get ironed out and I couldn't understand why such an exciting project had the entire household traumatized.

Father had to acquaint himself with the difficulties of communication between Calgary, Alberta (the nearest city to Buena Vista), and Grosse Pointe. He blithely tried to make contact with the contractor one day, and told the operator he wanted Calgary, Canada. The operator asked, "What Providence is it in?" Father said, "For God's sake, it's not in Providence, it's in Canada." A connection was made and he then had a brief conversation with a bricklayer in Seekonk, Rhode Island. He soon learned to say, "Please get me Calgary. Calgary is the city. It's in the Province of Alberta. That's in western Canada." Then we hired an architect from Chicago—the "bulwark of the nation"—and he began coming to our house with cases full of oversized papers and bundles of brochures. The architect went to Buena Vista to "have a look at the organics" and my father went to the Detroit Library and read everything ever printed about the Canadian Northwest. He referred to the project as "his baby." He would say to Mother, "Laura, this is *my* baby." Mother referred to the project as an enormous undertaking. She did have to be consulted about furnishings and draperies and kitchen equipment, but where my father could rummage around in brochures and swatches for hours, each detail seemed to fatigue my mother. We all noticed her becoming more and more lethargic, less and less interested.

"Look at this," said Cook one morning.

"What?" I asked.

"Your mother's breakfast tray. Look at it!"

"What's the matter with it?"

"There's no *food* on it! There's only *pills* on it! Pills for waking and sleeping and headache and nerves. She'll be put in an asylum before that lodge gets built."

As the difficulties began to mount—the problems of building into a nearly vertical piece of rock, the problems of a "dishonest" contractor in Calgary who apparently thought all Americans were wealthy idiots, the fact that my mother was convinced that the stores in Calgary were little better than trading posts—as all of this rose to a climax, she became hysterical. She reproached my father and me at dinner one evening, calling the Buena Vista venture a horrendous mistake. Couldn't we see that she was at the end of her tether? Couldn't we, while tallying costs, see the terrible toll it was taking on her mental health? There was nothing to do but write Grandmother MacAllister and tell her the thing had escalated to a point beyond all endurance.

She wrote Grandmother MacAllister that evening, pleading with her to come and "settle the thing." Grandmother MacAllister wrote back that it was high time Laura learned to finish what she started. Mother then called Grandmother MacAllister long distance, and said *she* hadn't started it. God knows, she had no desire at all to go to some godforsaken place in the Canadian Rockies every summer. Well, then, who *had* started it? Mother replied: Jimmy, Josh and Jay started it and before she even had a chance to think of all the ramifications, a bunch of dishonest people were drilling into a piece of rock and sending her exorbitant bills that were written in Arabic or something. Grandmother MacAllister asked Mother if she wasn't signing the checks. Mother replied, "Yes, I've signed reams of checks!" "Well, then," said

Grandmother MacAllister, "you must have it under control."
My grandmother believed that, in any imaginable circumstances, the person who signed the checks was the person in
control. Mother said she wasn't in control of anything. Why,
even Cook, who was as sensitive as a fossil, was predicting a
nervous breakdown. She wept, and said she was ready to jump
off the Foshay Tower if someone didn't come and settle the
thing.

My mother was born in Detroit, and she died in Grosse
Pointe. On the two or three desperate occasions in her life
when she threatened suicide, she said she would jump off the
Foshay Tower. It made no difference that the Foshay Tower
was in Minneapolis. She was so distraught at those times no
one ever questioned it. I used to think that I'd find some
placid period in her life and ask her why she had chosen the
Foshay Tower for her suicide. Even now, as I write this, it
seems humorous. You'd think you could ask someone a question like that, with a gentle little smile, during a placid
period, and get a reasonable answer. I never did find the right
moment, though I continued looking for it through her sixty-
eighth year.

At any rate, Minneapolis was saved from another statistic
when Grandmother MacAllister came and settled the thing
in short order. I regret that I never knew my grandmother
better. She was a strong, decisive woman (German, though
she married a Scot), and I have always been drawn to people
like that. After my grandfather died, and after she had gotten
my mother settled away for better or worse, she decided that
she didn't want to finish her days in Detroit. She said that
it certainly was a good place to make your first million, but
no one had ever accused it of being civilized. She had a large
house on Seminole, in Indian Village, which I remember
visiting only twice. I recall that she had a definite bent toward
Oriental art and furnishings. The house was crammed with
huge vases, jade ornaments, Chinese rugs, rosewood tables,
old scrolls and a myriad of ginger jars atop every flat surface.

I remember thinking that it all must have cost a lot of money. Yes, Grandmother said, the MacAllisters had a lot of money. "How did we get it?" I asked. "From trees," she said. She said it was probably sacrilegious, but just between the two of us, she asked God to bless every tree in Michigan at the end of her prayers every night. God would forgive her because God knew how poor she had been as a child, and God kept track of these things. She sold her house and bought a train ticket to San Francisco. She purchased a house on Nob Hill and, according to murky allusions made by my father, she conducted herself very badly. Because of what I'd heard of San Francisco, and because she was, to me, old and decrepit, I imagined that the worst she could do was take a puff of opium now and then. Whatever she did, she was loath to leave it. She complained bitterly whenever she had to come back to Grosse Pointe. I like to think it wasn't entirely the fault of the town, but rather that when she returned she stayed with us, and saw at first hand what she had wrought with the MacAllister Purchase.

She came, and went through the house like a whirlwind. She frowned at my stooping posture and she frowned at Cook's bulging belly. She ordered me into a chair, and stuck a ruler between my shoulder blades, and she ordered Cook into a corset. And then she looked at the blueprints for Timberline—studied them, actually, for two whole days. She called the White Glove Secretarial Service and hired a typist. It must be clear by now that I have a talent for remembering minutiae like this. I remember that particular secretarial service because I've always believed that names should mean something. I fully expected the girl either to arrive wearing white gloves or, better yet, to type with them on. Needless to say, she did neither. It's just one of those silly little memories that clutter up the brain.

Grandmother and the girl locked themselves in the library and wrote a twenty-page order to the Hudson's Bay Company in Calgary. Furniture, linens, rugs, draperies and kitchen equipment were ordered. A Nile-green bedspread was ordered for my mother's room. And then Grandmother set about ordering skins. Bearskins for my father's room and sheepskins for mine. She didn't question my mother on any of this and Mother didn't seem to want any input. She only said, when Grandmother was ordering some chalk drawings of Indian chiefs, that she hoped Timberline wouldn't turn out to be "hokey." She suggested that Grandmother look up a Canadian artist named Tom Thomson, who did brilliant, bold oils of northern scenes. Grandmother expressed surprise. Who in the world was this man Thomson?

Now, my mother read a great deal and knew a great deal. However, people were always surprised when she said anything that reflected it. I remember one afternoon when she and I were sitting together at some sort of fund-raising tea. A question came up. "What *is* it called?" said one of our neighbors, recently returned from Africa. "You *know*," she said, "when that little bird lives on the rhinoceros and eats the bugs off its hide?" Mother waited to see if anyone would answer. No one did, and just as the subject was being changed, she said, "Symbiosis," very quietly. They all held their teacups in mid-air and, rather than looking pleased at having the answer, looked, I thought, rather miffed. When we went out to our car, Mother asked me if the tea hadn't been a terrible bore for me.

"Terrible. You sure know how to pick 'em."

"I didn't mind it too much today. I enjoyed having the answer to that question."

"But didn't you think they looked rather miffed when you said it?"

"Did you notice that? I always get that reaction when I know something. Really, I might as well be the proverbial dumb blonde."

I didn't quite know what to say, but I wanted to reassure her.

"Gee, I'm glad you're not."

"Are you?"

She pushed the gear into first. "I'm not."

We ended up with a dozen reproductions of Tom Thomson's paintings at Timberline. Maybe it's because these paintings are so intimately tied to my youth, maybe it's because I lack the truly catholic appreciation of art that Pat possesses; whatever the reason, I have never seen nature paintings, anywhere, that convey to me such sublime communion between the artist and the outdoors. I don't know much about Thomson—he was apparently as remote in personality as the northern Ontario terrain he chose to paint. He died (drowned), in 1917, at the age of forty, and I understand that he didn't actually hit his artistic stride until the last few years of his life. I don't know of any American museum where his work can be seen, but there is a large selection in the National Gallery, in Ottawa, and another collection at the Art Gallery of Ontario, in Toronto. There are no self-portraits, interiors, Bohemian friends sprawled on cushions in lofts. He painted rivers, rapids, waterfalls, clouds, wildflowers, saplings, sumac, birches and pines. He painted these over and over again— the pictures, combined with each other, give a full array of the northern day. Birches at dawn, at high noon, at sunset, in moonlight. The changing seasons also fascinated him, so there are maples deep in snow, maples steeped in autumnal woodland decay, buds breaking through frost.

Not too long ago, I took Debbie up to Montreal to see "Expo." We were walking past an art gallery on Sherbrooke Street when I stopped dead in my tracks. Several of Thomson's oils were exhibited in the window. I was suddenly transported back to Timberline. My mother flashed through my mind, glowing, happy, with a garland of purple wildflowers in her hair. My God! Standing there on Sherbrooke Street, shaking, looking at Thomson's wilderness, trying not to look at Thomson's wilderness, I heard her laugh again the way I never had before and never did afterwards. I felt dizzy. My eyes blurred. I began to topple and finally had to support myself against a wall. "What in the world's the matter?" asked Deb. "Oh," I said, "I'll be all right. I've just been reminded for the umpteenth time that I must never go back to Buena Vista."

The dozen reproductions provided me with a great deal of cheer and enjoyment, in among the chiefs and squaws, tomahawks, antlers and bearskins. Additionally, there was a forty-foot-high totem pole just outside the front door. Grandmother ordered it that day, telling the White Glove typist that it was last but not least, and that it would be the Rutherfords' *pièce de résistance*.

I V

I have often thought that our day-to-day existence in Grosse Pointe could be described as a continuing estrangement. Never lesser, never worse, never dwindling, never developing —simply continuing on a line. There were days, weeks, when my mother and father had no contact at all, and it was not until much later in my life that I realized how very quiet our house was when compared with other houses. And then there were times when the animosity between them was palpable, and I was convinced that mine was the worst of all possible worlds. Occasionally there were arguments, odd, knock-down-drag-out affairs in remote corners of the house, remote, that is, from wherever I happened to be. The worst, of course, was yet to come. I have only one other memory of our days at home, prior to going to Timberline. It was a morning in March 1932, the day after a record snowfall. It is the last thread in my mind that connects me with any semblance of belonging, of safety and security, of protection. That is, of family.

The sun came streaming in through the library window, and bounced off the blueprints I had spread on the floor. The windows in the library were leaded glass, and as I looked out onto Lake St. Clair, I could see a big freighter slowly centering itself in the diamond-shaped panels of the window, like a ship enclosed in a bottle. Across the lawn, on the patio, giant icicles hung from some heavy metal furniture that had been left there. It was, for me, unbearably exciting to think of moving into Timberline that summer. It was so far away, the journey would be so long and arduous and nothing, absolutely nothing but the essentials could be taken with us. My bike, my comic books, my chemistry set, *all that junk* in my room had to be left behind. It would be enough of a job just getting three human beings across the plains. And this was something of a departure on Lake Shore Road. Servants generally went ahead of the family and opened the summer place. We were not taking servants. Mother announced, without the apprehension that usually accompanied her announcements, that *she* would cook for us, and she would hire a local woman to clean out the rubble once a week.

I had told all of my friends about Timberline, but I couldn't seem to communicate to them that this was going to be the rarest of experiences. My closest pal during my thirteenth year was Dougie Clark—a very hard boy to impress. Dougie lived in Flint, Michigan, but attended Croydon, our school in Grosse Pointe. His parents were divorced and his mother lived permanently in Paris, while his father was an executive at the Buick Motor Company, in Flint. Dougie went to Paris every summer. Whenever we accused him of being from the sticks, he would intimidate us with stories of Paris and how, under those bridges, you could see just about everything you'd care to see and some things that were so sickening they made you barf.

I would try to counter with tales of my visits to the old Baldwin place on Jefferson Avenue. It was a nineteenth-century mansion which had been sold to a real estate developer. Collectors and interior decorators had ransacked the place and taken whole fireplaces and paneled walls and marble pillars out of it, and what was left was pretty scary after eight o'clock in the evening. The preceding summer Dougie brought home, tucked away in a copy of the *Leather-Stocking Tales*, a used condom he had found near Les Invalides. I had found, in a shower stall on the fourth-floor servants' quarters at the Baldwin place, a douche bag. I alluded to this exotic piece of equipment one day and Dougie replied, "Great! Where'll we rendezvous?" We met in our garage that evening.

"You may be interested to know, Red, that this little item is a French Safe."

"What's it for?"

"Oh, Jesus, Red. You slip it on just before you come."

"Just before you come to Les Invalides?"

"Oh, Jesus, Red. Just before you come all over the goddamn vagina!"

"Oh. Boy, it's awful big."

"Listen, dumbo, this one's been used."

"What do they look like when they're new?"

"How the hell should I know?"

"Well, Dougie, take a gander at *this*. I've been saving it for you."

"Big deal. What are you going to do with it? Sprinkle the petunias?"

"What are you going to do with your French Safe?"

"Educate all those goons at school."

"Geez. I thought you'd be interested."

"I'm not. I'm afraid it's a singularly uninteresting find. I'll tell you something, though. You know what the whores in New York use for a douche?"

"No idea."

"Coke."

"You're kidding!"

"Listen, they carry a bottle with them. They shake it up till it gets all bubbly and they put it in. Then they're clean and ready for the next trick. What do you think of that?"

"Geez, Dougie. I think I'm going to barf."

I could not convince Dougie Clark that there'd be much of interest at Buena Vista. I asked him to come over Saturday morning and look at the blueprints with me. I told him they were really super, and I wanted to show him some photographs our architect brought back with him. He declined, saying he could care less, and that he hoped I had a lot of fun sitting around some mountain watching the caribou screw. So I looked at the blueprints alone that morning.

Timberline sat halfway up Mount Binnie, overlooking the small town of Buena Vista. Dad said it would be quite a hike up from the road, but that the hike would be good for all of us. Especially for Mother, he said, because she was altogether too sedentary in her ways. On the blueprints the living room looked cavernous. It ran the entire width of the house and was, actually, two living rooms with stone fireplaces and furniture groupings at each end. It was a two-story lodge; however, the second floor stopped short of the living room, and there was a beamed cathedral ceiling. There was a wooden arc-shaped balcony around the upstairs bedrooms—the four bedrooms and two bathrooms opened onto a view of the living room beneath. There was a space labeled "gallery" under the balcony. You had to walk through it to enter the kitchen, dining room, utility room and bathroom at the back of the house. I looked at the gallery on the blueprint, and a chill went over me. I thought it would be dark and gloomy. I thought the chiefs and squaws and antlers were destined for that space. I was right. However, since the entire back of the house and the front of the living room were glass, there was not a gloomy corner anywhere in Timberline. From the back of the house you would be able to see Mount Binnie's twin peak, Mount Elizabeth. The rooms were labeled: "Bedroom, Mrs. R.," "Bedroom, Mr. R.," "Bedroom, J.R.," and "Guest Room." There was something frustrating about the blueprints. I wanted to see the view from the living room. I wanted to smell the air and run up the staircase and roll down the hill. I wanted to peer down into the living room from the balcony. I wanted to ride a *palomino mare* up Mount Binnie! Perhaps I had, already, invested the place with qualities it didn't have. I fully believed that our family would somehow be different—behave differently—within those rooms I saw outlined on the blueprint.

I've always been that way about any new venture. I like to think that at some other altitude, in some other clime, in different rooms with different decorations, Pat and I and Debbie will be able to shake off all the niggling little petty days that make up our past. We'll meet each other freshly each morning and trust each other to be gracious and kind. And we'll tell stories none of us has ever heard before, and laugh instead of grunt. And the advertising won't be so obnoxious and the newspapers will carry good news and people will gladly give you directions to wherever it is you want to go. The airlines well understand people like me. I wouldn't be surprised if they've got my number on a chart in one of their market research offices. I'm the guy you see on the billboards. I go to luaus and Oktoberfests and the Mardi gras. I fly American; I fly the friendly skies. I come away with them; I get away from it all at the drop of a hat. Pat says I am the eternal child in this respect. But then, Pat is one of those people who've gone through life holding up the line at the counter while they count their change. Pat expects to be short-changed and, of course, generally is. Even when it isn't pounds or lire or francs. Even when it's right over on Kercheval, among the natives, buying Vicks cough drops—poor old Pat is invariably shortchanged.

My father entered the room, and was surprised to see me on the floor. "Hey, Bucko! What are you doing?" I told him I was having a fine time looking at the blueprints. "Oh, yes. I thought Dougie was coming over this morning." I told him Dougie wasn't very interested in Buena Vista. He went over to the fireplace and threw a log on the grate. "Dougie's a pretty sophisticated kid," he said. He poked the fire a couple of times. "Isn't it the damndest thing? We always build fires

when it snows. We never build fires when it's just plain cold."
He turned and looked at me. The blueprints were spread all
around me, every which way. "Careful not to crush those.
They're pure gold, you know." "Yeah. How much is all this
going to cost, anyway?" He paused, and looked as if he intended to sit down. Then he decided not to, and started for
the door. "Oh, I don't know. Fifty—sixty thousand, I guess.
Your mother and I don't often discuss money."

He stopped at the door and looked out the window. This
time an ore barge was making its way up the lake. He stood
there uncomfortably, not really in the room, not really out
of it. I had rarely seen him so pensive. I knew if I didn't say
something he would wander out, and I wanted him to stay.

"Boy, those ore barges are the ugliest thing on the lake."
He came into the room and sat down on the floor beside me.
"I've always thought so. Have to be careful where you say
that, though, Jay. On Lake Shore Road those ore barges are
manna from heaven."

He looked down at the blueprints, and began playing with
some loose rubber bands.

"You're excited about this, aren't you?"

"Yes, I am. I can hardly wait to move in. I think it's going
to be terrific, having Mom doing the cooking."

"Yes."

"I guess she'll have to buy a recipe book."

"Yes. And wear an apron."

He got up and sauntered over to the fireplace again. He
rearranged some logs and watched the new flames jump for a
moment.

"You know, Jay, it's going to be a lot of fun. But you
mustn't expect too much of your mother."

I don't know why I asked the following question. The room
and the fire, and the conversation, had all been pleasant up
to that point. Something tugged at my brain, and I asked,
"Will you have to go out so often in the evenings at Buena
Vista?" I felt that, at that moment, he removed himself from

the room, and the conversation. He mumbled, almost inaudibly:

"I don't know. Small town. Probably quite constricting. Maybe I'll exhaust myself. House should be large enough. Need a large house when people don't do anything. Hike and fish and swim. Really exhaust ourselves. Go to bed early."

He moved about the room, idly touching things, not lighting anywhere. I knew he'd leave soon. My question had ruined it. "Who's the guest room for?" I asked. "Oh, Josh Whitcomb is coming up for a while. He and I are going to do some climbing." He paused again, and suddenly a look of relief passed over his face.

"*That's* what I was going to do today! Have to see about ordering some climbing gear. Ropes and picks, boots with cleats. Better get right to it!"

He moved out of the room quickly, happy to have a designated task.

V

At lunch yesterday, Pat was in the doldrums. I assumed that something had happened at the Art Institute. She volunteers there three mornings a week, taking groups of schoolchildren around on tours. Her face was immobile. She looked like a candidate for the fifth head at Mount Rushmore. We began our soup without a word and it was, as usual, up to me to break the sound barrier.

"Rowdy bunch today?"

"Run-of-the-mill teen-agers. Pawing each other."

There she was again, right there between Abraham and Teddy. Nothing more was said until the soup was finished, and a crab salad was set in front of us.

"I notice a great deal of wastepaper coming out of your study these days."

"Yes. I make a lot of false starts. But as you know, even Michelangelo threw away a lot of marble."

"Who said that?" (She starts for the library, and Bartlett's.)

"Dorothy Parker."

"Oh. Jay, I don't see how you can write that story and still respect your mother's memory."

"I can do it, Pat, because to my mind the one doesn't contradict the other."

"You have to admit that she behaved abominably. The saga of Winger Burns was a terrific *lapse* on her part. And now you want to write it all down for the whole world to know."

"I'll use a *nom de plume.* Nobody'll know."

"Oh, well, I suppose I shouldn't waste breath on it, since you'll have to publish it *privately.*"

"Right. I'll publish it privately and use my own name. Then only a few close friends will know."

"God help us all!" she exclaimed. "If you had any respect for your mother's memory you wouldn't write it at all."

A pear and a piece of Gruyère were placed in front of me. Nobody in the world peels and quarters a pear quite so deftly as Pat. I somehow always end up with juice running down my wrist, into my cuff. I don't like eating fruit at table. I sometimes stop at the market when I'm driving alone. I buy a pound of cherries and sit in the car and spit the pits hither and yon, all over the place. The business of getting the pits to the plate, at table, is an ordeal.

"You're so sloppy with fruit! It gets noticeably worse as you get older."

No matter how your stomach may be churning, you can appear relaxed and calm while fiddling with a pipe. You can sit back and light a pipe and puff on it gently. You can loosen your limbs and cross your legs and pause many times between sentences. You can play for time while folding up the pouch and putting away the reamer and matches. You can also spill tobacco all over the cloth, but she didn't notice. I imagine it's easier to watch me lighting a pipe than it is to watch Pat lighting a cigarette, if you were, say, a fly on the wall. Pat turns the package sideways and gives it a swift tap on the bottom. Then, heaven help me, she *sucks out the cigarette with her pursed lips!* That one gesture—sucking it out of the pack with her lips—is something I simply cannot watch. I don't mind the nervous huffing and puffing, I don't mind the hacking, bronchial cough, I don't mind the smoldering smell of her clothing. I don't even mind the way she closes her right eye when the weed hangs off the right side of her bottom lip. But when she sucks it out of the pack, I avert my eyes and concentrate on our centerpiece—a porcelain peacock.

"How's it going, really?"

"How's *what* going?"

"*Roams.* How far along are you?"

"It's awfully hard to discuss out of context. I'm way back there where Josh Whitcomb came to dinner and talked about Buena Vista."

"My God, that was the *beginning!*"

"Yes. That's where I am. At the beginning."

"Did you put in that stuff about the two Irish maids on Christmas Eve?"

"Yes, as a matter of fact, I did."

"I'll never forget the time you told me that. You've never been able to do an Irish accent."

"Well, I'm not quite up to your rendition of Abie and Rosie."

"Oh, come off it! Did you write it with an Irish accent?"

"I tried to."

"I'll have to read it and see if it comes off better in print."

She pushed her chair back and drank her coffee. The bloom has long been gone from Patricia's cheeks but something, perhaps the crab, has expelled the sallowness apparent at the beginning of the meal.

"Miss Fenstrom used to say it was all a matter of selection."

"What was?"

"Writing."

"I guess that's right."

"Miss Fenstrom had dinner with Edmund Wilson once."

"Oh?"

"She used to say you have to select the interesting parts and leave out the boring ones."

"Right. But who's to judge?"

"The audience judges. You have to know your audience. Have you thought about that? For whom are you writing it?"

"Oh, just a few close friends, I think."

She leans back and pinches the brown leaves off a nearby fern. She rolls them in her palms, till crumpled, and drops them on the floor.

"I'd like to help with the title, if I may."

"That's nice of you, Pat. Why don't you think about it for a week or so and give me some suggestions."

"Yes, I'll do that. If it's going to be about Winger Burns it should definitely convey something about Winger Burns."

"Not necessarily. It's also about *what might have been.* Irrevocable decisions. Unrecoverable youth."

"Nonsense! You must be more specific. If it hadn't been for Winger there'd be no *raison d'être*, would there? And what was Winger all about, really? *Sex.* So it should definitely convey something about Winger, and your mother, and sex. And it should be short."

"O.K. How about *Motherfucker?*"

As she left the room, I told her I'd see her at dinner.

There are only two words in the English language that Pat absolutely will not sit still for. "Motherfucker" is one of them. I didn't know about the other one until quite recently. My daughter, Deborah, was home from Poughkeepsie three summers ago, and she and her friends decided to have some fun. I know that Deborah didn't instigate this; she swore she only watched, but nevertheless, she was a fellow traveler. Over on Kercheval there is a supermarket which advertises its specials on a big, theater-type marquee. On that particular day I'd noticed the marquee because I'd stopped in at noon for my pound of cherries. I sat in the parking lot, spitting out my pits, and the marquee caught my eye. It said: "Jumbo cantaloupe, 39¢, best buy in town."

The following morning the police called and said that Deborah Rutherford had been part of a group that destroyed a marquee on Kercheval. I asked how they could possibly destroy that marquee without using dynamite. The officer said they hadn't destroyed it, they had stolen some of the letters from it. I assured him that I'd get the letters back and return them. No, he said, they just took some down and rearranged the others. What they left, he said, was disgusting, and all of the parents were being notified.

"Now, let me get this straight. They didn't actually steal any of the letters?"

"No, they didn't."

"They took some of the letters down and rearranged some of the others."

"That's right."

"And the words they left were disgusting."

"Just one of them."

"Well, you'd better tell me what it was."

"Sir, when we got there this morning, the sign said: 'Jumbo cunt, 39¢, best buy in town.' "

That is the other word Pat will not hear. Poor Debbie was on punishment for the rest of the summer.

VI

I return to my desk and am nagged, no, downright hounded by Pat's "knowing your audience" theory. She gets this from her lectures at the Art Institute. I ought to dismiss it, but I can't. She does a darned good job down there, always somehow managing to get her point across to an unbelievable spectrum of mankind. So let me reflect on it for a moment.

To the Multitude under Twelve:

Think of it this way: Michelangelo was painting just about the time that Christopher Columbus discovered America. *Just imagine! That long ago!* He lived in the beautiful city of Florence, Italy. When he was only thirteen years old he became an apprentice for three years. That is, he studied draftsmanship and technique under the supervision of another well-known Florentine artist. Florence means flower. City of flowers, I suppose. He did many drawings and paintings and many, many sculptures. His most famous painting is called The Creation of Adam. Adam was, of course, the first man on earth. The female figures here are a bit chunky. That's because Michelangelo's models were men. Shakespeare's actresses were men, too. Things certainly have changed. This, actually, is not called a painting but, rather, a fresco. Do you know the difference between a painting and a fresco? A painting is done on canvas. The Creation was done on wet plaster, that is, fresh plaster. Fresco simply means fresh. When one dines al fresco, one dines outside. This is a most complicated work, depicting many Biblical themes, and in the very center is the figure of Adam, touching the hand of God. Do you see how your eyes focus on that point? Michelangelo lay on his back for four years, painting the Creation. Just imagine, four years in a damp, unheated chapel! And today you can paint a canvas red, and frame it, and title it Enigma, and it passes for art! Things certainly have changed.

Michelangelo's most famous sculpture is the David. The original is in Florence. Now, you mustn't giggle. Please, don't giggle. You see, in Gothic times the human body was thought to be something shameful, something nasty, something to be concealed. But Michelangelo thought the body a beautiful thing, a work of God, and he strove mightily all his life to attain perfection in drawing and sculpting the human body in every attitude. Yes, well, giggle if you must, but realize, please: it's medieval to do so. Michelangelo devoted his entire life to his art. He never married. It is said that he was mean and nasty, and had a very bad temper. And though he was proclaimed a genius by the time he was thirty, and enjoyed tremendous fame and acclaim —he didn't enjoy it all. Not a bit! He died a bitter and unhappy man. Now, let me show you some Raphael. . . .

To the Multitude over Twelve:

Michelangelo's full name was Michelangelo Buonarroti. He was born in 1475, and he died in 1564. I've always thought it interesting that, in that year of 1564, Michelangelo died and Shakespeare was born. He taketh away and He giveth, so to speak. Michelangelo and Leonardo are the most famous of the cinquecento Florentine artists. When he was just thirteen years old he was apprenticed for three years to the workshop of Domenico Ghirlandajo, in the city of Florence. If you have never been there, truly, you should move heaven and earth to do so! He received a solid grounding in draftsmanship and technique in this workshop, but he disagreed emphatically with the kind of art Ghirlandajo was producing in those days. Ghirlandajo's art was rather dull and traditional. Namby-pamby stuff. Plethoras of Virgins.

In Gothic times, the human body was considered to be something shameful, something nasty, something to be concealed. Michelangelo believed the body to be a work of God, a noble and glorious and reverent thing. Instead of studying antique Greek sculpture, he went to work analyzing the human body, dissecting bodies, drawing nude men in every attitude. Yes, well, almost every attitude. Sculpture was his first love—indeed, it is commonly believed that he hated to paint. He felt that, in sculpture, the figures were simply slumbering there in the marble and that he alone could awaken the human spirit from the matter. He spent many months of his life in the great marble quarries at Carrara, selecting the exact size and quality for his needs.

In all likelihood, his most famous painting is The Creation of Adam, the magnificent fresco on the ceiling of the Sistine Chapel. The female figures are a bit chunky here. That, of course, is because male models were used. It is very hard to appreciate the full impact of the ceiling when seeing small sections of it in photographs. It looks rather like a jumble. But it is probably the most controlled and coherent of the Renaissance paintings. The figures twist and turn in violent movement, and yet they somehow remain firm and restful. There are immense images of Old Testament prophets—you see Daniel here—alternating with images of Sibyls. The Sibyls supposedly predicted the coming of Christ. Then there is the story of Noah, and in the center, the Creation, with God mysteriously creating a splendid young man, Adam. Notice that the fingers do not touch. They almost touch, but they don't. They leave something to our imaginations.

The fresco is an endless succession of men and women in infinite variation. They hold medallions and tie up festoons. They sit on marble chairs and benches that are, themselves, beautifully decorated. This fresco took Michelangelo four years to complete. During all of that time he lay on scaffolding, meticulously transferring his drawings to the ceiling. The work was finished in 1512, when he was thirty-seven years old.

Undoubtedly the most well-known of Michelangelo's sculptures is the David. (If you have time at the end of the tour you may wish to look up the Captives. I, personally, think they are his best work.)

The story behind the David is this: The Medici had lost power in 1494. The Florentines, then under the influence of Savonarola, demanded works of art on heroic-patriotic themes. Michelangelo was commissioned to do a gigantic figure of David. Now, past Davids had always been rather small and nimble, and clothed. Michelangelo wanted to give us a David that was huge and defiant, and nude. He wished to confirm man's supreme achievement against all obstacles. I might say here that most Americans traveling in Europe are confused by the abundance of Davids. Innumerable copies have been made. However, in Florence one sees the original David in the Accademia. There is another well-known copy in the Piazza della Signoria—the heart of Florence.

As so often happens with men of genius, they pursue their art, or their profession, singlemindedly—to the exclusion of their own personal happiness. Michelangelo never enjoyed what we might call normal relationships with other human beings. And, because an acute dissatisfaction with life, or reality, is generally considered to be the motivation of every artist, Michelangelo never derived contentment or pleasure from his accomplishments. He died a bitter, paranoiac man, tormented near the end by a feeling of incompetence and inconsequentiality. Now, let us proceed to Raphael Santi. Raphael was a much more cheerful man, though God knows why. He had a simply dreadful childhood. . . .

I don't think we can deduce from these two lectures that Pat knows her audience. No, I don't think so. We know that kids won't sit still for much information and we know that adults are expected to be patient with proper nouns and historical data and dates. And we know that most adults would let hell freeze over before they'd question a word like "cinquecento" publicly. Better to look it up privately, at the end of the day. I've always found it confusing, anyway, since it means "fifteen hundreds" rather than fifteenth century. Perhaps the point is not to illustrate that Pat knows her audience, but that her audience knows nothing of Pat.

First, she loathes and despises the Sistine Chapel. The place itself is dinky and dark and swarming with sweaty tourists every day of the year. Regarding the controlled coherence of the *Creation*, her comment was that C. B. De Mille could handle a crowd better. She says if there were *one more* writhing figure in the work she'd break out in shingles. She says it's too bad you have to read the whole Bible before you can look at it, then you have to look at it for several days before you can understand it, and by that time your neck has to be put in a brace. She also feels it's all very well to have a penchant for male nudes, but why all the fuss when he botched up every female he ever laid a chisel to? And, finally, she believes that Michelangelo did the *Creation* purely out of spite. He'd prepared hundreds of drawings for the proposed tomb of Pope Julius II. He intended to sculpt some forty figures for that tomb. But then His Holiness lost his enthusiasm for the project and set Michelangelo to work painting the Sistine. Michelangelo got mad and crammed all those figures onto that itty-bitty ceiling, waving his fine Italian finger at Julius II all the while. She concludes that it might not be a paean to the Glory of Man after all. It might be a prophesy. Of what? Well, there's the slightly limp-wristed Adam. And not too far off there is Eve, hovering behind the Lord. And then there are those platoons of people, falling all over each other, gasping for air and space. She says the whole thing would make a good poster for Planned Parenthood.

So much for the Sistine. The *David*, says Pat, could be seen in just about any Y.M.C.A. in the U.S.A. It's a fine, athletic body but the sculpture is static. We must appreciate it for what it is: a virile youth. Lovely to look at, delightful to know, but as a statement of man's powers of mind and spirit it is mute. Now, Bernini's *David!* Yes, it's a hundred years later— yes, of course, it's Baroque. But Bernini's *David tells* us something. He scowls. His brows are furrowed. His teeth are clenched. His jaw is set. His torso is bent and his arm is tense and ready to hurl that rock! By God, Bernini's *David* is going to *slay* that old Goliath, not simply blind him with his beauty!

I don't know what all of this proves. Only, I guess, that I enjoy having the last word.

VII

The first meal my mother cooked at Timberline was canard à l'orange. Her only other culinary experience had been at camp when, in their teens, a group of bloomered girls sought out green branches, whittled each to a point, impaled a weiner on the point and sang "I'm in Love with the Man in the Moon" while the meat charred evenly on all sides.

I sat on a high kitchen stool as she tremulously placed the bird on the counter, handling it like a newborn babe, examining each orifice with wonder. Father said that, since she was a novice, she really ought to begin with scrambled eggs. The cost would be less if she failed, and if she succeeded, we wouldn't have to eat dry cereal every morning. He said that, by the end of the summer, the Rutherford family alone would make millionaires of those fellows back home in Battle Creek. She explained that canard à l'orange was her very favorite dish in the world. It was good to start with that because past memories of other, delectable canards à l'orange would inspire her to lavish great care on this poor dead thing lying all akimbo on the counter. Father made a quick getaway, with the excuse that there were still pictures to hang, and he wanted to watch for the truck that was bringing patio furniture from Calgary.

"Do you mind having a spectator?" I asked.

"Not as long as you're only that. Don't comment and don't offer advice, no matter how badly I bungle it."

We had a great deal of fun that day. It was our third day at Timberline. In May, we received a wire from the contractor in Calgary. *Timberline ready Friday, June 10.* Friday, June 10, was the day I graduated from the ninth grade at Croydon. My father sent a return wire. *Arriving Timberline Wednesday, June 15.* We arrived fatigued and numb after a train trip across half of Ontario, Manitoba, Saskatchewan and half of Alberta. We were at each other's throats every hour of the first two days.

The man who drove us from the Buena Vista station to Timberline didn't realize what we had just been through, and was surly. We all had to go to the bathroom the minute we got into the house and all three toilets overflowed when we flushed them. When we washed our hands the hot-water faucets throbbed interminably. The venetian blinds hadn't been installed along the back rooms of the house, and the sun poured in mercilessly. When we opened the windows, harmless but strange and exotic flying bugs came in. Mother said she hadn't expected an introduction to Josh Whitcomb's fauna quite so soon. Everything was wrong. The glossy black tile hadn't been laid on the gallery floor and boxes of it were stacked in the living room. Nothing was where it was supposed to be, excepting Mount Binnie and Mount Elizabeth. They were there in all their glory. I looked forward to exploring every path and byway, if the adults would ever let me out of the house. There was nothing I could do, but they seemed to need me there to listen to the altercations.

We had a terrific argument the first evening. There was no food in the house; we hadn't yet rented a car and we were stranded halfway up the mountain. The bedspreads and skins had arrived, but none of the bedding. We would have to sleep on the bare mattresses with those animal pelts on top of us. I said we at least had beds, which would be glorious after three cramped nights in berths. I thought that was a rather bright and positive two cents' worth to throw in, but my timing was wrong and nobody listened. Father replied that we'd been so goddamned judicious about bringing only our clothes along, we hadn't even brought soap. Mother said she'd remembered her recipe book, why couldn't I remember my pajamas? She sat down on the living-room floor and wept. It was beyond her endurance. The contractor had promised that his agent would have the place livable. He was a liar and a cheat, he was not a gentleman, it was a horrendous mistake, she couldn't deal with it, it was just too much. She was going to call Grandmother MacAllister and ask her to come and settle the thing.

Father—tired, haggard, sitting on a crate of tiles—said, "Go ahead, call her! You'll need a megaphone because we haven't got a telephone!" I, fourteen years old now, told them they were acting like a bunch of children. They told me I didn't know my place. I said the only place for all of us was bed. Eight or ten hours of it, so that we could get up in the morning and *enjoy Buena Vista.*

The following morning, our second day, we awoke rested and energetic. Alas, our energy didn't see us through the day, and by evening we were hollering at each other again. We did accomplish a great deal that day and I, for one, was delighted with the state of flux. Nothing is quite so boring as absolute order. I felt that we'd enjoy Timberline all the more for having to straighten out these final snags without the help of servants, or Grandmother MacAllister.

I've learned since, through a variety of linguistic spurns, snubs and cold shoulders, that Americans have a worldwide reputation for being impatient and demanding. Back in 1932, that reputation had not yet been felt in Buena Vista. It was a lazy mountain town whose greatest challenge lay in getting through the brutal winters. I believe Buena Vista received its indoctrination the day Jimmy Rutherford strode down the main street for the first time. Jimmy Rutherford was going to get the show on the road. I had much activity to report to Mother at the end of the day.

We went to the little telephone company office, where Father told the girl we had to have some phones hooked up. "How soon do you want them?" she asked. "Yesterday," he said. He told her that she'd better put us at the top of her list. He said he didn't care *how* busy they were in June, we'd just spent sixty thousand dollars up on Mount Binnie. He called the contractor in Calgary from the telephone office. He said that back in Grosse Pointe contracts meant something. He said that if the gallery tile wasn't laid by the end of the day he'd lay it himself. He turned away from me and told the contractor, sotto voce, that he'd laid just about every-thing in his day but he'd never laid tiles. "So you'd better get your ass up here or I'll have a lawyer breathing down your neck. And another thing," he said, "those goddamn pagans in Pompeii knew more about plumbing than you do." We went to see Mr. McCabe, who had the Ford franchise. He had two cars on which he allowed summer rentals. Both were 1931 Victoria sedans with maroon bottoms, black tops and a vermilion stripe running in between. He gave us the keys. He asked my father if he'd ever met crazy old Henry back there in Grosse Pointe. We drove the car around the block and took it back. "What's wrong?" I asked. My father was fit to be tied. "This car smells like somebody died in it!" Mr. McCabe gave us the other car and said yes, somebody died in it, slumped over dead for a week in it, and when they finally found it on Mount Elizabeth it did, he admitted, have a peculiar odor. We drove to Mr. Samson's grocery store. We bought coffee, milk, corn flakes, bread, Campbell's soup and three bars of Lux soap. Father asked Mr. Samson if he delivered. Mr. Samson said that all depended where we lived. I told him we were halfway up Mount Binnie. He said we should have known better—we should have built in town. Father then told him that he'd be receiving a call from Mrs. James Rutherford, of Grosse Pointe Shores, Michigan, later in the day, and that it was high time they extended their route to include Mount Binnie. He added, without blinking an eyelid, "We'll be doing our share of entertaining, and it'll be worth your while." Mr. Samson looked at the Campbell's soup and corn flakes, and smiled that delightful, knowing, rural smile. He said he'd talk it over with Mrs. Rutherford and see just what it would amount to by the week, and let us know if it was worth his while. The man's son, the boy responsible for deliveries, muttered under his breath, "Mount Binnie gives you the hernia."

We went down to the railroad station and asked if our

totem pole had come in from Kamloops, British Columbia. The clerk, Mr. Joseph Hilliard, smiled and said, "You betcha!" "Where is it?" I asked. "Over there against the wall." We all looked across the room at the giant oblong crate. "And it's going to stay there till you find a truck big enough to haul it up Mount Binnie." My father commented that it was longer than we expected. "Shoulda bought the parts," said Mr. Hilliard, "and assembled it yourself." Interestingly enough, Mr. Hilliard had a son who owned a large truck. The son was busy hauling gravel all week but sometimes accepted odd jobs on Saturday, for time and a half. "I'd sure as hell call this an odd job, wouldn't you, Mr. Rutherford?"

Now, Father knew, Grandmother MacAllister knew, everybody at home on Lake Shore Road knew, that money was the universal lubricant. But in Buena Vista, in 1932, a certain amount of finesse was required in negotiating a deal. You couldn't just ask what the son would charge. You had to chat awhile about the gravel business, and how dangerous truck hauling was on mountain roads, the hazards of grizzly bears wherever you set up camp, and what alternatives there were in order to make a living. And sooner or later it was impressed upon you that mountain life was bleak, and nothing came cheap. We would have to go to the home of Mr. Hilliard's son any evening after seven, and make the arrangements with him. You got into a lot of hot water when you made arrangements for your kids, especially since they all went fishing most Saturdays these days and had no regard for the value of a dollar.

On the morning of the third day, the phones were connected, the tile had been laid, two of the three toilets worked efficiently, I had new pajamas and the bedding had arrived. We put sheets over the back windows to protect us from the sun and foreign insects. We ate our corn flakes. Father decided to call Seth Hilliard, hoping to catch him before he departed for the gravel pit. Seth invited all of us over for coffee that evening, after seven. Father asked if we couldn't just set it up on the phone. Seth said no, bring the missus and the lad and we'd talk it over after seven.

At mid-morning, our back doorbell rang. It was Arnold, Mr. Samson's boy, panting heavily, carrying a box that contained (1) the duck, (2) the oranges, (3) a pack of brown sugar, (4) a box of arrowroot and (5) and (6) a bottle of Madeira and a bottle of orange liqueur, both of which had been fetched from the liquor store by Mr. Samson himself. Father thanked him, tipped him and sadly noted that we still didn't have any eggs in the house.

All of this comes back to me in a veritable cascade of thoughts, feelings and impressions. I remember not knowing what time it was, even approximately, for three whole days. I remember walking into rooms and reaching for old, familiar light switches that were never there. They were beside another door, on another wall, placed higher or lower than my hand expected them to be. I would awaken several times each night and each time I would orient myself to the room anew. I needed to make a mental exit from the room. Where was the light coming from? Where was the rug? Where were the chairs? How must I navigate across all this to find the door? The sounds, the light, the smell of the air, flooded my senses, leaving me exhausted and dazed at the end of the day. And all those confirmed ways of judging people, and figures of speech, and buildings, and meals, and chinaware, were called into question. The touchstones were gone. The milk came in funny containers. The bars of butter were stubby and fat. The mirror on my door elongated my already lank and bony body. The water was full of strange-tasting minerals. The toilet-paper container in the bathroom was placed directly under the towel rack and was, therefore, forever hidden from view. In short, my fourteen-year-old body was awash with sharp, new sensations. And because I was only fourteen, I found these sensations curious and challenging. I would never again, in any other circumstances, be as fluid and flexible as I was those first few weeks at Buena Vista. I now must admit that luau, Oktoberfest and Mardi gras are but calculated mutations, intended to force me from my inertia and alter, for a moment, the uniformity of my days. The peculiar placement of objects and things is something I tolerate until I can fly the friendly skies back to my familiar Grosse Pointe sounds and smells, my Grosse Pointe mirrors reflecting my Grosse Pointe light, and my encroaching sixties which approach stealthily, methodically, hour by hour, day by day, without, thank God, surprise or variation.

But I mustn't leave the duck akimbo on the counter. It turned out to be delicious. My father took a picture of it but then ran into difficulties when he tried to carve it. Mother and I sat at the table watching him wield the knife. It was apparent that carving a bird was a complicated job, but we assumed, for the first few minutes, that the difficulties were due to his inexperience. He hacked away at the carcass and finally said, "Laura, there's no *meat* on this bird!" We soon discovered that she had roasted it upside down. Mother and I assisted in turning it over, dropping it once on the platter, splashing grease and sauce all over Father, but we eventually put it to rights on its sorely mutilated back. It was not a large bird and, since Mother hadn't thought to prepare any rice or vegetables, the three of us polished it off in short order. I must say, Father went out of his way to heap praise on this, my mother's first effort. But she was visibly disappointed when he had a bowl of corn flakes for dessert.

"I'm sorry, Laura," he said. "I'm hungry."

VIII

The matter of correct attire presented a dilemma to my father whenever he had to go out. In preparing for the evening at Seth Hilliard's house, he didn't know what to wear. I've learned, over the years, that only people who wear clothes superbly have this problem to this degree. People like me, and my mother, understand very early in the game that clothes really don't help us much where the larger world is concerned. But Father, who had a reputation to live up to in these matters, was known to stand at the door of his closet for hours, shifting from one foot to the other, deliberating. He didn't so much deliberate possible combinations of colors and designs—everything he owned was tastefully coordinated, and he never made a purchase without this vast master plan of hues and patterns in mind—but the final selection had to be made with one primary consideration: the *destination* of the costume. Certain shirts and ties went with certain people's houses and personalities. At certain people's houses you dressed to kill. At others it was important to fade into the woodwork. Certain people's houses and temperaments allowed you small, flamboyant touches, such as brilliant paisley ascots, or braided Italian straw belts, or suspenders hand-embroidered by those fishwives on Burano. Then again, some people were so forbidding, their drawing rooms were so austere, their mental armor so impenetrable, you felt obliged to gild the lily and venture out à la Eva Tanguay, not giving a damn, confident that whatever cheer the evening might contain would be provided by your own sartorial daring. In the case of the proposed visit to Seth Hilliard's, Father wanted to fade into the woodwork. He'd been half an hour, pacing up and down, unable to find anything appropriately drab. I suggested that he wear something slightly old and rumpled. But even his old, rumpled clothes had been expensive when new, and Seth would know it. And Seth would be uncomfortable. How about those old khakis he wore fishing? Mother said absolutely not, they smelled like a salmon cannery. It was, after all, a visit to the man's home. His home was his castle, no matter how humble. Luckily, the evenings were cold at Buena Vista, so the final decision was a pair of English tweed slacks with just the ghost of a crease left in them, and a heavy cashmere sweater. We agreed that he looked casual without being shoddy. We assured him that Seth wouldn't find him "dandy," and that assurance sent him out to the car in a huff, hollering back that he couldn't care less what some two-bit truck driver thought of him.

The house was situated in a valley behind Mount Elizabeth—a half-hour drive from Timberline. It was a small, shingled house, painted a pale pink. There was an old, warped prairie schooner, sans canvas, in the front yard. Mrs. Hilliard had set a row of geraniums on the seat of it. Five or six white chickens wobbled helter-skelter around the yard and, as we neared the house, we heard the lowing of cows from somewhere back of the yard. When we drove up the driveway a gigantic German shepherd plowed through the weeds and yelped at us. We must have been a sight, because the three of us, me included, were ridiculously nervous about this meeting. It was an imposition, having to go to this man's house, having to dress carefully so as not to offend him, having to talk about gravel and grizzly bears, having, probably, to dicker over the price, all because Grandmother and the girl from the White Glove Secretarial Service had seen fit to order a forty-foot totem pole some fifteen months ago. There we sat, petrified, as the huge dog jumped on the doors and bared its fangs at us. Mother was pale with fright and I actually felt like crying. But then Father rolled down the window, coated his voice with caramel and said, "Hello, there, pretty boy. How's about letting us out of the car?" The dog, unable to believe what he'd just heard, gave my father an incredulous glare and then snarled even more ferociously. Mother groaned, I laughed and finally Seth Hilliard stormed out of the house and sharply ordered the dog to a nearby shed.

Seth Hilliard was in his early thirties. He was short and stocky and very darkly tanned. His hair was blond, and there was a tight, curly red beard around his chin. His two front teeth were missing. He seemed genuinely happy to see us and immediately ushered us into the kitchen, where his wife, Elsie, was putting away the supper dishes. The kitchen was so large that I wondered if there could possibly be any other rooms in the tiny house. My father, upon catching a glimpse of a couch in the next room, began to head for the living room. But Mrs. Hilliard quickly said the kitchen was more comfortable, and sat us down around a heavy oak table. I must have hesitated, because she noticed me gazing across the room at a peculiar metal object which had an enamel basin under it. I was so terribly afraid of making a faux pas, I hurriedly fell into a chair. Mrs. Hilliard smiled and asked me if I'd never seen a pump before. She very gently took me by the arm and guided me to the pump, smiling at my parents as she did so. "I was just about to fill the coffeepot," she said. "You come here, sonny, make yourself useful." She took a big aluminum pot from the top of the stove and held it under the mouth of the pump while I swung the handle up and down. She then said that the fire was low, and asked if I had ever seen a cookstove before. She turned to my mother. "Can he put the wood in? He might get dirty." Mother came over to the stove, saying she'd like to watch. Dad said he'd like to watch, too, whereupon Seth said, "Hey, Rutherford, dontcha know about cookstoves?" He turned bright red, poked my father in the ribs and said: "Lifter-leg-and-pok*er!*" It was one thing to get a couple of logs in one hand, but it was another to lift the heavy round lid at the same time. There was a chorus of oohs and aahs as I clumsily completed the operation. We all watched for a moment until the hot coals singed the bark and the flames began to jump. I remember looking into Mrs. Hilliard's red, shiny face. She smiled down at me, searching my face with her bright blue eyes, and somehow we all knew that she'd let me fiddle with the pump and the stove because the adults had no easy way of breaking the ice. Still, we were on edge. Mother wore a plain, but finely made, yellow shirtwaist dress. Mrs. Hilliard furtively glanced at it so many times that mother became tongue-tied, and finally, unable to contain herself any longer, Mrs. Hilliard lunged forward and took a piece of the skirt in her hand, excitedly exclaiming that it was a lovely piece of stuff. This admiration was genuine, and when my mother then admired the cookstove, that admiration was genuine, too, but Seth and Elsie looked at her in disbelief. It was just a cranky old cookstove. It was just until they could see their way to an electric one. No, said Mother, it was a magnificent stove. It had that big space in the middle for keeping things warm, and that area at the back where you could keep all your utensils, and that heavy wide shelf at the top for roasting pans. Why, just that afternoon, she'd roasted her first duck, and nothing was near the stove, everything was in drawers a mile away. She included in the tale the admission that she'd roasted the duck upside down. When Elsie chuckled, Mother fed on the laughter, building her story with an amazing amount of animation until Elsie fell on her, and hugged her, and both women, God only knew why, cried, and buckled up, and wiped away immense rivulets of tears. Only then did the strain disappear. The Hilliards were relaxed—comfortable in the knowledge that my mother didn't put on airs. The adults repaired to the table, and I was sent out into the yard to look for Bob.

Bob Hilliard was, and always will be, my boyhood Huck Finn. He was twelve years old—two years my junior—and as I call him to mind now his image fits directly into a frame with Norman Rockwell's signature at the bottom. Did boys, *could* boys, ever really look like that? I never looked like that, nor did any of my friends, nor did any of the other farm boys around Buena Vista. Here was the consummate combination of torn hats, freckles, lost toenails, mashed thumbs and peeling scabs, all rolled into one. I saw him in a field beyond the shed and hollered at him. He beckoned me into the field and carefully spread the two lines of barbed wire widely apart so that I could climb through the fence. What he was doing, just then, was goddamned chores. Long as he could remember, sunup and sundown, his life had been plagued with goddamn chores. His particular chore that night was gathering cow pies. He pointed to one, a large round circle lying on the grass, and said he had to pick them up, put them in a box and then take a spade and crush them. This made powdered manure which his mother spread over her garden. I offered to help but he said no, I was wearing good clothes and, additionally, it took an experienced eye to spot the dry ones. All he needed, he said, was me getting hold of a fresh one, and him getting blamed for the ensuing stink.

It surprised me that Bob picked up the big dry pies with his bare hands. He got a good hold on either side and then quickly cracked the pie in two, and threw both halves into a box. I hauled the box along and tried to spot the pies around the field so that we could go from one to another without wasting time. The dog, Kaiser, came along with us. I noticed that Kaiser limped slightly. Bob said Kaiser was just a damn fool hound who didn't know thistle from clover. "Why don't you take him to a vet and have the thistle taken out?" Vets were too expensive, and anyway, Kaiser was ailing of one thing or another half the time. They just had to wait till it pussed up and then Bob's mother would put hot cloths on it, and lance it, and take out the thistle. I looked at Kaiser. He was enormous, irascible, and there was a hard, steely glint in his eyes. I thought of Bob's gentle little mother and made him promise to call me when the operation was performed.

We wandered around the field, collecting ten or twelve cow pies in all. Bob said it was a pretty good haul for one night. He spread the barbed wire for me again, and we went to the shed. "Wanna help smash 'em?" he asked. He handed me the spade and I went to work pounding the pies.

"You're a Yank, aren't you?"

"Not really. Just American. The real Yankees are in New England. Maine—Vermont—places like that."

"Your folks built that new lodge up on Binnie, right?"

"Right. You'll have to come up and see it sometime."

"Oh, yeah. Sometime. Canadians ain't got that kind of money for lodges like that."

"Some must have. We've got Canadians around us."

"I'll tell you something about Canadians. Even the rich ones don't build lodges like that. I mean, you ain't gonna *ever* catch no Canadian building a lodge like that."

"Oh, I don't know. I don't think it's all that palatial."

"That's 'cause you're spoiled. Where'd it all come from?"

"What?"

"The money."

"Trees."

"Yeah?"

"Yeah. Michigan trees. I don't see that it makes any difference."

"Dontcha? I do. I see a whole hell of a lot of difference."

He told me I'd get pains in my arms if I didn't hold the spade properly. He showed me where to place my hands in order to achieve the correct chopping action, and he noted that he was surely in for trouble because my shoes were covered with cow powder. It was dry, and harmless, but when it got up under the soles, and what with foot sweat and all, it haunted you for days.

"Have you met your neighbors to the west? The Mac-Millans?"

"I think my mother said hello. We've only been there three days. We've been busy straightening up the house."

"Yeah, I know. My granddad's got your totem pole down at the station."

I didn't much like his little smirk but, what the hell, the

totem pole was none of my doing. Not everybody could have a prairie schooner in their front yard.

"The MacMillans have a girl. Her name's Eileen. She's fourteen."

"Oh?"

"She's a real looker. And she keeps two horses down at the stables all summer."

"Is that right?"

"One's an Appaloosa and one's just a horse. She rides like nobody I ever saw."

"You mean she's good?"

"She rides like no girl I ever saw. But she's not rough. Y'know? She's no tomboy. She just looks so weak and pretty and then she gets on that old Appaloosa and, Jesus, you better watch out. She goes like hell. She digs in them heels and then she whoops like an Indian. Then she gets off and she's weak and pretty again. It's what you call a *phenomena*."

"What about the other horse? She ever let anybody ride it?"

"She let me ride it once last week. We went up a trail together for an hour or so. She was just bein' nice. I don't like that whooping stuff. She did it for me. Y'know? Because she don't like trails much. Can't get up much speed on a trail."

"Maybe she'll let me ride with her one of these days."

"Oh, yeah. Maybe."

I had finished crushing the pies. Bob poked the spade around, to see if I'd obtained the right texture, and then hung the spade on the far wall of the shed.

"She's probably a real brat when you get to know her."

"Why do you say that?"

"Well, I guess you know Mount Binnie's a pretty choice place. I mean, it's been choice for years before you even got here. Them MacMillans got money running out of their ears."

Just outside the shed there was a huge old elm tree. Bob had tied a heavy rope around one of the limbs and had run it through a tractor tire. We each had a turn swinging on the tire. During my turn I gathered momentum and swung out over the shed, high above the fields. Clearly, this should be the first step in gathering cow pies. At the highest point in the arc, just prior to the descent, you could case the field and see precisely where the pies were. I suggested it to Bob, saying that I had a bright idea which would make his chores more efficient and easier. "Swing out over the field and spot them first. Then you don't have to break your balls walking the field." He didn't think it such a bright idea. He grunted and rubbed his forehead. "You Yanks are all alike," he said.

We were on our way back to the house when a car pulled into the driveway. I thought it odd that Kaiser didn't accost the car. He sat, nursing his thistle, in the shed. "That's Winger," said Bob. "He's a friend of my dad's. He's going to help my dad get your totem pole up Mount Binnie." His tongue was in his cheek and he smirked again for a moment. Then a look of pride came over his face. "See that car? That's a 1928 four-door Dodge sedan. That color's called Safari Blue. Winger bought it secondhand and it *still* cost five hundred dollars!" Now it was my turn for the insufferable smirk. "They lived on my street, y'know—Horace and John Dodge." His reaction was predictable: wide-eyed and awed. "You pulling my leg?" "Nope. Both of 'em died in 1920. Mrs. Anna—that's Horace's widow—she married some actor guy and they're building a new place right now, coupla blocks from our house." But the supreme revenge I wanted slipped out of my hands. He beamed. "God*damn!* You gotta tell that to Winger!"

He ran to the car and gave Winger a big hug. Winger mussed up Bob's hair and they punched each other several times—Winger punching too hard and knocking Bob into the weeds. It was a rollicking, rowdy greeting with fists flying in the air, rising clouds of dust, shouts of *"Hey, Tiger"* and *"Sonofabitch!"* and, above all, a kind of ecstatic joy that made me feel oddly deprived. I thought it all very childish. Winger came over and extended his hand. I shook it and said that I was pleased to meet him. I must have cowered slightly, expecting a blow in the belly, but he grinned at me and shook my hand firmly. He was not particularly tall—under six feet, I think, and his arms and legs were extraordinarily taut and muscular. His head seemed too large for his body. This impression was due mainly to the dense mass of curly hair covering his head and part of his neck. I learned later that he cut his own hair whenever it began to feel "heavy." He was clean-shaven, his eyes were speckled hazel and he had perfect teeth, which I, after only three days in rural Alberta, knew to be rare. His skin, like Seth Hilliard's, was brown and leathery. Two other things were immediately visible. He had suffered a bad cut over his right eye. The eyebrow was split in two with a thin line of scar tissue separating the hair. And on his upper right arm there was a tattoo of a clipper ship. I was made, then and there, to tell him the saga of Horace and John Dodge. I embellished the tale with gossip pertaining to the exploits of the two Dodge widows (their huge inheritances, their new husbands, their new homes), Winger was duly impressed, and the three of us went into the kitchen.

Winger was obviously very much at home here. No effort was made to break any ice. He scooped up a handful of Mrs. Hilliard's matrimonial cake and then he scooped up Mrs. Hilliard, catching her by the waist and kissing her on the neck. She whirled around and punched him in the stomach while Seth looked on, laughing. She turned to my father and said, "This here ton o' trouble is Winger Burns." He nuzzled his nose into the top of her hair and kissed her again, saying we shouldn't mind Elsie, she was just an old bramble bush blown in off the prairie by a mean old northwind. She whirled around again, jabbed him in the ribs and said that bramble was better than *flotsam*. She turned to my mother and said Winger was just a piece of no-good flotsam, blown up on the Vancouver docks along with Chinamen and Japs and God knew what else. These people sure did enjoy rough-housing. I could see that Father found it all a little too robust, and was anxious to go. He rose from the table, looked at my shoes and asked what on earth I'd been doing. "Crushing cow pies,"I said, "for Mrs. Hilliard's garden." Elsie directed Bob and me to the pump. "Go scrub and I'll get you some cake." Father sat down again, resignedly.

I think it must be a curse to be as handsome as my father was. He most certainly was not fading into the Hilliard's woodwork. He wasn't in the least effeminate or sissified, but why was he so obstrusive in a wooden chair at an oak table? He was in top form—not a bit of flab anywhere—why did his lean physique make him appear suave and "dandy"? And why did Seth and Winger seem so unruly and rambunctious beside him? I wondered if, before he married Mother, his gestures had been so refined, his stance so controlled and graceful. Had he developed all this elegance for Lake Shore Road? Probably not, or Grandmother wouldn't have considered him for the Purchase. Mother didn't fit here, either, but she had the look of an eager witness. There was an aura of anticipation about her as she sat there in her plain Galey and Lord cotton dress, rocking back and forth in a wicker chair, watching the Hilliards and Winger jostle about. Goodness, where was the limit with these people? If they did all this kissing and fondling and punching in the first five minutes that you knew them, where would it lead? Would it get out of bounds? Would the language become raw and vulgar? Would we be forced to leave—to march to the car on righteous feet, with noses halfway to heaven? *Mr. and Mrs. Highborn were not amused!* Her head rested against the back of the chair. She'd put her feet upon a little footstool. Her hands were relaxed and clasped in her lap. She wanted to know what the limits were. My God, I thought, she's not afraid to find out!

"It's all set, then? Saturday morning you and Winger'll haul it up?"

"Yes, sir," said Seth. "You have that concrete ready and we'll sink her for you Saturday."

We were all on our feet, ready to leave, when Elsie asked my mother if she'd like to take some leaf lettuce home. Bob and I were sent to the garden, and when we returned with the lettuce, I noticed my mother standing near the cookstove with Winger Burns. Her hand was at her throat, and she was blushing. I heard her say, "Is there something wrong, Mr. Burns?"

"Oh, no, ma'am. Excuse me for staring. I never saw a redhead like you before."

"Oh, Mr. Burns, I think you've seen redheads many times before."

"Oh, sure, plenty of redheads. I never seen one without freckles before."

"That's right," said Mother, "I don't have freckles."

"No, ma'am, not a single, solitary one. Excuse me for staring."

"That's quite all right. I guess it *is* unusual. My son, Jay, doesn't have freckles, either."

"I'll be darned," said Winger. "I never noticed. That sure is unusual."

We thanked the Hilliards for their hospitality, took our two heads of leaf lettuce and carefully made our way to the car. Kaiser didn't bother to acknowledge our parting. It was a bright, crisp night, and I remember seeing the moon cradled deeply in the "V" between Mount Elizabeth and Mount Binnie. I told Bob that I'd make Eileen MacMillan's acquaintance as soon as possible, and I asked him to come to Timberline on Saturday morning when his father and Winger brought up the pole. He said he wouldn't miss it for the world.

The drive home was quiet. Father said only that he wished he'd worn a plaid shirt. There was something just a bit too *cosmopolitan* about cashmere sweaters, even old ones. That's what we had to find. Some cosmopolitan people with whom we could be comfortable.

IX

Winger Burns was thirty-eight years old in 1932. He was born and raised in the town of Trail, British Columbia, a stone's throw from the Washington border. He finished the eighth grade there and that was the extent of his formal education. The years between the eighth grade and his marriage, at twenty, have always been hazy to me, but he apparently spent some time as a migrant fruit and hop picker in and around the Okanagan Valley. When he was twenty his father died, and he was summoned home. Winger referred to his father many times, generally berating the man for not giving his ass—Winger's—a good kick around the block and making him go to high school. He would not tell me his father's name, nor would he tell me his own. They were one and the same, and when the father passed on, Winger saw to it that the name went into the hole with the old man.

Winger was a very strange name. Was it a nickname? Was it some infantile mispronunciation of William? He refused to tell me. It was just a name he chose to use because the goddamned moniker his father hung on him was embarrassing. O.K. Was it Algernon? Or Horace? Was it Percival? Was it Shadrach, Meshach, Abednigo? Hell, no. It was worse than all those. Wild horses couldn't drag it from his lips.

The father had been a watchman in one of the zinc smelters in Trail. It was easy enough to visit his father's old cronies and let it be known that he was ready to settle down. He would have to take the red-eye—the eleven-to-seven—shift, but it would be a steady wage. He was tired of being a gypsy. The farm owners treated you like mud, fed you crap and wouldn't give you so much as a Band-Aid if you accidentally mashed a hand or foot. In addition to all this, the owners posted rules with strict provisions for the social behavior of the pickers. There was to be no hanky-panky.

So there, in a field of hops, Winger obtained his scar. He was caught, bare-assed, atop a very pretty Ukrainian girl at noon one day. The farmer raised his hoe and brought it down on Winger's skull, splitting his right eyebrow in two.

"Geez, Winger, what did you do?"

"I pulled on my pants, and I quit."

"But you said there were posted rules."

"Shit, man, I don't read so good. Besides, he had no right to gripe. It happened on the lunch hour."

He had the most appealing grin I have ever seen on a man. He had what my mother called "smiling eyes." There were tiny, minuscule laugh lines which ran like triangles from the corners of his eyes to his hairline. He was quick-tempered, and quick-witted, but he had a reserve which amazed us on more than one occasion. He was thunder and lightning at thirty-eight; I oftentimes wonder what he was at twenty, when he married. I asked him about this once, saying that he must have had the pick of the crop around Trail in his youth. "Well, yes," he said. That was true. But at twenty quantity was all he cared about. All the fellows in Trail at that time cared only about quantity. As a matter of fact, there was a wooden pole in the middle of the pool hall, and you were required to carve a notch in it every time you struck. Winger busily applied his jackknife to the task until he found that some of the fellows had delusions of grandeur. Once he was assured that it was not an honest tally, he quit. But that was at twenty. In the intervening years he'd given some thought to quality.

During his first year at the smelter he met a seventeen-year-old girl named Gladys. She had been a virgin when he met her—he was sure of that. And he therefore felt more than a little responsibility for her welfare when she became pregnant. They married, had a boy they named Keith and moved into a three-room apartment. The apartment left permanent memories in Winger's mind, although he put it differently. He said the apartment left permanent damage. The rooms were small, but that wasn't the trouble. That particular apartment made him wonder whether there were any rooms, anywhere, regardless of size—any rooms, any four walls, anywhere in the world, where a man and woman could live together peacefully. He thought that, if you had to get away from a woman, even Buckingham Palace would feel like a chicken coop. She was still there, somewhere, down some corridor, and you had to pay attention. You had to make excuses. You had to explain. You had to sympathize. And if you got mad and said to hell with it, and closed yourself off somewhere, you kept running into traces of her. Garter belts and bobby pins and bath oil, all of which proved you still shared a roof and your life was not your own. Without the excuses and the sympathy and the explanations, you were barred from the bedroom. Gladys, in particular, made a habit of being unwell twenty days of the month. She was either going to die of anemia, or he was going to kill her.

After four years of marriage, Winger hated the sight of her. She was a nice girl, a pretty girl, it wasn't her fault. Apartments just did that to people. He knew that she, too, was permanently damaged, because they'd both been nice people in the beginning, and they weren't nice people any more.

I have felt the most peculiar attachment to Keith, Winger's son, for forty years now. I never met him, I have no idea what sort of person he is, or where he is. I remember a snapshot Winger carried with him. Keith was seventeen then, and in high school. He looked like a personable boy, with dark-blond curly hair. Gladys and Keith continued living in Trail, and Gladys worked part-time in a dry-cleaning plant. Winger sent them money every month, with an extra fifty dollars in August so that Keith could outfit himself for school. Winger never corresponded with Gladys—he was ashamed of his handwriting, couldn't spell and had no patience with a dictionary. However, he did call at Easter, at Christmas and on Keith's birthday, which was July 25.

Every now and then over the years I've had an inexplicable urge to find Keith. Winger was so determined that Keith would finish high school. Winger said he was smart, and Gladys said he was ambitious. He might even get a scholarship to go to University. In my mind, the boy in the snapshot was rather like a half brother. I knew Winger, and came to love Winger, and surely I ought to keep track of Winger's boy. The deterrent is simply this: Whenever I envision our meeting, it takes the following form. I would find Keith in Vancouver. I would make an appointment to have a drink with him. I would tell him his father had meant a great deal to me at Buena Vista. And then I would offer him money. His clothes were neat; there was no hint of a mend or a turned collar. Nevertheless, there was some sort of perturbation, and money would fix it. And so, there on the barstool, I reach into my billfold and offer to help. This ridiculous fantasy, which continues to haunt me, pains me deeply. It pains me because Winger had such high hopes for Keith. And it pains me because Winger Burns would die before he'd take a nickel from the Rutherfords.

No, no, no. The fantasy is not the deterrent. The real deterrent is sloth. I am the laziest of lazybones. The premonition is there, though, and God knows, I've never been one to look for trouble.

At twenty-five, Winger went to Vancouver and became a stevedore on the docks. He didn't divorce Gladys because he was certain he'd never marry again. If she wanted to jump into another can of worms, he'd gladly give her a divorce, but in the meantime lawyers and courts were expensive, and there was no need to mess with them. In Vancouver he met an Oriental woman. Her name was Cheeoh—I spell it as he pronounced it. Cheeoh worked in a beauty salon. She owned a small house on Burrard Inlet, a house whose hind quarters rested firmly on the earth, but whose front quarters were supported by three poles which were sunk in the Inlet. Because of this, Winger never felt at ease in the front of the house. He swore you could actually get seasick in the living room. The kitchen and bedroom were at the rear of the house, and Winger spent three years living quite comfortably at the back of Cheeoh's house.

His face, his smiling eyes, suddenly saddened while telling me this. It got bad. After only three years it went sour. They were fighting—why, he didn't know. She paid the monthly mortgage, he paid the utilities, bought all the food and took her out every weekend. She was sewing by hand when he met her. He bought her a Singer sewing machine, second-hand, but he toiled like a bugger to get it shipshape. He dismantled the whole thing, washed and oiled all the parts and bought a new belt for it. He got down on his hands and knees with a toothbrush and cleaned the intricate scrolls on the treadle. He went with her to the little Japanese fabric shops and bought yards and yards of silk and cotton for dresses. When her legs ached, after a day of stooping over shampoo basins, he rubbed them for her. He thought he'd learned how to take care of a woman. He thought he knew where the pitfalls were, after all the years with Gladys. Still, the house became a prison. It got bad, it went sour, and he couldn't figure out why. He left Cheeoh and moved into a room at a boardinghouse.

Between Cheeoh, in his late twenties, and my mother, in his thirties, no other woman had meant anything to him. He was not, generally speaking, a reflective or introspective man, but he had spent more time than he liked to admit pondering his break-up with Cheeoh. She was the best barber he'd ever seen. Nobody else could cut his hair right without shearing him. He'd watched Cheeoh carefully. When he moved out, he cut his hair himself. She didn't criticize him. She didn't up and want a baby. She never mentioned marriage. What went wrong? He vowed he'd never move in with a woman again. It was the sharing of the roof that led to catastrophe.

Winger admitted that you couldn't really call a woman yours until you paid some of the bills and took on some of the responsibility. But she couldn't call you hers, either, in those circumstances. Nobody took anybody for granted. You couldn't demand too much in the way of conjugal rights with your head in the window and your foot out the door, and that always led to some hooting and hollering. It led, Winger said, to the same old question every time.

"Winger Burns, just who the hell do you think you are?"

"Nothin' more than Winger Burns, and, lady, I am *temporarily on loan to you!*"

They generally settled for his terms. I found all of this fascinating. Why, Winger? Why did they settle for your terms? He grinned like a Cheshire cat, but was mute. O.K. I'd ask my mother. He gave me a rough clout across the ear. If I wanted to get on in this world, I'd better learn to keep my eyes wide open and my big mouth shut.

He worked on the docks for five years altogether. He acquired the tattooed clipper ship the night he left Cheeoh's house. He got so roaring-eyed drunk on rot-gut whiskey, he couldn't even remember the episode. And he formed the philosophy that was to get him through his relationships with women for the next ten years: You anchored yourself mentally to your shaving kit. If you were roaring-eyed drunk, if you were halfway to Timbuctoo, if she fell on her knees and resorted to pleas—three, four, five in the morning—in a car, on a bike, shank's mare if you had to—you went home to your kit, and your cot, and your room, and you greeted the dawn alone.

In 1926, while loading wheat on a ship, he paused and looked behind him. He saw the mountains rising up out of the bay, behind Vancouver. He was sick to death of ships and water and cities. He rode the rails east for three days, examining each town until one caught his fancy. When he reached Buena Vista, he couldn't believe his eyes. The train stopped and he jumped off without a moment's hesitation, and went into the station. Joseph Hilliard saw him ambling around. When the platform had cleared, and no one came to meet him, Mr. Hilliard approached him. "Son, you look to me like you're riding without a ticket." Winger said, and I had no reason to disbelieve him, that he asked Mr. Hilliard pointblank whether he was friend or foe.

"That depends. My wife says I'm hospitable to strangers and inhospitable at home."

"Well," said Winger, "I'm a stranger."

"Right. Are you going to settle here awhile?"

"I don't know. It sure looks good to me."

"That depends whether you're looking for work or looking for trouble."

"Well, sir," said Winger, "I've worked in Trail and I've worked in Vancouver. All those places got the same definition for work. But the definition for trouble—that varies from place to place. I guess all I can say is when I work, I work, and when I party, I party, and I learned a long time ago not to mix 'em."

Mr. Hilliard said he had a friend on the Road Commission. He said the roads were the government's number-one concern because the summer visitors were coming in swarms and the roads weren't fit for horse and buggy. He took him home and gave him a meal. Mrs. Hilliard unabashedly asked for his dirty underwear. She said her son, Seth, had married six years before and the one thing she missed was his bulk of dirty laundry. It was hardly worth running the machine after Seth left. The following morning, with clean clothing and a full stomach, Buena Vista looked even better. He decided to stay until it went bad, or got sour, or the job became monotonous. The place was so beautiful—he vowed he'd do everything in his power to prevent any of those contingencies.

X

They did not give me my manumission until there was a place for everything and everything was in its place. And while they scurried about, accomplishing this feat, I loomed over them like Marley's ghost. They wanted me seen, but not heard. God knows, they didn't *need* me. My presence served no useful purpose.

"Please, can I go out now?"

"NO!"

"Hey, listen, can I just take a walk over to the hotel?"

"NO!"

"Look, you guys, I want to go meet that girl next door."

"NO!"

"Give me just *one good reason* why not?"

"NO!"

Sit, Jay. Stay, Jay. Eat, Jay. Sleep, Jay. There's a good boy.

Finally, Father drove me into town and bought me a spanking-new Schwinn. Me and my Schwinn were hell on wheels back in Grosse Pointe, but Grosse Pointe is, of course, flat as a pancake. I knew I had some hard peddling ahead of me on mountain roads but we all agreed, once again, that it would be good for me. We stopped at Mr. Samson's with a list Mother had given us. We had to buy eggs, not because Father yearned for a proper breakfast, but because Mother had those two heads of lettuce. Her luncheon effort was to be a Caesar salad. We also bought some bologna so that I could pack a lunch and go exploring for the whole day. I remember that first day out on the road very clearly. I had a map of the area, and I'd decided to take a back road that ran behind Mount Binnie and ended at Acorn Lake. Mr. Samson told me about Acorn, saying it was a perfect gem, impossible to reach by car, because there was only a thread of a trail for the last mile. It was a small, glacial lake, only a dot on the map. Tourists seldom went there, due to the perilous last mile. It would be about twelve miles in all—six there and six back. My sandwiches were placed in my basket, I heeded the warning about bears and falling rock, kissed Mother goodbye and finally, after nearly two years of talking about it, was off to have a look at the majestic mountains.

Be it God, Buddha, Mohammed or some gaseous mass—I am eternally grateful to whatever it was that gave us the Canadian Rockies. It's very difficult to look back over forty years of World War II, Korea, Vietnam, tainted air, ravaged land—close at hand the dormant slough that once was Lake Erie—and not wax eloquent about Buena Vista. I remember, back in the sixties, I'd reached a point where several months passed by without my thinking about it. It had receded to the darker reaches of my brain, and I bumbled along for whole seasons without ever giving it a moment's thought. Then, during the Detroit riots, in 1967, it became a fixation. Twelfth Street was in flames, Grosse Pointe had a curfew, the National Guard was posted everywhere with fixed bayonets. Black youth was on the rampage, filling all of us with blood-curdling fear. The six-o'clock screen lacerated us with close-ups of young sneering black men, arrogant politicians in pin-striped suits, old, wincing white men being driven out of furniture stores and pawnshops. The refugees of the holocaust sat on the doorsteps of burnt-out buildings. Hyped-up reporters approached them, vapidly asking where would they go now? Did they have anything left? What did they think of it all? And elderly black women stared at us through the six-o'clock tube, and assured the quivering white majority that it wasn't intentional—they hadn't raised their sons to turn out this way. Where was God? Where was mercy? Where, oh, where was the Fire Department?

None of the Pointes was harmed, but I found little comfort in that. Since the beginning, we'd always breathed a rarefied air in the Pointes, and now the seething, smoking city was more than I could bear. Disgruntled revolutionaries stood in the rubble, on the eleven-o'clock screen, and made it clear: my turn was coming. My days, so many of my lazy, slothful, trust-protected days reared up before me. I had never in my life felt quite so inept, inadequate and downright obsolete. My nights, then, became a panorama of floating visions. I stood, serenely peaceful, at the edge of Bear's Hump, gazing down at Acorn Lake. It lay there, five hundred feet below me, a clear emerald green with pink edges. I raised my eyes and looked down into the Mistaya Valley, a broad expanse of fifty miles, ending at the Yoho. I peddled for miles over razorback ridges the entire length of Lake Moraine. I saw the jagged white peaks of the Seven Sisters all around me, and saw them again reflected in the water. Fourteen snow-capped mountains, all over ten thousand feet, encircling me, enveloping me, overwhelming me with awe and wonder. I could feel, in my hands, those old, corrugated Orange Crush bottles. I would place mine in the Bow, the Sunwapta, the Athabasca, and return three hours later to find them glistening there, between the rocks, icy cold. I could feel, deep in my groin, Eileen MacMillan's Appaloosa below me. We would stop every half-hour or so, beside rippling streams or frothing waterfalls under Mount Norquay or Mount Assiniboine. We rode long and hard, and when we spotted moose or goats or sheep or antelope on rocky ridges or deep in the evergreens, we never stopped. They had seen us, too, and if we stopped or even slowed to a trot, they disappeared, gauging the speed of their departure with that of the hooves on the trail.

I awoke, drenched in sweat, the bedclothes twisted and knotted. I turned on the radio over my bed and heard Walter Reuther, Edward Cole, Henry Ford vowing that something would be done. The fires would be put out, the wretched, charred buildings would be replaced. The unskilled and untrainable, the displaced and dispossessed, would all be taken care of. General Motors, Ford, Chrysler, the U.A.W.—*all* had better ideas! They, with their vast resources, committed themselves to new projects and programs. The riot was photographed and documented. The costs were tallied. Committees were formed. Panels were convened, replacing the vapid reporters on the eleven-o'clock screen. Detroit had been neglected. There was going to be a New Detroit.

I didn't believe a word of it. Pat was furious with me. What cause had I to be so despondent? Ed Humboldt and all those other auto men on Lake Shore Road—*they* had cause. They'd made their millions, scraped them off the laboring backs of thousands of men on the lines and in the pits. You only had to look at the Diego Rivera mural at the Institute to know who was at fault: the men who owned the machines. MacAllister money—forests—lumber—none of that had anything to do with the turmoil on Twelfth Street. Ours was old money, innocent money, clean money. My conscience should be clear. The belching smokestacks of River Rouge were far, far away. I would hie me to my trundle bed fast as catch can, and shut out her voice, and the screen, and the pounding migraine headache. Two Demerols and I was off on my Schwinn, cruising through Kicking Horse Pass. Three Demerols and I heard the bagpipes filling the air at Lake Louise.

After two weeks of this, Pat was hysterical. What I was doing, according to her analysis, was cuddling up in that cozy Buena Vista womb. What I'd better do, before the men in the white coats got wind of it, was seek professional help. Now, I try to listen to Pat whenever possible. I have given her very little in marriage and it seems the least I can do. I went to see a psychiatrist, and I have to admit it was worth the fifty dollars. I told him the riots had gotten me down and I spent an inordinate amount of time in bed, dreaming of a magic place I'd known in my youth. I figured that, since everybody who goes to see a psychiatrist is in for prolonged analysis, I might as well be hung for a sheep as a lamb. The

Demerol bottle was empty and it seemed altogether too late for reticence, so I blurted it out:

"You see, it's the womb."

He impressed me mightily. He smiled. He said it would all go away when the smoke died down. Everybody he'd seen in the last two weeks was doing the same thing, with small variations, and in two particular cases, deviations, on the theme. We'd both been in Ann Arbor at just about the same time, so we reminisced about that for the last fifteen minutes. He rose and shook my hand. I didn't need analysis. I wasn't deranged. (Why, in God's name, didn't I get that in writing? I could use such a document now, in my daily defense of *Roams.*)

He was right. The National Guard went home. The network cameras returned to New York and left the ashes to the local stations. The gardeners, chauffeurs and day maids came back to Grosse Pointe without suspicion. And I slipped into my lazy, slothful, trust-protected days once again.

XI

When I returned from Acorn Lake, I sensed a strain even as I approached the house. It was early evening; I could see Mother and Father in the living room as I walked up the hill. I was hungry to the point of dizziness, but I was anxious to tell them about my discoveries. My excitement was soon squelched. Father didn't acknowledge my presence at all. Mother handed me a letter, received that day from Dougie Clark, and perfunctorily ordered me to the kitchen, where a plate of cold ham and wilted Caesar salad awaited me. Sit, Jay. Eat, Jay. They continued whatever it was I had interrupted.

"Josh isn't coming for two more weeks, Jimmy. You can't go on like this in the interim."

My father made no reply. I got a knife and fork from the drawer and sat down in the kitchen.

"It's too damned *late* for this, Jimmy! We agreed it was isolated. We agreed it was too remote. We agreed all that at its *inception!* Josh himself said so. Did you really expect to find a Canadian facsimile of Polly Adler smack in the middle of Buena Vista?"

I cut my ham very quietly, waiting for his reply. He made none.

"Well, *did* you? Did you envision wall-to-wall roadhouses from here to Calgary?"

He replied, not in anger, but with a weary, vague lassitude.

"I thought there'd be some people."

Mother thought there were some people. Mr. MacMillan, next door, was an affluent rancher from Medicine Hat. Mr. Dickinson, two hundred yards on the other side of us, was a pharmacist in Red Deer. Why didn't he try to make their acquaintance? Weren't they people? No, said Father, they weren't people. Mr. Samson was a very pleasant man, full of interesting yarns and historical data. Why not get something going with him this weekend? No, he wasn't people, either. He was a grocer. He was even less people than Mac-Millan and Dickinson. Seth Hilliard and Winger Burns apparently liked to fish. Mother had noticed hip waders on the Hilliards' back porch. I glanced through the gallery to the living room. Father was sitting by the fire in his maroon kimono. He looked askance. Was she trying to be funny?

There were tennis courts, a golf course and a pool at the Amberley Hotel. The Amberley was a monstrous old place, very expensive, very Victorian, and all of the clientele looked to Mother very much like people. Father, too, thought they resembled people, but he'd investigated the Amberley yesterday afternoon and found, to his dismay, they weren't. They were old ladies and old men who seemed to be suffering from a variety of bone diseases, and they were families who went on bus tours together and wore baggy clothes. The only people who were having any fun at the Amberley were the waitresses. They were lodged in a building at the back of the hotel, and not one of them was over twenty. Then, too, they weren't your average waitresses. They were clean-cut schoolgirls; many of their families had cottages around Buena Vista. He had talked to two of them. They were less mature than Jay. They *liked* being waitresses. They were kids, not people.

Mother, being unbelievably reasonable about all this, paced up and down in front of the fireplace, with her hands in the pockets of her slacks. Pity now took the place of agitation in her voice.

"Would you like me to run over and ask the MacMillans in for a drink?"

"That would be awkward. What would you say?"

"I'd tell them we're lonely and we'd like to get to know them."

Up he shot, in a fit of anger. Who the hell said he was lonely? He wasn't lonely. He'd had a great time yesterday, taking pictures. If she thought he was lonely, she had another thought coming. He waved me hello, he bade me goodnight and pounded up the stairs to bed, making a glorious, truculent exit.

Mother came into the kitchen and sat down at the table with me. I had thought the scene with Father would leave her distraught, but no, like a chameleon, she adapted to the bright yellow kitchen and left the tempest behind. For well over an hour I told her about Acorn, groping for adjectives, describing every ferny dell in purple superlatives. She was relaxed and interested. She seemed relieved to spend the time with me, relieved to simply listen.

How strange—paradoxical—that she would suggest going to the MacMillans' and Father would decline. Her hair didn't look so undone here at Timberline, perhaps because she'd given up all those strait-laced dresses with capes and boleros. She now rattled around in pants and sweaters. Her face didn't look so pale and gaunt—it occurred to me that I hadn't seen any women, anywhere, wearing make-up. And then I understood what Father meant. I, too, hadn't seen anyone around Buena Vista who looked like people. Maybe that's why Mother flourished here. There was no social calendar, no appointment book by the phone. Mr. Bates, the headmaster at school (that's right, Master Bates!), wasn't calling to say he had noticed the first, disturbing signs of sloth in my behavior. Mr. Samson charged exactly what the food cost, without that annoying ten percent tacked on for Cook. Our meals here were simple, one-course affairs with one lonely fork to the left of the plate and a plain cotton cloth beneath it all. No Flemish tapestry covered our dining-room wall and there was no buzzer on the floor connecting us, umbilically, with the kitchen. Our towels weren't changed for us daily—mine, indeed, became a stiff, charcoal gray before Mother noticed it and carried it, between index finger and thumb, to the basket.

As for civic duties, the church—the United Church of Canada—went to the natives whenever it needed bailing out, and called the rest of us summertime heathens. That was it. We were transients here. We didn't belong. We didn't vote, we didn't sit on the town council. In our case, we weren't even citizens. We had a vague, but not a vested interest in the other ten months of the year. We'd all go home soon and in the meantime we weren't worth bothering about. I looked at Mother across the table. Timberline became her.

Beside me, here on my desk, I have Dougie Clark's letter from Paris. It is addressed in an adolescent hand that had not, as yet, found its final form. He must have been striving for a certain boldness, for the writing is, after four decades, thick, black and upright. I read it to Mother that night, before we retired. It capped the evening off nicely, with a good laugh.

10, rue Marbeau
Paris 16ᵉ, France
June 20, 1932

Dear Red,

Listen, I am having one helluva time finding a private moment. My old lady decided to hire me a companion this summer, since she's all tied up with some guy who designs the sets at the Comédie Française. This companion has turned out to be more of a governess, and let me tell you, she is one royal pain in the ass. Her name is Huguette, and she is a student at the Sorbonne. She's only twenty and she's already got sagging tits. I figure she's got about five good years left and I keep telling her: nix on the books, Huguette, your salad days are numbered.

So here I am, caught between these crazy excursions with crazy Huguette, and boring, *dismally* boring, evenings hanging around backstage at the Comédie Française with my mother. I can't for the life of me see what my old lady sees in this set designer. He is one helluva freak, and so are all of his friends. The bunch of them would be tarred and feathered and hung from trees by the balls, back in Flint. Except I find no evidence of balls in any of them.

Boy, Red, have I ever got a smashing case of the old *ennui*. I've seen all this damn stuff before, and I never could get excited about rose windows. Jesus, I really envy you, sitting around up there in the wild, listening to moose calls. I keep telling Huguette: you've seen one *arrondissement*, you've seen 'em all. She keeps telling me she's going to show me *her* Paris. No question her Paris is more normal than my mother's Paris, but she ruins everything by lecturing at me, long past my saturation point. I just don't want to know that much about anything. I finally got all those syphilitic old kings straight and now she wants me to memorize their offspring—nearly all of whom were illegitimate. Huguette charmingly calls these bastards "natural children." I am trying like hell to get a crush on her. Problem is, by the time I'm old enough to shave, poor old Huguette's sun will have set. Paris is jam-packed with women whose suns have long ago set, and boy, are they pathetic! That kind of trouble I don't need.

We've turned up only one interesting thing in the past three weeks. There's a seventeenth-century convent, way the hell on the outskirts of town, and about fifty years ago they discovered a huge graveyard out back of it. This is not one of your ordinary grave-yards, full of senile old stiffs. This one's full of babies. For hun-dreds of years those priests were knocking up the nuns in there and burying the babies out back of the place. I always see paint-ings of those guys scratching away on parchment, surrounded with books and compasses. I'd sure as hell like to see just one of them depicted out back of a convent with his robes rolled up and a shovel in his hand. Old Master Bates keeps harping about the his-tory of the Catholic Church. I'm really going to give him an earful when I get back, because he's nuts if he thinks any of this stuff is recorded in books.

Crazy old Huguette is knocking at my door again. Time for a Visit to Another Historical Place. The guards at the Louvre are so used to me, they don't even watch me any more. I'm gonna sneak out one of those Fabergé eggs one of these days. I'll sell it in Detroit and maybe you and I can use the bounty to get our-selves a Taste of High Life.

You better get that piano off your arm and write, Red. Keep it clean, though, O.K.? My debauched old lady might read it. She thinks I've come this far with blinders on.

Miss ya,
DOUGLAS

XII

Saturday, the Day of the Totem Pole, began when I pulled open my newly arrived venetian blind and saw something move near our back door. It was a fawn. I ran down to the kitchen, bounded in and was met with a loud ssshh! from Mother. She, too, had seen the fawn, and she signaled to me to come to the door. The fawn was nosing around our patio and we could see, twenty yards away in the foliage, the doe. Mother got the corn flakes, filled my cupped hands, and I padded out to the patio in my pajamas. The doe immediately stood at attention, but the fawn wobbled over and ate the corn flakes. He—it was a *he*; I established that posthaste—had very good manners. He didn't make any noise and he didn't wet my hand too much. He had those eyes that I always think exaggerated when I see them in paintings—enormous, velvet eyes. Mother was whispering something about not letting him bite me, and Father was behind Mother in the doorway, taking a picture. I fed the fawn three handfuls of corn flakes. He thanked me with a blink from the limpid pools of velvet brown and climbed up the hill to his mother. Father took another picture of me in my pajamas. I've just been looking at that snapshot in our old album. Under it, in my mother's handwriting, in white ink, it says: "Jay, in pajamas, at B.V." The one with the fawn didn't turn out.

So it goes.

An hour later, Mr. Samson's boy, Arnold, delivered a box of groceries just as Seth backed into the driveway with the totem pole. Arnold asked if he could stay and watch and we said yes, of course. The pole, or rather the carton containing the pole, had a big red rag hanging off the end of it. At least ten feet of it extended beyond the truck's limit. Winger and Bob Hilliard were in the back of the truck, steadying the carton, and Seth was in the front with two women. One was Elsie, who wore a blue polka-dot scarf and carried two more heads of lettuce. The other was Nancy Worth, who startled Father, Mother and me, because she looked like people. She was a small, elegant woman, nattily dressed in white pants and a navy blazer. She looked fairly old to me—taking my fourteen-year-old standards into consideration, I would now place her somewhere in her mid-thirties. She owned the Petit-Pointe Bone China Shop, which was located on the main street, next to Mr. Samson's grocery. She was, to my father's astonishment, accompanying Winger Burns. Seth and Winger looked at my father and then exchanged glances. Father was wearing a plaid shirt but he, also, wore white pants. White sharkskin pants. They guessed he wasn't about to pitch in and help with the pole, certainly not in that get-up. Eileen MacMillan spotted Bob and came over. Her primary interest was in watching the erection of the pole, but she made my acquaintance as a fringe benefit.

Winger and Seth began to grouse. The bunch of them were going on a picnic, and they'd expected Mr. Harmon to be here already. Mr. Harmon was the man we'd engaged to dig the hole and pour the concrete. Mother went into the house to call while Father tried, futilely, to strike up a conversation with Miss Worth. Miss Worth had eyes for Winger Burns exclusively. Arnold and I went and sat down beside Winger, who continued to grouse.

"God*damn* that old Harmon! Don't he know ten A.M. means ten A.M.? Don't he know some people got better things to do on Saturday?"

Mother came out with the news that Mr. Harmon had left his house and would be here any minute.

"What's that red rag hanging off the carton for?" said I, innocently.

"Oh," said Winger, "them's a pair of Nancy's old bloomers. We hung 'em there so's everybody'd keep a distance."

We all laughed at this, excepting Father. Miss Worth laughed, too, and came over and ran her fingers through Winger's curly hair. She did this compulsively, and frequently, during the following two hours. It must have been her predilection for Winger's hair that made me notice Eileen MacMillan's long, chestnut tresses. Eileen was a spindly little girl who talked of nothing but Ginger and Storm, Storm and Ginger. I liked the look of her, and I remember hoping that I might, on some occasion, get her off the subject of horses and onto something that would yield fodder for a letter to Dougie Clark.

"God*damn* that old Harmon!" said Seth.

"Where the hell is he at? That old bugger'll be late for his own funeral."

Old Harmon heaved his broken-down truck up the driveway, in a cloud of exhaust fumes. He got out, raised his fist and hollered at Seth.

"What the hell kind of bird-brained parkin' job is that, Seth? You gotta park on the road and let me get my truck up there by the door!"

Seth and Mr. Harmon climbed back into their trucks. Mr. Harmon drove down the driveway, followed by Seth. Seth pulled into the road while Mr. Harmon backed up his truck to the corner of the house. Seth, then, decided to back into the driveway again, in front of Mr. Harmon's truck. They both got out, slamming doors, Harmon screaming this time through his unkempt, steel-gray mustache:

"Seth, you got the whole goddamned Gobi Desert 'tween your ears, I swear! Dontcha see you'll have to pull out when I get done with the hole so's to let me pull out so's you can pull in again and get that pole up here somewhere's near the door?"

He turned, and scowled at me.

"Musical trucks, son, that's what we're playing. Musical trucks."

Seth tried to introduce Mr. Harmon to my mother and father, but Mr. Harmon had no time for amenities. He climbed up on his truck and started to throw down his gear. He acknowledged Elsie's presence and, upon seeing Miss Worth, whispered something to Seth. Seth laughed, Winger grinned, Mother blushed and Miss Worth came over and ran her fingers through Winger's hair again.

These three men had never before sunk a totem pole, but it was clear that they had worked together many times. There was a flurry of activity, but there was no wasted motion. Each man anticipated the next man's move and went, without instruction, to fetch the appropriate tool. A rhythm of gestures and movements developed, interrupted now and then by harsh expletives. Harmon, who was sixty if he was a day, knew this earth like the back of his hand. When they hit rock,

Winger and Seth groaned and cursed. Harmon delighted in ridiculing them. Didn't they take their vitamins? Didn't they eat their Wheaties? There was nothing under this crust that wasn't familiar to him. While Winger and Seth rolled back on their haunches, bemoaning the rock and shale, Harmon laughed with glee and turned, proudly, to my father. "This here old Binnie holds no surprises for *me*." He talked of the mountain as if they were intimate friends.

"She's a good old soul, old Binnie. Kind of a lamb, as mountains go. She ain't carrying no grudge. That old Lizzie, now there's a cantankerous piece of rock. That old bitch, I'll tell you, in 1916 she let go one whole side and killed all the folks in the lime quarry underneath. Seventy-five folks in all, didn't know what hit 'em. I knew what hit 'em. I said to Joe Hilliard—that's Seth's paw, down at the station—I said, 'Joe, you know what? Old Lizzie's going through the change.' I said I'd steer clear of that mountain for the next five years and he would, too, if he had an ounce of brains. By God, I was right! Three years later they're just getting that quarry together again, and old Lizzie starts agitatin'. She shakes and she rumbles, and them boulders, twenty foot wide and a zillion of 'em, they come flying down that slide and killed fifteen men buildin' up the quarry. Old Binnie sat and watched it all. She ain't carrying no grudge. She went through her change long time ago—who knows, maybe when them dinosaurs was roaming around here. She's a gentle old soul, and her innards is at peace.

"For Chris*sake*, Seth, will you watch that pick? Are you trying to blind me, Seth? Swing it over that way—blind all them snot-nosed little buggers running around here, gettin' in the way."

I was never able to look at Mount Elizabeth after that without a tinge of fear. She was a cantankerous old bitch. She harbored terrible forces—unspeakable secrets lay dormant inside of her. She was not to be trusted.

During the following hours the aforementioned snot-nosed little buggers (Bob, Eileen, Arnold and I) generally made nuisances of ourselves. Harmon bellowed at us; Winger thought it would solve everybody's problems if they dug an extra-deep hole and threw all of us in. Father was at loose ends until he remembered his camera, and then recorded every step of the hole digging, the concrete pouring and the pole sinking for posterity. Mother and Miss Worth had a pleasant, relaxed talk about Josiah Wedgwood. Here, again, Mother had a wealth of information and talked in such a quiet and unassuming manner that even Winger Burns took an interest. Miss Worth prided herself on her knowledge of English bone china. This was not one-upmanship; Mother had no wish to put Miss Worth to shame. She simply had facts that she wished to share. While at school in London, twenty years before, she had visited the Wedgwood works in Staffordshire. She saw them making Queen's Ware. Did Miss Worth know it was named that after Josiah presented a set to Queen Charlotte in 1762? She saw them making the famous blue and green salt-glazed Jasper Ware. Did Miss Worth know that the white bas-relief medallions were Hellenic in provenance? Josiah had visited the British Museum just after Lord Elgin brought the Marbles back from Greece, and proceeded to decorate his Jasper Ware with miniature cameos. No, unfortunately, Miss Worth didn't know any of those things.

I began to get anxious about all this. There was my father, jumping up and down like a Mexican bean, shoving his Kodak into Mr. Harmon's disgruntled face, exerting all sorts of precautions to keep his sharkskin pants clean. There was my mother, going on just a bit too long about Wedgwood and Greece. I thought Winger would come up with a super-deflating wisecrack at any moment, but he didn't. He listened. He asked a couple of questions. He watched her like a hawk. He told me about this later, in his own words. He couldn't believe his eyes and ears. Here was a woman entirely without guile or artifice. She'd never learned how to be coy. She was just there, among us, without defenses, without façades, like a newborn pup. But she was forty. How had she survived all these years without some kind of protection?

The real difficulty came when they couldn't manage to get the pole at right angles to the ground. They tried and tried, but it stubbornly tilted forward. Harmon had Arnold and me haul three long boards off his truck and we placed them against the front of the pole; however, the pole was so high and the boards were so short, nothing was accomplished. Winger said you couldn't really expect those Kamloops Indians to know anything about engineering. Mother—my God, what was she doing?—took him to task for this. She said the Indians knew a great deal about engineering, they knew it instinctively. She said it wasn't very nice to make deprecating remarks about the Indians when the fault clearly lay in our own ignorance. Now, I thought, right now, Harmon's going to throw a shovel at her and call it quits. But there was no retort, no grimace. He rubbed the sweat off his forehead and admitted there must be some special trick to sinking a forty-foot totem pole. I heaved a sigh of relief. She was getting away with it. "Just a minute," she said. "I've got some papers that might help." She ran into the house and returned with a brown envelope. On the front of it, in my grandmother's handwriting, it said, "Laura—read this." Harmon, Winger and Seth sat down at the base of the pole and Mother proceeded to read the printed contents of the envelope.

Dear Customer:

You have acquired a totem pole which was carved by the Haida Indians who live on the Queen Charlotte Islands in British Columbia. The pole was erected there in the early nineteen hundreds and remained there until our company purchased it, ten years ago.

It belonged to a family in the tribe, and the figures represent family crests from both the man's and the woman's ancestral line. Many Haida families erected these poles, having obtained permission to do so from the Chief. The Chief's fee for granting permission was one hundred blankets.

There are six carved heads, topped with four small crouching figures. These figures wear tall, cylindrical hats. They are called "Watchers" and are common to the poles of the Haida tribe. You will notice that the head at the bottom has a large tongue which falls out of its mouth and is held by a hand. This head represents a grizzly bear. The other heads have hooked noses, enormous black eyes and large even rows of oversized white teeth. The hands at the bottom of the heads hold a variety of birds, fish, frogs and other animals.

We sincerely hope that your Haida pole brings you much aesthetic pleasure, and that you will tell your friends about our company. We have a splendid array of totem poles. They are described and photographed in our catalogue, which is available for the price of $1.00.

Mother folded the paper and put it back in the envelope. Mr. Harmon slowly rose from his sitting position and spat on the fresh, black mound of earth. "Mrs. Rutherford, it's good to know all that, but there ain't a single word in there about installation." Well, said Winger, he was damned if he was going to stand there supporting it until the concrete dried. So it was left, tilting slightly toward the road. We all applauded and cheered. Miss Worth said it was an impressive piece of carving and added that those big white teeth were almost as perfect as Winger's—and ran her fingers through his hair again. Father said he'd take a run up there some night and throw down a stone, à la Galileo. We all stopped dead in our tracks, stared at him and wished he'd stop trying so hard. Old Harmon left right away. He had to pour some stairs for another new family—a Mormon family from Salt Lake City. Between the totem pole and the polygamists, it sure was turning out to be an interesting Saturday. Mother wrote out his check; Bob and Arnold and I loaded the last of his equipment, and he was on his way.

At this juncture there occurred a certain strain between Bob Hilliard and me. Eileen had asked me if I had a girl friend back in Grosse Pointe, and for some reason this question promptly put his nose out of joint. I couldn't understand his attitude—he was, after all, only twelve. And he was the one about to go on a picnic. And, even then, I envied him the company of Winger Burns. There seemed to be an added strain over all of this check writing my mother was doing. Seth, God knows, had worked like a Trojan, and deserved every penny. But when Seth took the check from Mother, Bob looked away and sheepishly glanced at Eileen. Elsie, beaming cheerfully, thanked my mother profusely, and offered her hand to my father. I learned that day that Elsie was Dutch. For four decades now, I've admired the Dutch. They have a settlement at Holland, Michigan, and Pat and I try to go up each spring for the Tulip Festival. At the risk of being simplistic, I must say I've always found them to be just like Elsie Hilliard. Squeaky-clean, friendly and generous to a fault.

Now, nobody else noticed it, nobody else heard it. It lasted a second but it was, I think, where my story really begins. We were standing in clusters, at the front door, around the base of the totem pole, against Seth's truck. Mother and Winger were at the rear of the truck. He was gazing into her face again, as he had two nights before at the Hilliards'. I assumed it was a repeat of the conversation about freckles. I was fooling around with Arnold and Eileen. I had no reason to eavesdrop. But why was she standing in that peculiar pose? Her head was cocked toward him and she was holding her arms back, with her hands on her hips. This made her bosom protrude. I had never been particularly aware of Mother's breasts. At home they were always hidden somewhere under folds of crepe de Chine or those terrible lace boleros. I found myself wishing she'd hunch over a bit, so they wouldn't be quite so noticeable.

Winger bent his head, said something inaudible and grinned. She left her head where it was, very near his face now, and she smiled ever so slightly. I heard her say: "No, Mr. Burns, there aren't any. Not a single one—anywhere."

Part Two

XIII

Saturday Night with Pat and Jay

"Miss Fenstrom used to say writers can't understand the universe until they understand the smallest grain of sand."

We are in the car, going out to dinner. Pat looks lean and trim. Her evenings on the Exercycle are paying off.

"Professor Trumbull used to say 'particularize.' Same thing, I guess."

"Do you presume to understand the smallest grain of sand?"

"No."

"Then we can't anticipate a universal truth imbedded somewhere deep in *Roams?*"

"We can anticipate, but we'll be disappointed."

"Goodness, we don't want to be disappointed!"

"Goodness, no."

"But nevertheless, you're writing a novel."

"Trying to."

"Well, what *can* we anticipate from this novel?"

"Oh, various reflections on a couple of people during a magic summer a long, long time ago."

"That's all?"

"That's all."

"You don't want to bite off more than you can chew."

"Goodness, no. Better to do a small thing right than fuck up the universe."

"Your language is atrocious. You're picking it up from Deb."

"Wrong. I picked it up a long time ago from Douglas Clark. I'm just reviving it in my old age. Hey, I'm going to send a telegram when we get to the Humboldts'."

"To whom?"

"To the President's Commission on Scientific Affairs. I'm

going to say: 'Better to do a small thing right than fuck up the universe.' "

A long pause. She is wearing a charm bracelet and a crocheted dress. The problems inherent in this combination are enormous. The charms get caught in the lacy holes every time she moves her hand. Pat moves her hands continually when she talks.

"Gee, I hope you don't have to sit with your wrist hooked to your thigh all evening."

"Why don't you just shut up?"

"Good idea! I'll turn on the radio."

"Please don't."

"I'll turn on the windshield wipers."

"Oh, God!"

"How'd you like a little heat?"

I've gone too far. My pitiful little attempts at levity are lost. We are back on Mount Rushmore again.

"Patricia, let me tell you how I feel right now. I'd rather be banished to an island of lepers than go with you to the Humboldts' tonight."

She is concentrating on the glove-compartment knob, and biting her lip. We pass the house I grew up in. It's only about half a mile from the one I presently own. It must be keeping its secrets well. I'm told a big happy Catholic family lives there now.

"Oh, Jay, everything's out of whack now that you're bent on this public penmanship. It's terrific that you're finally doing *something*, but writing, at your age, is grasping at straws. An aberration of middle age. An attempt to portray a rosy, marvelous youth, with the conclusion that it's been lousy ever since. And another thing. You really should let me help with the title. Only an illiterate would buy a book called *Roams*."

"Illiterates don't buy books."

"They buy *comic* books, don't they? They buy *Mickey Spillane*. Look. I just want to get it on the record and then we'll change the subject. I think it's a dalliance at middle age. Wouldn't you know you'd choose to write a book rather than run off and sleep with a twenty-year-old, the way Ed Humboldt does. I really do want to change the subject. But one other thing before I do. For the record, once and for all, I hate this stupid little car. I hate going out in it. I hate the way it sits there, in the driveway, like something from F. A. O. Schwartz. Henry Ford drives past our house every day and he sees it, sitting there, and I'll bet he knows as well as I do *cars like this are aberrations.*"

"Are you done?"

"I am."

In case none of the above makes sense to those people who don't happen to live in the Detroit metropolitan area, foreign cars are anathema on Lake Shore Road.

Too quickly, before the mercury has a chance to recede, I say:

"I get a real bang out of the Humboldts."

"Ed Humboldt is your closest friend. Spare me, please, disparaging remarks about your closest friend."

"All right."

"I *would* like to know, though, why you get a real bang out of the Humboldts."

"Oh, they've gone to so much trouble to build a streamlined, ultra-modern, no-nonsense house, and then they put those awful stone lions on either side of the gate. Nellie told me they got them from an English country house."

"They're nice people. I can forgive them the lions. They're just people. They make mistakes. Human beings make mistakes, Jay."

"Oh, I know. I know. Most people don't display them quite so pretentiously on Lake Shore Road."

"Most people don't air their dirty linen in a book."

I see the lions dimly, a block away. I decide that they are one of Nellie Humboldt's aberrations, and I guess that's all right, as aberrations go. It seems a safe time to stop the talk and compose ourselves. We're not in a rage, our hearts aren't thumping. However, as we pull into the driveway and approach the series of rectangular concrete slabs that are the Humboldts' house, Pat says:

"Why don't you go to London for a while? You always come back from London refreshed and sane."

"I only go to London in the spring, when I need refreshing. I don't need refreshing now because I'm busy writing a book. If you want to know what I think, Pat, I think you're afraid I'll make a balls of it and finish my days in infamy."

Furiously, she waves her right hand across her chest. We leave the car; I go around to help my lady disembark. She's in trouble again with the bracelet, but, being Patsy, she'll greet the morning sun before she'll ask for help. I poke in my paw and disengage a miniature Eiffel Tower from her right breast. Twenty-five years together, oh Lord, twenty-five years. But at this moment she's pubescent Pat and I'm the big bad child molester. She slaps my hand and widens her eyes and gasps at my effrontery. As we silently approach the house, Herbert the butler opens the door and smiles at us. Herbert the butler is the spitting image of Arthur Treacher. He was part of the Humboldts' package deal. They found him, and the lions, somewhere in Surrey, about ten years ago.

The concrete slabs are eerie in the moonlight. I feel like a Druid entering Stonehenge.

Sunday Morning with Pat and Jay

I am standing in our attic in front of a full-length mahogany mirror. I am wearing a pith helmet and holding a BB gun. I am singing "On the Road to Mandalay"—vigorously. Just as the sun comes up over Rangoon Bay, I hear her foot on the stairs. We have spent an unbearably silent morning making hasty entrances and exits from rooms which couldn't contain the both of us. We haven't passed like ships in the night; no, the battleground is the one place where we excel. Verbal warriors we, silence is something we cannot tolerate. We sideswipe each other, grinding gears, not quite colliding, hoping the sparks will ignite a skirmish. We perform this rite at least once a month, the last hundred yards leading, irrevocably, to an apology. The apology must be hers, this time, because her behavior at the Humboldts' was inexcusable. I shudder. I cringe. Pat is inept at apologies. The rest of the ceremony is fun—gnashing teeth, matching wits. We've had so much practice, we've developed a marvelous élan. It's too bad it has to fizzle out with one of Pat's pathetic apologies.

"Jay, are you in the attic?"

"Yes, I am."

She can't ever apologize when I'm sitting comfortably in my wing-back chair, smoking my pipe. She gets me cornered in the attic, strutting with my pith helmet and BB gun. The attic stairs are a steep climb. Up she comes, pausing at the top to look at me. She's out of breath. She huffs and puffs, and gives me a careful once-over.

"Pukka, pukka," she says.

"Hello, Patricia."

She enters the room and reaches down into the pocket of her dress. She pulls out her pack of cigarettes and gives it the swift whack on the bottom. No porcelain peacock here, so I avert my gaze to a pair of Deb's old roller skates.

"What in the world are you rummaging around up here for?"

"I'm looking for something."

"What?"

"Oh, you know. My lost youth."

"Well, you won't find it here. You'll have to go back to Buena Vista for that."

A distinct lack of élan so far. But wait! It gets better.

"I'm looking for some old letters. I've got them in a shoe box up here somewhere."

"What do you need them for?"

"The novel."

She shoves a sheaf of theater programs onto the floor and sits down on a steamer trunk. Nearly all this stuff is hers—the pith helmet was her father's, the BB gun was her brother's. Boxes of hideous antimacassars, a samovar, a crate of Caruso records, snowshoes, Mexican serapes and a Mexican silver tea set which turned out to be Bolivian tin at the first polishing—it's all her family's. So I have to snicker when she says I'm a veritable magpie and I'd better clean out the attic one of these days.

"Whose letters are you looking for?"

"Dougie Clark's."

"Oh, yes. When did he ever write you letters?"

"When he was in Europe and I was at Buena Vista."

"You mean you've put Dougie Clark into *Roams?*"

I nod yes. She blows out a mushroom of smoke.

"Selection, Jay, selection! It's imperative!"

I move to the corner of the attic, hoping to find Dougie's letters and be gone. I can't remember what prompted me to keep the first one in my desk and tie the others up with three or four I later received from Eileen MacMillan. I vaguely remember a light-brown shoe box with a dark-brown lid. I remove a large canvas I bought twenty years ago, in London. It is called *Sunrise on the Doge's Palace.* I bought it under the impression that it was the work of J. M. W. Turner. It turned out to be the work of Lazlo Olzewski, of Budapest, when I had it checked in New York. We ought to put that and the fake Russian icon and the Bolivian-tin tea set all together under the label: International Swindlers I Have Known. I lift my copy of the complete works of the Marquis de Sade, which I put up here so that Deborah wouldn't read it, and I note that she has rabbit-eared the sections she liked best, while sitting up here, reading it. I spy a shoe box. It has, alas, a pair of patent-leather dancing shoes in it.

"Jay, I'm afraid I had one too many at the Humboldts'. "

She's going to tell me she got so high she can't remember what she said.

"I think I owe you an apology. Although, quite frankly, I was three sheets to the wind and I can't remember what I said."

"I remember very well. You wanna hear what you said?"

"No, I don't. I would appreciate it very much if you'd accept my apology and forget about it."

"Oh, no, Patricia! You are saying that you were under the influence and therefore don't know what you're apologizing for. I think you should know what you're apologizing for. You began by walking in, hunched, like Quasimodo, blaming your misshapen frame on my MG. You announced that I was writing a book and then collapsed on Ed Humboldt and told him you'd rather have me dally with a nymphet, the way he does. When Nellie ran to the bathroom, crying, you had your fourth martini and banged on the bathroom door, and apologized, and said this was proof positive—the wife is always the last to know. You stood, like a goddamned apparition, in front of that awful white grand piano of theirs, with your arm hooked to your hip, and informed the gathered throng that no one is master of his fate, no one is captain of his soul, and you finished with a flourish, saying we were all no better than a hill of swarming piss ants. Ed Humboldt, bless his soul, handed you your fifth martini and said we'd really rather have you give us a little of your Edna St. Vincent Millay. You obliged, mumbling, unintelligibly: 'Life in itself is nothing, an empty cup, a flight of uncarpeted stairs.' You find an appropriate apology for that, Pat, and I'll eat my hat," I said, as I took off my pith helmet. She stands, and straightens her shoulders, and lets her arms fall to her sides. She is an attractive woman, when sober, and I envy those sleek, tanned arms. They are the result of hundreds of days on the tennis courts. Mine, slack and flabby, are the result of hundreds of days in my wing-back chair. I don't mean to belabor the subject of sloth; I only mean to illustrate that it has taken its toll on my arms as well as my brain.

"It was a nightmare, Jay, for me as well as you. I called Nellie this morning and she cut me dead. I am simply not responsible for my actions when I'm drinking."

Pathetic. But wait! It gets worse.

"I have been a very bad girl, I know, a really naughty girl. And I want to do penance so that we can talk again and get back to normal. Normal, that is, for us. I'll gladly do penance, Jay. Anything. I'll pray. I'll hail Mary. I'll deprive myself. Tell me what I should do. Don't tell me to go to hell. We both know that'll be my just desert when the time comes."

Mea culpa.

I have a paucity of imagination where penance is concerned. It's a very fertile field to plow when you're young, and fuming, and words still mean something. I used to relish the thought—the infinite possibilities of sentences beginning with "Why don't you . . ." I've exhausted my repertoire over the years, and she knows it. The last time I was asked to dish out penance I said, "Why don't you try growing up?" which is scraping the bottom of the barrel when talking to a fifty-three-year-old woman. Anyway, once we get to the mea culpa we're long past the élan. Additionally, I now have my literary career to consider. Several hundred blank pages await me, downstairs. I can no longer waste time on this penance crap.

"If you'll excuse me, I have more important things to do."

"Goodness, we don't want to neglect the Muse, do we?"

"Goodness, no."

I have found Dougie's letters in a Florsheim's box. I take them out, and move to the stairs. As I pass Pat, she hands me the Marquis de Sade.

"Deb's old enough now. You might as well take this wordy bugger downstairs."

Wordy bugger? I exit laughing. We've broken the stalemate, we're verbal again. I go directly to my study, where I place the wordy bugger prominently on a shelf.

XIV

Josh Whitcomb came to Buena Vista two weeks earlier than expected, arriving on June 30. He had planned to stay with us at Timberline for several days, prior to taking a camping trip with my father. Mother looked forward to the visit, mainly because Mr. Whitcomb was to be our first houseguest. She had never handled a houseguest alone, and she eagerly accepted the challenge. A grand supply of groceries was laid in, and she personally cleaned the guest room— discovering, for the first time in her life, that rooms contained baseboards, and baseboards collected dust. I looked forward to the visit because my father's general tone and demeanor had descended to an all-time low. I felt that the summer, and all future summers, were in jeopardy unless his attitude improved and he could somehow be made to feel comfortable. It had not been brought to bear on him, until these first two weeks at Buena Vista, that he was unable to get along when left to his own devices. The realization frightened him, I think, and when he was frightened he became petulant. I'd noticed this at home, but at Timberline there was no escape. The lodge seemed to make new requirements of us. It forced a familiarity. It was without the luxury of libraries, dens, sewing rooms, solariums, butlers' pantries, game rooms, etc. And so, huddled together in close proximity, microscopic truths were revealed. It was as if, along with all the other perplexities of puberty, I underwent a cataract removal. New facets of the man were exposed to me and I was disturbed at what I saw. In his present frame of mind his looks, his charm, his Lake Shore Road sophistication were no solace

to the rest of us. We were not moved to comfort him in
his misery. We only wished that he'd hibernate somewhere
until he got his sagging jowls back where they belonged—
until he was fit for human company.

My God! Had he been carrying on like this all these years?
I stumbled over him one morning, just after breakfast. He
was sitting, dejectedly, in the living room, listening to the
record player. The song was "Am I Blue?" He seemed deep
in reverie, and I apologized for interrupting. For no apparent
reason, he exploded:

"I simply have no control here, Jay! Do you know what I
mean? I mean control over my *life*. Your mother's temperament is very deceiving, you know—she seems frail as a poppy
but she's really very strong, and of course, she's independent.
One has to be careful with independent people, or you're
relegated to the tail, you know—the tail of somebody else's
comet. My friends, at home—I don't know, I could pluck
them out of the phone book, just like that. You simply had
to call and say hello, and people knew you wanted company.
You didn't have to beg for an audience. You didn't have to
get down and kiss the ring! You just picked up the receiver
and there you were, connected with fun, and people who
were ready to try anything—you know?—go anywhere, pay
any price, for a kick or two. Ready and willing. You name
it, it was worth the effort. Couple of years ago, in Europe,
among strangers, same thing. Paris, Venice, hordes of people
ready and willing to try anything. Jesus! Maybe it was the
crash. Hell, I don't know. I met Ray Graham the other day—
he's the manager at the Amberley. I said, 'Gee, Ray, I hear
the trout's awful good at Lake Pinto.' *Dead as a doornail!*
I said, 'How'd you like to drive up Saturday and spend the
day?' He said he'd love to, but he couldn't. He said I was
on vacation, but he was a working man. Hotels, he said,
weren't a nine-to-five proposition. He doesn't even take Sunday off, he takes *Tuesday!* The assistant pitches in and
Graham spends Tuesday with his family. Rest of the time

he's holding hands with all those old fogies up there, fetching hot-water bottles and liniments and trusses, probably. I'm *goddamned* if I'll get down and kiss the frigging ring!" He stared at me vacantly for a few minutes. Then he waved me out of the room with an exasperated gesture. He lifted the needle, and Ethel Waters continued her seventy-eight revolutions per minute.

Mother didn't concern herself half as much with my own moods and frailties and I was, ostensibly, the kid in the family. When I got on my high horse and complained about it, she said, "Jay, I must spend the rest of my life with your father. You'll go away and do marvelous things, but I'll have to greet him at breakfast each morning for another thirty years. One can either adjust to these things or jump off the Foshay Tower. I see no alternatives." I thought she was either being stoical or she'd suffered brain damage at birth. Maybe that was the reason behind the MacAllister Purchase. Maybe that was the skeleton in Grandmother's closet. Maybe my mother wasn't all there.

We didn't discuss our hopes for Mr. Whitcomb's visit, but there was an unspoken urgency to it. We both knew it was crucial that Mr. Whitcomb's familiar Grosse Pointe face assist us in rescuing Father from the pits of gloom. For my part, I had envisioned three or four sumptuous lunches at the Amberley. I knew that Father had been saving his impressions of Mr. Samson and Mr. Harmon, and I looked forward to hearing the fully performed anecdotes as they were passed to Mr. Whitcomb—one sophisticate to another.

None of this occurred—at least not in my presence. Mr. Whitcomb arrived in a frenzy and announced that the sooner they left for Jasper, the better. There was a hurried huddle with my parents, some whisperings and exclamations of heartfelt grief. I thought perhaps Mr. Whitcomb's ex-wife had died, or that his house had burned, or that his boat, the *Lady Baltimore,* had come to a bad end. The cause for the grief, and for my being sent to my room at 8 P.M. that evening, was something I did not understand. I kept hearing the words repeated, in disbelief and horror, whenever I had my back turned. A "paternity suit" had been brought against Mr. Whitcomb. He had fled Grosse Pointe and had left his lawyers to deal, in whatever manner they could, with the "floozie."

So, there was no canard à l'orange in our kitchen, no sumptuous lunch at the Amberley and no witty anecdotes illustrating the incredible stupidity of Mr. Samson and Mr. Harmon. Mother agreed that Josh looked ten years older. She commiserated with him over his futile negotiations with the floozie, and urged him to spend his time in the Rockies in any way that would help him get his feet on the ground again. He thanked her for her understanding. He hugged her, he hugged my father and, being totally distraught and undone, he hugged me, too. All of this hugging embarrassed him and for some reason he did exactly what my father did after a moment of unbridled emotion. He dug into his pocket and flipped me a quarter. The following morning they left for Calgary, where an agency had made arrangements for them to pick up gear. They were then to travel north to Edmonton, and hire a guide who would escort them into Jasper National Park and stay with them for two weeks of camping, fishing and climbing. Mr. Whitcomb, who evidently never did anything without a motive involving money, had a contract with a Detroit newspaper to take photographs for the Sunday magazine.

I remember that farewell mainly because of its hypocrisy. Mother said, "Goodbye, Jimmy, we'll miss you." I said, "Goodbye, Dad, we'll miss you." Mother assured him that we could get along very well without the car; Arnold would bring up the groceries and I could run errands on my bike. I assured him that I'd become adept with hammer and wrench; I knew how to cut off the water and work a plunger and replace blown fuses. And finally, Mother promised Mr. Whitcomb that if the floozie attempted to contact him, both she and I would say we had not seen him, we were not expecting him, the last we'd heard from him was a postcard from Morocco.

This, for the record, is the point in my story where Patricia loses all logic and rages incoherently at a man she never knew. It is beyond her ken to accept the subsequent events as spontaneous. Her Jay, who later was proved, at Croydon, to have an I.Q. of 160, and her mother-in-law, who was called "an intellectual," for want of a better term—two such clever, perspicacious people would not willingly be led down the primrose path. As long as she breathes she will believe that we were the innocent victims of a calculating, conniving, cloven-footed Winger Burns. Her argument that the abundance of one's brains should somehow be commensurate with the fervor of one's passions is erroneous. I'm the proof of it: she's known me intimately for twenty-five years, and still she will not believe it. *My God*, we were willing! As we stood there that day no two people were ever more vulnerable. We were ripe for adventure: our affections were quite literally up for grabs. We waved goodbye and stood and watched until the car disappeared around the bend. We looked at each other, smiled and began our walk up the path to the house. Unquestionably, at that moment, there was a subtle change between us. We were not little boy and Mama left alone to fend for ourselves. Mother put her arm through mine as we slowly, lazily climbed the path. We were perfectly at ease with each other. We were friends—comrades—soon to embark on a venture that would make us, in my father's eyes, partners in crime.

Even as I write, I feel an airiness of spirit, a sense of *remission*, similar to what I felt that day. I don't think either of us realized just how heavily Father's saturnine presence had weighed upon us. And now, with the master off in the hinterlands, what fantastic freedom we enjoyed! We both possessed sweet teeth; however, Father watched his weight so carefully we were rarely able to indulge ourselves. At home,

Cook would never leave me unsupervised in the kitchen, and she didn't consider the making of fudge part of her job. We decided to try our hand at candy making, and I was sent down to Mr. Samson's to buy a candy thermometer. We went on a wild, syrupy binge. Our first, and worst, effort was peanut brittle. We followed the recipe exactly, pouring the chunky molten liquid into a buttered dish and anxiously checking the refrigerator every half-hour to see if it had brittled. It never did. We sat at the kitchen table that evening, ladling it out with sticky spoons, listening to "The Lux Radio Theater." The following evening we made Fannie Farmer Chocolate Fudge. We ate the sloppy chunks while listening to "The Green Hornet." The next day I was a mass of pimples and Mother suggested that we wait a few days before trying Divinity, which was next on the list. But I had resolved to grab the iron while it was hot. Undaunted by the awful, mottled spectacle in the mirror, we threw caution to the winds and sat, that evening, listening to "Cavalcade of America," eating mounds of Sally's Best Divinity. We were soon at the point of addiction. Neither of us had the will power to remain in the house and ignore the ten-pound bag of sugar in the cupboard. I remember distinctly, it was a Friday night.

"Well," said Mother, "there must be an *infinite* number of things we could do. I could do the crossword, and you could play solitaire. Or vice versa. Or, we could walk downtown and look at the tourists. Or walk up to the Amberley and look at the tourists. Or we could wash the kitchen floor—you know—make a project of it. I noticed that I stuck to it this morning in my bare feet. Or we could both go and take good, long, relaxing baths."

"I don't want to take a bath."

"Or, we could go and visit the MacMillans, if you wouldn't mind."

If I wouldn't mind! I was itching to go. Eileen's *modus*

operandi, by day, was familiar to me by now. The previous afternoon she and I had tramped up Binnie. I went first, blazing the trail, confident that I could fight to the death the Abominable Snowman when he appeared and made lecherous advances at my fragile damsel, bringing up the rear. At one point I stopped to pick berries and she went on, ahead of me. Eileen, from behind, was almost more than I could bear. Eileen, by day, made tentative, sensuous suggestions, implicit in which was the pledge that Eileen, by night, would turn fancy to fact and provide me with some small favor. We quickly combed our hair and went to visit the Mac-Millans.

Mrs. MacMillan welcomed us in, apologizing for the absence of her husband. Ross MacMillan owned a thousand acres of land just south of Medicine Hat, in the southeast corner of the province. He returned to his farm every couple of weeks during the summer, and Mrs. MacMillan confided that she was glad to see him go. He spent most of his time at Buena Vista listening to the market quotations on the radio. The Lord knew, he had a very plump nest egg put aside, but he didn't approve of summers away from the farm. There was something dishonorable about a farmer who vacationed in July and August, especially during these lean, depressed days.

Mrs. MacMillan had been a forty-year-old schoolteacher when she married Ross. He was forty-five, and so set in his ways that the only concession she'd been able to wheedle out of him during the intervening fifteen years was the house at Buena Vista. Even that was not without strings. She had to accompany him to the Calgary Stampede for a week every July. Ross MacMillan's prize Aberdeen Angus bulls were shown at the Stampede, an event that he regarded as being approximately equal in importance to the Second Coming. Mrs. MacMillan told all of this to my mother in the first five minutes, summing up the marriage by saying that Ross had the Stampede, she had Buena Vista, and they shared Eileen, who was the greatest shock of their lives, coming along, as she did, when Mrs. MacMillan was forty-three.

She sat us down in the living room and asked Eileen to bring two dishes of chocolate ice cream. "Just two?" asked Eileen. "Yes," said Mrs. MacMillan, "Mrs. Rutherford won't want any, and I'm fat as Patty's pig." She commented on our totem pole, saying it was the talk of Mount Binnie. Mother naïvely replied that she hoped the talk was good talk. There was a silence. Whenever Mrs. MacMillan was caught off guard she lost control of her eyes. They stopped tracking. They shot to the corner of the room. The truth was, Mr. Hamilton, who owned the house just above the MacMillans', had come around with a petition. He said that our totem pole was cutting his view in two, and he needed twenty-five signatures to get it taken down. Though Mrs. MacMillan hadn't talked with Mother, she had introduced herself on the day of our arrival. She had seen my father greeting trucks from Calgary. She told Mr. Hamilton that we weren't the lunatic Yanks he said we were. She told him Mother was straight as an arrow and Father was the best-dressed man she'd ever laid eyes upon. Mr. Hamilton had no business stirring up trouble amongst neighbors, even if his view was split in two. Besides, Mr. Hamilton lived up there with a thirty-year-old housekeeper from St. Eustache, Quebec, and everybody knew what that was all about. The Rutherfords may have their little idiosyncrasies, but there were no kept women on the premises. And then, to my utter chagrin, and with Eileen present, she momentarily lost control of her eyes again. She cast a diabolical leer at Mother and told her that she'd spent the best five years of her life living with the principal of John MacDonald High in Medicine Hat. No one was the wiser, since she taught fourth grade at Princess Alexandra.

"Perhaps Jay and Eileen should take a little walk," said Mother.

"Oh, no," said Mrs. MacMillan. "They're going to play checkers."

She rose and opened a drawer in Mr. MacMillan's desk. She took out the checkers and board and sat Eileen and me down at a table near the front window. She told Mother, with the accumulated authority of twenty years in the classroom, that children were always happiest when playing near a window. "You look like a very smart lad, Jay." And she cautioned Eileen: "Careful with this boy, Eileen. Don't get caught with your pants down." I felt the heat rising in my cheeks, but Eileen was cool as a cucumber. She let me choose my color, and when her mother returned to the sofa, she rubbed her ankle against mine. I wondered what Dougie Clark would do in similar circumstances, so I returned the rub. It seemed like an auspicious beginning; however, we did not finish the game. We got caught up in the discussion on the sofa.

"I've promised Eileen for two years now to take her down to the pavilion one of these evenings. I thought we might go tonight, since Ross can't dance worth a hoot and Ross is away. Tell me, Laura, do you think she's too young?"

Mother asked what they did at the pavilion. Mrs. Mac-Millan said they danced, that was all, and that seemed innocent enough. There was a small band, six or eight men, on a small stage. There was a vast dance floor surrounded with pine benches. Everybody went there nearly every evening. The staff of the Amberley was always there, and storekeepers and farmers and tourists, and on the weekend people came from Okotoks and Carstairs and other nearby towns. Mother asked if Eileen knew how to dance. Mrs. MacMillan proudly stated that Eileen was just a dancing fool around Medicine Hat. Those Medicine Hat dances left a lot to be desired, though, because all the teen-agers snuck off into the cloakroom and felt each other up. There were no cloakrooms at the pavilion; the adults were all mixed in with the kids, and nothing could transpire but good, old-fashioned dancing.

Mother was familiar with my feelings about checkers. I thought it a childish game. I was bored and uncomfortable. The tablecloth offered me a good opportunity for ankle rubbing, it was true, but that horizon had its limitations. A dance floor would permit fleshly contact over a larger area and would be vastly superior. Mother glanced at me, dolefully unhappy there by the window, and with the smallest rearrangement of my facial musculature I conveyed to her that she had it in her power to rescue me from the checkerboard and deposit me, mercifully, at the Buena Vista Dance Pavilion. Mother, who knew the gamut of my facial expressions intimately, quickly complied.

"I certainly don't want to impose, Mrs. MacMillan, but if you'd be more comfortable, Jay and I could come along for an hour or so."

Eileen was ecstatic, and her mother's eyes shot to the corner of the room again. Yes, said Mrs. MacMillan, the idea of going alone had troubled her. She didn't want to appear to be *on the prowl* with Ross back at the farm. She alluded to my father, saying it was really too bad that he'd gone off hiking. She couldn't fool me. Another man would be a fly in the ointment. Ross or no Ross, Mrs. MacMillan was on the prowl. She was fifteen years older than my mother. She looked ancient to me. I thought there was something faintly odious about this female Methuselah, plainly chomping at the bit to get down to the pavilion. This, surely, was the acquaintance that laid the foundation for that hint of nausea I feel whenever my own Patsy affects girlish wiles. ("Is my widdle house-bum angwee with Pat-wisha? Confooshus say seek-wet of happy mah-wedge is big smooch at bedtime.") Deborah, on the other hand, has never felt compelled to affect girlish wiles. Perhaps it's the influence of Women's Lib. Whatever it is, I am forever grateful that, even through the most awkward stages of her early teens, Deborah has refrained from batting her eyelashes, wrinkling her nose and twinkling her toes. Mrs. MacMillan, at fifty-five, was a champion at all three.

X V

The pavilion was a half-hour, downhill walk from Timberline. Eileen and I walked ahead of our two mothers, and I heard the monotonous drone of Mrs. MacMillan's marathon conversation in the background. I felt a little guilty. I had inflicted this woman's company upon my mother for the whole evening, but I recall that any guilt I ever felt, at fourteen, was decidedly short-lived. Whatever grief I might cause adults couldn't be too serious, because, after all, they were adults. They had drivers' licenses to prove it. Their fortitude was greater than mine. They were expected to cope and keep a stiff upper lip through every tribulation. And, aside from floods, fires, hurricanes and, in Grandmother MacAllister's case, the San Andreas fault—what tribulations could there be when society bestowed upon you a driver's license, a checkbook of your own and freedom from those warnings, dictates and words to the wise which we commonly call parental guidance.

Eileen, to my surprise and horror, was an A student in her eighth-grade class in Medicine Hat. She excelled in science, which put me on the defensive because I was at that time, and am presently, more inclined to investigate the mysteries of human behavior than the mysteries of nature. I didn't know the difference between stalactites and stalagmites, and have only once in my life felt the need of this information—during a one-hour visit to the Carlsbad Caverns in New Mexico. She also knew *C. Hopkins Cafe*: carbon, hydrogen, oxygen, phosphorus, potassium, iodine, nitrogen, sulphur, calcium and iron. And she was fascinated with the ways in which locomotion occurred. All sorts of locomotion. Steam engines, car motors, trolley cars, sailing ships, right down to the ambulatory aspects of the human anatomy. Oh, the night was so black and the stars were so plentiful! The outline of the mountains so severe and dramatic. Why couldn't she have told me all of this during the daytime? What cared I about the ambulatory aspects of the human anatomy when the sins of the flesh were an untapped well in one small, very particular area of my groin? I knew that Eileen wore a bra, and suddenly, right in front of Mr. Samson's grocery store, it struck me that she must have begun menstruation. My God! This sometimes pedantic, sometimes giddy girl was throwing off eggs every month! One could, if one didn't play one's cards right, impregnate Eileen MacMillan! Now, there was an anatomical consideration much more fundamental than feet, a consideration of mind-boggling proportions compared with the steam engine or the advent of the wheel. Mr. Fulton's steamer was but a cog in our industrial revolution, but Mr. Darwin's evolution encompassed the millennia and was born, not out of heat and water, but of Eileen MacMillan's ancestral ape who magically, miraculously, threw off eggs every month. My God! I was walking down the main street of Buena Vista with a *woman!*

So it began that evening with two of us harboring lusty motives, Eileen ranting on about Thomas Alva Edison and Mother innocently tagging along. What did she imagine her role to be that evening? I suppose she thought she was with us primarily as a chaperon, to keep Eileen and me in line, to keep Mrs. Macmillan an honest woman for another week or so. I expect she imagined an isolated pine bench, somewhere off in the shadowy corners of the hall, a sanctuary where she could see everyone and no one could see her. When I think back on it, I don't for a moment believe she expected to dance. (She was, according to Father, an octopus on the dance floor.) I don't think she even expected to be called upon for conversation. She could not have known that liquor flowed like the Ganges in the bushes and shrubs around the hall, or that those who imbibed the most were the single men, farmers mostly, who left the fields and came to Buena Vista for a weekend of revelry. These men were cut from a cloth she could not deal with in the most sobering of daylit circumstances. In the smoke-filled, noisy, crowded hall, unable to find an isolated pine bench, she cringed like a sparrow that had inadvertently swooped out of clean, clear skies into a foul, fetid alley, and was caught there in the midst of tomcats. Mrs. MacMillan, too, was prey, but easy prey. She was approached the minute we entered the hall, replied, "Yes, I'd love to!" and off she went, wrinkling her nose and twinkling her toes. Eileen and I followed, anxious to take part in what had been aptly described as good, old-fashioned dancing. I remember seeing old Mr. Harmon doing a Virginia reel, apparently all by himself. I don't recall being concerned about Mother. She had so readily suggested our accompanying the MacMillans, I simply took it for granted that she would manage. I didn't realize that the evening was fraught with peril, and when I saw Seth and Elsie Hilliard, I thought they would eventually find Mother and spend some time with her.

For nearly an hour I caught glimpses of her, refusing to dance with what seemed to be battalions of seedy, sixty-year-old men. After each set of songs I would head for the spot where I had last seen her, but she would not be there. When Eileen and I went back to the floor, I would spot her again. Each time she appeared to be less in control and nearer the back of the hall, where the bandstand was located. She was flushed, but the hall was hot, and I really did not calculate the degree to which she was suffering. I am not a reader of lips, but each time she was accosted her reply was visible to me: "No, thank you. I don't dance." I remember that there was a chair, one of those folding metal chairs, near the bandstand. A very pretty young woman sat there, obviously attached to the clarinetist, who played directly above her. I

noticed her because she was extraordinarily pretty and because she was clearly not for public consumption. I saw this
woman whisper something to the clarinetist, and then rise
and make her way to the ladies' room. Immediately—a split
second later—I saw my mother running, frantically, to the
chair. She was followed by two burly men who literally chased
her to the chair, shouting angry insults at her. I was horrified.
I left Eileen and ran through the crowd to the bandstand.
The two men accused Mother of snobbery, calling her a high-
class hussy, asking her if they weren't good enough for her.
What the hell did she mean, she didn't dance? What business
did she have, coming into the pavilion on a Friday night,
rebuffing every man who paid her the time of day? What was
she trying to prove? The accusations escalated into a full-
fledged scene when the clarinetist bent down and insisted that
the chair had been placed there solely for the use of his girl
friend. Mother tried, vainly, to leave the chair, but a crowd
had gathered around, and I, unfortunately, was but an ineffec-
tual member of the crowd. I remember crying out that she
was my mother—if they would let me through I would quickly
remove her from the chair. The farmers laughed and asked
if I was her escort. One of them called me a gutless wonder
and pushed me farther back into the crowd. Mother sat, near
hysteria, penned on the chair with the bewildered dancers
encircling her. I was astonished that, when she began to cry, I
still was not allowed through the mass of hot bodies. The air
was oppressive and there was a stench of stale liquor, sweat,
hair oil, perfume and, over it all, occasional whiffs of manure,
wafting up from the boots on the floor.

Seth Hilliard, short and thick, came to our rescue like a
bantam cock. He wedged his body into the crowd, bulldozing
his way to the chair, where he quickly put his arms around
Mother. I heard Winger Burns's voice shouting, a few feet to
the left of the scene: "For Chrissake, will you let her out?"
The farmers were a tenacious duo, grabbing at my mother,
clutching her blouse, calling her a whore now and wishing her

good riddance. One of them turned to a bystander and offered a glassy-eyed judgment.

"She thinks *hers* don't *stink!*"

My throat was so dry at that point, I could not speak. I had seen some activity at the door, and I tried to croak out my message to Winger. Two policemen had swung into the pavilion, brandishing clubs. They followed us out to the sidewalk. Our coterie included me, Mother, Seth and Elsie, Winger, Mrs. MacMillan and Eileen, all of us in various states of disarray. The police brusquely moved Mother to one side and demanded an explanation for the fracas. When she began to speak, she gagged. She doubled up and folded her arms across her stomach. Winger impatiently—brutally, I thought—hoisted her into his arms and carried her to his car. The entourage followed, jabbering senselessly, leaving me alone on the sidewalk with the two policemen.

I had never before experienced a brush with the law. Their uniforms, their clubs and pistols, their beefy bodies, conjured up images of bread and water pushed through bars—dank, windowless cells. I forgot the neat little Buena Vista jail, which I'd passed many times, and envisioned the Buena Vista dungeon, vermin-infested, with shelves of mechanical devices designed to pull out tongues and toenails. I had trouble controlling my urine and, at the same time, was aware of a dearth of saliva in my mouth. I raged at the lot of them, waiting for me in the car, leaving me alone with these two cretins.

"What kind of tricks was your mother trying to play in there, sonny?"

"She came to the hall to chaperon me and my girl friend. She doesn't dance—she doesn't know *how* to dance. None of the men believed her. They insulted her and attacked her. They said they'd like to get into her fancy pants. They trapped her on a chair and wouldn't let her out. She's in very bad shape right now, and I'd like to take her home."

They asked me if I lived in Buena Vista. I said, yes, we had just moved into a new lodge on Mount Binnie. They

asked me if we owned a totem pole. I said yes, we did. They
nodded at each other and I saw their tight, square shoulders
relax. Only then did they replace their clubs and take me to
the car. Winger was at the wheel, with the motor running.
Eileen and her mother were in the back, flustered, thank God,
to the point of silence. Mother sat, rigidly, next to Winger.
The sleeve of her blouse had been ripped, so that her right
shoulder was bare. I climbed in, and the five of us went,
mutely, down the main street and up the hill to Timberline.

When we emerged from the car, Mrs. MacMillan said her
first words. "Laura, your husband will have me to blame for
this." Mother didn't answer. She had her key in one hand
and was trying to cover her bare shoulder with the other hand.
She stealthily made her way to the front door. She didn't say
goodnight to the MacMillans, and she didn't thank Winger
for our transportation home. She moved, like a sleepwalker,
into the house, leaving the door ajar behind her. I said goodnight to the MacMillans, and apologized for the outcome of
the evening. When I turned to thank Winger for his help, he
was standing in the doorway. "I'm going to come in, Jay." I
replied that I didn't believe he should. I said I knew my
mother very well, and I was certain that she wanted to be
alone. "You know what she's going to do now, don't you?"
he said. I hadn't thought about it, but I said that she'd probably take some pills and go to bed. "No," he said, "she's going
to crumble. Crumble, like a lump of clay. You think she
wants to be alone, and she'll say she wants to be alone, but
they don't really want to be alone when they crumble." I found
his confidence insulting. His use of the word "they" seemed
to reduce my mother to the lowest common denominator. She
was not like other women I had known; Winger didn't know
her at all. I chafed at his impudence in making such a glib
prediction of her behavior. I wouldn't allow him to shroud
my mother in a blanket of generalizations dredged up from
past associations with God knows what kind of trash. All of

these noble sentiments were finally expressed by me in the following manner:

"You're a bunch of animals—all you guys—and I want to go home to Grosse Pointe!" Whereupon I began to cry. I fell upon him, dug my head into the zipper of his suede jacket and sobbed uncontrollably.

I remember that the next time I saw Mother she had replaced her torn blouse with a green sweater. I was lying on my bed, in my room. She was unzipping my fly, and Winger was removing my socks. Somebody rustled in my closet for my pajamas and somebody pulled the draperies across the windows. Somebody nearly suffocated me, getting my shirt over my head and off my arms. Somebody methodically did up all the buttons on my pajama tops, and somebody asked me if I wanted to go to the bathroom. Mother kissed me goodnight and Winger ran his fingers under my chin. Somebody pulled up the quilt, and somebody turned off the light.

I had glanced at my watch when I said goodnight to the MacMillans. It was midnight, so I therefore must have slept about two hours before waking. I awoke at two o'clock and relived the entire scene, from *C. Hopkins Cafe* to the Buena Vista dungeon, in a matter of seconds. I knew the minute I woke up that Winger was still in the house. I opened my door and crept out on the balcony. I had no desire to see my mother crumble, but I imagined she would have already done that, and I would witness the aftermath. There was but one lamp on in the living room, and it took me a moment to see which person was where. Mother was sitting in the corner of a couch and Winger was sitting in a chair across from her, in front of the coffee table. She was surprisingly calm; I could see no traces of crumbling. She held a coffee cup in her hand and listened to Winger with a wide-eyed intensity that seemed out of place at two in the morning. Winger was hunched over the coffee table, lighting a cigarette. My father had called Winger a vagabond and a nomad, so I hoped that I would hear a yarn of danger and intrigue on the Vancouver docks. What I heard was hardly worth getting up for:

"Gladys bought stuff cheap, right off the rack—met herself coming everywhere she went. But that little Cheeoh was an artist. Only table we had was a card table in the kitchen, so she'd get me moving all the furniture in the living room so there'd be a big space in the center for her to work. I sure as hell hated the front of that house 'cause it rocked to and fro and it raised merry hell with your dinner. I got back to the kitchen fast-as-catch-can, and then I'd watch her lay out the material. Only woman I ever met who really enjoyed that kind of nit-pickin' work. She enjoyed it 'cause she did it *slow*, painful *slow*, working with pins and chalk, and making them things called tailor's tacks. Then she'd put the whole thing together by hand. She'd piss away a month of evenings jabbing up and down with that thimble. But I will say she had some pretty stuff—lined and everything so it hung right. I've still got a couple of shirts she made for me, and I look at all those eensy-weensy stitches and I remember all those evenings we pissed away before I bought that old clinker of a Singer."

I was back in bed at two-fifteen. It seemed to me they were both pissing away perfectly good sleeping time on empty conversation.

That was the first time I'd seen my mother hang on anybody's words with that amount of concentration. I remember, when Deborah was little, I used to take her to the library for the Saturday-afternoon Story Hour. All of the children would sit in a circle, on the floor, with one of the librarians sitting on a chair in the middle. The librarian would read, and gesture, and grimace, and make voices.

Somebody's been sleeping in my bed, said Daddy bear.

The kids would sit with gaping mouths, totally involved in the unfolding tale. It always reminded me of those endless conversations between my mother and Winger Burns. No matter what he said, no matter what she was doing, all activity screeched to a halt so that she could fully absorb every pause and intonation. Which now reminds me of another, somewhat allied memory. Years later, Pat and I and Mother attended a fancy dinner at the Waldorf-Astoria. David, the Duke of Windsor, was at our table. He talked to Mother about the days when Wallis Simpson was first entertained at Fort Belvedere. Mother could barely keep her eyes open, and made no attempt to stifle her yawns. I was alarmed at her blatant boredom. When the Duke got up to dance, I hastily took her aside and whispered to her:

"For God's sake, look alive! This is history! The man is telling you about the quintessential love story of all time!"

"Nonsense, Jay, do you really think it is?"

"Of course I do! Don't you?"

She paused, yawned again and thought for a moment.

"No, I don't. Boy meets girl. Boy gets girl. That's not your quintessential love story. That's marriage."

The following morning I descended the stairs to find Winger in his suede jacket, Mother in her green sweater and a pan of bacon sizzling on the stove. I thought they had sat in those clothes all night, like two protective watchmen guarding my sleep. I soon discovered a new-found intimacy. It hung there, delicately, and for all of their furtive glances and surreptitious touches, their feelings were transparent. I had lived for fourteen years in a house where bodily contact occurred between adults only for reasons of expediency—carrying a box of books to the attic, struggling with a Christmas tree, moving a bureau from one wall to another. And so, when Mother leaned over the counter, causing a piece of hair to fall over her face, and Winger lifted the lock and replaced it behind her ear, I distinctly felt that they were the company and I was the crowd.

Winger saw my confusion and quickly banished all discomfort by siding with me, against Mother. He teased her mercilessly. He threw his arm around me and flashed his wonderful grin. He said it was a terrible thing for a boy to see two horny old gorillas in hot pursuit of his mother. He cradled my head on his shoulder and bemoaned the after-effects of such a traumatic experience. He said he once knew a man who took his wife to court and accused her of being an *unfit mother*, because she had caused a similar scene in the presence of her son. In one swooping movement he left me, and put his arms around Mother. He asked how come she'd attracted the two most notorious shit kickers in the whole province. And then, amidst gales of laughter, he waddled across the kitchen like a pouter pigeon, imitating Mrs. MacMillan's harried exit from the pavilion.

It seemed the most natural thing in the world to have Winger at our breakfast table. Pat has often asked me if I wasn't shocked at the realization that they had not, in fact, sat in those clothes all night. I remember nothing even faintly resembling shock. I remember only the closeness, the intimacy, the essence of which comes back to me now as I write. It is as if I had uncorked a forty-year-old vintage and was suddenly overcome with warm, languid feelings of euphoria. It's impossible to speak of this intimacy to Patricia. Regrettably, she and I have never achieved it in twenty-five years of marriage. Pat tried, in the late fifties, to achieve it with someone else. The man's name was Lawrence Motta. It was a difficult time for us, and I don't wish to go into the details of it here. I did not have the audacity to ask why it failed, and Pat has never volunteered the information. Her continuing presence in the marriage seems sufficient proof that the results were not what she'd hoped for. At any rate, I am luckier than Pat by far, for I was once at least privy to it.

Macbeth:	What is the night?
Lady Macbeth:	Almost at odds with morning,
	which is which.

An hour later on that brilliant Saturday morning, remorse set in with cataclysmic speed. We arose from the table, pushed our chairs in place, stood behind them and stared at each other. We stood, like three pillars, realizing that a whole day stretched out before us. As the hours went by, it stretched so tautly it seemed to me another bedtime would never come and relieve us of daylight's terrible clarity. It's easy enough to assemble what Mother and Winger must have brooded about that day, but at the time I was only aware of a round of relentless motion. I felt that I was watching an old silent movie, where words were not spoken, people moved in silly spurts and jerks, and I was too young to provide my own subtitles.

Winger's shaving kit was far, far away: he had broken his vow. Additionally, it was Saturday. He must have felt nagged by his own Saturday routine. He generally cleaned his cabin and did his laundry and then went out with Seth and Elsie and Bob. Perhaps he feared that the Hilliards would be looking for him. Conceivably, if I had not been there, he might not have felt a need to preserve appearances. He might have simply said goodbye to Mother and left for his appointed rounds. Perhaps something unknown to me, something that transpired between them in the night, compelled him to stay. The staying was plainly torture for him. He had, like an actor, to take on a role, but what role? Casual visitor? Guest? Father/lover/husband/handyman? He opted for the latter.

He began by doing such unmanly things as washing up the breakfast dishes and helping my mother make the beds. He grabbed me by the collar, told me that I had a fourteen-carat ring around my neck and pushed me into the bathroom, throwing a rough washcloth after me. He said it would sure as hell help if I used a little soap and elbow grease. He spent the early part of the afternoon swooping through the brush around the lodge with a scythe. He went at it so ferociously, murderously flaying the stands of grass and weeds, I began to wonder what it was about the day that made him work so fanatically. As afternoon drew to a close the strain became more obvious. He worked compulsively and erratically, without plan or order. His brow was deeply furrowed and, when asked to stop for tea or lemonade, he scowled and dove into another project. Our garage was overflowing with large, empty cartons from all of our furnishings. He set about knocking them down into flat sheets, banging them, kicking them, dealing terrific blows to one after another. He hollered for a knife, some wire, some cord. I scurried for a knife that was too small, wire that was too heavy, cord that was *string*, goddamn it!: he asked for cord, not string. Next time I washed my neck I'd better wash my ears. When my mother demanded that he stop and rest while she prepared dinner, he said no, *he* would provide the dinner. What the hell kind of a freeloader did she think he was? He climbed into his car and drove to his cabin, informing us that he had three prime T-bone steaks waiting in his refrigerator.

Those were the last words spoken for well over two hours. Winger's cabin was only ten minutes away from Timberline. As the minutes passed, the atmosphere in the house became so dense I dared not utter a word. Mother looked through me, past me, around me; her eyes played some sort of holographic trick that excluded me from her line of vision. She paced back and forth restlessly, through the gallery to the kitchen, through the gallery to the living room. Her footsteps became as monotonous as a metronome. She stopped, thought, agonized, heaved voluptuous sighs. She gazed down, for long periods, at her image in the black tile. She rearranged the length of her sweater a hundred times, pulling it down tightly over her hips, then loosening it so that it fell in folds over her abdomen. And then, when the light was gone from the sky, I saw her do something I'd never seen before. She ran her hands up under her breasts and held them there for a moment, cupping her breasts and letting her hair fall back on her shoulder, while her pelvis thrust forward, like a house-bound cat in the throes of heat. She made no effort to remove me from the scene. She could have asked me to go to the MacMillans', or given me a chore, or sent me to my room. She was not hampered by my presence, she was not restricted or confined by it; she was oblivious to it. I sat, like a piece of statuary, in the corner of the living-room couch, and watched with astonishment. She was strange, removed, not related to my past—an unknown woman struggling with a seizure. My brain told my feet to make a distance, a space between us—to at least get up on the balcony and watch from there, but my eyes were fastened on her and I could not move. She mindlessly touched things, straightened pictures, bit her fingers. In the soft light of dusk, I became hypnotized by her movements. The mood eventually became so eerie, the light became so thick and hazy, my eyes were unable to ascertain the outline of her body, and I lost track of where she was exactly. Then she would be close to me, materializing, Ophelia-like, out of the half-light, supporting her breasts as if they were too heavy to be borne.

It was close to nine o'clock when Winger finally returned. I remained, a nonentity, hunched up grotesquely on the couch. The only light in the room was a glow from the front window. It rose from the streets and houses in the town below. I was not visible to either of them, but I cannot believe they didn't know I was there. Winger crossed the broad expanse of our living room and went directly to where my mother was standing in the gallery. His voice was calm and quiet.

"I didn't bring the steaks."

"I know."

He moved slightly away from her and shoved his hands into his pockets. They both stood, looking down at themselves in the tile, the way children do in pools of water.

"I hated you for a while today. I really hated you. And I'm not prone to *hate*—you know? I've learned to be at home with *compromise*. God, you were playing *hired* man! I have tried all afternoon to erase that damn swinging scythe from my mind. Don't you ever do that again!"

"No chance," he said. "No possible way. Had a big chat with my shaving kit this last hour."

He moved his arm in an arc that encompassed the gallery.

"Can't take it on, Laura. Too risky. Can't tangle with it. Too much money, too many *things*. Books. Totem poles. Rutherford. Grosse Pointe. And most important, your boy."

His hand fell on a small obelisk which sat, with the other objets d'art, on the gallery table.

"What's this stuff?"

"Alabaster."

He picked it up, ran his finger over the apex and put it down.

"I got out of my Buster Browns too long ago, Laura. Christ—for how long, anyway? Six-seven weeks? Hiding in the bushes? Sneaking—lying—quickies in the clover while he's taking a nap? Summertime gigolo? And then what? Go lay down on Nancy again come September? Uh, uh. Dried behind the ears too long ago, Laura."

He swung around and looked, I thought, directly at me.

"Shit! Sock him in the jaw? Kick asses up and down Binnie all next weekend? 'Took over for you, fella, while you was camping. Snuck in under the door. Big cocksman.' Uh, uh. Only insects do that. Under the door. I'm going to wake up in my cabin tomorrow morning. No chance to do it again."

I don't think she was crying. I could see only the blurred outlines of their faces. I heard her move and I saw one arm go around his neck. The other arm dangled by her side. What was she doing with her other arm? My God! She was holding him, there, between the legs, fondling the front of his trousers. My silent movie ground to a halt and, for the second time in twenty-four hours, I had trouble controlling my urine. I wished there was more light so that I could see them clearly. I wished there was total darkness so that I couldn't see at all. I wished myself in bed—at home on Lake Shore Road—at Croydon with Dougie Clark. I wished I didn't have to pee so badly. I felt at once sexually aroused and horrified. And then, her elbow made one short downward motion and her hand went into his trousers. That proved too much for both of us. Winger quickly, roughly, held her at arm's length. My brain surrendered to my bladder, and I wet my pants.

He moved like a thunderbolt to the front door. He paused there, breathing heavily, and turned back into the darkness. Once again he moved his arm in an arc over the living room.

"I can't take it on, Laura. I'm sorry. I think I could, and I'd like to, if it weren't for coming in under the door. There just ain't no way I can do that. I'm sorry."

I lost all track of time. The day seemed stuck, frozen forever in twilight. I heard the door bang. I heard him start the Dodge and roll down the hill. After a moment, or maybe half an hour, I felt the air go out of the cushions as Mother sat down beside me on the couch.

"Are you all right, Jay?"

"Yeah."

She put her arm around me and stroked my hair.

"Mama has to make some changes, Jay. There's something I want and I must have it now, Jay, because I'm forty, you know, and you must understand this isn't something I want for a second time. It isn't something I had, that palled, that I want to retrieve or repeat. I feel rather like a newborn babe, Jay—you know, the way they hold them by the feet and slap them and they make a squawky noise, and you know the lungs have cleared and the life is ready to live. I'm going to have to make some noise, but I can do it. I can do it without harming you because I have a great deal of love for you, and I have a great deal of money. This is a very mean thing to say, Jay, but your father has neither. If you don't know that already, I think it's only a matter of time until you know, because parents can't hide things like that. Sometimes I think all the parents in the world walk around their houses harboring all kinds of things, very sure that the rest of the world won't ever be able to decipher their most private thoughts, and a child always knows. By osmosis. Like that. He knows. Lord knows, when I was a child, *I* knew!

"So I must spend the next week very quietly, thinking out all the details of what I have to do to clear the way. Do you remember, I used to drive you to school every morning, but I expected you to walk home? I used to say, 'Don't dawdle. Walk right home or I'll worry.' And I used to say, 'But if it's *raining*, look for me. I'll be there.' I want you to know in your heart that I'll always be here, we'll always be together. I can take care of you and protect you from all kinds of things because I love you so much and because nobody can ever take that away. Your grandmother very wisely set things up so that nobody can ever take my money away either—you know, that's always a possibility when marriages are arranged against everybody's better judgment."

She rose from the couch and turned on the light.

"You do like Winger Burns, don't you, Jay?"

"Yes. I like him a lot."

"Yes. And Mama loves him. I love him and I love you. Do you know, he told me he has a couple of shirts another woman gave him. When he told me that I wanted to drive to his cabin and tear those shirts to shreds. Can you imagine *me*, wanting to do a thing like that? I'll do it yet, Jay! I'm going to play this game for keeps. I'm going to clear the way so that I can love you both without having to dole it out in skimpy little parcels. I refuse to love anybody any more in skimpy little parcels. That's what I've been doing, Jay. Paving a path to my grave with skimpy, niggardly little parcels. I have so much left over I'm sometimes fit to burst. I don't think it's written down in any great book of laws that I have to live that way. So, I'll make some noise next weekend, and then I won't ever do it again. Now, go throw those pants in the laundry, and I'll get us some eggs or something."

XVII

Deborah is home for Thanksgiving weekend. It will not be a warm, friendly reunion because Pat resents the fact that Deb refuses to live at home. She graduated from Vassar two years ago, brought her diploma home in a piece of Saran Wrap and sat in her room for a whole week, on the edge of her bed, resolutely cast in the mold of Rodin's *Thinker*. She didn't perk up at any of our suggestions. She didn't want to go to graduate school. She had no intention of getting married; she didn't want to fool around Europe for a year. She had even less interest than I have in the Grosse Pointe Yacht Club. "Her interest in the club is *nil*," said Pat. When she finally climbed out of the debris in her room, she said she wanted a job. Great, we said, how about giving New York a whirl? My friend Jim Benson was a bigwig at *Time* magazine. Jim wouldn't mind making a few phone calls. No. Did we realize that, in her entire twenty-one years, she had been in downtown Detroit only eight times? Pat didn't find that so startling. There was little reason to go downtown—less and less reason every year. Pat herself went to the Art Institute, had lunch there in the Garden Court and didn't dare venture an inch off Woodward Avenue. Deborah had thought it out, knuckles to chin, and came to us with the ultimatum. She wanted a job in downtown Detroit, she wanted to find it herself without our interference and she wanted an apartment of her own. She got all three within the next month. She became a "typist-re-searcher" for a lawyer in the Penobscot Building. (They've recently changed the name of this building, apparently in the belief that change is progress. I've called it the Penobscot since 1928 and shall continue to do so until my dying day.) At the Penobscot, she presented her own credentials and blew her own horn. She then rented three pleasant rooms in a complex near Palmer Park, just north of Six Mile Road. Notice was served upon us: we could come to the apartment by invitation only. When she came home, which was every weekend in the beginning, and once a month toward the end of the first year, she seemed satisfied and happy. Her satisfaction, her cheery smile, pleased me immensely. Pat, however, after passionately begging Deb to return home, confronted her with the same questions every time the child pulled into the driveway. "What are you doing with your evenings?" "Who are you seeing?" "Are you entertaining?" "Would you like to borrow my fondue pot?"

Well, for one thing, she was discovering the intricacies of The Law. There were a lot of people who got up in the morning with the single intention of breaking The Law. There were others who devoted their lives to twisting it and bending it to suit their own purposes. She had also discovered a restaurant named Hellas, near the Court House, in Greektown. She often went there for dinner with girl friends from the office. Sometimes her boss took her there for lunch. Who were these girl friends? Where did they come from? They came out of business schools. Many of them came from small towns in the Upper Peninsula. What about this boss? Was he married? Where did he get his degree? He got his degree at Columbia University. He was married and had three teen-age children. He was a "driven" man who took downtown Detroit very seriously. He was dedicated; he worked twelve hours a day, and he was not sullied with political aspirations. No Philadelphia lawyer this, he was devoted to the plight of the common man. He belonged to an organization which acted as a grievance board for downtown businesses. He went, in person, on his own time, and pleaded with distraught concerns to stay in Detroit. He had, single-handedly, persuaded six firms to stay in the last year. He was curbing the flight to the suburbs, but he shunned recognition, publicity, awards and other tokens of appreciation. Nothing fazed him. There was no aberration, no schism, no *behavioral fissure* he hadn't seen at least twice before. Gee, Deb, we're sorry we asked.

Yea, verily, there was nothing Robert Silver couldn't do. He played the violin like a virtuoso; his daughter played the flute. They had Sunday-afternoon concerts in their home, eclectic gatherings, to which Deborah was invited. They welcomed her during Passover, too, and patiently explained their religion and the history behind, and reasons for, every platter on the table. They were not self-righteous, they could poke fun at themselves:

Knock-knock.
Who's there?
Menorah.
Menorah who?
Menority shall overcome.

Judaism made a lot of sense to Deb, but she could see, from our faces, we couldn't understand. We didn't know anything about Detroit, we didn't care anything about the common man, we didn't even know anything about our own religion and certainly didn't practice it. *Thank You for the food we are about to receive.* That's as far as it went. We donated five hundred a year to the Episcopalian summer camp on Lake Huron! Yes, said Deb. That's when our religion had meaning for us. In April. As a tax deduction.

She was very sorry to have to say it, but her new experiences with Detroit, and The Law, and Bob Silver, called the lives of her parents into question, and we were found lacking in almost every regard. I protested. Since there's a grain of truth in all of the above, I protested feebly. I said I cared deeply about all of these things and, what's more, I was well versed on these subjects. I had all the figures on white flight to the suburbs. I read the *News* and the *Free Press* cover to cover every day, and the whole *New York Times* on Sunday. Try me, I said. I can talk rings around Bob Silver. I can show you that I care. "Oh, yes, Dad," she said. "I know you care. The trouble is, you care from your wing-back chair." She climbed into her Mustang and drove home to the excruciating reality of Six Mile Road. She returns now for birthdays, anniversaries and most major holidays.

Most major Christian holidays.

Today, Elise, our French maid, has the Butterball in the oven. Pat has Indian corn on the door. The Alençon lace cloth is on the dining-room table. Deb has placed a pot of yellow chrysanthemums in front of the fireplace. "Oh, Deb," we say, "you shouldn't have!" "Two bucks," she says, "at the Eastern Market!" We float around the house, not wanting to begin anything or go anywhere because it's Thanksgiving. It's too soon to dress for dinner and too late, and improper, to toil in the garden on this day. Anyway, fall gardening is one of those after-the-fact clean-up chores. When I am not immediately rewarded for my efforts, I prefer to leave it to our lawn service. I have retreated to the study for an hour. I hear Deb's rap on the door. She enters, carrying a book. I'm glad to see she's given up Vonnegut for a while. This one's something called *The Bell Jar*. She looks terrific in fall clothes. She's like my mother in this respect; heavy fabrics—tweeds and tartans—give her a substance she lacks from May to September. Only Pat, Pat of the amber tan and sleek, athletic arms, does well in sleeveless linens.

"What's all this about writing, Dad? Mother says you're trying a novel." I tell her that I've always wanted to write about my mother because my mother had an interesting life. She does a double-take. "Grandma Rutherford?" Yes, I say. Years ago, when I was kid, and we owned that lodge in Alberta, she fell in love with a local man up there and was very happy for a time. Deborah frowns and fidgets with her pleated skirt. "Grandma Rutherford?" Yes, I say. I was witness to it. It had a tremendous effect on the course of my life. "Wow!" she says. "Grandma Rutherford!" I tell her I am astonished at the ease with which I bring these memories back. I tell her I remember whole conversations. I tell her I sometimes have to quit, and go to bed, because the clarity of the memories raises havoc with my ulcer. "Jesus," she says. "How did she manage it—like, I mean, your dad was there, wasn't he?" I tell her she managed it all right. She managed it as if her life depended on it. She says that she hopes I'm serious about the novel. She hopes it won't be like everything else I start and never finish. She sounds, for a moment, like her mother. There's two thousand dollars' worth of photographic equipment in a darkroom downstairs. Five years ago I painstakingly assembled it and proclaimed that I would follow in the footsteps of Yousef Karsh. I then got interested in hi-fi equipment, and never took a picture. I tell her I'm serious. My encroaching sixties are weighing heavily upon me, and I have *intimations of immortality*. I'll finish it if it kills me. "What's it called?" she asks. She must promise not to tell Pat. She crosses her heart, but asks why.

"Your mother believes that particular summer signaled the end of my days as a useful human being. You can decide when you read it. It's called *Reflections on a Mountain Summer*."

"This guy Grandma fell in love with. What was he like?"

"Well, Deb, he wasn't one of *us*. He gave of himself the way we never could. He laughed, and he loved, and he worked. He was kind, and open, and never self-serving. He was funny and trusting, and he thought I had the world by the tail because of MacAllister money. He thought I'd set the world on fire—end up in *Who's Who*— Ambassador to the Court of St. James's in a pin-striped suit. He loved your grandmother and me very much and he didn't know—he couldn't believe—that people like us could need someone like him so badly."

"Daddy, you're *crying*."

"So I am."

She thinks my title too prosaic. She'd like something racier, something that'll catch the eye on the stands at the five-and-ten. She's probably right. I remember when Douglas Clark went to Hollywood and became a screenwriter. He submitted a script to Jack Warner and Jack Warner thumbed it down. It was called *Lady of the Camellias*. Douglas wrote me that Jack Warner didn't know from camellias, so he changed the title to *Lady of the Evening*, submitted it again, and it was accepted.

"What the hell," she says, "the title doesn't matter. It's wonderful that you're doing something, really working at something. Even if you never finish it, it's exciting that you're trying."

Oh, ye of little faith! I have the tears of forty years to speed me to my destination.

She crosses her legs and lights a cigarette. She is sheer heaven to watch; the cigarette is not an appendage. She doesn't even inhale.

"Guess what I've been doing."

"What?"

"I'm taking a sociology course down at Wayne State. Bob Silver talked me into it."

"Good for you! In the evenings?"

"Yeah. Twice a week. Don't tell Mother. She'll sign me up in Ann Arbor, and I'm getting a big kick out of Wayne. It's a kooky campus, y'know? I mean, like, a *real* campus. Thirty-six thousand enrolled. Poles, blacks, Jews, Italians. I don't tell anybody about Vassar."

"Why not?"

"It's nothing to be proud of."

"Yes, it *is*! Mary McCarthy, Edna St.—"

"Aw, come on! Can it, will you? You just don't dig."

She rises and says it's time to dress for dinner. I shuffle my papers, get my pipe and tobacco and search around under the desk for my slippers. She quickly blurts out another sentence.

"I've also got a boy friend."

"Hey, that's great. What's his name?"

She doesn't reply.

"What's his name?"

"Promise you won't tell Mother?"

I cross my heart, but ask why.

"His name is Christo. He's Bulgarian. He's a real sweet guy. Poor as a church mouse. If you want to come in some evening you can meet him. If you want to come in, like—alone. Dig?"

I dig. I thank her for the invitation. We agree that I'll sneak in the following Wednesday, when she's not in class. We'll all have dinner in Greektown. I open the door.

"Don't breathe a word of this to Mother."

Never in a million years would I breathe a word like Christo to Patricia.

XVIII

The little noise my mother spoke about was eventually heard halfway around the world. The following day she expedited part of her plan to make our lives as similar to the mainstream as possible. She began with her bedroom. When I think of that room, and I think of the various articles and accessories she chose to bring with her to Timberline, I am faced with a truth so intensely personal I hesitate to write about it. It was a little girl's room. It was frilly and frivolous—a room that made no concessions to time, and certainly not to a masculine presence. She had never, in her forty years, shared a room with a man. The things that she brought to Timberline, the souvenirs, keepsakes, memorabilia, were the same things she brought from Indian Village to Grosse Pointe Shores when she married my father. They were things that must have held fond memories, and it seems to me extraordinary that she only viewed those objects from an adult point of view with the advent of Winger Burns. What a hodgepodge it was! There was a frayed pajama bag with a rabbit's head (a bunny's head?) appliquéd on it. There was, stuck in the hinge of the dresser mirror, a miniature bamboo cane with a kewpie doll in a pink, feathery skirt tied to the top of it. There were three cheap, poorly executed china monkeys. (See no evil, hear no evil, speak no evil.) A school friend had given them to her, on the docks at Southampton, when she departed England in her twentieth year. There was a neon-green clay piggy bank with "Mackinac Island" stenciled down its back, undoubtedly a purchase made during her bloomered camp-fire-girl days in northern Michigan. And there were two little pictures with starched lace frames containing elaborately printed poems—"The Duck and the Kangaroo," by Edward Lear, and "Little Orphant Annie," by James Whitcomb Riley—all of it so much schlock, as Deborah is fond of saying these days. Mother had never thought about these things. She never looked at them or called attention to them and yet they traveled with her across the Canadian prairie, to Buena Vista. Now she abandoned them peremptorily, packing them away in a carton without a trace of nostalgia. They simply didn't fit into her future plans for that room.

A Swedish woman had been coming once a week to clean. The woman was told we would no longer need her services. She told Arnold that she would be doing her own marketing in the future, and that she would haul her own groceries when my father returned with the car. She had been accustomed to throwing away my socks and pants when holes appeared in the toes and knees. We went to visit Elsie Hilliard one afternoon, toting a shopping bag full of worn-out garments. Elsie taught her to mend and patch. I'm quite sure that Elsie had a glimmer of what was afoot. I think it quite likely that Winger had visited the Hilliards and related a part, if not all, of his mental turmoil to them. And Elsie must have felt some amount of turmoil herself. She had met my father, and though she couldn't relate to his aloof and elegant manner, I doubt that she was readily able to sanction this present duplicity. Still, she liked my mother. She was polite, and had even to instruct Mother as to what one did with one's fingers while tying the knot at the end of the thread. She sent Bob and me to the cucumber patch, with a salt shaker, and told us to eat our fill. When we returned, distended and bloated with cucumber pulp, Elsie seemingly had accepted the current events, all in the line of friendship and duty toward Mother and Winger. Her hug, and her shrug, at the end of the visit seemed to say, "If anyone's dispensable, the father is."

In the evenings, Mother got out the envelopes of diagrams and instructions explaining our appliances. She set herself the task of understanding the intricacies of our mechanical aides.

"What happens, Jay, is the refrigerant—some kind of ammonia, I think—goes into an evaporator and becomes a vapor. The vapor absorbs heat given off by the air, and the food on the shelves. It then goes into a compressor, where it's condensed back to a liquid, and the cycle is complete. There are no moving parts. Now, really, Jay, that's simple. And so *interesting*."

All of this was superficial to the core of the problem, and we both knew it. Father and Mr. Whitcomb were expected back from Jasper on Saturday, July 16. As the day approached, I developed a spectacular case of nerves, which manifested itself in a near-constant stream of urine. Mother maintained a methodical calm during the daylight hours, but I heard her stirring around the house hours after I went to bed. I tried to imagine what tack she would take with my father.

I imagined it all precisely as it occurred, but for one thing. I was sure that, at some point in the holocaust, I would be asked to take sides. I was sure that, if he returned to Grosse Pointe, he would ask me to go with him. In this fantasy he accused my mother of being unfit, and threatened to take her to court. I, of course, wanted to be with my mother, at Timberline, in the company of Winger Burns. I told him so, in my fantasy. I told him as gently as I could, with the stiffest of upper lips, and I said that maybe we could be pals when I got older and shared some of his interests. (Shirley Temple, I think, played this scene so many times she had it down to perfection.) I'd worked it out down to the last, heart-rending embrace, there by the door, at the foot of the totem pole, at high noon. As luck would have it, it didn't happen that way at all.

Quite honestly, after all these years of twisted, tangled memory, I still have to smile at the return of the woodsmen. I must give them their due; they had spent fourteen nights in the forest, sleeping on the ground. They had carried canoes past miles of untraversable rapids. They'd been caught in rain, hail, swarms of mosquitoes, quicksand and a rock slide. Mr. Whitcomb had an infected finger from a rusty fishhook. He said he wouldn't complain; it would heal. He'd seen the best damn (Castor and Pollux, Damon and Pythias) flora and fauna this old planet had to offer. My father complained at length. He had fallen into a northern river and now had persistent cramps in his feet. It took Josh so long to maneuver the boat around boulders my father was chilled to the bone for twelve hours after. Josh had some sort of survival book along, and he recommended that Father sleep with his bare feet on Josh's bare belly. This didn't work because Josh had a habit of sleeping on his belly. The cold feet were then crushed under Josh's considerable weight. The tendons were the size of telegraph cables the following day.

And the guide. The guide was a sullen, half-breed Indian,

twenty-five years old, with one shoulder which tilted much lower than the other one. Father said that was because of the enormous chip on it. The man called himself "Gaggles." He hated both Americans and Canadians, but mostly he hated his job. After the evening meal was cooked, Gaggles crept off somewhere (he preferred to sleep high up in the trees) and didn't return till dawn. The worst of Gaggles' failings, however, was his forgetfulness. He forgot to take along toilet paper.

"This *savage*," said Mr. Whitcomb, "forgot to bring the goddamned toilet paper! It wasn't *our* bailiwick. It was *his* bailiwick. He forgot his own damned bailiwick. Every step of the way, something was amiss. We kept saying, 'Gaggles, where's the whatchamajig?' He never knew. 'Gaggles, where's the thingamabob?' He never knew. He never knew his own damned bailiwick!"

So the men were forced to use broad leaves and bunches of weeds to cleanse themselves. They naturally didn't say too much about this latter, touching on the subject only to explain the acrid, somewhat mephitic odor exuding from their clothes.

Still, they were able to put on a show for us. It was late at night, eleven o'clock or so. I was allowed to get into my pajamas and wait for them. They paraded around the living room, proud of their matted beards and their black, splintered fingernails. My father had bought some beaver pelts from an Indian, dirt cheap, and he thought the Scully Brothers down on Woodward would be able to whip them up into something nifty for next winter's skiing. Unless—unless Laura would like to have a jacket or a stole. Would she? He'd be willing to let her have them if she wanted them.

"No, thank you, Jim. I have no use for them. Just as soon as you've bathed I'd like to talk with you, privately. I want you to go back to Grosse Pointe with Josh."

He stood, with some poor beaver's hide hanging loosely in his hand. His mouth opened gradually, until it looked like a piece of black coal stuck in the middle of his face. I noticed a ball of spittle rolling on his lower lip.

"For Chrissake, what happened?"

"I think you'd both better go and get cleaned up. I'll wait for you in the kitchen, Jimmy, and we'll discuss it privately. Kiss your father goodnight, Jay. It's past midnight."

I hadn't been asked to kiss my father since I was taken out of rompers. And I hadn't kissed him voluntarily in the intervening dozen years. It seemed a strange request, but the three of them lingered there, waiting for me to comply. I looked at the beard and I looked at the spittle. I planted a smack on his forehead, and went to my room.

For the next fifteen minutes all of the faucets in the house were turned on. With the air so heavy and the nerves so frayed, it should have been a quiet time, used for the gathering of our variously shattered wits. Instead, it was pandemonium. The faucets creaked and throbbed. The water rumbled and belched through the pipes—harbingers of the dreadful noises that were soon to sear our ears. I don't know what my mother was doing in the kitchen; whatever it was, it required gallons of water. Father ran a tub and Mr. Whitcomb ran a tub. My bedroom, unluckily, was between the two upstairs bathrooms. They bathed quickly. I thought about Gaggles and wondered if they did the thorough job they should have done. But then they didn't have to pass inspection, as I did. They didn't have to submit to the ignominy of a spit-wet handkerchief applied behind the ears. They shaved quickly. I heard the banging of brushes and mugs, medicine-cabinet mirrors, razors, the splattering of a fortnight's growth against the sink, the curses when they nicked themselves and the roll of the toilet paper, which they used to sop up the blood. I heard Father hoisting suitcases on his bed, throwing shoes into the closet, dumping piles of miscellaneous coins, knives, bullets, nails onto his dresser. And there was cacophony in the kitchen. Mother learned, in later life, to prepare for turbulence with careful organization of thought. She learned to marshal systematic arguments and deliver them with marvelous economy of word and husbandry of gesture. But now she was slamming cupboards and banging pots, throwing utensils into drawers, clanking glassware. There would be no rays of logical thought emanating from her brain tonight. She would exhume a portion of the insults, the slights, the neglect, and lay it, like a hollow, malformed bone, before my father.

When I heard him go downstairs, I was ready. My blankets were pulled down so that I could dive into bed at any moment. I knew it would be a long concerto, without intermission, so I moved a chair over to the door. I put on my robe and my slippers so that cold discomfort wouldn't thwart my concentration. I turned off the lights in my room and opened my door about four inches. When I heard Father moving under me, through the gallery, I put my slippered foot in the crack of the door and glanced down the hall. I saw, at the far end of the balcony, another slippered foot, another robe, another dim chair. Josh Whitcomb and I locked glances, fumbled with our belts and receded into the darkness of our rooms, where we sat on our respective chairs and listened.

For the longest time only my father's voice was audible. I could not make out any of Mother's words, though I was able to hear some indistinct murmuring for the first few minutes. Then, when Father's voice became harsh, she apparently resorted to whispers, and couldn't be heard at all. Father began sardonically. There was a tightness in his throat, as if he were loath to release the words. And when he did release them, they were like short, staccato jabs in the air.

"All right, Laura, I'm clean. Needless to say, I found your pronouncement devastating. What's it all about?"

.   .   .   .

"Well, that's nice, Laura. I'm always happy when someone falls in love."

.   .   .   .

"Oh, I'm sure you're serious. You couldn't even let me get a good night's sleep in a proper bed. What a thing to come home to! Little Laura's in love! Well, tell me. Have I had the pleasure? Samson, perhaps. Jumped over the counter and took you by force, on the sawdust."

.   .   .   .

Laughter. High-pitched, almost supernatural laughter. Not like a human's, not like a man's. Like a eunuch's cackle.

"That is *funny!* That is absolutely hilarious! What? Thirty-forty dollars a week at most?"

.   .   .   .

"I *know* it! Money's the last thing in the world you'd think about. Little Laura thinks that love will conquer all. You've *never* thought about money! You've never had to. But, Jesus Christ, surely you don't think *he* hasn't given it a thought or two?"

.   .   .   .

"I'm not insinuating anything! I'm telling you he's a freight-riding, freewheeling hobo. A vulture, Laura, for silly rich women like you. Forty-year-old, silly, rich, homely women just itching like hell to get that last train out before the tunnel closes. Wait till Josh hears about this!"

I heard Mr. Whitcomb clear his throat and move his chair a few inches farther from the door. Several moments passed.

"Is that what you imagined? Josh and me holding hands in a Pullman, hashing it over across the goddamn prairie?

I'm not going, Laura! I'm going to sit in there by the fire. I'm going to make me a big hot-buttered rum and you can sashay down to his cot, or his bunk, or his heap of straw, and let him screw you there. I am going to sit in cozy-assed comfort right here at Timberline. And, Laura, I don't care if the whole town knows and calls me a cuckold. I've been called worse. A parvenu. A whoremonger. I'm immune, Laura. It's so much water off a duck's back. I've always thought you just might dig yourself up a stallion one day or another. And I thought, so what? If I'm going to be cuckolded, I'll do it in comfort. That was the bargain, Laura. That was the *Purchase!* God, I thought if you understood anything in this world, you understood that! You've always let me play my little tiddlywinks, now I'll let you play yours."

.   .   .   .

"My, my, my, aren't you sly? Renard the fox! You won't cancel my accounts, Laura, you haven't got the guts. It's easy enough to say, up here in these godforsaken mountains. But the accounts—our life—is back in Grosse Pointe. Back in Grosse Pointe you couldn't face the music."

A glass is hurled into the sink. It smashes to smithereens against the hard white enamel. I hear Mother's long, agonized moan. It seems to travel up a scale, gaining momentum, until it finally turns to rage.

"Let's just talk a minute or two about *guts*, Jimmy Rutherford! Talk about a *bargain!* Talk about a *Purchase*. Where the hell were you when my mother verbalized the fine print? 'Of course,' she said, 'Laura will probably want children.' 'By all means,' you said, 'as many as she wants.' Just let me have my clothes and cars and boats; my crossings on Cunard and Grace! I had to come crawling to you, damn it! I had to get down on that parquet floor and beg for a baby. I thought I'd go mad without a baby! And where the hell were you when the baby was born? Laying bets—laying anything in skirts—at Saratoga! For four whole days there was a three-by-five card on his bassinet. *Baby boy Rutherford.* I didn't want to name him all by myself! I was damned if I'd haul you from the track to the phone to get your advice. And the thought of James, Jr., sickened me. Do you hear me? I'd have sooner strangled him than call him James, Jr.! The doctor helped me find a name. The doctor drove me home. The doctor sent me his bill, for services rendered. Why the hell are people always rendering services and tallying it up in neat little columns, and sending me the bills? I'm sick to death of the whole thing. I was never a girl, or a bride, or a wife, or a mother! I've been some sort of inept, ill-trained accountant all my life. And none of the work is satisfactory. It's all cheap, shoddy work! It can't be satisfactory, it can't have any meaning. It's an adulterated marriage. There's no support, no love, no respect. I'm starved for these things, Jimmy! It's like a hunger. A malnutrition of the soul!"

"Malnutrition of the soul? Sounds like a job for the Salvation Army. Or the Red Cross. Or both. Remember, if you will, the last night of our honeymoon. You forbade me, Laura, to ever touch you again. You sat on that bed at the Huntington, in Pasadena, and you said if we both lived to be a hundred you'd never let me touch you again. That hurt like hell, Laura. Was I so repulsive? Was it so awful—"

"It was a screaming bloody nightmare, and you know it! Oh, what's the use of dredging it all up again? It's all so much stinking sewage under the bridge."

"Nasty talk, Laura. Nasty. Unbecoming to a woman of your class."

"Now you listen to me, Jimmy. What does old Sophie always say, eh? Old Sophie always says the person who signs the checks is the person in control. I'm in control, Jim. I can cut off your water like a master plumber! I can plug up those accounts of yours till you're lucky if you've got trolley fare for transportation. I can do a whole lot of dirty little things I've contemplated *ad infinitum* over the last fifteen years. You don't have to sleep on it. You don't need a week to think it over. You haven't got a leg to stand on. But a bargain's a bargain, right? I'm not your slippery little run-of-the-mill street Arab. I'm not asking for a divorce. I'll pay your bills; I'll give you your monthly stipend. I'll come home at the end of the summer and put Jay back in school. But you have to leave with Josh and let me have the rest of the summer alone with Winger Burns."

Laughter again. Staccato little babbles, without a trace of mirth. The clink of ice cubes in a glass, the slap of a palm on the table.

"Leapin' lizards! Will you listen to the lady call the shots! Must be your Teutonic blood, Laura. Yes, that's it! The Wessel contingent has been heard from. Got it all figured out like so much territory. Your territory, my territory. No, no, no!! I've got it all wrong. It's all *your* territory. You're going to be the four-star general, and I'm going to be the little tin soldier. Well, if that's your deal, it's not a bad deal. Relieves me of a lot of responsibility, actually. Hell, I don't think I'd make it here anyway, the natives being what they are. Bunch of rubes. But listen, just in the interests of prudence, I'm going to call old Sophie and tell her about this. I'll want her to keep a sharp eye on the books. Ten to one that hobo tries to rob you blind."

I hear a final clink of ice cubes, and realize that he is leaving the kitchen. But then I hear a voice. Whose is it? It seems more like a windy howl, blowing down from the top of Binnie and in the back door. It contains violence and loathing, horror and humiliation.

"Jimmy?"

"Yes?"

"There was no need for *Vaseline.*"

He makes his way through the gallery, and by the time his foot reaches the bottom stair, my door is closed, my chair is back in place and I'm in bed.

Now, what do we perceive in all of the above? Among other things, a glaring omission. Not once does the father give mention to the son. I might as well admit it. It's galled the hell out of me these forty-odd years.

XIX

Two days later, on Monday, July 18, my father and Mr. Whitcomb left Buena Vista. The house was solemnly quiet for those two days, due, in part, to Mr. Whitcomb's sudden attack of diarrhea. I'll never know if it was brought on by his outdoor attempts at meals or by his eavesdropping. Mr. Whitcomb, like my father (and, alas, like me), didn't "go to business." He had an inheritance from sand pits, and held considerable stock in a large plate-glass company—to which the sand was sold. But his alimony payments were stiff. Whenever he talked about having to "tighten the belt," my father laughed and picked up the tab for their various excursions. Perhaps he foresaw, in my mother's edict, the threat of penny pinching. At any rate, his diarrhea provided an excuse for our not having to confront each other past the point of pleasantries.

"Mom!"

"Ssssh! Mr. Whitcomb's indisposed."

"Dad!"

"Ssssh! Mr. Whitcomb's indisposed."

"How're you feeling, Mr. Whitcomb?"

"Sorry, Jay, can't talk now. I'm indisposed."

I think, at that juncture, I was just too tired to notice much of what happened around me. I woke up with a long itinerary of things to get me away from the adults. I was going to ride with Eileen; I was going to go and watch Elsie Hilliard butcher a hog. I was going to go up to the top of the Amberley and take some pictures. I was going to write Dougie Clark. By the time I'd finished breakfast, I only wanted to go to bed again. And, though I tried to drink very little liquid, my very saliva seemed to turn to urine as it went down my esophagus. Too lazy to stand, I sat, lethargically, on the toilet, or I sat, lethargically, in the living room. Mother finally contrived to include me in her work.

Her work those two days involved load after load of Father's and Mr. Whitcomb's laundry. I was given the job of taking all the damp, knotted-up socks and straightening them right side out. I then had to turn out all of the pants' pockets and remove whatever debris I found there. I helped her sort the heaps of soiled, mildewed garments so that she could alternate the loads from light to dark. While the machine chugged away, I dozed in a nearby chair. When the machine clanked to a stop, I fed the sopping garments into the wringer. Mother caught them on the other side and then proceeded to do something or other with bluing and starch. We learned, together, that Shetland sweaters, six of them in all, come out of the wash in shapes fit only for midgets or dwarfs. And we learned that, with a little effort and careful selection, one could coordinate a clothesline so that when you took it all down it came off in convenient categories: socks, underwear, things to be dampened and ironed, things to be folded and put on shelves or in suitcases. It was the first time I'd ever assisted with "woman's work." I formed the opinion then, and have held it ever since, that it was interesting work for the first couple of hours, and tedious drudgery ever after. (Oddly enough, Patricia disagrees with this judgment. She has said, for years—through a dozen housekeepers and maids and half again as many dayworkers —that housework can be creative and rewarding. "It may not be a bowl of cherries, Jay, but I'm sure it's not, as you say, a *crock of shit.*")

I remember that Mr. Whitcomb, whose own marital situation seemed insufficient testimony to warrant it, decided to play counselor that evening. He summoned my mother to the guest room and tried to convince her that Winger Burns was a freight-riding, freewheeling hobo. I had gotten down to writing Dougie Clark. I was seated at the desk in my room, and I remember feeling very sorry for Mr. Whitcomb. God knows, he was trying. He was trying to wax poetic about the joys of hearth and home, but the more he waxed the more he waned. I pieced together the phrases that wafted my way; my only comfort being his numerous allusions to me and my welfare. Whatever kind of life he was proposing for my mother and father was certainly the antithesis of anything I'd ever known. It sounded rather like one of those rosters of homespun virtues compiled by *Good Housekeeping* magazine after a national sampling of opinion. He talked about what great fun picnics were when the mother loaded a wicker basket full of pickles and tomato aspic and everybody piled into the car and sang good old songs down by the old mill stream. He talked about the ceremonies of life, the christenings, the birthdays, the graduations, the anniversaries, and asserted that these days were deadly ordeals unless celebrated in the bosom of the family. Parades and pyrotechnics on the Fourth—cider mills in autumn—carnations for Mother in May—red satin hearts in February—Easter hams and painted eggs—Christmas turkeys, ancient carols, chestnuts roasting, Jack Frost nipping—this familial utopia was being heartlessly wrenched away from little Jay because Laura'd gone and gotten *the hots* for a hobo. He talked of the importance of a man's example in the house, and listed those Grosse Pointe families where divorce had occurred and the sons had shortly thereafter gone to Broadway and joined the chorus of Earl Carroll's *Vanities*. He talked of what the neighbors would think—not here, at Timberline; these neighbors didn't matter. The people in the Shores, the people at the Yacht Club, the people at Croydon. How would she endure the silly smirks of servants and shopgirls and hairdressers? Oh, yes, yes, it was done all the time. It was done for movie stars and Ivy League athletes, expatriate novelists and impoverished noblemen. It was never, ever, done for hoboes. They were in there, with the door closed, for about twenty minutes. When they came out I could immediately see that Mr. Whitcomb's common pleas had had no effect whatsoever on Mother. As he zoomed past me in the hall, I realized his indisposition was the reason for the meeting's brevity.

The following day, nary a word was spoken. Perhaps there is a great deal to be said for silence. The breakfast, the packing, the drive to the station were all conducted as if we functioned in a soundproof shelter. Coffee cups were set down in saucers, drawers were opened and closed, suitcases were snapped and locked—all soundlessly. Even the water pipes failed to throb. The tasks we had to perform were very much like the tasks I have since performed after the funeral of a friend or relative. It was as if the living personage were gone and a group of delegates gathered to disperse and relegate the material belongings. Most of it was done arbitrarily —every trace of Father was emphatically removed, including his Kodak. There was no need to question whether or not certain items should be left for some future visit. He would never again come back to Timberline, and I had only to look in Mother's eyes to know it. It was a disconnected, tormented day for all of us, but I think especially for me. Mother moved about, watching the clock like a hawk, with silent, but confident determination. I tried to find reassurance in that, but I couldn't. Father moved silently, watching the clock with a sense of defeat and resignation. Josh Whitcomb went to the guest room after breakfast and stayed there until it was time to drive to the station. I felt the time slipping through my fingers like so much sand in an hourglass. Why didn't he say something to me? Throw an arm around me—hand me a five-dollar bill—extend his best wishes for a good summer. No warnings, no dictates, no words to the wise. We loaded the car and drove to the station, traveling up the main street and passing the Petit-Pointe Bone China Shop. There, Father turned to Mother and the following exchange took place:

"Nancy Worth doesn't know one never wears blazers in July."

"Oh, perhaps the laws that govern those things are different in Buena Vista."

"So it would seem. And the name is dubious. Worth. There's something flat and Slavic about her forehead. I'll wager there's a Pole in Nancy Worth's woodpile."

"Well, perhaps the laws that govern that sort of thing are different here, too."

"I seriously doubt it."

"Oh, well, who knows? Mustn't forget Chopin was Polish."

That was the extent of it until we reached the station, where Mother and I lingered behind the men while they bought their tickets. Joseph Hilliard was surprised at Father's request, but he had long ago learned not to register inner feelings or questions. He looked searchingly into Mother's face and saw there only the aforementioned determination. She was very much in control and wanted simply to get it over with.

"Urgent business, Mr. Rutherford?"

"Yes. Unexpected."

Mr. Hilliard passed the tickets through the wicket and took their money.

"I never envied people with money. Too much responsibility."

"For some, yes."

"I always taught that to Seth. I used to say, 'Seth, uneasy lies the head that wears the crown.' "

"Quite true, yes. Thank you."

The redcap took their luggage, and Mr. Whitcomb suggested that we board with them for the ten-minute wait. Inexplicably, I again felt the pressure of my bladder, although I had gone to the bathroom just before we left the house. I excused myself, and hurriedly went to the men's room on the train. This abundance of urine puzzled me. I filled the small metal bowl quickly and noisily. I obeyed the sign—refraining from flushing the toilet while the train was standing in the station. When I made my way down the aisle, I saw Mother standing near Mr. Whitcomb. They weren't talking; however, their bodies formed a twosome, and Father sat, by himself, on the plush arm of the seat. Clearly, the goodbyes were being left to me. I went, with as much assurance as I could muster, directly to him and shook his hand.

"I sure hope you have a good trip, Dad."

He held my hand for a moment, and ran his thumb over my school ring. There was ineffable sadness in his face. There was a weakness and resignation about him, making me wish that some large-bosomed woman would come along and take him under her wing. He pulled back his hand and shoved it into his breast pocket, reaching for his wallet.

"You've been done a great disservice, Jay."

I thought he referred to Mother's involvement with Winger. I wanted to make it clear that I had no qualms about that involvement. I shrugged.

"She didn't plan it this way. She'd never purposely do me a disservice."

"Nor would I," he said. "You don't understand. The disservice was done years ago. By your grandmother, I think. Although I'm sure she thought she acted with the best of intentions."

When, oh when, I thought, will all of these folks stop passing the buck? He handed me a five-dollar bill. It was that odd blue Canadian five, which always reminded me of Monopoly money. Just then we heard the familiar "all aboaaaard." There was a flurry of kisses and wishes, some handshaking, brushing of cheeks and patting of shoulders. Our voices climbed into a nasal, upper register, and we spoke in quivering falsetto. As Mother and I pushed our way past the passengers, to the platform, I was aware of leakage: moisture in my underwear. I headed into the station house but Mother caught me by the arm and directed me down the platform.

"I don't think I want to see Mr. Hilliard right now."

We circumvented the building and found our Ford in the

lot. In the car, we saw the train moving slowly away from Buena Vista. She threw her arms around me and burst into tears.

"*Baby! Tell* me! Are you sad? Are you heartbroken? Do you understand any of this?"

"I think I understand."

"Are you depressed? Worried? Anxious? Is there *anything* I can say to make you see that the world hasn't come to an end?"

"Well, I'd like to know. Is Winger going to move in with us?"

"Oh, I hope so! I'm going to do everything in my power to persuade him to, Jay. I want to go to his cabin tonight around five—I'd like to go alone, if that's all right with you. You'll be O.K. for a couple of hours, won't you? You see, I have to convince him that we won't interfere with his routine or his work. I have to explain that there'll be no need for lying or sneaking—you know—that I need his love and I'm prepared to pay the piper for it. And if he does move in, he'll go to work all week—you know—won't that be *strange*? Having a man leave at eight and come home at five? A whole new way of arranging one's day, don't you think? So we'll have plenty of time together, and you can see Eileen, and I'll drive you over to Bob's anytime you want, or he can come to Timberline, maybe even stay a weekend and roast marshmallows or something like that.

"And, Jay. When there's talk, and there will be talk, what you must do is this: you must first write off half of it as sour grapes. Some people get very upset when people with money appear to be making their own rules. And some people get very upset, really, Jay, they get so *surly* simply because other people are enjoying themselves and finding pleasure in things. And then you must remember that some people, well—nobody. I expect there's not a single soul in Buena Vista with the vaguest understanding of our past. Yachts and grand tours and the Scully Brothers—things like your dad's

Ruxton Roadster at home. I mean, who could imagine that enormous pile of bills and all those paperweights all over my desk, holding them down?

"But then, for the other half of the talk. That's very hard to write off. So you must do this: look and listen. And see if we don't manage to fill that great big lodge with oodles of fun! And if we succeed, and I know in the marrow of my bones we will, then you'll learn to look at and listen to the people who are doing the talking with a very compassionate eye. I mean, damn it, you'll know who you are, and where you belong, and what really matters. And I know for a fact there are zillions of people walking this earth who never, *ever* find that out! And pretty soon you'll get a perspective on things so that— What's the matter? Oh, *baby! Tell* me! Do you have to go to the bathroom again?"

"Yeah. Something awful."

We drove home. I filled the bowl again, and changed my underwear. I went to my room and finished my letter to Dougie Clark. Mother went to the kitchen and cleaned up the breakfast mess we'd left behind. I could hear her humming bits of "Embraceable You" while she puttered in the sink.

It was over. He was gone. And I found hope and solace in the fact that I did not have to urinate again, not so much as a tinkle, until I went to bed that night.

Part Three

I finally find a parking place on Monroe Street, across from St. Mary's Church. I've admired this vast, pink-brick church all my life, and have always wanted to go inside. It was built in 1885, and certainly must be the most beautiful church in Detroit. I've dragged myself through Notre-Dame, the cathedral at Chartres, St. Mark's in Venice, and St. Peter's in Rome. I've done all that as a tourist. But there is something so overwhelmingly immigrant-Catholic about Detroit's St. Mary's, I don't dare enter it. I wouldn't be able to rattle around with a herd of other gawkers and touchers; I'd have to hover near the statues and try not to disturb those elderly, kneeling, black-shawled souls who came to pray. It would be a voyeur's visit, and I would feel like a Peeping Tom.

I pause in front of a shoddy, paint-peeled magazine stand, and glance over *True Confessions, True Stories, True Experiences.* Is this what the teeny-boppers are reading these days? "We Traded Our Baby for a Secondhand Car." "The Swedish Sex My Husband Demanded." "The Jack-Rabbit Love Technique I Had to Endure." And, "I Followed My Heart, Now I Can't Look in the Mirror." Remarkable, all of it, if true.

I am to meet Deb and Christo at Hellas Restaurant at seven-thirty. It's just seven twenty-five, so I wander up St. Antoine, hoping that the doors of the church might be open and I can get a glimpse of the altar. The doors are closed, so I cross the street again and make my way past the Ambrosia Market. I see trays of baklava in the window, three-pound pouches of beige pistachio nuts, gallon cans of Minerva olive oil. On the shelves there are grape leaves in brine, bottles of ouzo and retsina. Inside, I spy barrels of peppers and ripe olives, bins of rice and beans, tied bunches of dried oregano. All of this whets my appetite and I quickly stumble into the darkness of Hellas, right next door.

I am immediately thankful that Pat wasn't included in the invitation. The place is packed; and none of the occupants seems to be having a quiet conversation. They are all involved in spirited discussions. I see husky black men holding hands with china-doll blondes. I see four young men with braids down their backs. There are two Filipino doctors from nearby Detroit General, still wearing their greens. There is a table full of portly Polish policemen. Booths and a jukebox line the walls. The tables in the center have no cloths. And at the back, above a trellis full of artificial grapes, there is an enormous photograph of the Acropolis at night. I quickly surmise that there are two kinds of waiters: those who have just passed through puberty and those who have just entered senility. The latter appear to speak—grudgingly—a few words of English. The former are ingratiating, and smile a lot. The swinging front door whacks me in the back as Deborah and Christo enter the restaurant. Surely, the meeting of father and boy friend is the most awkward of all introductions. Christo is not at home with English and I am not at home with Christo. I notice that they both wear Levi's and tie-dyed shirts. Christo's, of course, are authentic and appropriately faded and frayed. Deb's are natty, and come from a boutique.

Oh, this Christo has the biggest, brownest eyes I've ever seen! And eyelashes that put Deb's pale blond ones to shame. God! Why am I remembering that awful old song?

Oh! how I hate Bulgarians.
Big Bulgarians, small Bulgarians
Short Bulgarians, tall Bulgarians
Oh! how I hate Bulgarians—
With their big Bulgarian eyes.

We are seated and given menus which, when opened, display a mimeographed sheet of hieroglyphics. All this menu tells me is that the three of us will eat for well under fifteen dollars. I am not one of those people who try to be suave, botch up the pronunciation and end up with a plate of sheeps' eyes staring up at them. I tell Christo I'm a fish out of water and I need help. I say yes, I like lamb, yes, I like eggplant. Christo smiles. I will be in the good graces of somebody out behind the Acropolis. Christo orders a variety of dishes—moussaka, dolmathes, pasticcio and spanakopita. We share and swap and settle down to a delicious potpourri of aromatic Greek tastes.

For openers, Christo says he would very much like to hear about the novel I'm writing. I get out of that one like quicksilver and ask him what he's studying at Wayne. He is a senior in mechanical engineering. He says he doesn't envy the guys who will graduate and work for Ford or General Motors. He speaks with some authority about the Ford River Rouge plant, saying he is supporting himself now by working on the assembly line, which he loathes. His plan is to return to Sofia and make a name for himself. He then tries to tell me what his father does. We have a language breakdown here, and I am left with the impression that his father is somewhere between a dogcatcher and the president of the Sofian equivalent of the S.P.C.A.

I find myself asking a series of inane questions pertaining to the differences between Detroit and Sofia. I know they are inane because Deb is groaning audibly but, hell, I don't know what else to talk about. They've got each other, there on the other side of the booth, and I'm doing the best I can all by my lonesome. I find out a little about the Bulgarian weather and the Bulgarian standard of living. I learn that Varna and Burgas are the principal Black Sea ports. The population is about eight million and the country is divided into thirty provinces. He touches on politics only once, with a mention of the Soviet Union. He glances at Deb, hesitates and doesn't continue. Deb then tells me that Bulgaria's second city, Plovdiv, contains many ancient Greek ruins. We all realize that it's getting rather like a taped travelogue. I decide to tie it up with a definitive statement.

"Detroit must have been quite an adjustment for you."

"Yes," he replies, "but it has been easier since I have been with Debbie."

They now do something to each other under the table. I can feel the reverberations cross my knees. *Been with?* Oh, boy. I pour another glass of retsina and thank my lucky stars Patricia isn't along. I wonder, did that lose something in translation? Does he mean, "Since I *met* Debbie"? "Since I've become *friends* with Debbie"? Does he mean, "Mr. Rutherford, the adjustment has been easier for me since I *made the acquaintance* of your daughter"? I look at Deb and am met with the coldest and boldest of stares. No doubt about it. Deb's the one who's lost something in translation. He means, *Been with. Lying with. Having carnal knowledge of.*

I am moving my napkin across my mouth too many times. My arm is going back and forth like a windshield wiper. Deb reaches over and stays my hand. She is smiling beatifically and Christo is blushing and batting his bushy eyelashes.

"We're together for a while, Dad. That's all right with you, isn't it?"

My hand is pinned under hers, on top of my napkin, which is just as well because the napkin will hopefully absorb the globules of sweat now gushing from my palm. Why is she confronting me like this? I've been plunked in the middle of a tournament and nobody's explained the rules. Why isn't she sneaking off to a motel? Why isn't she acquainting herself with lumbago in the back seat of some old Chevrolet, the way I used to do? I don't like all this honesty. I liked it much better in the old days when everyone pretended to be virtuous, boys were told to look for blood on the sheet, and more than one young bride I knew made a prenuptial trip to the butcher to buy a vial of it. I notice a certain inscrutability now on Christo's countenance. He has tuned in to my thoughts.

"Mr. Rutherford, I understand your feeling. I understand because in my *con-try* such things are not confessed."

And he continues, somewhat upper-handedly:

"If it is worry in your mind you should know I have deep care inside your daughter. Is not—how you say?—*fly-by-one-night stand.* Is not *permanent,* no, but is very deep true care I have inside. Your daughter."

He is holding his stomach, which I take to signify depth of feeling rather than dyspepsia. I should either rise like a phoenix, read the riot act and make a hasty exit, or say something like I hope they'll be happy, and careful, and as considerate as possible when it all falls apart. Instead, I lean over and say, earnestly:

"Listen. How're you kids fixed for money?"

There is a terrible, embarrassed silence. Clearly, I'm being a terrific prick about this whole thing. Deb says that between them they have seven hundred a month. They are doing just fine. Christo gilds the lily by saying that I am their guest this evening.

We're now into roditis, for some reason, and we finally reach that pleasant, mellow, full-bellied plateau where talk comes easily. Probably because we are downtown and not too far from Gratiot, I begin to tell them about my great-grandmother Wessel, who emigrated from Germany in 1860. Grandmother Wessel was Grandmother MacAllister's mother. She married a young German baker in 1865, and they opened a bakeshop in what should have been their living room. Grandmother Wessel assisted her husband there until, somewhere around 1890, he had a stroke. Grandmother MacAllister was in her late teens then; they lost the bakery and were reduced to poverty. Deb asks why I've never told her this before. I really don't know. The story of Grandmother Wessel was told to me only once, during our last, tortured days at Buena Vista. As a child, my mother had visited Grandmother Wessel. Her account of the visits is blindingly vivid. She was lying on the floor at Timberline in clothes she hadn't changed for three days. My intestines begin to churn, and I know I'm in trouble if the moussaka and dolmathes get caught in the whirlpool of this memory. So I tie this one up quickly, too. I say the matter apparently caused some discomfiture in the family. The visits were clandestine; Grandmother MacAllister went to visit her mother secretly, and took my mother along. Grandmother Wessel spoke no English and could not read or write, even in her native tongue. Grandmother MacAllister, née Wessel, had agreed, when she married her lumber baron, never to see her family again.

Deb and I are surprised and startled at Christo's reaction to this. He brings his fist down on the shiny black table with tremendous force. He snorts, and his huge eyes are ablaze with fury. "I will *kill* the lumber baron!" he announces to our half of the restaurant. Deb pats his arm and says, "Now, now, Christo!" but he will not be silenced. He thrusts his face into mine and blurts, "*You*, Mr. Rutherford! *You* must kill the lumber baron!" Our language problem is of immense proportions. Has he understood anything I've said all evening? I try to explain that I am speaking of incidents that bridge four generations. When he finally understands the time span, he nods fitfully, and I privately pray that we'll leave it be. But no. He leans forward again and peers into my eyes. A hushed silence falls over the diners in the immediate vicinity. "How did he die?" he whispers. "Wracked with pain," I answer. "He was escorting a United States senator through one of his mills. He was explaining the procedure to the senator and his arm was cut off by a huge saw." Christo throws himself against the back of the booth. "His *right* arm?" "Yes," I reply. "Gangrene set in and he died a week later." "Good!" shouts Christo. And he turns to the middle-aged couple seated behind us and murmurs, "*That lumber baron was a son of a bitch!*"

Well, I guess I like Christo. The three of us move out of the restaurant and seem now to stand on a footing that's much more harmonious than the hazardous ground on which we began. It's unseasonally balmy for the beginning of December. I've been wondering all night if Deb will spend the holidays with us. I broach it now, trying not to convey how fervently we need her in the house to help us patch up the chinks in what would otherwise be an ordinary day.

"Will you be coming home for Christmas, Deb?"

She and Christo exchange looks. I like him all the more for that look of his. It's a look that's unencumbered with misplaced verbs and dangling participles. It says: *Of course you will! The old folks must come first.* I'm so taken by this look I make a magnanimous offer. "We'd certainly like you and Christo to at least spend Christmas Day with us." Deb's look, now, at me, is wholly encumbered with the vernacular. *For Chrissake, have you lost your marbles?*

"Why don't you plan on it? I'll make the arrangements at home."

"That'll take some arranging."

"Nonsense! An extra plate at the table, that's all. O.K.?"

"All right," she says, as she kisses my ear.

Christo pumps my hand and smiles.

"Hey, Mr. Rutherford! Everything is *copacetic!*"

They climb into Deb's Mustang. I pass the Ambrosia Market and detour up St. Antoine again for a second try at the altar. Still no luck, so I find my little MG and start for the freeway.

What I do next is madness. I have a curious urge to drive over to Gratiot and take a look at what is left of the German community. I know damn well there's very little left. The Italians were the next wave of immigration, pushing the Germans eastward, and the Italians were followed by the blacks. This pattern is common to all metropolitan areas; however, in Detroit there was no noble request to be given the tired, poor, huddled masses. The offer was singular and it was made by Henry Ford. It was heard in such disparate places as Warsaw and Naples, and it was carried, personally, by Henry's agents, into the American South. Five dollars per man per day.

It's sheer folly to take my white face, red hair, green MG onto Gratiot at ten o'clock at night. Once there, I realize my only hope is to beat all the red lights and get the hell out as quickly as possible. Much of the street is "Riot Renaissance"—boarded up, shut down, barred. The gutters are filled with trash and broken glass, and on every block there is a broken-down car with its hood up, and three or four black men bending their upper halves over the ailing engine. The billboards show me beautiful blacks smoking Kents and drinking Pepsi. I am jarred at the sight of a young girl sitting on her porch steps reading—yes, Vogue magazine! She is a skinny little girl, very pretty, no more than fifteen, with a short, tight, cappish Afro. When she catches me staring at her she puts the magazine down and swiftly raises her arm. I expect the familiar Black Power fist. No, wait! She is giving me the finger! And while I am sitting there, thinking how preferable—how much less threatening—the finger is to the fist, the light up at the corner turns red. Rather than sit any longer opposite the girl, I roll up to the corner and take my chances there. God, the light is interminable! I am vaguely aware of someone approaching the left side of the car. The door, of course, was locked ages ago, but still, I am ensconced in the frailest of automobiles and I feel catastrophe inching nearer. A very old, nearly feeble black man knocks on the window. He doesn't look dangerous, and God knows, I can spare a dime for a cup of coffee. I roll down the window.

"You look like you're lost."

"Oh, no. I'm just taking the long way home."

"Oh, yeah," he says. "I thought maybe you were looking for one of the old *biergartens*." He pauses. "They're all gone now."

"I know," I reply. "It's too bad."

"Yeah. They've all gone out to Mount Clemens."

"Thanks, anyway."

The light turns green, and I go. I go with caution. They are so very hard to see at night.

XXI

Winger Burns moved into Timberline the day after my father left—mid-July. I'd been out with Bob and Eileen most of the day, and came home red as a beet, painfully sunburned, eyes smarting, nostrils swollen; my scalp was so scorched I couldn't comb my hair. I had, of course, been given a tube of salve, Formula ZB-2, a concoction culled from some unspeakable part of a halibut. ZB-2 was for the delicate skin of redheads and I was, of course, damned if I'd smear the goopy, chalk-white stuff on in front of Bob and Eileen. So I sat near the front window that evening and I clearly remember that my face emitted so much heat it actually steamed up the glass. I saw the Safari Blue Dodge coming up the road far below me, and much as I wanted to run out and greet him, the thought of a rough-and-tumble encounter with Winger was too much to bear. I called Mother and told her he'd arrived. As she ran out the front door, I cautioned her: "Tell him I'm burned to a crisp! Tell him I can't be touched!"

He bounded out of the car with such ebullience and joy I found the transition difficult to comprehend. He had been so resolute in his leaving the lodge that last time I'd seen him. He had stalked through the living room and out the door, pulling up his zipper, making a final pronouncement: we were too much for him; he couldn't take us on. As I reflect upon his about-face now, I realize it surprised me because it didn't fit into my past associations with reversed decisions. Nothing of this nature occurred on Lake Shore Road without considerable wheeling and dealing. When my grandmother told my father that he was being altogether too extravagant, when she begged him to harness his appetites, he relented only when bribed. She gave him a bright-yellow Ruxton Roadster, and he promised to curtail his expenses for the next year. In other words, the attitude that accompanied

all such reversals was this: *Fine. What's it worth to you?*
And I had watched my mother and father negotiate with an
acumen that made Shylock look like a pussycat. Mother
habitually bought freedom from Father's social obligations
with what seemed to me to be an infinite number of ploys—
she really did find the Olmsteads insufferable—why didn't
he go alone? Why didn't he run down to the Scully Brothers
and buy something special, something daring, something
dazzling. Here's a check, Jimmy. Here's an extra fifty, Jimmy.
Take along a nice bread-and-butter gift; stop in at Stoddard's
and buy a piece of antique crewel. Have it gift-wrapped. Have
a good time. See you Sunday. Give my regrets. Give my
regards. Go away now, Jimmy. Go dazzle the Olmsteads all
by yourself.

Conversely, the only time Mother felt motivated to go
along with him was when there was travel involved. Travel
afforded her food for thought. People were all the same, but
places varied sufficiently in customs and cultures to warrant
one's leaving the house. I remember, one Easter, a group of
Father's friends had chartered a cruise to Bermuda. Ten days,
ten nights; Father plainly did not want her along, cramping
his style. Wouldn't she really rather stay at home? She *knew*
what to expect: dressing to the nines or tens for dinner,
competing with other women's designer labels, cards and
gambling, bathtub gin till they reached Bermuda and got a
bellyful of the real stuff—wouldn't she really be better off at
home? Besides, that Jewish fiddler—whatsisname?—Elman,
was playing with the Detroit Symphony with—whatsisname?
—Gabrilowitsch conducting. That was more to her liking.
She'd have a good time listening to Mischa Elman. Maybe
even get to shake his hand. Maybe get his autograph! He'd
gladly run down to Orchestra Hall and pick up a ticket. He'd
give her regrets and regards. He'd bring back something nifty
from Hamilton.

It may be that I'm ignorant (if so, it's blissful ignorance)
of any complexities in the transaction between my mother and

Winger. She went to his cabin the night before, at five o'clock, and was home by quarter of six, bouncing in like a cheerleader, effervescing with the news that Winger was to be ours for the rest of the summer. As far as I know there were two major bones of contention, and two points which might properly be termed addenda.

1. She must allow him to buy all of the food and pay the utilities.
2. She must never, ever, suggest that he leave his job and retire under the wing of that great MacAllister dividend.
and
3. His cabin would remain his cabin as long as he resided in Buena Vista.
and
4. She must promise, on pain of death, never to order him monogrammed towels from Moseley's in Detroit.

Points 3 and 4 probably wouldn't have been mentioned had not she, too, been conditioned by past experience. Winger later told me that, for a woman gifted with consummate tact, she lost her touch on point 3. After agreeing without pause to 1 and 2, she then insisted that, when we returned to Grosse Pointe for school, Winger would stay the winter at Timberline. He refused to let his cabin go. He'd lived there for six years; his name was on the mailbox. His name was not on the mailbox at Timberline. She became flustered at his obstinacy. She pleaded with him to cut his ties with the cabin. She said we'd put his name on the mailbox at Timberline, and we'd call up the gas and electric and have those accounts put in his name, too. She expanded, nervously, concentrating on this matter of appellation. She said she'd taken Father's monogrammed towels and dumped them in the rag bin. Now, she said, she'd write to Moseley's in Detroit, and order a whole new set, teal blue would be nice, with a satin "W.B." on the border—in scarlet. He listened to all of this speechlessly, incredulously, and when she was done he said that (3) his cabin would remain his cabin as long as he resided in Buena Vista and (4) she must promise, on pain of death, never to order him monogrammed towels from Moseley's in Detroit.

At the end of it, he felt a need to make a distance between them. He moved to his cot and sat down. Disturbing, disquieting thoughts were tumbling around in his brain in such profusion that he stammered. He took several moments to arrange his doubts and fears into words, and then he told her this:

"Now, Laura, there's going to be times when certain things'll have to be said in order to get around the snags. This'll fall more to you than me because I got to thirty-eight with a passel of snags. I don't mean in my temper. I think you'll find me a fair man in most everything. What I mean is, you're going to want to call attention to my snags and smooth them out. Oh, yes! Don't interrupt! I never met a woman yet wasn't bent on altering a man. What I want to say is hard to put right. I guess it's a half-assed kind of compliment.

"This is a whole new ball game 'cause I never before met a woman I felt was really *qualified* to call attention to my snags—I mean things like manners and grammar and such. You're so qualified and nice, I'll tell you, I'm real anxious to just lay around with you and let you set some of these snags to rights. Trouble is, no matter how you stack it, what all these snags amount to, is *criticism*. I'm going on and on like this because, honest to God, it's been my biggest worry where you and me are concerned. I figure I'm big enough to take it, but what'll kill me, Laura, what'll just finish me off, is if you don't do it gentle and you don't do it *private*. Like, in front of Jay. Or Seth and Elsie. You got to understand, Laura—that'd just wipe us out like a busted dam."

He needn't have said any of this. She never criticized him, I think not even privately. I never heard her turn a "lay" to "lie," a "me" to "I"; there was never the hint of a suggestion that his manners were in any way offensive or unacceptable.

I remember, after dinner, the very evening he moved in, his coffee was scalding hot when she brought it to him. He took the cup, poured out half the coffee into the saucer and drank it from the saucer as it cooled. Well, I didn't jump up and down and flap my arms, but I did look directly into Mother's eyes, expecting that old familiar expression of disdain to pass silently between us. She stubbornly avoided my stare. She poured half of her coffee into her saucer, lifted it to her mouth carefully and practiced her first sip. Having mastered it, she put the saucer down on the table and looked at me, and smiled. We were never again to share those looks of disdain. They were forbidden in his presence.

I must now clutch myself by the collar and talk of their nights. And as I broach this point, and try to capture the substance and the essence of their lovemaking, I fear I must also grapple with my own set of circumstances at the time. I was, just then, fourteen years old. The summers weren't too bad for me, but during the school year I had my hands in my pants more than I had them on my books, and when I finally did lay them down on printed material, I sought out the dirtiest printed material I could find. Since things weren't nearly so enlightened and explicit back in those days, I did this with some difficulty. At Croydon we occasionally got hold of eight-page bibles and, of course, we had access to the juicier passages of the Bible itself. But in the former, Popeye didn't adequately fire our imaginations, and in the latter they beget and beget and hedge, forever, on the specifics. We were, in fact, so hard-pressed (!) for dirty books at Croydon we had to depend on two particular boys for our adventures into erotica. One was Dougie Clark, who generally appeased our lust for a week or two with a variety of anecdotes brought back from Paris. The other was Vincent Pellegrini, an Italian boy who was the class dunce but who could draw pictures like nobody's business. Vincent, for a fee, drew us some pictures of penises and vaginas. For a larger fee, he put them together. At the suggestion of Dougie Clark, he began to use carbon paper, and eventually made a small killing for himself, selling copies. (The first time I saw a Xerox machine in operation I did not consider it God's gift to the world of industry. I thought—and this was a good twenty-five years after the fact—how lamentable it was that we didn't have such a machine for Vinnie's use at Croydon.)

Vinnie's penises were predictably enormous, always reminding me of water towers with bulbous tops. There is no way to describe his vaginas except to say that the poor boy was working in the dark. Having no prototype to go by, Vinnie's vaginas varied only in size from month to month. Douglas begged him to improvise—extrapolate—use his imagination:

"Listen, Vinnie, I'm just sure as hell it doesn't look like the Black Hole of Calcutta. You're getting away with *murder*, Pellegrini, charging all that loot for the same old fuzzy hole!"

Vinnie cried all the way to the bank, as they say, because we were insatiable. Douglas even went so far as to ride in the coach, rather than the parlor car, on the weekend train to Flint, and pocket the difference for a supply of Vinnie's pictures. And I, with that canny MacAllister blood coursing through my veins, flourished for a time as a loan shark. Any boy who was broke could borrow a dime from me. I charged a nickel a day interest on the loan, an interest which amounted to criminal usury in 1931.

These pictures, however, palled after a while. The last, pitiful resort was Webster. There was a list at Croydon, an ancient list originally compiled by an inquisitive and, God knows, a dedicated group of ninth-graders. They labored to set down their collective knowledge for the edification of the entire class, and they provided asterisks denoting the worthier, more titillating definitions for the convenience of those of us who were in a hurry. I have this minute reconstructed the list on my note pad. I'm a little ashamed of the facility with which I recall these words. They are indelible in my memory

—they flowed to the paper alphabetically, all of a piece, which illustrates that this desperate last resort was almost a daily ritual for nearly three years. Whatever else it illustrates. I leave to the reader.

anus	menstruate
castrate	nipple*
clitoris*	nymphomania*
coitus	orgasm*
copulate*	ovary
ejaculate	penis
fetish	pervert*
gonorrhea*	pubic
homosexual*	sadism*
impotence	scrotum
intercourse	semen*
labium	sodomy*
libertine	testicle
libido	vagina*

And at the bottom of the list, this note:

Not in dictionary: fellatio—blowing.
cunnilingus—eating.

Having confessed all of this, I am compelled to clinch it with the truth. My consuming interest in the subject dissipated, abruptly, at my own bedroom door in my own house! I don't know what the explanation is for that. It might be conscience, it might be cowardice—oftentimes, I know, it was simply a case of fatigue. Once, I remember, when there was heavy breathing and multiple moans, it was a painful combination of athlete's foot and poison ivy. I knew, at fourteen, that some boys listened at their parents' door. I had never developed any expertise in that area because my parents never shared a door. I knew that some boys hid in closets, some hung perilously on window ledges, some listened with a tumbler at the wall. A peculiar, psychological quirk made me accept whatever was the status quo. I never seriously questioned the sterility of my parents' relationship for fourteen years and, when Winger went to my mother's room, I must honestly admit I did not view it as an event charged with opportunities for my own sexual enlightenment. (Actually, I hesitate to delve into the reasons for my detachment. The answer would probably alarm me.)

To sum it up, I was far from being either apathetic or oblivious to the vibrations in the air—what was overt, was overt. But only once, when my curiosity was piqued beyond restraint, did I actually *investigate*. And that occurred when Winger had been with us only two days.

They had, after sipping their saucers dry as a bone, cleaned up the kitchen very quickly. Mother was in a hurry to unpack Winger's two suitcases and lay out his clothing in what was now to be "Winger's half" of the bureau. She saw, in this bit of business, something irrevocable, something de facto— a final casting of the die. I recall them chatting amiably about the road gang—what time did he have to be there, what would he like for lunch, what time did he want his dinner? Now that the horse was gone from the stable, I dug out my Formula ZB-2 and spread it on thickly. Winger scowled at this, saying all I was doing was clogging up my pores so that they couldn't breath—so that the heat would turn inward on itself and I'd awaken with a big, molten mess in my stomach—*like the core of the earth!* He came over to me several times, stood behind me, pulled back the neck of my shirt and blew cold air down my back. Mother gave the kitchen table a lighthearted swab, and we all went upstairs together.

I remember that climb very clearly because, as is so often the case when one is sick, the vitality of those healthy souls around us is hard to tolerate. Mother, that night, was as nimble as a puppy. She skipped, she pranced—her acrobat-like agility made me wince with pain. When we reached the balcony, Winger put his suitcases down and peered out our front window. He put his arm around Mother and scrutinized the totem pole. We were now on a level just slightly below the six carved "Watchers" at the top of the pole. He waited a few minutes, in hopes, I think, that I would take the hint and continue to my room. Again, it wasn't curiosity that kept me there, but rather a certain haziness of the brain. I leaned against the wall, emitting my conspicuous heat, waiting for them to make their comments and get on with it. Winger turned, and grinned, and whispered to my mother:

"It's a damn good thing them Watchers is facing on the town. If they was looking in here, they'd be blushing in the morning!"

She nuzzled her head into his neck, and they went to her room to unpack.

I limped into my room, took off all of my clothes and tried to arrange my body so that it contacted the bed in as few places as possible. My ears were sore, my knuckles were sore—the heat had penetrated and inflamed every muscle. It seemed to me that I had no sooner fallen asleep than I heard an alarm clock ring. This startled me because alarm clocks signified school days. It took me a few minutes to get my bearings, and then I realized that it was six-thirty, and time for Winger to go to work. I stiffly, tortuously, made my way down the hall to the bathroom and just as I reached the door, Mother came out of her room. She was wearing a heavy chenille robe. She inched her way, snail-like, to the stairs. "How's the burn today?" she asked. "Torture," I replied. "Sheer torture." She ran her hands down her thighs and grimaced. What in the world was the matter with her? "You don't look so spruce yourself. Are you all right?" A strange little smile crossed her lips. "I'm a little sore this morning. Stiff, actually. Nothing serious. Come have breakfast with Winger and me."

When Winger came down, he seemed unduly concerned with her infirmity. Dotingly, he watched with large mellow eyes as she groped her way from stove to cupboard. He ran his own hands down her thighs and looked searchingly into her eyes to see if the pain was literal and present, or if this was only the remembered aftermath of pain. He made throaty little moans of sympathy while affectionately, devotedly hovering over her. But in the midst of this dramatic agony they were clearly enjoying private recollections, and were stifling secret, confidential chuckles. They repeated this spectacle when Winger returned from work that night, only by then the drowsiness of the morning had worn off, as had the throatiness of the moans. They now simply looked at each other and grinned, and now, when he ran his hands down her thighs, it seemed to me there was more tension than sympathy in the gesture. I heard him mutter sections of sentences. She would have to adapt . . . limber up . . . she was out of shape . . . it would take time. And she, my poor, timid, virginal mother, flushing, breathing heavily, stood back against the counter like Jezebel, arching an eyebrow, running one index finger over the other, saying, "Oh, shame on you, Winger Burns!"

I come now to the incident which demanded my investigation. I have treasured this incident for years because it seems to me to demonstrate conclusively the sexual ambiance between Mother and Winger. It also demonstrates that this ambiance existed right from the start. It wasn't something they discovered, or worked at, or grew into with the passage of time. And it demonstrates an aspect of my mother's humor which I cherish for its wit and originality. I found this humor all too infrequently in other women of her generation. (Deb's generation, now, is another story, but a different story, and not my own to tell.)

The following morning I was again awakened by the alarm clock. Shortly thereafter, no more than two or three minutes, Winger's voice boomed through the lodge:

"What the hell is *this?*"

And then my mother's laughter, naughty and mischievous, rang down the hall. His voice boomed again. There was a tinge of drowsy terror in his questions.

"Did you do that?? Well, you *dickens!* What does it say? Take it off! Ouch! Christ! What does it say? My God, it's *adhesive!* Let me do it. I swear to God, Laura, you're titched! *What does it say?*"

Then there was laughter again. Shared, mutual hilarity, echoing through the quiet rooms of Timberline. It was, needless to say, a rude awakening. I determined to get into their room and look for the evidence—to find out what it was and what, in fact, it said. I pretended to sleep until Mother banged on my door on her way to the kitchen. When Winger followed her downstairs I padded into their room and quickly surveyed the surfaces of the dresser and bureau. That produced nothing of interest, so I rumaged through the wastebasket near the bed. And there I found a piece of white adhesive tape, about two inches long, shaped in a semicircle. It said, in large, black, printed letters:

HARMFUL IF TAKEN INTERNALLY.

She had taped it around his penis in the night.

XXII

These were long, lazy days marred only occasionally by passing clouds from what my mother called the "real world" —that is, the world beyond our totem pole. There was tension in the house on July 25, when Winger called Keith to wish him a happy birthday. It was an innocuous conversation. Keith was fine, Gladys was fine, everybody in Trail was fine. Keith had passed with a B-plus, the weather was holding up real good, Keith was being real good. He was being real good to his mother, he was minding her, he was keeping his nose clean. When Winger put the receiver down, my mother inexplicably, I thought, began to cry. Winger didn't seem to notice. He trudged up to their room and, even more inexplicably, Mother didn't follow him. She sat with me in the kitchen, listening to the radio, playing cribbage until well after ten. When I went to bed she brewed herself a fresh pot of coffee and remained there. Another cloud passed in the form of another telephone conversation, this one from San Francisco. My father had written my grandmother, apparently saying that Mother was intent on flushing the family fortune down the drain. It was awkward for Mother because Winger and I were present. We didn't feel the need to remove ourselves until Mother became angry and then, somehow, our exit would have been skulking and conspicuous. Her hand trembled on the receiver and beads of perspiration surfaced across her forehead. Her complexion became pie-bald, spotted with rash, and her voice was that of a ten-year-old girl.

"Hello? Mama? What a nice surprise! . . . Oh, did he? Well, I thought he might. I hope you took it all with a peck or two of salt. . . . No, you needn't read it. I can imagine. . . . Well, yes, he's back there now. . . . Yes, they're both here. . . . His name is Winger Burns. Pardon? What? Extraction? English and Scots, I think. I really don't know. How's your bursitis? . . . Oh, I'm sorry to hear that. . . . No, not a single word. I wish he would, for Jay's sake. . . . Fine, fine, just over a terrible sunburn. Blistering now—you know how we do. . . . Yes, ugly. . . . Of course I did, but he wouldn't use it in front of his friends. . . . Pardon? Oh, Mother, the man is certifiably crazy! There's not a shred of truth in that. . . . Pardon? I really don't think I'm obliged to tell you that. You might remember, if you will, that I'm forty. . . . You know, I really don't want to hang up on you—you *are* my mother and we've done a lot of time together, haven't we, but it's all quite simple. . . . Head over heels in love, yes. Dizzy with it. Seeing stars. . . . I'm *not* being brazen, I'm stating the truth. He is, in my opinion, God's appointed gift to your little girl! Pardon? Well, they build truck trails. . . . *Truck trails*, yes. Forest *maintenance*. . . . Well, you may be as snide as you wish out there on Nob Hill. I continue to sign the checks, I've never felt more in control in my life, and I'm not being rash. I'm taking Jay back to Croydon in September. . . . *Mother?* Will you stop *nattering* and listen to me? I'm going to hang up now because I'm angry and this conversation has become untenable. . . . Oh, yes, I'll keep you informed. . . . Well, put the heating pad on it and see if that helps. Listen, thanks again for the totem pole. . . . Oh, some old man up the hill doesn't like it, but Jay and I are getting used to it. I don't think Winger likes it. . . . Pardon? No, you don't understand. If Winger doesn't like it we'll take the damn thing down and *burn* it. *That's* what you don't understand. . . . Oh, you're being unbelievably *odious!*"

She hung up violently, after groaning her goodbye into the phone. That night she went to her room very early, and Winger and I made fudge. The evening dragged by in deadly sluggishness. We hated each other and hated, especially, the vulgar interference of an insensitive, real, outside world.

The fudge was doomed from the beginning because the butter in the refrigerator was rancid. Mother was cooking daily, experimenting, and enjoying it immensely, but still hadn't quite managed to get on top of the planning. (Less and less frequently, though, did we open the refrigerator and find ourselves faced with fuzzy green growing things.) I realized that I was feeling irritable, and was being rather carping with Winger. When I tried to analyze why, it occurred to me that I'd heard Mother justify their relationship time and time again, always with avowals of love. But no pronouncement, stating his exact feelings and intentions, had ever come from Winger. I knew as certainly as Mother did that he wasn't a gold digger. He wasn't out to rob us blind. Still, she had on so many occasions been called upon to defend her feelings, and part of my annoyance that evening stemmed from what I took to be a certain nonchalance on Winger's part. God, I was fatuity personified! It's a wonder he didn't boot me out. I placed myself in front of the sink, folded my arms and tried for an imperious, magisterial presence.

"See here now, Winger. A phone call like that is very disturbing for Mother."

"You don't have to tell me that. I know it. If you're wondering why I didn't go up, it's because I know when I'm not wanted. You're looking pretty silly, Jay. You got something on your mind?"

"Yes, I have. I'm very glad you're here, Winger. I like you a lot. But with my father gone, and my grandmother up in arms, I'm the only one left with Mother's interests in mind. It's pretty clear to everybody that she's not Greta Garbo. And she does have considerable private means. Do you really love her, Winger?"

The first and only time I ever saw him blush was then. I was being ridiculous, and a little impetuous, yet there was a solemnity to my question that required an honest answer.

"I'm in this house because I love her. Shit, Jay, I'm in here among the alabaster and the paintings and them carved tusks and all, because the woman *moves* me something terrible. But, Jay, that don't mean much. I don't want you putting stock in that, because it's just words. I mean, it ain't like insurance. It's just so much blather to say those words. There's lots and lots of complications, having to do with where she came from and where I came from and what's been done to the both of us over the years. The question is, can we put these two things together with any kind of workable result? And feel comfortable with the match. Not just for ourselves, for everybody. Old Harmon and Mr. Samson—even your grandmother. We got to be able to look 'em all in the eye and honestly say we put it all together and it's working pretty good. But, oh my, it's fascinatin' in the meantime."

He poured the hot chocolate into a casserole and, as if acknowledging the failure of the venture, handed me a spoon. He seemed relaxed—almost pleased that I'd brought the subject into the open.

"Didja ever see a Chinese Jang box, Jay? They're a crazy kind of construction, about so big. They got some kind of engineering inside I don't know what kind of brain dreams these things up. This Jang box's got lots and lots of little compartments in it, and there's a locked door on each compartment. Now, one of these doors isn't locked, but, of course, there ain't no instructions anywheres telling you which one it is. So first you gotta diddle with all these little doors and gnash your teeth and curse the guy who designed it in the first place. Then you find it, and open it, and it automatically opens another one! Course, they don't provide nothing to tell you which other one it opens. So you gotta diddle around with the whole lot of them till you find the next one. And when you open that second one, it unlocks the third. And on and on till you've got the whole bunch, maybe fifty in all. And if you really concentrate, and make a few notes along the way as to what leads to what, you get all done with a pretty good understanding of what them little hinges and gears is doing back there in the innards of the thing.

"Well, Jay, your mother's the goddamnedest Jang box I ever seen. She's been storing away booty in there for years. If I can get this all opened up where I can understand it, we'll be O.K. If I can't, if there's places where I can't get to, or where I'm not allowed 'cause of the difference in where I came from and where she comes from, then I'm going to fail again.

"So, yes, I love her. But love—shit, Jay, it's nearly always got an expiration date stamped right on it. It ain't no insurance at all. So don't ever hold me to it, or I'll regret having said it."

All the same, he said it, and I felt better.

I've always derived a comfort and sense of well-being from hearing those words. Pat hasn't said them in years, but Deborah still whispers them at unexpected moments, generally when I'm bedridden with some undiagnosable virus. Then I'm never sure if I've heard them or if, at the height of a fever, I've imagined them. Too, in my late teens, in Ann Arbor, there was a raven-haired girl named Valerie who said them many times. She died, at twenty, of leukemia, but now and then I still feel a sense of euphoria, sitting in my wing-back chair, recalling Valerie and the ease with which she said those words. Douglas Clark said the words once, on the day he was expelled from Croydon. However, he was so agitated over the explusion, and the events leading up to it, I wasn't sure he realized what he was saying. They are the most tenuous words in the language, but through the ages one mortal fool after another has risked life and limb, property and integrity, to hear them. And even from my spectatorial stance out there in the wings, I am as unprotected as the rest, and am thankful for any crumbs of affection that happen across my path.

I felt rather superior when I went to bed. Josh Whitcomb, my father, my grandmother, all of them professed an interest in my mother's fate. But none of them had gotten Winger on the carpet and asked him, point-blank, to voice his intentions. I felt very old, very competent, very accomplished. I fell into a peaceful sleep, secure in the knowledge that I had acted prudently.

There were no more disruptive phone calls that I remember, and I soon learned to pay little attention to the innu-endoes and guffaws that trailed after us three when we passed those townsfolk in the real world. We found a natural pattern for our lives—depending on the time of day, day of week, prevailing moods inside, prevailing weather outside. My mother called it our "spontaneous routine." She and Winger rarely went out on weekday evenings, and generally, before being sent to bed at ten, I would sit with them in the living room. I suppose it would be shocking to an outsider—certainly to Patricia—to have witnessed those moments. We always built a fire after dinner, and Mother and Winger sat on the couch while I sprawled on the floor reading, or pressing flowers. We would talk for a while, and sometimes Winger would ask riddles: *What is it that's black and white and read all over?* or tell jokes—expurgated versions of traveling salesmen and farmer's daughters. After an hour or so, we all felt rather mellow and drowsy, and I would crawl up beside them on the couch. He would occasionally run a hand over one of Mother's breasts; sometimes, with an arm around me, his other hand simply fell over her shoulder and rested on her breast. Very often, when she sat with her legs crossed, his hand rested there, between her thighs. These gestures were not freighted with secrecy or shame, and when the town's whispers and guffaws did infringe on my peace of mind, I recalled what Mother had said that day at the train station. I was, I knew, beginning to get a perspective on things. I liked what I saw. *I knew what I knew.*

On weekends we saw a great deal of the Hilliards. Seth and Elsie came to Timberline for Friday-night dinner, after which the four adults often went down to the Tivoli, the local movie theater. Saturday night we all went to the dance pavilion. Under Winger's tutelage, and with his persuasion, Mother became quite proficient on the dance floor. Saturday and Sunday afternoons, Winger and Seth sometimes had a chance to pick up a little extra cash, helping in one way or another with construction around Buena Vista. They would try to schedule this moonlighting so that it didn't interfere with the entire weekend. When it did interfere, Mother valiantly held her tongue. The amount of money the two men earned on weekends was a pittance, but times were hard. Winger had to accumulate fifty dollars for Keith's school bills in the fall, while Seth and Elsie were saving toward an all-electric kitchen. Though Mother was always disappointed, she showed her disappointment only to me, if she showed it at all. And sometimes this disappointment took an odd turn. Eileen was over one sunny Saturday, and questioned our presence at Timberline on such a glorious day. "Oh," said Mother, "Mr. Burns has to work today, so we can't go out. You know," she said, "Mr. Burns has to *bring home the bacon*." The italics are mine.

But on one of the two weekend afternoons, we always managed to drive up to the lake and swim, play ball and eat Elsie's picnic supper. We even sang good old songs. I learned "It's a Long Way to Tipperary," " Pack Up Your Troubles in Your Old Kit Bag" and "There's a Long, Long Trail" on the shores of Lake Marne. While the men played catch with Bob and me, Elsie knitted and Mother read. She had set herself the task of reading *Antigone* that summer. One of my fondest memories is a picnic, early in August, when Winger noticed that she hadn't brought her book along. She had finished the play, and now was reading *Sonnets from the Portuguese,* which she'd obtained from the little Buena Vista library. We had eaten to the point of gluttony, we lolled around on blankets, not yet wanting to go indoors. It was about seven o'clock, the sun had disappeared behind the mountains and the fish were jumping in the lake. Winger laid his head down in Mother's lap.

"Laura, I'm so damn sick of chewing the fat about gravel and roads. Tell us that *Antigone* story you been digesting all summer long."

I naïvely hoped for a ten-minute synopsis, but no, she took a good half-hour. During this time it got dark. The men, and Bob and I, listened attentively, while Elsie's needles clicked speedily. The scene was played on the blankets, in the dark, amidst bread crusts, wilted lettuce, wet towels and the pungent smell of damp sneakers. When Mother's voice finally petered out, Elsie threw down her needles in a fit of disgust.

ELSIE:

That man Creon was *no* Christian! I'll have nightmares tonight, thinking about that man Creon, and that body laying out in the sun, decaying.

WINGER:

And them birds, pecking at the bones.

SETH:

Oh, Creon don't bother me none. The man was a king. He had a lot of responsibility. He had to make an example of—whatsisname?

LAURA:

Polynices.

SETH:

The real humdinger in that story is the prophet—whatsisname?

LAURA:

Tiresias.

SETH:

Tiresias. You skimmed right over him, Laura. He's the most interesting of the bunch. Antigone sounds like one of them spoiled, bullheaded brats—needs a good whipping, s'all. I mean, Jesus Christ, there's times when you got to put family concerns aside for the good of the country. Like in '14 to '18, when Dad went. Jay, would you mind moving them sneakers? The wind's changed. Jesus, think of it. If I could live as a man, and as a woman, too, I guess I'd know just about all there is to know.

LAURA:

He wasn't a man and a woman at the same time.

WINGER:

He shoulda counted his blessings for *that.*

LAURA:

He was first a man. And then he saw two snakes, uh—they were coupling, and he killed the male snake with a stick. Then he was changed to a woman.

WINGER:

By who? Who did that? Did he drink a magic potion?

LAURA:

No, the gods did it.

SETH:

Greek gods, Winger. They had a bunch of them. One for winter and one for summer and one for trees and one for rivers. Like—specialists. 'Member old Miss Cheesencrackers, Elsie? With her slip showing a mile? She taught us about the Greek gods.

LAURA:

And after a while, he saw two more snakes coupling, and he killed the female. Then he became a man again.

BOB:

(*Whispering, to me.*) How in *hell* do snakes do it, anyway?

LAURA:

But *also*, Tiresias was blind!

ELSIE:

Dear-dear-*dear!*

LAURA:

There are two theories about his blindness—

SETH:

How in *hell* do you know all this, Laura?

LAURA:

Oh, I read it somewhere, years ago.

WINGER:

And stored it away in her Jang box.

LAURA:

One theory is that Tiresias saw the goddess Athena naked, while she was bathing. The story is that she punished him by blinding him, but she tried to compensate by giving him powers of prophecy.

WINGER:

Some compensation!

SETH:

Damn white of Athena!

ELSIE:

Bobby, this story isn't true. It's a myth. It's no cause for nightmares.

LAURA:

The other theory is that the most powerful of the gods, Zeus, had an argument with his wife, Hera. They were arguing about—well, about love. That is, actually, about who enjoys love the most. I mean, who takes the most pleasure from love—the male or the female. Zeus thought the female did.

ELSIE:

Zeus was wrong.

LAURA:

Do you think so, Elsie?

ELSIE:

Don't you?

(*Silence falls over the blankets. I can't see, but I feel blushes emanating from the two women. A few minutes pass.*)

ELSIE:

Well, maybe gods are different from ordinary people.

ME:

Hey, Tiresias shows up again in *Oedipus.*

BOB:

Oh, who the hell *cares?*

ELSIE:

Bobby, watch that tongue in company!

LAURA:

This play, *Antigone,* was sort of a forerunner for *Oedipus.* Tiresias is the one who tells Oedipus that he's murdered his father.

ELSIE:

Dear-dear-*dear!*

LAURA:

And then, of course, Oedipus married his own mother. But, Elsie, he did all of that *unintentionally.*

ELSIE:

I should hope so.

SETH:

What's that called, Laura? That's got a name.

WINGER:

It's called incense.

SETH:

Nah, it ain't. That's the stuff they burn in Bombay and and places like that.

LAURA:

(*Timidly, as if afraid of repercussion.*) It's called incest, I think. But I'm not sure.

I looked at Winger, hoping that he wouldn't take the correction as criticism. He laid his head back down in Mother's lap and smiled. He wasn't miffed, he was proud of her. "Laura," he said, "you're the genuine article."

But away—away from the Hilliards, the work gang, the townsfolk, the telephone, away from all the niggling demands that other people forced upon us—we indulged ourselves wholeheartedly in ourselves. There was affection in our house then, and we wallowed in it openly, with unabashed sentiment which often spilled over into sloppy sentimentality. We became compulsive gift givers. We could not do *enough* for each other. We were so totally immersed in each other's moods and needs that, when I tried to remind myself that there was, in all probability, an expiration date stamped on those days, my internal arguments were quickly refuted by the evidence around me.

The gift-giving ritual began when Winger whittled me an instrument he called a flute. It was a recorder-like piece of hollowed-out branch, and I was never able to achieve a tune with it. What I achieved was a piercing monotone. Winger called it a "shrill." When it became clear that I had no aptitude for the flute, I was banished out back, to the far reaches of the patio, and I made my "shrill" there until both Mrs. MacMillan and old Mr. Hamilton up the hill complained. I tried, once, to play it in the Hilliards' barn, but Elsie said, quite seriously, that the hens didn't lay for a week afterward and the cows became dyspeptic. Undaunted, I made my "shrill" down the main street of Buena Vista one quiet Sunday morning and got home to find that the Reverend Alistair Fraser had called Mother to say that his parishioners were not Arabs and did not need to be summoned to prayer. I never played it again, that I remember. Winger then made me a kite and that, compared with the flute, was a huge success. He also bought me a set of jacks, which disappointed me at first because my father bought me jacks when I was twelve, and I never got the knack of it, all by myself, in my bedroom. But Winger, unlike my father, was prepared to play the game with me, and did so, for half an hour or so, nearly every weekday evening. He created, and installed, a number of gadgets that were gifts for Mother. One was a simple board with a magnetic plate across it, to which she attached her carbon-steel knives. Another was a broom handle, painted yellow. He added hooks and suspended it from the kitchen ceiling so that Mother could hang her saucepans and skillets there, over the stove. And one evening, he and I drove to the maintenance toolshed, where we pilfered materials to make a spice rack and then pilfered more materials to sand it, stain it and wax it.

Mother and I began our reciprocation by driving to Calgary for a sewing machine and yard goods. She devoted herself to the task of making two shirts for Winger—I say "devoted" advisedly. She turned our dining room at Timberline—a room we never used—into a sewing room, and there measured and basted and pinned for hours. She made, in truth, five shirts in all, but three were disasters. A disaster was defined as a shirt into which she could not set a sleeve. She accused the Butterick Company of gross malpractice because the sleeves were several inches wider than the hole. She finally learned to "ease" and made two exceptionally handsome shirts for Winger. The other three were destined to become peculiar, rectangular handkerchiefs, two dozen of them, which ended up in my dresser drawer. Her dictum was: *Waste not, want not.* The italics, again, are mine.

We found ourselves driving to Calgary as often as twice a week. I bought Winger a new fishing rod, a catcher's mitt and a large, illustrated book about Michigan. It was something of an adventure for Mother and me—trying to buy inexpensive gifts that wouldn't overwhelm him, that he could return in kind. My manly judgment was brought to bear on these occasions, and I remember selecting a very fine English leather belt, and a clothes brush with a long, walnut handle.

On rainy days, when Winger and his crew couldn't work, he and I drove into Calgary to look for "store-bought" gifts for Mother. This was even more adventuresome. His limit, per gift, was fifty cents—a sum that sorely tested our wits. We shopped solely at the five-and-ten, and it was these gifts that gave Mother the greatest pleasure. At Christmas and birthdays all through her life, I would find these gifts flashing through my mind. I thought of them on her sixtieth birthday, when Pat and I gave her an emerald pin, and on her sixty-fifth birthday, when we gave her diamond earrings. I think of them, and the expression on her face while receiving them, every time I visit her grave. I think of them then, probably, because I found them in a trunk, wrapped in brittle tissue paper, shortly after her death. They included a rolling pin, a teapot caddie, a wire whisk, a cheese cutter, a meat thermometer and two potholders in the shape of pineapples. I also found in that cache two leather bookmarks that Winger made for her during the winter of '32–'33.

In Buena Vista, Mother never returned from any errand empty-handed. If she went to the library, the filling station, the post office, she always picked up some small item from the drugstore or from the catchall stand near Mr. Samson's cash register. A key chain, a nail clipper, a jackknife, bootlaces. When Winger mentioned that the soap we used at Timberline was too highly perfumed, that he preferred plain

Ivory, six bars of Ivory were packaged and ribboned. She meticulously printed a card to go with them:

Roses are red
Violets are blue
They smell good on me
But not on you.

When he mentioned that the sun chapped his lips, I was sent for lip balm. And when he mentioned that his feet ached after a long, hard day on the trails, we ransacked all of Calgary, bringing home a fantastic array of Dr. Scholl's yellow foot preparations. We would drive home about four in the afternoon, with the bundles, packages, envelopes and cans sliding around the back seat of the car on the hairpin turns.

Whenever I am in that frame of mind that Patty calls my "regression" ("Hello, Nellie? My God, I'm going mad! He's off on a regression again!") and I call up my travel agent and tell him I'm going to Buena Vista next summer, by Jesus, and no one's going to stop me, it is because I have heard Ravel's *Bolero*. Ravel's *Bolero* spiritually thrusts me back to the drive between Calgary and the foothills. It has me in its clutches, that drive. It never became second nature to me; the sequences I sought in it forever eluded me. I tried time and again to find a point, a line of demarcation, when one left the grassy hills and entered the mountains. There was ranchland, then there were foothills, then there were mile-high peaks. I searched in vain for landmarks that would divide and separate the three stages into entities. I sat beside Mother, peering out the window, more and more befuddled each time. How had it happened so quickly? Had I cat-napped? Or were we talking and I missed it? Was my attention span that brief, my concentration that flaccid? It all rolled by inexorably, with mounting tension, evolving into a climb that bore no movements or segments or divisions, a crescendo that climaxed at Timberline. One was on bustling

Eighth Street and, shortly thereafter, one was halfway up Mount Binnie, bursting out of the car, hollering his name to see if he was home, distributing the largesse to the man with the smiling eyes. It was entirely different in reverse. When you left the mountains, you left them. Behind. In the rearview mirror, you saw them receding. I knew I was in the foothills when a terrible sense of loss came over me, a sense of emptiness in my stomach, bordering on hunger. And when I approached the grasslands, the rearview mirror told me, emphatically, the mountains were gone. I had left Buena Vista. I must then adjust to a world of concrete, steel and asphalt, people who wouldn't make flutes for me, or play jacks with me, or care whether or not I washed my neck. Regrettably, all through my life things have become emphatically clear only in hindsight.

I played another game in vain, this one with the mailbox. I knew, in my bones, that my father wouldn't write me, yet I never passed the box without hoping there might be a note, or a postcard, perhaps even a five-dollar bill accompanied by his signature. On those days when I didn't actually investigate the box, I found myself flirting with it, rather reluctantly. It became a sort of masochism: the dark, empty cavern hurt me, and there was always a need to recover, to reconcile myself with the day, after looking. But I hoped, right down to the last gasp of August, that something would move him to write. Nothing did. However, there was another letter from Douglas, and that letter, in the absence of any from my father, took on an importance entirely out of proportion with its contents. The letter represented a continuing contact with my other world; I felt secure that, though our life on Lake Shore Road had suffered irreparable damage, Douglas' loyalty would enable me to pick up where I'd left off, at Croydon.

In this second letter, I detected a note of maturity that was missing in the first, although there was a lapse of only five weeks between the two. Perhaps that had to do with the influence of the older woman, Huguette.

10, rue Marbeau
Paris 16ᵉ, France
July 30, 1932

Dear Red,

I've just received your letter. Unfortunately, all the information is concealed between the lines. What the hell does this mean: "My mother has taken an interest in a local man"? Leapin' lizards, I hit the ceiling when I read that! *My* mother, yeah, her past is pockmarked with local men, but *your* mother? I think I know your mother pretty well—I always liked the way she combined the inscrutability of the Far East with the innocence of twentieth-century Michigan. The latter, evidently, has gotten the upper hand and I think she's going to get screwed. Either by your father (forgive me, Red, but Rutherford, Sr., is a very shifty character) or by the ubiquitous local man. You gotta be hard as nails with snakes in your hair to really excel at that game. I know for certain your mom hasn't got the savvy/savoir to survive in that league. You better fill in all the gaps for me when I see you in the fall. (Your allusions to your man Hilliard are droll, and I also want to hear more about him. I do not really believe he exists. Huck Finn was fiction, you know, created in the mind of Twain/Clemens. My own theory is that Huck Finns exist only in the minds of old men. And, perhaps, barren women.)

The big news here is that I've fallen in love with crazy Huguette. I knew for certain last weekend, when Mother sent the two of us down to see the coliseum at Nîmes. She—Mother—had some sort of high jinks planned for the apartment, so she bundled Huguette and me off to rather superb lodgings for three whole days. We had separate rooms, of course, but— On the Saturday night Huguette imbibed a bit and then, after dinner, took me to her room. All we did, really, was talk for an hour or so. I got hornier and hornier till I finally told her I was really nuts about her and I tried to kiss her. Then we got into a big discussion about our age difference, and she said she thought it was unhealthy (*insalubre*) for boys to do it before sixteen. Anyway, she was tired from tramping around over all those busted stones, and wanted to go to bed. Here's the clincher: She let me watch her undress. She stripped right down to starkers and let me have a good look. I'll have to tell you more about this when I see you—a gentleman doesn't divulge such things in the mail—but I will say that I'm not buying any more pictures from Pellegrini. His efforts are but infantile abstractions. These new feelings are growing like a cancer and are torture for me. The bitch has me firmly impaled on my birth certificate!

Your girl MacMillan sounds sort of pert and robust. Persist, Red! It's high time somebody at Croydon separated the goons from the men and lost his virginity, *insalubre* or not.

Only one other item. My old lady's been yapping at me about my lousy marks in math. She wants me to be a doctor. I've been giving this some thought and I think what I really want to do is either go to New York and work on a newspaper—give Benchley a run for his money—or go to Hollywood and write for the movies —give Fitzgerald a run for his money. Anyway, screw math and the A.M.A. I'll be off to greener pastures.

Not much use your writing me now, I won't get it. I think they use canoes to get the mail across. I leave August 31 on the *Europa*. I hope you are, as the English say, keeping your pecker up over this thing with your mom and the local man. Tell her from me: *that way lies madness.* See you back at the salt mines.

Miss ya,
DOUGLAS

XXIII

Once, sometimes twice a week throughout the summer, I accompanied Winger to work. Other than my occasional trysts with Eileen (her mother was quite undone by Winger's presence on our premises), those days were the best for me. Remote, Waldenesque days spent with men and machinery, huddled together deep in the forest on the side of a mountain. We had to be at the toolshed by seven-thirty in the morning, so we left the house not later than seven-ten, carrying lunchboxes, wearing heavy, high-laced boots and denim pants and jackets. The Dodge was cold and inhospitable at seven-ten, and I remember that we had to run the windshield wipers all the way to the shed because of the heavy fog and dew. I never really woke up until we got there; I was aware of the deathly quiet of the drive, the gray-green mists coming out of the woods, the bumpy, carbuncled surface of the gravel road and the cruel, biting cold of the morning.

Winger had been, for four years, the gang foreman. There were three groups, containing five men each, working under him. Each group had its own "boss," who took his directions and instructions from Winger. I have thought many times of Winger's innate managerial ability. He commanded respect from the men, he rode them long and hard, he was ever concerned for their welfare and safety, but he was not friends with any of his gang. He couldn't risk friendship, he said, because:

"There's this line I call my no-shit line. This is a hard, fast, rigid kind of a line you got to observe 'cause everything works like a dream long as that line don't wiggle. But if I'm drunk with a guy on Tuesday night and Wednesday morning he's hung over, he's lookin' to me for favors. He ain't going to say it, but he's lookin' to me like—'Ease up, old buddy, let's be pals.' And then this no-shit line I took so long to establish gets all wiggly and gray and you piss away a whole day sometimes that way."

All of the men drove their cars to the toolshed each morning and picked up trucks and equipment there. The shed was an oblong, tar-papered building in back of Mount Binnie. It had been built in a clearing at the base of the mountain in the early twenties. During the winter Winger spent much of his time repairing the shed itself, repairing and ordering tools and equipment, making "inventory" (his own code of scratches and checks) in stacks of old dusty ledgers, and laying out plans for the following summer's work. In the summer, the work divided into two areas—cleaning and maintaining firebreaks, and building and maintaining truck trails. Winger viewed both jobs as crucial. The forest maintenance and conservation crews couldn't get into the heavily timbered areas without the truck trails, and the rangers had no hope of preventing massive fires without the firebreaks.

The men all stood around at seven-thirty, blowing on their hands and shuffling and knocking their feet against the ground. I remember watching the steam from their breath as they stood, silently listening, while Winger gave out the day's assignments. The youngest of his crew was an eighteen-year-old schoolboy who had worked for Winger for three summers, and the oldest was a one-armed man named Calvin Hurd. Calvin was in his late fifties. He was the only man among them deemed so mean and irritable, so tough and cranky, that he worked alone. His eyes, when they met yours, contained a contempt and a mockery that belied his intelligence. He seemed to me just recently removed from the cave—ragged and primitive, and always within an inch of eruption and violence.

When they spent the day on firebreaks, they took along crosscut saws, rakes and sledge hammers. The firebreaks were located approximately three hundred yards apart throughout the forest. They were not trenches; they were paths about fifteen feet wide. When we reached them, they were a confusion of broken branches, whole trees, brush, weeds, leaves, pine cones—leftovers of old man winter's wrath. All of this had to be cleared and put on trucks and hauled away. The paths were sectioned off into hundred-foot lengths; the men separated into their familiar gangs and hacked out the debris. Sometimes a large fallen tree would require the cooperation of the whole gang and all of their saws. Sometimes boulders would have tumbled down the mountain and settled in the break. The men then went in with dynamite and blasted the stone into pieces that could be lifted. They were not finished until they could leave a swath that was inky black and immaculately clean. No twig or piece of bark was neglected;

otherwise low fires would jump the break and hundreds of acres would be devastated. My contribution to all of this was negligible. I concentrated most of my efforts on keeping out of Cal Hurd's way.

The truck trails were more complicated and arduous. These were gravel roads, twenty feet wide. Every year they had to be filled with gravel and smoothed out with a steamroller. However, at that time most of them were yet to be built. For the building of a trail, we also took bulldozers and tractors. The area had first to be cleared, which required several days of chopping and sawing and hauling through the tangled jumble of trees. Stumps and stones had to be lifted onto trucks before the bulldozer could come in and dig. It dug out a road about eighteen inches deep, and while the digging forged ahead, the gangs of men brought up the rear with loads of coarse rock and large stones. This was the first layer to be laid, the one that provided a drainage bed for the trail. The next layer was finer shale and smaller stones; the final layer was the gravel, which was brought to the site by Seth Hilliard. The hardship, and the most time-consuming aspect of the procedure, was that there was no separate crew providing the rock and stone and shale. Winger's men had to fetch it—*manufacture* it—themselves. And this was unimaginably grueling work.

Winger would look for a glacial retreat, a moraine, and then instruct his bulldozer driver to pile into it and rip out a corner. The dozer rammed up against the layer of shale again and again, until it had crashed away enough pieces for another few feet of trail. At this juncture, Cal Hurd descended with his one arm and his specially cut, short-handled ten-pound sledge hammer. Pieces that had broken away in chunks too large to handle had to be smashed down to size. Calvin, with his thick, veined, knotted arm, would jump across the piles of rock, wielding his hammer, cursing like a maniac. He was spectacular to watch—old and leathery and toothless and mean, never bathing in a month of Sundays, sludge and grime embedded in every crease and crevice—he balanced his body precariously, strangely throwing his arm- less shoulder away from the heave, and mightily hammering down with his one thick pillar of an arm. And just when the metal hit the rock, and his feet left the earth with the pres- sure of the blow, he let out a whoop: *Cocksuckin' sonofa- bitch, yer no match for me!* Then, reverting before your eyes to infancy, he got down on his knees and gently ran his callused palm over the soft, velvety cleft in the rock. He caressed the new surface, stroked it, fondled it and made sensuous, sucking sounds with his gums while admiring what his own force and will and muscle had wrought in the rock. And when the pieces were rolled onto the lift, he stood back and lowered his head, infinitely sad that the moment had been heartlessly wrenched away from him, before he could sufficiently savor it.

By eleven o'clock the heat was high, and the men threw down their coats and windbreakers. In the forest they kept their shirts on, because of swarming mosquitoes; out on the rock piles they stripped down to their pants. When brush had to be cleared, only Calvin was eager to do it. Everyone else avoided brush like the plague—it was always full of bees. Calvin pulled on his long, heavy glove and dashed in head- first, using his one arm like a sickle. He was stung once, on the nose, in my presence. He slapped his hand against his face with such force he knocked himself down. He lifted his glove and peered at me with his mocking, reptilian eyes.

"Don't look at *me*, you young turd! He stung me, but I killed the cocksucker!"

At eleven-thirty, they broke for a forty-minute lunch pe- riod. The habit was to eat quickly, gulping down sandwiches and coffee in six or eight minutes, then to stretch out and sleep soundly on the ground for half an hour. Calvin Hurd never brought sandwiches. He never, in fact, ate. He had in his bag a flat, rectangular box of bones. Sometimes it was just one large soupbone. He went off by himself, under a tree, and sucked his soupbone, tunneling his tongue down into the center and lifting out pieces of marrow. One had to watch him furtively at all times. If he thought you were staring at him he snarled and threw something—a stick or a log or a stone. One day the soupbone sucking was so noisy and fascinating it caused me to linger on him a moment too long. He came over to where Winger and I were sitting, bent over and passed wind in my face. Winger ordered him away, in tones appropriate to master and dog, and Cal went back to his tree, cackling merrily, leaving a sulphuric effluvium behind him. As I think of it now, the man must surely have been deranged. But no comment was ever made by anyone to that effect.

Seth Hilliard often brought Bob up to the site for lunch and left him for the afternoon. When Winger moved into Timberline, I anticipated the need for an explanation, or a discussion, or an argument with Bob. Worse, I thought he might chide me, or cast randy aspersions upon my mother. "Must be serious this time," he said. "Winger never moved in before." And when I thanked him for his acceptance of the situation, his reply was portentous:

"Oh, I was a bit jealous when I heard the news. But then I remembered what my maw said last Christmas when Winger spent the day with Nancy Worth. I just couldn't understand why he had to be with Nancy Worth when we had such a nice present ready for him. And Maw said all his life Winger was just on loan to people. She said 'less I understood that, I'd get hurt. I wanna tell you, though, that's one hell of a hard thing to understand."

It was during those afternoons that we did most of our exploring. Bob was a great talker, and he talked most consistently about sex. I listened attentively, for Bob's experiences were at once outrageous and authentic. I collected his stories as part of an ever-growing repertoire, and passed them on to Douglas in the fall. I remember the first one he told me most clearly, and the ones that followed were but variations on the theme.

"One time we went out to this old farm to buy some raw honey and I made friends with this boy named Matthew. Never saw him since, but I sure would like to go back there sometime—maybe take you along to prove what I saw. Wasn't too far away—round Okotoks somewheres. My folks was talking and talking with his folks and pretty soon it got dark. And him and me was out lookin' at his dad's beehives when we heard this crazy noise coming from the barn. It weren't coming from the barn so much as it was coming from a *cow*. But it sounded like no cow noise I ever heard. This kid, Matthew, got all nervous when I asked him what the hell kind of a funny cow noise was that I was hearing. Then he gets this snotty look on his kisser and says if I'll be real quiet he'll show me something fit to write home about.

"So we sneaks around the barn and looks in the door. Now, I'm gonna tell you what I saw. No way to say it but to say it blunt. Matthew had an uncle, worked there with the bees as kind of a hired man. Well, Matthew's uncle was up on a goddamn ladder with his pants down, friggin' that cow! Sure as God made mountains, he had his dick sunk deep in that cow and, by Jesus, he was humping back and forth something furious. And that poor old Bessie was making the weirdest cry and not enjoying it half as much as Matthew's uncle. That was one time when I sure wished I had a Kodak."

On those days when sex was uppermost in our minds, we received further gratification from hiding in the bushes whenever Cal Hurd had to relieve himself. God knows what terrible brutality would have fallen on us had he ever caught us. I risked it the first time because Bob promised that Cal was as big as a stallion. I risked it the other times because Bob turned out to be right. It was an awesome member, as thick and knotted and veined as Cal's one remaining arm.

There was a bizarre contrast in all of this talking Bob and

I did in the forest. He talked of the same two topics day after day, and they seemed to me the strangest of bedfellows. Pederasty and wildflowers. Bob, his father, Seth, and his grandfather, Joseph, were renowned around Buena Vista for their knowledge of wildflowers. I, who had never known either of my grandfathers, and had never had ten consecutive minutes' talk with my father, felt a sense of continuity in this association with three generations of selective pickers. And so, after watching Calvin take his lunchtime leak, Bob and I went looking for wildflowers. He had a fine collection of dried, pressed blossoms glued in a loose-leaf at home, and therefore was now very particular about what he picked. This worked to my advantage; I was beginning my own collection and was starting from scratch. In short, it all looked good to me. The more we went out, the farther afield we had to roam, the more exciting the collecting became. My collection was no threat to Bob because he had all of the spring violets and most of the fall berries; both of which would be forever omitted from my book.

I found this book of faded flowers among my souvenirs in the attic this morning, and have spent more than an hour looking through it. I logged them in as I found them—that is, chronologically rather than geographically—and for some reason it pleases me that I can now categorize them according to location. And as I do so, the locations themselves, the scents, the intensity of the light or the lack of it, the burnt umber of the earth, are with me again and I am transported back to the creeks and ravines and meadows. Yes, Patricia, it was rosy. It was marvelous. *Those were my halcyon days.*

In parts of woods and thickets where there were dark pockets of moisture, we found the wispy white Spikenard with its purple, speckled berries. We found Solomon's-Seal, Lily of the Valley and pink Wood Sage. In dark, eternally wet gorges and chasms we found Green Orchis, scarlet Smartweed, Dwarf Cassandra, Bunchberry, Coralroot, Laurel and, best, Pitcher Plants flashing opulent crimson and purple blossoms. In the open valleys and meadows there were Silverweed (Bob called it Goose Tansy), Fireweed, Blue Vervain and Wild Basil. In and around dry beds of rock, we found pink Corydalis, Mountain Flax and Bedstraw. In and around waterfalls and wet rocks, we found the low, crawling Saxifrage, the tall, slender Venus Looking Glass and aromatic Wild Mint. And in ponds, and slow streams, there were deepgold pond lilies, feathery Water Parsnip, ferny white Crowfoot. As a fringe benefit, I also became familiar with some of the trees. The peculiar characteristics of Paper Birch, Balsam, Poplar, Quaking Aspen, Lodgepole Pine and Black Spruce were easily distinguishable, and would be if I went back to Buena Vista today. And yet, here at home, I'm only vaguely aware of sumac and maple screaming red at me in the fall, and am decidedly bored with the rest of the species the rest of the year.

We often brought back small cupfuls of wild strawberries and used them to bribe the men in Winger's gang. In return for the berries, they would hand us rakes and hoes and let us perform a final purging on the clean wide swath. We could then, of course, legitimately act out our masculine roles, and spit, and cuss, and fantasize that fiery holocaust that would be stopped, dead in its tracks, by the Rutherford/Hilliard firebreak. And we could imagine the bronze plaque the citizens would place there:

> Here, in August 1932, a monstrous fire threatened the western border of Alberta. It was stopped, dead in its tracks, by the Rutherford/Hilliard firebreak, now known in these parts as "Salvation Gap."

One lunch hour, while sitting with Winger on the back of Seth's truck, I began crying. I had looked into his smiling, hazel eyes, and I experienced a shattering revelation. Someday he would die. The man had become an integral part of my days and my thoughts: I felt the morning cold when *he* huddled down into his collar, I felt hunger at noon when *his* stomach growled, I felt fatigue at five when we collapsed, together, on the seat of the Dodge. I scanned his separated brow, his dark, earth-stained hands, and I felt rage and fury at a life process that would age him and stoop him, dim his smile, slow his walk and, finally, omit him from the scheme. For the first time in my life I was struck by the tenuous, transient nature of the whole procedure. When I tried to explain my sadness to Winger, when I tried to articulate what I felt to be the absurdity of the scheme, he said he couldn't comprehend it, either. It was masterminded by God, that was all he knew. I thought it wasn't *masterminded* at all. It was a mindless, random scattering of blood and bones without special rules and decrees for special people. I glanced at Winger again and he was sad, too, with his extraordinary talent for communion with those he loved. He put his arm around me and said that it was even more shattering to think of *me* in *my* dotage. But, as was always the case when we touched upon my future, he quickly rallied and talked at length of my bright prospects, which, to him, originated not in my own abilities, but in a silver spoon. When he talked of me, or Keith, it was always the same. Everything was ahead, rich with expectation, fertile with potential. We, especially me, would receive a stellar education. I would make wise, expedient decisions and choices, I wouldn't bungle my relations with women, I wouldn't end up, at thirty-eight, on a boulder with a thermos. But while he sat, deriving total, all-encompassing pleasure from the thought of my limitless possibilities, I was overcome with primordial fears. I wanted to stroke him, savor him, engulf him, the way Cal Hurd did with his bit of velvety rock before it was taken away. So for the first time I was laid spiritually bare, not at actual loss, but at the very *contemplation* of loss. Around me the terrain became a barren chasm; within, all purpose and reason were momentarily rendered null and void while I speechlessly clung to his shirt sleeve.

We talked, groused, mused, wondered, debated through I

don't know how many hours. At the end of the day we took home bunches of frail, mauve laurel. Winger gave them to my mother. The three of us would stand, with our arms around each other, on the patio at the back of the lodge. We would stand, silently, glad to be together with the evening ahead of us. The shadows we cast were two long and one short at first, then melding into one narrow black shaft which stretched across the brick and up into Binnie's trees, and the end of it was not discernible to the human eye. I was very happy.

XXIV

I must, this morning, deal with menopause (Patricia's), deceit (mine) and ornithological tragedy (Elise's). The women in my house are more than a little erratic in their moods. I try to think of this variety of emotions and expressions as my spice of life, but still, I resent their bad timing. If I had magical or, better yet, surgical powers, I would lobotomize these two till noon each day. By noon I'm wide awake and ready to take the weight of the world on my shoulders.

Poor old Patsy's all broken out in herpes. These mounds of ugly, wet sores erupt around her mouth whenever her nerves flare up. The dermatologist says it's a virus that has no connection with one's state of mind. This dermatologist practices on ladies in Grosse Pointe, and for that reason I find his conclusions spurious. The string of women who darken his door are mainly interested in creams, lotions, potions, salves —magical concoctions—to obliterate the footprints of passing time. Eye of newt, toe of frog, wool of bat, tongue of dog, *anything*, at any price, to erase the sag from the jaw, the crepe from the neck, the crow's-feet from the eyes. He caters to them, holds their hands, listens to their tales of woe and then prescribes a lubricant to ease them through the vale of middle years. I hate like hell to pay his bills at the end of the month. I don't think he knows psoriasis from hemorrhoids.

The pat on the pack, the strike of the match, the porcelain peacock. Breakfast time at the Rutherfords'.

"That herpes seems to be spreading. Better make an appointment with Ponce and get some salve."

She inhales and blows the filthy dregs directly across my bran muffin.

"I've already been to see Ponce. I was in a terrific state going, and I was near collapse leaving. Nellie Humboldt was there, under a pound of clay. She actually had the assistant chip a patch away from her mouth so she could tell me that she and Ed spent Wednesday evening in Birmingham, with Nellie's niece. Isn't that *nice?* She and Ed spent Wednesday evening in Birmingham with Nellie's niece."

Ahem. I had told Pat that I was going down to the Detroit Athletic Club to have dinner with Ed Humboldt last Wednesday night. I called Ed and said I had to meet Deb, and Pat wasn't invited, and I asked him to cover for me. I have covered for him through every imaginable contingency, with everything from little white lies to big black frabrications. I raced to Belle Isle at eleven one night, when a streetwalker ran off with his car. And when a certain itch resulted from that encounter, I arranged for him to go, sub rosa, to a doctor in Port Huron, for a dose of penicillin. For *weeks* I roamed around Lake Shore Road bemoaning the fact that Ed Humboldt's car had been stolen right out of that parking lot across from the Fisher Building in broad daylight. This is the thanks I get. He owed it to me to go down to the D.A.C. and take a shower or something.

"Isn't that *nice?*"

"Yeah, that's nice. Ed's nice. And Nellie's nice. No doubt Nellie's niece is nice, too. What did Ponce have to say about your herpes?"

"He said he didn't know you were an author. He said if

the book was troubling me to this extent, I should ask you to put it aside and find another topic. He said professional authors have no problem finding topics. I told him you weren't a professional author. You were a professional loafer bent on spilling your mother's dirty old beans all over the place. I told him this scribbling of yours has changed our routine, and our lives, and I can't sleep. I lie awake and think about your mother. The main thing I remember about your mother is that bilious green gooseberry jam she used to give us every Christmas."

I can see the herpes getting more and more inflamed with every word she speaks. She may call me a liar, which I am, but she may not malign my mother's jam.

"Remember, it was homemade. Best damn gooseberry jam to ever cross a palate."

"Oh, I wish you'd stop this insane nonsense and go back to your hobbies and your collecting and your stodgy old routine! You're getting so *spooky*. Where the hell *were* you Wednesday night?"

"I went Christmas shopping."

"I don't believe it."

"I went down to the Stadium. The Wings were playing the Bruins."

"You haven't cared about the Wings since Gordie Howe retired. Now, Jay, let's have out with it."

"Pat, in the book I'm touching on the life of my great-grandmother Wessel—the old German woman who died penniless. I needed to sort of case that area on Gratiot where they all used to live. I poked around there for a couple of hours—"

"You poked around *Gratiot* for a couple of hours?"

"Right. Then I stopped in at one of those Coney Island places and had a foot-long weenie. Then I came home."

"Hobnobbing with the people."

"Right. Something like that."

"That must be why your stomach was so upset Thursday morning. I saw you empty the Bromo."

"That was it. The foot-long weenie."

"You didn't have to lie, Jay."

"I felt I did."

"Why couldn't I come along and hobnob too?"

"It takes a certain knack. Let's just call it research. Please don't question me again. The sooner you accept the idea, Pat, the better off you'll be. I'm writing my mother's story, and that's that. The *why* of it, at this point in my life, is not so hard to understand, really. To borrow a phrase from Deb, I'm letting it all hang out. I *will* do it. I *will* finish it. I *am* captain of my soul. I am not, in other words, your average swarming piss ant."

Patricia likes me when I'm assertive. She nods her head now, as if to say the matter is settled for the moment, and she glances at her watch. She is due at the Art Institute. Pat is really a very dependable, responsible person, when sober. She made a commitment, so she's going down, herpes and all. She bolts for the door.

"Hey! I forgot to tell you—"

"I'm in a *terrific* hurry, Jay!"

"Listen, Deb called. She's befriended a Bulgarian kid and this kid's got nowhere to go on Christmas. She thought it might be nice to share the cakes and ale."

"Good! Fine! By all means. Male Bulgarian or female Bulgarian?"

"Male, I think."

She's out in the hall, jangling her bunch of keys. She shouts:

"Remember that awful old song?" She sings: "Oh! how I hate Bulgarians . . ."

"Yeah, I remember."

"Do you suppose he'll have *big Bulgarian eyes?*"

"We'll see, soon enough."

She runs through the kitchen and out to the garage. I envy her wholehearted commitment. She believes those inner-city kids need Michelangelo like mother's milk. I, too, ponder this question frequently. Late in the evening. In the warm cocoon of my wing-back chair.

I'm about to rise and start my morning's reverie when Elise comes in to clear the table.

"Bonjour, Monsieur Balzac."

Up yours, Elise.

She's scraping at the crumbs absent-mindedly. Her hand is shaking. Jesus, what now? I've given her a raise, new shoes, her own TV and complete Blue Cross coverage all in the last six months. She pushes at the puffs of gray hair encircling her worried face. Her chin is quivering.

"Monsieur, Philippe is dead."

Philippe was Elise's pet parakeet. He has lived with her, on the third floor, for ages.

"Oh, Elise, I'm very sorry. When did it happen?"

"It 'appen zees morning."

She falls into Pat's empty chair. The tear ducts open, and rivulets stream down her pale, wizened face. She sobs with grief, but at the same time I see a trace of embarrassment and shame. She takes Pat's napkin and wipes her eyes.

"He was all I 'ave in zee world! Since thirty years, I leave Grenoble, I 'ave no family, I find Philippe! I make Philippe my family. He speak zee Anglais better than me! I say, 'Hello, Philippe.' He say, 'Hello.' I say, 'Philippe, who eez pretty boy?' He answer, '*Philippe* eez pretty boy.' He follow me all over my room. When I comb my hair, he sit up on zee mirror and watch. Oh, monsieur, I love him so much! When I take zee shower, he go with me to the bathroom. He sit up on top of shower curtain and make a little cheeps. Zees morning, oh, monsieur, he sit on top of zee curtain and make a big, sad squawk. He 'ave a heart attack! He fall down backward, into zee toilet, and splash! he drown!"

I am at a loss for words. Familiarity, especially with servants, always leads to contempt. And yet, try as I may to live by this maxim, time and again I end up with my arms around one or another starched uniform. Pat reprimands me for this, but I just don't know what else to do in times of extreme stress. Elise remains seated while I stand, with her head resting, tentatively, against my abdomen. We are both aware that this intimacy is strange and awkward, and we cannot look each other in the eye. After a moment, I return to my chair.

"I wish there was something I could do."

"There is," she replies rather abruptly.

I imagine I'm to be asked to dig a hole under the elm at the back of the garden and preside over some sort of burial. But suddenly I see, in Elise's face, a glimmer of the old cunning. Her mouth has returned to its firm, thin line.

"You could put Philippe in your leetle book."

"Pardon?"

"You could make for Philippe zee *immortality*. You 'ave some lady in your book, no?"

"Well, yes."

"Zees lady you could give a bird named Philippe. And when she say, 'Philippe, who eez pretty boy?' Philippe answer, '*Philippe* eez pretty boy.' Eez not too much space to take—a few lines—and we make for Philippe zee—how you say?—zee *commemoration*. Eez possible, no?"

"Well, yes, it's possible. But in the meantime, why don't I dig a little grave at the back of the—"

She is incensed. It's December, and the ground is frozen. She'll not bury Philippe in frozen ground—indeed, she won't bury him anywhere. She has already called a taxidermist. Philippe is to be stuffed and permanently perched on top of her dresser mirror. She will continue to talk to him while she combs her hair; he'll be there while she watches television, he'll hear her say her prayers at night, he'll be company when she awakens every morning.

I find all of this decidedly morbid, and vaguely necrophilic, but I agree to drive her, and the dead parakeet, to the taxidermist right after lunch.

XXV

I had been hearing, off and on all summer, that Mother would take me back to school in September. The semester began on the nineteenth, which led me to believe that we would leave Buena Vista no later than the fifteenth. As best I can recall, it was shortly after Labor Day when Mother's extraordinary crying began. It was extraordinary because it was a mode of grief that did not give vent to emotion. It was not accompanied by any degree of drama; it was not produced by verbal warfare or alarming incident. I noticed it, first, when she confronted Winger and me at breakfast with a question: "How about some French toast this morning?" A bright suggestion, the hint of a smile around the lips, readiness in the body to make an extra effort, to make up a batch of something she knew we'd appreciate. Tears welled up in her eyes and stayed there, like a liquid film floating on a horizontal piece of glass. But her eyes, of course, were vertical, and these few tears seemed to lie there indefinitely, not enough of them to spill over and roll down her face, not enough of them ever to be described as an outburst. They were, in short, at odds with the rest of her demeanor. The effect was to make the vision of the beholder hazy and blurred, while she herself carried on her routine, methodically breaking eggs into a bowl. Later in the day they came again, even more surprisingly, when she read Dougie's letter. She laughed out loud, roaring out the word *"insalubre,"* and there, amidst the evident mirth, the tears surfaced again. For several days she made beds, ironed, grocery-shopped, washed dishes— none of this activity put a halt to the tears, and not even the most arduous stooping, bending, kneeling caused them to overflow.

I was at a loss to deal with this quasi crying. Mother had been, especially in August, hovering on the brink of beauty, and that was something of a revelation to me. I had concluded long before that she'd been double-crossed in the womb by a wayward set of genes and chromosomes. Now, even Bob Hilliard commented that her ease among us, her glowing tan, her lack of restraint, all of this combined to make her something of a "looker." The sudden regression shocked me, the permanent, stagnant mirage covering her eyes, the apparently inoperative tear ducts, made me want to run for a handkerchief and pluck the mote away. I wanted a groan or a gasp, even total collapse, anything that would warrant a pat or an embrace or at least an inquiry into the cause.

It was not until then that the impact of our leaving became fully realized. One evening—it must have been about the ninth of September—Winger was fiddling with a package of black rubber washers, attempting to fix our ever-faulty plumbing. My own eyes began to water, my body suddenly felt ungovernable and I experienced a momentary hallucination. I looked at Winger and saw, instead, my father. I shook my head and blinked, wanting to cast out the vision. As if in a trance, I saw a spectacle before me that was not a man, but a dummy: a mannequin. Smooth and hairless molded-plaster limbs, round, glass, cobalt marbles in the eyes. Mute as a sphinx, it would not respond to touch, its shell concealed a hollowed-out cavity. The hair lay dormant, permanently enameled across the head. It wore an unctuous smile and it stood on an Oriental rug in the window of the Scully Brothers. The vision lasted but a minute and when it passed I saw Winger again, cursing the washers, all of which were the wrong size.

I knew then that we couldn't go home. Home was there, at Timberline, with Winger. Why had Mother told Father we'd come back in the fall? It was either a bald-faced lie or she had seen the interim with Winger as little more than a summertime fling. Neither reason fit comfortably on her character. Certainly, if she had told Father we wouldn't return he would have balked. To his lights, the affair couldn't be anything *but* a summertime fling and, to his lights, it was acceptable as such. I think now that Mother was actually playing for time. She was uncertain of herself, far beyond the surface concerns of sexual fulfillment. She had held physical love in abeyance for so many years, she knew she could give herself to the man with complete abandon. The real tests lay elsewhere. Could she wake up with him, manage all of her hitherto, God knows inhibited ablutions before him. Could she cut back on her accustomed extravagance, sniff out danger areas, trespass lightly on his past, cook for him, *do* for him, satisfactorily? Would he be kind to her son when the loving was done, would he walk abroad with her publicly, proudly, or would he guide her through the sexual gamut, leave his ration and return to Nancy Worth?

All of her fears must surely have been worsened by Winger's silence. He too had heard all summer long that we'd return to Grosse Pointe in the fall—the assumption being that we would pass the winter apart and pick up again the following summer. That assumption didn't fit well on his character, either. His love for us was evidenced in multitudinous ways; he was not so cavalier as to take us on a whim and send us packing after Labor Day. But what in the world were they waiting for? Now it was the tenth of September and they were moping about casting furtive, penitent glances at me. Now not only was Mother drowning in a slough of wet despond, but I, too, was suffering nightly perturbations. My tension manifested itself in recurring dreams of my father; the plaster smile began to haunt me in my sleep. Surely, if Winger cared for us I should see, shouldn't I, similar signs of stress in his behavior? My turmoil manifested itself in another, more disturbing way. My latent feelings of superiority came to the fore. He was, after all, a vagabond, a rolling stone. One did not have to probe very deeply to see that he lacked the credentials to warrant one's faith and trust. What did he amount to, really, in conventional terms? A foreman on a forest work gang, a man without means, a man without substance. He had never, in his adult life, sought to involve himself in a family unit. Perhaps we were, after all, two indispensable pawns on the notably defective game board of his life. Yes, I had jumped the gun. I'd been rash in thinking that Winger accepted me as his son. He already had a son; he didn't need a surrogate. But he had become a surrogate father to me, like it or not. He should have thought of that when he moved in. He should have known we Rutherfords had two vacancies to fill. He should have known the child's needs were as great, if not greater, than the mother's.

I began to brood, quite irrationally, on the possibility of hiding out in the mountains and letting Mother travel home alone. There were an infinite number of places, places where I'd ridden with Eileen, places that would shelter me until I could take my bedraggled self down to Winger's cabin. In the cruel Buena Vista winter he'd have no alternative but to take me in. He could go about his business; I wouldn't interfere. I'd even approve a winter liaison with Nancy Worth and understand it, male to male. I gave this matter, the matter of desertion, serious consideration for approximately two days. I made a midnight requisition in the kitchen, taking a knife, fork and spoon, a box of matches and a drinking glass back to my room in preparation for my getaway. I wondered, though, if something wasn't in the wind. We were conspicuously ignoring the calendar; not once had we mentioned the date. No plans were afoot to pack, cover furniture, order coal for the winter. We seemed to hang in limbo, all of us aware that we were near the end of our sojourn, none of us able to shatter the silence and open the suitcases.

Then, beginning on Sunday, September 11, I saw the signs

of stress I had so eagerly awaited. Winger was, at Sunday breakfast, haggard and morose. I had heard them talking through most of the previous night. In the puffed eyes, the sallow complexion, the weariness with which he languished through the day, I saw hope that he was, after all, party to our plight—he was loath to lose us. The following day, Monday, he did not go to work. I burst into their room at eight o'clock, saying that we'd overslept. He was due half an hour ago at the toolshed. They were dressed and talking, but not closely. Mother sat in her dressing-table chair, he sat on the bed against propped pillows. I was asked to leave the room, but when I saw the gravity of their expressions, I felt reassured that they were addressing themselves to our mutual fears of separation. Winger went to work at noon, but returned an hour later, saying that he couldn't work. There was too much at stake. Our days were numbered and the matter needed further discussion right now. They closeted themselves in their room and that night I heard them again, only this time there was anger. I was amazed to hear Winger, the hobo, the man without substance, calling my mother a babe in the woods, a pup, a sapling. She was green, he said, innocent, born yesterday. He tried, whenever the accusations became too volatile, to lower his voice. This was no mere discussion; at its lowest ebb there was smoldering passion in his voice. His anger mounted to a point where I felt I should run for help. I had never, even when Mother was involved in harangues with my father—I had never felt that she would be physically harmed. My father, though, was a known quantity, a quantity that was, at its roots, shallow and without moral wherewithal. At the pinnacle of the argument Winger brought his fist down on the bed with a dull thud.

"*This*," he said, "is all you're thinking about!"

And again:

"This is the one damned thing you never had!"

I heard her start to cry, and I was relieved. I hoped she'd

cry a waterfall and rid her eyes of their watery fog. In exasperation, he finally shouted:

"The world's full of cocks, Laura! I never met a man yet didn't have one! You're acting like you want the Nobel Prize for the discovery!"

Cruel talk, I thought, concentrating on a dilemma I couldn't fathom. What was the point of it all? It didn't seem to hinge on any technicality. It apparently wasn't money— our too much, his too little. It wasn't class differences, or the complexities of Mother's Jang box. It wasn't Nancy Worth. Father wasn't mentioned once. But then:

"Irresponsible, Laura! Whadayacallit?—*negligent*. He's laying in there sleeping like a baby and all you're thinking about is *this!*"

Once again I heard the air go out of the mattress. He left their room then, and went down to the kitchen. A hush fell over the house. I was aware of her quiet sobbing as I fell asleep. The argument had been so heated, I had been so tense and now was so exhausted—it didn't occur to me until morning that the dilemma was, of course, me.

I awoke to a banging on my door. Feelings of apprehension and foreboding overwhelmed me. Mother ordered me to dress and meet her in the kitchen. With an odd, untimely concern for Winger's continuing employment, I asked if he had gone to work. He had not, she said. He was depressed just then and would try to go later. In the kitchen, in the bright morning light, I saw how tired she was. Her shoulders were stooped, there was a faint tinge of jaundice in her face and her hands were shaking. She looked, in a word, old.

"Winger and I have been talking," she said.

I had no reply that would not sound facetious. There was no rapport between us; her attitude was remote and chilly.

"We're not going home, Jay. We're staying."

This was the news I'd hoped for. I felt as if my life span had suddenly been extended. I wanted, terribly, to bridge the chilly gap between us. I whooped and ran to her, kissed her, whirled her around the kitchen. She did not share my enthusiasm. She pushed me aside and struggled for composure. She went to the counter and began scooping coffee into the pot.

"It's ambivalent though, you know? I never thought I'd look at my own child and feel pangs of jealousy. Of course, I never met a man who was truly concerned about children. He feels that he and I are adults—we're responsible for ourselves. You are not responsible; you have no choice but to do what we decide. If it were pride—that is, his poverty, my money—or if it were fear of disgrace, I'd have arguments for those things. He says *suffer the little children*. He says we'd make you the sacrificial lamb of the piece. I ran out just now because he got quite beastly with his accusations. The truth is, I'm sick to death of hearing him speak your name.

"To cap it off, he asked me how much money I actually have. *And I didn't know!* He laughed at that, of course. Uproariously. He thinks your grandmother will disinherit me if we stay. I once told him that she wields those trust funds like an anvil—of course he threw that back at me. He said I ought to find out exactly where I stand, because Jimmy Rutherfords don't come cheap.

"This afternoon we're going into Calgary, you and I. I'll retain a lawyer and find out, once and for all, what I've got. I don't have any papers here, everything's in the safe-deposit box at home. I'm confident we're secure as Brinks financially. Within a week, if we do it by phone and wire, I'll have a piece of paper to prove that his fears of calamity are unfounded.

"Now, go up to him and do whatever you can to show him you're happy with the decision."

As I went to their room I knew, first, that the decision to stay was hers. Secondly, I knew that she'd edited the argument. She had made it appear that she herself did not even figure prominently in any of this. It was Winger who was being unreasonable in this version, ignorant of the true facts, selfish, somehow, in his obstinacy. However, I must admit that if she was thinking only of ecstatic nights, I was thinking of ball games and picnics. I visualized, in the little McMaster school, the rustic romance of a one-room schoolhouse. I saw a lone, spinsterish schoolmarm wearing amethyst broaches and calico frocks, carrying a hickory stick. I imagined a potbellied stove, a homemade rink for hockey in the winter. In my book of wildflowers I saw spring violets and fall berries—plentiful enough to rival Bob's.

When I knocked on the door Winger didn't ask me to come in. Rather, there was a barely audible "uh huh?" I went in, cautiously, and as soon as I saw him I knew that I mustn't actively enter the room. I closed the door and remained there, leaning against it. He was standing, looking out the window, with his back to me. I had never before, and have never since, seen a man cry; nor have I felt so helpless at another's anguish. He hung on, with one arm, to the drapery rod above him, and moved his face back and forth, wiping his eyes on his extended shirt sleeve. He didn't sob, he gulped convulsively. His sorrow welled up in spasms, expanding his rib cage. The back of his shirt, stretched tightly across his torso, was wet with perspiration.

"Jay?"

"Yes?"

"Go away."

I was riveted to the floor and could not go. Surely, he didn't really want me to. I wanted to convey to him my need to stay with him; at the same time, something, probably pride, moved me to defend myself. I found the specter of the sacrificial lamb rather frightening. I wanted to lay it to rest then and there.

"Winger, our life at home was awful."

"Your life at home was damn comfortable. You just don't know. You've got the silver spoon right there between your teeth. Christ, kid, you've got it by the tail."

"Winger, you know how I see my father? I see him as a dummy in a shopwindow."

"Jay?"

"Yes?"

"Go away."

When I didn't, he swung around in anger.

"You want to be a *shit kicker*? Is that really what you want? You want to go to McMaster with Bobby Hilliard, learn to count if you're lucky, end up at sixteen behind the wheel of a gravel truck? Marry dumpy Dora at twenty, raise a flock of scabby kids? Buena Vista will *get* to you, Jay. It'll creep in there and ruin you. It ain't a summer resort, it's a state of mind. Scabby and mean and narrow, and you don't know it, but it's cruel. Money don't help—even the rich ones, Jesus, those old farmers could buy me and sell me a dozen times over, they're still a bunch of shit kickers, living like pigs, no book learning, don't know nothing but *work* and *hard-ons*.

"Listen. I screwed it up for Keith, it'd kill me if I screwed it up for you. I mean, if I had to *live* with that. You got Latin back there, you got calculus. That's *collateral*, man! You'll go to one of them good colleges—there's a thing I read about at Princeton—the Triangle Club. I'll bet you'll even get in there! You better listen to me—you sure as hell won't get in from Buena Vista. No shit kicker from Buena Vista ever applied and got in. Shit, what am I saying? No shit kicker ever even knew enough to *apply*.

"Your education, the people you know, the year of your car, the cut of your clothes, the balance in your savings account—you're bare-assed without those things, Jay. You got a cat-o'-nine-tails up against your back, you're crawling into bed with catastrophe every other night without that kind of collateral."

He paused, and banged his head against the wall, his fist against the dresser, and then slumped down on the bed. He threw both pillows on the floor and moaned.

"Jesus Murphy Christ, I never misjudged anything so badly in my life. When I came here, in July, I'll tell you what I thought. I thought, well this fancy lady's going to have at me for a while and then she'll pick up her moneybags when she's had her fill and it'll make a fat little entry in her private diary. Fancy ladies *do* that, Jay, when they're away from home, believe me. I know. They always go home *for the season.* And it's kind of a feather in the cap for a guy; he gets his piece of quality goods and then he goes back to his remnants, but he's had a shot in the ego in the meanwhile.

"I'm going to be forty soon, Jay. I took one look at your father in his sharkskin pants and I thought, Jesus, this lovely lady is *wanting.* I must sound crass, Jay. You gotta understand, I've played this game all my life, and I never misjudged anything so badly. I never thought she'd *love* me. I never thought anybody that looked like that and talked like that could be weighted down with so much old fear and hurt—all that stuff about old Granny Wessel. I wanna tell you, that is one bunch of monsters you got in your blood lines!

"It happened so quickly I couldn't believe it was happening to me. Neither could Seth and Elsie. The way you both latched on, accepting me right from the start. I mean, right away I saw this was more than acrobatics in the bed. I was really up to my neck this time, and I got scared then, because all I've got to offer, really, is goddamned acrobatics in the bed. But you were crying that day on the back of Seth's truck, and she was tramping all over Calgary for foot powders, and I thought: Fella, the shit has finally hit the fan. Judgment Day for Wenceslaus Burns. That's my name. Wenceslaus. My granddad had a pal in the zinc smelter, his name was Wenceslaus, and he hung that moniker on my dad, and my dad hung it on me.

"*Shit*, will you get the hell out of here? What am I doing, telling you all this, telling you my goddamned *name*, for Chrissake!

"Get out of here and go find your lawyer. She thinks she's

going to get proof your grandmother won't touch the money-bags. You know what it'll be, really, don't you? Proof, oh yeah, sure enough, proof all right. Proof that she's got half of Michigan up her sleeve. And what do I bring to the part-nership, Jay? *Nothing.* Goddamn acrobatics in the bed.

"Two years, buddy, I give you two years! You'll walk funny, you'll talk funny, you'll have hayseed coming out your ears. S'pose you'll learn to hunt with the rest of them, miss the first two months of school running around after venison. And you better get that *sass* off your face 'fore I wipe it off! I lived in Vancouver, buddy. I *seen* what col-lateral means. I know what it takes to live civilized. These Buena Vista shit kickers *don't even know. Get,* now! I mean it this time! *Go!*"

He left for work at noon, and Mother and I drove to Cal-gary. Indelible in my mind is her clothing. She wore a mauve tweed suit with a dark-brown sweater under the jacket. We went to the offices of Grant and Merchant, attorneys at law, and there, for the better part of three hours, we tried to untangle the web of our finances and see what could, or could not, legally be taken away from us. Mr. Grant was in a quandary to help us because Mother's knowledge of actual holdings was vague and unspecific. He was an elderly, schol-arly man, and he proceeded with logic and patience.

Mother thought her income was around seventy-five thou-sand a year, but she couldn't be sure. She received, she thought, in the neighborhood of sixty thousand a year from her mother. Not exactly from her mother, from an account of her late father that her mother administered, until her moth-er's time of death. She somewhere got the idea that she was to inherit approximately three million when Grand-mother MacAllister died, although she couldn't precisely recall whether she'd read it, or been told it, or overheard it. My son here, she said, will come into a million or so of his own at his grandmother's death. Too, there was a fund set up, not in Detroit, somewhere else, for tax reasons—one of those lenient states out west somewhere—a fund that would guarantee Jay fifty thousand dollars a year, beginning at his twenty-first birthday. She believed her own will made provision for more, for Jay, and some for her husband. She wondered if Mr. Grant would be kind enough to wire our lawyers in Detroit and ask them to pin some of this down.

It seemed to Mother that there were some municipal bonds that were supposed to go to Jimmy; a thousand shares of Great Lakes Shipping were to be his, too. There'd been a large investment at Hancock, in the copper country. That was exceedingly profitable in the years 1916 to 1920; someone said it probably wouldn't be profitable again until the United States got into another war. Mr. Grant had to understand that it was very difficult to keep track of all this. It was all she could do to run the house in Grosse Pointe, and pay the servants, Jay's tuition, Jimmy's club memberships, and it seemed that we were always in arrears at the Scully Brothers. There was considerable shoreline property along Lake Superior in the Upper Peninsula, and also along Burt and Houghton lakes. Her mother, she believed, was in contact with developers regarding that but she seemed to think she'd heard somewhere that they'd hold off further negotiations until the depression ended. There was an orchard near Port Sanilac, five hundred acres, but all we knew of that, really, was the crate of lovely McIntosh apples they sent to Lake Shore Road every autumn. She apologized for her lack of knowledge, and then, exuding as much charm as she could muster, said it had always been her understanding that lawyers were paid to straighten these things out and give you an honest accounting. With rather astounding candor she asked Mr. Grant if his firm was honest, and he assured us that it was. A good thing, too, I thought. She expected from him, then, a piece of paper making it all clear. She gave him our lawyer's address, our broker's address, and my grandmother's San Francisco phone number. "Do you mind my asking why," said Mr. Grant, "you're gathering this information at this particular time?" Not at all. She had fallen in love with a man in Buena Vista and he was without means. She planned to file for divorce just as soon as Mr. Grant provided the piece of paper that made it all clear. I remember her closing speech, and her continuing candor, as if it happened yesterday.

"I don't know how it is here in Calgary, Mr. Grant, but in Grosse Pointe we try to accomplish these things with discretion. We try to keep scandal within, as it were, our collective family. It's my understanding that we don't, among our people, we don't go before the judge with loose ends dangling—such things as custody of children, for instance. We try and settle those things, those touchy things, before we get to the court and the court reporters. This matter of settling is sometimes called, I think, collusion. I'm told that collusion costs a great deal of money, and with my particular marriage arrangement, we can't take the matter lightly.

"I think if you talk with my husband you'll understand immediately. Our marriage certificate is very important to him—you see, if he didn't have that kind of official sanction he'd just be a *kept man*, wouldn't he? I imagine he'll suggest, rather rhetorically, a custody fight over Jay. And then I'll counter with, perhaps, the orchard at Sanilac—if indeed it is mine. And that's the way we work things out. I think, once you've spoken with him, you'll be able to surmise the approximate cost of this collusion. I'd appreciate it so much if you'd include that in your statement to me."

Mr. Grant said no, they didn't do things quite that way in Calgary. And he added, with a touch of nationalistic fervor, that Canadians were, of course, behind the times.

As we walked to the car we were happy for the first time in days. We laughed at our own lack of guile, and on the drive home our spirits were high. We knew that we appeared to be babes in the wood to Mr. Grant. In my ebullience, I did an imitation of Mother which finally had her rocking with laughter.

"It seems to me though I can't be sure someone mentioned once though I can't be exact I have an idea but it's not certain somewhere or other I think in a mattress someone stashed a million or so I don't recall who actually I think if I'm right you'll find it in one of those apple crates from Sanilac. I hope when you find it you'll tell me it's mine."

"The cupboard's bare," she said, as we left the outskirts of Calgary. "We'll have to shop at Samson's before we go home." But we arrived in Buena Vista late, at six o'clock. Winger would already be home, so she decided to let the shopping wait till morning. She was anxious to tell Winger that the decision was, as she said, "in the works." As we entered the driveway we saw the sturdy figure of Seth Hilliard, leaning against the totem pole. The windows of the lodge were closed, as was the front door. The Dodge was not in the garage. We saw, and assessed the situation, as soon as we saw Seth's long, sad face. Mother didn't get out of the car, she leaned out the window and looked down at the gravel for several minutes.

"Where is he, Seth?"

"He's gone, Laura. So help me God, I don't know where."

XXVI

Seth told us what little he knew. Winger apparently went to work only to quit. He sold his car to Arnold Samson for seventy-five dollars. He then came into Buena Vista to collect his back pay; he went to his landlord and settled on the cabin. He must then have gone to Timberline to pack. He caught the four-o'clock train, whose final destination was Toronto, and gave no word of explanation when he purchased his ticket from Joseph Hilliard. With quivering chin, Seth went on to say that Winger had not bothered to say goodbye to him or Elsie or young Bob.

Seth accompanied us into the lodge; however, in the living room Mother turned upon him abruptly and asked him to leave. She escorted him back to the door, saying that she wanted to be alone, and that she would call him the following day. She ran upstairs, where I heard her banging the drawers in Winger's half of the bureau. She ran downstairs and found, on the kitchen table, a note. I can't be sure that she read it; she seemed to glance at it briefly. She then threw it at me and hurled herself into the gallery, where she paced back and forth in a fit of fury. The note was difficult to read. It was full of misspellings and was barely legible. I had never before seen Winger's handwriting, and I remember his strange, erratic use of hyphenation.

Deer Laura,

I can't take it on, Laura. I'm go-ing all the way East this time, plees don't look for me. I love you, and if theirs a God hell make you under-stand. You no me and my wri-ting. I hav to make this short.

I hop youll send Jay a-way from Grosse Pointe to a reel good coledge. He's got to get some milage on him in the world or he's go-ing to end up all sad and stranje.

Promiss me Laura, that youll never agane get so scard as you was that nite I met you in your yel-low dress at Seths.

I gess what Ive never reely under-stood is how any-one with so much $ can be so scard and un-happy.

love

WINGER BURNS

p.s. Promiss me you won't show this to any-one and I meen es-peshly Jay.

I read the note carefully, twice. Upon finishing it, I felt an urgent need to get out of the kitchen. The kitchen had been the center of so much of our activity—his spirit loomed largest there and I knew I would cry if I didn't get out. I wanted to pass through the gallery, to the living room, but I hesitated to do so. I saw no way to get past Mother. It was as if, in her anger, she had expanded and filled every inch of the way. I left the note on the table and moved, headlong, into the gallery. She whirled on me, pouncing her two hands on my shoulders. She pushed me to the wall and there, with a firm, almost inhuman grasp on my shoulders, she began banging my head against the wall. I can't explain my own lack of strength; I was like a rag doll, flopping back and forth, feeling pain, praying that she would stop. She screamed:

"You are a *leech!* You have *finally* bled me dry!"

I ran, crying, to my room. I closed the door and locked it, and prayed that she would not follow. Her strength was so awesome—if she wanted to hurt me further I knew that somehow I would have to protect myself. So I stood, panting and crying at my bedroom door, holding a baseball bat in my hand. A part of me found the scene ludicrous. I was at the point of bludgeoning my mother with a baseball bat. I threw the bat to the floor in anger, but when I heard her enter the living room, I quickly picked it up again and waited. She stayed in the living room and I remained in my room, with the door locked, for approximately two hours. I think it was around nine o'clock when I dared to open the door and move out to the balcony. She was sitting on the couch, in the tweed skirt and brown sweater. I asked: "Can I come down?"

She didn't reply or make any sign of acknowledgment. I went back into my room and fell asleep. At eleven I awoke and went again to the balcony. I was not sure she was still in the living room. It was dark, and I heard no sound.

"Can I come down?"

"Yes."

I asked, when I got there, if I could turn on a light. She said no, I couldn't. When my eyes became accustomed to the dark I saw that she had a bottle in front of her, on the coffee table. The liquor cabinet, which stood across the room near the phonograph, was open. My father had laid in four bottles of gin during our first week at Timberline.

Two were what the Canadians called "forties"—forty-ounce bottles—and there were two "twenty-sixes." We needed that much, he said, for a summer's worth of fizzes, slings, Collinses and martinis. The cabinet had not been opened in the eight weeks since he'd left. Mother had a "twenty-six" on the coffee table, and was drinking it straight, without ice.

"Can I get you some ice?"

"No."

"What about some supper?"

"No. The cupboard's bare."

I could have, at that moment, gone into the kitchen and gotten something to eat. I hadn't eaten since breakfast and I was dizzy with hunger. My fatigue outweighed my hunger, so I sat, thinking I'd wait half an hour or so before going to bed. She was, after only three drinks, intoxicated.

I tried, twice during that interim, to begin a conversation.

"I guess I won't go to McMaster after all."

"No, I guess not."

"He says, in the note, not to look for him. Maybe he didn't really mean that."

"He meant it."

"I think it was shitty of him to sneak out like that."

"That's the way you have to do it sometimes."

"You mean you condone it?"

"Oh, shut up!"

At eleven-thirty I rose, and stretched, and said that, since she didn't feel like talking, I'd go to bed. She gestured to me to sit down again, which I did, and she then began to talk.

My father, you know, was twenty-five years older than my mother. The term back then was "sawdust millionaire." Confirmed bachelor, everybody thought. Lived at the old Russell House in downtown Detroit, lived there at the Russell House in some sort of overdecorated baroque elegance, very fussy about furnishings and service and clothes. Self-made man from a farm near Lake Erie, not unattractive in the face but very, very tall and very, very fat with a big round bushy red beard. I remember the way the fat buckled in a bulge over his collar and above his knees. He looked like a caricature Scotsman. You expected him to open his mouth and say: *Ach, I'm vurry vurry thrrufty.*

He was too self-reliant to open up and give anything deeper than the depth of his pocket, like Rockefeller, throwing dimes walking up Woodward Avenue on Sunday with a gold-knobbed cane. Plenty of chances to marry and marry well, never had time for it till forty-five. All those mills—Saginaw, Bay City, Muskegon—I remember the pins with round red heads stuck in the map of Michigan on the wall of his office. He was always shucking off small talk, small favors, little incidentals, paring down, stripping away normal little courtesies, simple howdoyoudo's. They took time and there was too little time, too many red pins needing policing, assessing. He was glued to the map till at forty-five in 1890 he had no niceties left. No pleasantries, very gruff and narrow-minded, brusque answers to questions and such successful paring away of friends and associates only two or three even dared to venture an opinion. Other ideas were fiddle-faddle, fuzzy thinking, horse feathers.

He was invited to all the parties but declined most. Too stingy to reciprocate and always looking for motives. The more red pins, the fuller the map, the more gold diggers. He knew he was not at all personable, bad at conversation, not well read or widely informed, talked only of mills and efficiency. Like Carnegie, thought that idle money was a sin, working money paved the way to heaven. Not interested in music, sports, animals, weekend recreation, so what could they want of him but showcase houses, unlimited wardrobes, lording it over the others with bigger stables, costly excursions to New York. He used to say no one loved him for himself. You couldn't get an inkling of that self. It was subcutaneous, under all the lard, imprisoned like the crown jewels in the Tower of London.

So he took it out then on the immigrants, calling them filthy scum, said they needed fumigation, just as soon run a knife through you as look at you. Hating, in his loneliness, the way they grouped, stuck together, he raged at their cheap beads and tacky clothing, terrible jewelry, he ridiculed their native costumes. I saw him once in a kilt. This, he said, is the noble tartan of the Clan MacAllister. The bulging fat between hem and hose was distinctly ignoble, and I thought to myself, Oh *wad some power the giftie gie us to see oursels as others see us!* He ranted about the way they ate, the things they ate, so much garlic, horseradish and those winter root things they cooked in Europe, beets and turnips, radishes stinking up the buildings. Poles and Jews were worst, the Irish served and went unnoticed but for their religion—he hated the genuflecting, he thought the women bullies, thought the men as soft as porridge. Didn't think about the colored at all, considered them vermin, beneath contempt.

Anyway, from his office to the Russell House he wasn't exposed to much, he kept that pocketful of dimes for the scabby palms along the route. Finally wouldn't even read about them in the newspaper, bought the paper in the lobby of the Russell House, threw away all the sections but financial, kept on paring away so it, the city, wouldn't infringe. Mother said he drank alone sometimes across the street at Churchill's bar. Quite psychotic finally, seeing beggars in the doorways everywhere, walking a mile out of his way avoiding missions, convents, hospitals, homes for the blind. Dreaded the mail wanting contributions, dreaded the doorbell wanting donations, dreaded any gathering where a plate was passed.

Hateful, spiteful, misanthropic, he felt all the poor were vultures haunting him from broken tenement windows, lifting pot lids as he passed, fumes of cabbage on his clothing, slate-gray underwear strung on lines across the streets. He had to go occasionally, unavoidable, had to check on buildings that he owned, shameful places but *working capital* nevertheless. What a panacea! He pretty much stuck to the felling of trees, collecting of rents, never diversified like the other lumber men—Alger, Newberry, Whitney, Ward—they'd stick a bit in shipping, railroads, merchandising, finally automobiles, they informed each other of what was hot. He was never there to be informed. The suite at the Russell House became the inner sanctum; he found solace there, sitting in a Jacobean chair, fondling the noble tartan of the Clan MacAllister.

The Wessel bakery brought cinnamon buns to the Russell House every Sunday morning, baked all Saturday night, Mother and Granny and Grandpa kneading, punching, shaping, baking tray after tray for the Sunday-morning breakfast at the Russell House until that fateful day when Grandpa had a stroke. No cinnamon buns for the clientele that Sunday. Well, damned if he didn't hire a hansom, down he went to the Wessels' on Gratiot—odd for him, I think so even now, but wanted his buns, you know. Banged like fury at ten o'clock with his cane on the door. Your grandmother answered and knew right off he was carriage trade. Sawdust clinging to his great red beard, there he stood so enormous, bankrolled to the hilt, demanding cinnamon buns. She thought: *the last thing in the world this fat man needs is starch*. But bowed, and said her mother was at the hospital with her father, he'd had a stroke, was paralyzed, terrible turn of events. It looked unlikely they'd fill the Russell House order ever again.

Lord, she was pretty! All my life she was pretty, though I know you don't think so. Just hard to get along with now, but then nineteen, pink and rosy, with dark chestnut ringlets down her back. She pretended to be cowed by him; he liked that immensely, cowing people, jangling dimes, accentuating his gruffness with raps of the cane, and always that great belly stretching the threads of his tailor-made trousers. He asked if there was money to pay for the hospital. Mother wasn't so cowed she'd lost her spunk, she said whatever it came to they'd take care of it. Of course, she didn't know from Adam what coffins cost and couldn't foresee the six months lying paralyzed while the bakery floundered. All the big orders were lost excepting over-the-counter penny items, pastries and strudel, not enough from that to heat the ovens. I'm awfully glad she was uppity at the start because a week later he smuggled her into the Russell House and jumped her on his bed, and after he'd done his business offered her money. Again she said no, she didn't need his money, she had two strong hands, she could always work and she had the will. God knows, she had the will!

The way she tells it she laughed in his face the way you do when you're nineteen, insolent to the tips of her nipples. She said what he'd just done was the saddest excuse for lovemaking she'd ever seen. If he didn't mind, she said, and could spare the time from his two-by-fours, she'd like to instruct him in the fine points. The way she tells it she took the feather quill from the inkwell on his desk and ran it down his penis. If you truly understood efficiency, she said, you'd know this thing is good for more than passing water. She told me later in a gale of laughter she had him swooning, heaving his big belly on the bed. I know what she did but I can't tell you.

That was it then, you see: he offered her thrice the original price. No thanks, she said. Well, he said, at least I'll give you the hansom-fare home. Oh no you won't, she said. Put on your shirt and take me home or I'll cause a scene. Even on Gratiot we observe the formalities. Two days later he was back at the door not so arrogant this time, wanting more than buns this time, wanting to jump her again at the Russell House. You must be crazy, she said. God knows it's no fun for me! She told him, if you can take her word for it, she told him his basic equipment was all right but it took a lever and fulcrum to get him moving. Next came an offer to set her up in a private house on Canfield. Even on Canfield, she said, it still won't be any fun for me.

When Grandfather died their life savings was two hundred dollars pinned in Granny Wessel's bra. They had to mount a funeral, those Lutherans, you know, they want the finest for the grave. Mother watched it go on a big walnut casket with six brass handles, fluted and ruffled inside with yards of white velvet. It was the final straw, the two of them were destitute. MacAllister, the elephant (Granny Wessel called him *der Elefant*), came knocking the door down, panting at the thought of his newly acquired efficiency. He didn't look like an elephant at all, by the way, I always thought he looked more like a walrus. He couldn't work, he said, his office was a tomb. There was no more pleasure in puncturing the map with little red mill pins, so he said: Sophie, define what you mean by fun. She said: That's a waste of breath, you can't provide it anyway, but I'd settle for missus. So he married her and built the house on Seminole in Indian Village. You were only there twice, I think. . . . Really? It seemed to me it was only twice.

The hell of it was she agreed never to have Granny Wessel in the house. Granny knew no English except for counting change; she had that foreign look, big loose skirts, homespun kerchiefs, furrowed hands. He said—can you imagine what he had the gall to say? He said she was *without the niceties*. When I was little, six or seven, I didn't understand why we lied to Father. She and I snuck off to this place called the Garrison Block, aptly named, a horrid apartment building. Father owned it. Long dingy halls steaming with the smell of those root vegetables cooked to mush. One small room was all she had, she slept on the couch. We snuck off with meat from our kitchen, steaks and chops. We couldn't take too much in summer, but in winter Granny Wessel put it just outside the window on the ledge. It kept cold there with her bottle of milk and dish of butter. I remember being over-dressed, lending credence to Mother's lies. When Mother and Granny argued they sent me down the hall to a maiden lady who played the piano dawn till dusk. I sat on an ottoman in

my tea-party dress. *The woman was glad to have company.
She played rinky-tink gay nineties.* There was no sink in Granny's room. *When they had tea
they gave me the kettle and sent me down the hall. There was
a gray stone sink for the use of the floor.* One bathroom for
the use of the floor, not a tub on the premises. The landlord,
mein Papa, paid no attention. I wondered about that, it
seemed to me that niceties most certainly began with cleanli-
ness. *She hated our visits, took a ten-dollar bill one time, held
it over the lamp flame till it curled up in ashes, said she
wouldn't take money from an elephant.* In the corner there
was a carton full of yarn and needles. *Granny went from door
to door in downtown Detroit selling mittens and gloves.*
People in the building gave her scraps of material, old lisle
stockings, she braided them into mile-long strands and wound
them in circles, sewing it all together for rugs in the old
German way. She called me a term—*I hope it was affection-
ate*—I think it was because she smiled when she said I was a
Rusenuck. It means little Russian. Sometimes she offered me
tiny citrus candies shaped like lemons. *She kept them in a
drawstring bag.*

Is it Tuesday? What are you eating? You shouldn't eat from
a can, you should put it in a dish. String beans. Green string
beans. You should at least heat them up. They must taste
awful cold. You were gone just now getting the beans, I
guess. Didn't you hear the phone? Seth called, said they were
worried, passed by and saw all the drapes drawn. I said we
were fine, having a lengthy siesta. If he comes, don't, whatever
you do, let him in. He said we had to understand that Winger
was just on loan. I told him to go to hell and hung up. He
has to understand I'm not Gladys or Cheeoh or Nancy
Worth. I'm not like Elsie, I kept nothing for myself. I gave it
all, I'm an empty vessel, parched, bone dry, all my natural
juices are gone. We do that, we late bloomers. A man becomes a sponge, we let him soak us up, my mouth's so dry I
can't even salivate.

Oh, for Christ's sake, no, I don't want cold string beans!
While I was at the phone I called Calgary. I told the contractor to find a good realtor, place Timberline on the market,
sell it for a song if he has to. He said he'd have to, what with
the depression. I told him to go to hell too. I said, listen: I'll
suffer a capital loss. I called whatsisname too, that pro-
fessorial barrister who found us so amusing, Grant. I said,
forget, if you can, that we ever came to your office. Oh, Jay,
you look so sad with your can of beans. If my natural juices
weren't gone I'd console you. I can't even lift my arms, I'm
drained. Some discus thrower's got this room in his hand,
he's whirling around preparing to hurl it off into space. Everything's whirling, you and me, all the furniture, even Tom
Thomson's birches are whirling.

From the Garrison Block to the mansion on Seminole, I
found it very hard to fathom the difference. It was on Seminole that Mother showed her true colors. Newly rich are hateful to their servants. She forbade me to hang up my clothes
or fold my underthings, took them once and threw them on
the floor, saying that others were paid to keep me neat and
tidy. As a matter of practice I took off my little white anklets
and turned them right side out. She caught me once and
rolled them up in a tight, knotted ball and said *others* were
paid to unwind them. We had a laundress named Fiona.
Sometimes I'd visit Fiona in the laundry room, she'd sing me
funny old songs while she rubbed on her scrubboard. When I
stopped turning my anklets right side out, when I threw them
down the chute in a ball, she got mad and never sang me
songs again.

My father didn't like me, I think I reminded him of how I
was made. You see, Jay, all those years he'd believed that
death was the great equalizer. He thought that only in death
he'd be leveled with the rest, the Poles and Jews, the genuflecting Irish. But Sophie showed him the fallacy of the
theory. She made him swoon, she liberated the core of his
subcutaneous self. The result was a man no longer an island

unto himself. Strait-laced for forty years, his laces became lax then, slack and raveled, she'd got him down on all fours and made him at one with the rest of the animal world. So then he felt corrupt, our very presence caused him shame. He thought he'd forsaken the little red mill pins, the road to heaven, for the swoon on the bed. He showed his resentment in a million cruel ways, he became unaligned and malicious. Of course, no one's more easily reduced than a one-dimensional man. You might chalk that up for the future, Jay, one of Mother's little maxims: Never tilt the axis of a one-dimensional man.

He became morose, he tired easily but she urged him to work, especially to travel. She saw in his death a lumber empire. His heart was bad, pumping laboriously, choked by all that blubber, the doctor said he wouldn't see sixty. On his sixtieth birthday he told me the Clan MacAllister was known for both its lard and its longevity. It wasn't the heart that got him anyway. He was escorting a senator from North Carolina through one of his mills, he was sixty-two then, truly obese, got stuck in chairs, couldn't fold his arms his girth was so great. Mother got prettier and prettier, full bloom at thirty-five, thin and stylish Gibson Girl, dressed to kill, cost was never the question. Jesus, think of it! He would have been hideous to any woman.

He caught his arm in a saw. Lost gallons of blood before they reached the hospital in Saginaw. We had to go, he couldn't be moved. Gangrene set in. I sat in a chair at the side of his bed, his belly under the sheet like a mound, some ancient Druid earthwork, and the stench like sewers, putrefied dead tissue. Only three years ago, Jay, I vomited in a Venetian canal, the oldest part of Venice. Your father of course was sipping wine under an umbrella listening to Mozart in the Piazza San Marco. Silly me had Shylock on my mind. I wanted to see where the Jews had lived. I went alone to find the ghetto, the worst neglect and rubbage all along the canal, shredded sanitary pads and excrement, rusted cans, dead fish on the banks, skeletons of cats: it smelled like the hospital room in Saginaw before he died so horribly. Mother sat across the bed, I saw the ostrich plume in her hat flutter when he issued his final breath. She rose and smiled and left the room. It was over for her, she had the empire. I looked at the little concave niche in the sheet below his belly, the area of his genitals. I thought, my God, that's where I came from! I felt contaminated by their union, the weakness of his flesh, the terrible abundance of his flesh, the magnitude of her greed, the stinking, draining, gangrene poisoning.

There she was with me in one hand, the empire in the other, wanting her belated fun. She had high hopes for me, God knows they were unwarranted. Cat always had my tongue, I couldn't talk, I was so tall, I felt so contaminated. I didn't understand how the other girls fixed their hair, how they attained that ease and looked so comfortable in their clothes. I sat before the mirror, combed and primped. My best friend, Sharon, had a double row of eyelashes. She came and tried to help me once, help me with my hair. When it was dry it still sprung out in corkscrews. Even Sharon threw up her hands in despair. I was beyond improvement.

Mother said I couldn't relate to people. She was wrong. I could, but only from a distance. Born melancholy, I understood it all at an age when I should have been frivolous. Something prevented frivolity, the easy laughter of girls. I saw their stupid rivalries, watched them vow eternal friendship, saw them breaking promises. One day's heroine was the next day's despot, always needling, slipping a knife in the back of the prettiest girl—that's why Sharon liked me. I thought she was beautiful, I liked looking at her, she couldn't help her double row of lashes, why should I hate her for that? She went to New Orleans with her mother once. When she returned she'd brought a gift for me, for no reason other than friendship. Two little pictures with lace frames, I had them in my bedroom for years, do you remember? The worst of the lot was a blond girl named Hope, she defamed you daily with a vituperative tongue. Sharon called her Whispering Hope, I called her the tongue depressor. I came in for some of it too because I was the richest. They said the riches of Croesus couldn't get me a beau, well, they were right, you can't buy beaux but you can buy husbands. Every time there was anything public I let Mother down. I was made to recite at Christmas, there was a concert, forgot my lines, stood like a ninny, bald-faced, the blankest of brains, the embarrassed audience coughed so much I thought they suffered from massive catarrh. And at games, my God, I had dropsy! They'd boo and heckle: *Get off the court!* Sophie was always in the stands with plumes and boas, sent me to England for a year, hoped I'd acquire a finish like a piece of fine linen. Letters of introduction coming out of my ears, well, even impoverished earls didn't want me. Better to sell off ancestral Gainsboroughs than face the altar with a string bean from Michigan.

One summer at the Grand Hotel in Mackinac I slashed my leg with a piece of glass. I didn't want to swim with the others. They held me under the water till I quaked. I sat on that enormous porch in a rocker with a bandage rolled around my leg and who should happen by but Jimmy Rutherford. He said he came from the Toledo Rutherfords, ha! There weren't any Toledo Rutherfords. He does have a sister, she might as well be dead. His father had been disgraced for peddling fake stock. There he was at Mackinac, scavenging. Resorts were his forte, still are to this day, that's why we came to Buena Vista. Always intrigued with resorts, loving the ambience of idle people. I'll admit he was handsome, Mother said he was a dream of a man. Spitting image of Douglas Fairbanks. He bought me lemonade and catered to Mother, the poor lady, if you want to know the truth she's been afflicted all her life with penis envy. In the dining room he pulled out our chairs, on the porch he ran for lemonade. He dropped all the proper nouns from Detroit and Chicago; oh, he'd been there all right, scavenging at their parties, lounging on a chaise with a highball. And his speech! Well, you know his speech. He thought that speech received pronunciation. I knew right off it was *compensated* speech. They sure as hell don't talk like that in Toledo. Mother, of course, thought it upper crust.

You know, Jay, someone once told me they wouldn't do business with Jews. When I asked why, they said that Jews were unethical opponents, they used the analogy of stepping into a boxing ring with both hands tied behind your back. Jews stooped to methods too odious for Gentiles. Well, I thought, that takes the cake. They ought to meet old Sophie, purest of Aryan. I've always been in the ring with Sophie, always had my hands tied behind my back. I'm so disastrously timid, a beggar for her brand of punishment, she's always thrived on Byzantine intrigue. Beats me how she reconciled it all. Prayed every night, you know, down on her knees before her maker. I wonder what the old walrus thought of her doing that after she'd finished with him. Maybe she prayed while he swooned. My God, the whole story's such a *corker*, isn't it? He was damned good-looking, Dougie Fairbanks was. I thought a baby would be nice, and especially my own house away from Seminole. She wanted that more than I. She called me her albatross.

Have I slept? I see you've finished your beans. I heard banging. At first I thought it was raps of a gold-knobbed cane and then I realized it must be Seth. Did you open the door? That's a lamb, you handled it well. We'll go around at the end of this and make our apologies. I think I'll wear widow's weeds and put a black band on your arm. When they ask who died we'll say we did. We're ghosts in mourning, for our lost selves. This glass is smeared, I need another, run and get another, that's a lamb. What is it now? Wednesday? He's gone, hasn't he? All the way East this time. He left a note. People like that always hope God will forgive them, as if God gives a tinker's damn. It's I who've gotten mangled in events. I don't imagine you'll come off unscathed, either.

All I knew on the porch at Mackinac was the Sunday-school lesson taken from Noah: it was preordained that we board the ark in twos. It materialized to marriage, I think I know why. They talked the same language, Mother and Jimmy, had the same mentality. Always thought they were the cagey ones and me the puppet on the string. You can't imagine the machinations surrounding the idea, I swear they take a hog to slaughter with more kindness. I decided long before they broached it I'd say yes, I figured Sophie too cunning to enter it unarmed with legal documents. He met his match with Sophie, she'd been at it longer, had her finger on the loopholes before he returned with the lemonade. He didn't know she wrote the lawyers in Detroit, asked them to draw it up like a contract that night, the very night he happened by the porch in Mackinac commiserating that I couldn't swim. So he was plotting and she was plotting and I sat back and nursed my leg and sipped my lemonade and watched them fence awhile. I really can't tell you how preposterous they were. All I could think of was people I'd met from Toledo. Not one of them talked that way, they used to sound a little bit like that in Mayfair years ago. Even they've given it up to some extent. Your father continues, though. I often wish he'd gag on his upper crust.

Damn old Sophie, knowledgeable as a courtesan, never told me a thing. At twelve I started to bleed. I thought, my God, I've ruptured something! Flew over to Jefferson where Sharon lived. I said, Sharon, there's blood on my bloomers, I'm going to die! Sharon hadn't started yet but knew the rigamarole. She said I should be happy, now I was a woman, this was my *portfolio*. Some damned portfolio, the uterus engorged, cramps and a wad of cloth between your legs strapped like a hammock. I went to the theater once in London, wore a white coat, couldn't get up at intermission. Stained the coat and the seat, wouldn't get up till the building emptied and the management brought me a blanket. I wore it like a cape all the way back to school in a taxi. I offered to pay for the reupholstery but they looked askance, as they do, and thought me gauche for the suggestion. I do believe Africans are smartest. They take their bleeding, braying women and lock them in a mud hut till it's over, all the while mumbling that old Swahili saying, loosely translated: misery loves company.

Well, I couldn't have been more ignorant and I think Sophie enjoyed it. She thought all revelations should come like thunderbolts, jolt you out of your wits. All I'd seen was a dog standing up on the back of a bitch and a stallion behind a mare. I thought Jimmy would do that though Sharon insisted he wouldn't. Jay, are you there? Are you listening to this? You probably shouldn't. I must be mad, telling you this at fourteen, but I don't want you to learn it at forty or maybe never. He came out of the bathroom naked, with a jar of Vaseline in his hand. I thought, well, maybe his lips are chapped or he's got a scrape. He said the most injurious thing, he said that women like me never enjoyed it—didn't provide the right secretions to make it work. Handed me the jar and told me to smear it on, with the light on, still in my negligee, what a monster! Oh, I hate that man. He told me to take hold of him and guide him in, I thought either he was handcuffed or the great throbbing thing wore a blindfold. Quick like a rabbit it was over. I didn't like the way I smelled when I went to the bathroom, I couldn't seem to wash enough. Like Lady Macbeth all the perfumes of Arabia couldn't sweeten or cleanse me, I felt contaminated again, I thought these goddamn men all they do is drain from one end or the other, all they really need is receptacles in one form or another. For the first time in my life, in Pasadena I made such a splendid ruckus! Those people at the desk at the Huntington, they'll never forget me. When I went back to bed there were spots on the sheet. I got on the phone, I said I wanted a chambermaid with a cot, yes, at one in the morning, I was damned if I'd sleep on that soggy sheet in his precipitant drainage. I wanted a chambermaid with a new set of linens and a cot for Mr. Rutherford. I'll bet there were hoots of laughter in the linen closet in that infamous year 1916. Jimmy was asleep already, he couldn't have been more embarrassed—ran to the bathroom and hid while they came. A white woman with new sheets and a colored man with the cot. They were so poker-faced, afraid they'd laugh. I was bold as brass, stood right there and watched her miter the corners and tipped them royally, five dollars each when they were done. Out in the hall I heard them whispering. The colored man asked the maid, Do you think she lost her *virgility?* Oh, yes, said the maid, no doubt about it. I'd lost my virgility all right, what a farce the whole thing was. I went to bed and slept quite soundly but had to get up at four and wash again. I remember there was this smell—doughy— bready—rather like yeast. I thought: It's Granny Wessel come back to haunt me from her bakery in heaven. She didn't like Mother's elephant, now she disapproves of my gazelle.

One day in July Winger had gone to work and you'd gone with him. I went upstairs to make the bed. I saw semen on the sheets, I automatically began to change them. Then I did the strangest thing, I kissed the stain and left the sheets, patted the spread, happy knowing it was there, knowing that I'd shared it. Don't ever love like that, Jay, don't love so much you love the very residue. Always hold something in reserve for yourself. All you have to do is witness what you see before you. I'm empty, spent, wrung out, entirely without resources, I want to die.

What's that smell? Are you cooking something? I won't eat soup. My hands are shaking, I couldn't lift a spoon. Why are you pestering me about food at a time like this? I ate the toast, was it yesterday? It's dawn now, isn't it? Funny time of the day for soup. Well, everything's ass-backwards. I'll try a spoonful or two, just the broth thank you, what a lamb you are to bring it here and feed me. I can't control my hands, where did you find it? The cupboard was bare. It's bouillon, isn't it, you found the jar of cubes. That's enterprising, Jay. Maybe you'll make a good social worker feeding soup to indigents, dispossessed ladies like me, late bloomers itching like hell to get that last train out before the tunnel closes. Oh, I'm going to vomit, I can't take any more, I want to stay like this, addled until I pass out. My head is sore, I must have a lump, I fell on the sink when I went to the bathroom. Have I got a lump? Bring me a mirror, hop to it, boy, I want a mirror. I told you *what for!* To *ascertain* the *dimensions* of my *lump!*

My God! Is that me? Mirrors are the bane of my existence. If only they'd fib a little, soften the rough edges. I'm going to break this, smash it to bits with the gin bottle. There, look at that! Seven years' bad luck! But look, I've multiplied. Twenty lumps on Laura's head, twenty shards of Laura in her cups, I must smell bad. I can see from your face, I've spilled and dribbled, drooled like a baby or some sad old geriatric, I need a bib. Run upstairs and get the Arrid, do as I say, it's in the medicine chest. I want Arrid, I want it *now,* is it such a foolish request? You look as if I'd asked for arsenic—don't cut your feet on the broken glass. Don't make a mistake and bring Vaseline, bring Arrid. We'll tend to my secretions, you and I, that's a boy, fetch it for Mother. There's blood on your foot, you caught a sliver of glass, the Band-Aids are there, get them too.

Jay, we must be in hell. Our bodies won't contain us any longer. Two days now or is it three? I can't keep track, I see the squalor, cans of string beans, stains on the rug. Our skins are too frail for life's lacerations, like gossamer they're splitting and oozing. The skimpiest of wrappings, really, the poorest of panoplies. The inside's quite marvelous, jeweled like a Swiss watch but the casing's bad. God must have been cutting corners when He made our skins.

Where were you? Time has passed, several hours it seems to me. I sent you for something, I can't remember what. You must have fallen asleep, you look rested. Shame on you, sneaking upstairs, falling into bed when I'm putting on such a wallowing good show down here in the mire. You've picked up the glass, haven't you? I noticed when I went to get this bottle there's only one more left and then I'll have to face the music, the most discordant of my life. Everything I've told you I told to Winger, he'd sit and shake his head, cradle me in his arms, he said, oh, if only I were *there*, I wouldn't have let these bad things happen. Then I'd get a vision of Winger in Grosse Pointe. I saw how helpless he'd be on Lake Shore Road, each of us on Lake Shore Road, no matter how vile we may be I think we've all prepared for the run on much the same turf, birds of a feather. Our fortification lies in our similarity, we speak in tongues—all but your father. He's only fortified with that phony broad A. My God, he's come a long way on that phony broad A.

I think I did sleep awhile, dozed off into oblivion. We were walking, you and I, in a grove of wildflowers, little streams, exotic trees, I think it was Eden. And he was there, Winger, naked and unspoiled, smiling. You and I were not unspoiled, we were contaminated, both of us dull, sluggish, feckless, not a freckle to recommend us. Too long in the world, thin-skinned and pale, all pigmentation bred out of us, albinos from some wasteland of a planet exploding into Eden. We pounced upon him, half-crazed, love-starved birds of prey, devouring him and giving nothing in return.

After I talked of sawdust and pins he dredged down deep and cried one night, telling me he'd applied for a job, he took a written test and failed it. The man said the job required filling out reports and forms. He said Winger was worse than a foreigner, shoved the paper across his desk, look at this, he said, it's gibberish. A fourth-grader writes better. I thought you graduated from the eighth grade. I did, said Winger, but I've forgotten it all. Well, said the man, if you want a decent job you'd better get a stack of books and refresh your memory. He went to the library, he was thirty then, he found himself in the children's section and asked two boys to suggest some books. For his son, he said, his son in the eighth grade. One was a detective story and one was about Napoleon. He read them and understood them but he couldn't reproduce the sentence structure. *He was so frustrated telling me this, beating his head on the pillow, telling me he could read, he knew proper language when he heard it, but he couldn't reproduce it. Spelling for him was a trial, like Greek for me, or maybe Russian with all those cases.*

Do you remember he said *salary* for celery, *knifes* instead of knives, he said: Laura, your hair sure *are* red. He decided it wasn't natural to work indoors and fill out forms, he decided nature was natural, he could function that way feeling somehow in tune with God and creation, timeless things, eternal elements. But it nagged him every waking hour: he wore his illiteracy like a hair shirt. I opened my mouth to comfort him but, God, how that man could anticipate platitudes. He said I couldn't speak to the subject, migrant labor had taught him poor people lived within an inch of jail. For no reason at all, he said, they'd throw you in the pokey. Education brought money, commanded respect, a permanent address, a savings account, the year of your car, the cut of your clothes, those things made you immune to trouble. They were the trappings that insured social security; they began, he said, with a job filling out forms, a white collar.

I think he'd be here today, Jay, but for you. He could swallow it all, he knew I could accommodate, he'd watched me assimilate, he knew I had nothing to lose in a break with the past, nothing of value. But he saw you as victim. He'd die before admitting it, but I think he felt me selfish, absorbed in my own passions without regard for you, calculating my future without concern for yours. He believed in Croydon, Latin, calculus—these were your ticket to custom-built propriety, collateral against destitution. He hurt me unintentionally, he scoffed at my timidity, the way I sometimes stammer, all my tortuous inhibitions. He made light of these things, he said, what the hell, if I were you I'd never even try to talk. He said: Lady, *money talks. Let your money do your talking for you.*

I want to stress that for him these mountains were a sanctuary away from cities, offices, elevators, monuments, banks, all
the bureaucratic crap. He didn't feel the whip so keenly at
his back, he'd sought and sought until he found these mountains. But for him they were a geographical extremity, a last
resort, excuse the lousy pun. A place to hide when you weren't
acceptable anywhere else. Do you see why he saw you as victim? He felt our decision ruinous to your future, he felt we'd
deprive you of some Elysian destiny, strip away your collateral.
Oh, Christ, I can see it doesn't make an ounce of sense to
you, it never did to me either. Perhaps that's because we
were, as he said, to the manner born. Perhaps it was rather
like those high-pitched noises only dogs can hear. I listened,
but didn't have the right apparatus to truly relate. At the
root of it I think he felt this: we were behaving irresponsibly.
No, it breaks my heart to say it, he felt that I, as your
mother, your sole protector, wasn't behaving responsibly. So
we'd begin on a faulty foundation, ridden with guilt, scourg-
ing your future for the needs of my flesh. It would fester
there between us and undermine our love. Oh, it makes him
sound so lofty and moral, he'd have a conniption if he heard
any of this because *he* saw himself as some sort of burrowing
mole. The truth of the matter is, he was, God help me, a
lofty, moral man, the first and only one I've ever met.

I might as well tell you, while I'm taking Gilbey's dry
cathartic medicine, I might as well tell you why Winger's
fears seemed so unfounded. I think he saw you eventually
holding a seat on the stock exchange, or in the diplomatic
corps, in that Elysian destiny he saw you attaining some
ultimate status: Ambassador to the Court of St. James's in a
pin-striped suit. I'm a silly, sheltered woman, Jay, I don't dare
speak aloud on half the subjects in the world, but I'm so in
tune with my own limitations I'm almost omniscient where
other people's are concerned. I seem to know how much
latitude everyone's got, I mean the circumference of their
souls. My darling boy, I think you'll be likable and kind but

you'll never be interesting. Interesting people originate things, they have a kind of psychic energy that repels the conventional. They rile against the laws of nature, their questing is implacable.

I can see right now, Jay, you'll take your experience from other people, you'll take for your own what you read in books and newspapers, your knowledge of things will always be superficial, a patina. You'll be too afraid of the consequences to ever dare to be different. And what you'll want more than anything else by the time you're thirty, all you'll want is to be left alone to collect your patina without sacrifice or impingement, to have a quiet corner from which to observe, a solitary place to be alone in. Up on old Lizzie there's a lake, we only went there once because it's so dreary, do you remember? It's called Lake Crypt, it lies in a volcanic crater, is has no inflow, it has no outflow, it's self-contained. It's not the source of anything, there are no dependent rivers or streams, it exists through the good graces of melting snow and rain that happen into it. Oh, it's *placid* all right, but you visit there and you take the obligatory picture and you leave essentially untouched by Lake Crypt. So here I sit, Madame Laura, your friendly neighborhood reader of palms, I peer into my crystal ball and see a lackluster future, a quiet acceptance of whatever's foisted off on you. Whatever collateral you'll have you'll inherit from mein old walrus. My darling, I know the truth always hurts but personal distinction isn't in the cards.

Oh, my *baby*, don't cry like that! I don't mean to hurt you, I'm too deep in ether to edit my words. Come and lie down with me, cry on this cushion. Well, I don't blame you, I must be horrid, my smelling so bad with this lump on my head. Sit there and cry then, bawl your head off, release the bad vapors. Listen. I'll make amends for all of this one day. I think I'll have a long convalescence, trays of pills again, but one day I'll see the sun, I'll wear an enigmatic smile, I'll be at your beck and call. *Blood is thick as silica when the chips* are down. Can I tell you something? I was in the labor room having terrible contractions, I thought I was giving birth to a Galápagos turtle. The nurse kept checking and checking, waiting for your head to show. She said it's almost time to get the doctor, I can see it now. Stupid me, I didn't, quite literally didn't know which end was up. I said, oh, nurse, is it a boy or a girl? She laughed, she said all I can see is the head, thank your lucky stars it's not a breech. She looked again and you know what she said? Whatever it is it's got lots of red hair! I think that makes you squeamish, doesn't it? I guess I'd rather see you sickened than bawling.

The next thing I knew you were crying, I was awake, my legs were in those stirrups, I was numb from the waist down. The doctor was sitting on a little stool at the end of the table. There was blood on his gown, the nurse was running away with a pan of placenta. My God, he was *sewing*, there at the end of the table his hand went back and forth with a needle and thread. What on *earth* are you doing? I asked. Stitching a sampler? You tore, he said, you need a few stitches. Don't worry, he said, your husband will never notice. Well, not from Saratoga he wouldn't. When he finally left the track he bounced into the house so jocular, like Wordsworth's daffodils, wanting to see Rutherford junior. I wanted to hurt him; I said, Jimmy, his head was too big. I tore and had to have stitches. Too bad you weren't there to grease the way with your trusty jar of Vaseline. You know what he said? He said the most injurious thing, he said poor little Laura's been defiled again.

Jay, you *must* stop crying, you're red as a beet, there's mucus on your mouth. The gin's all gone, is there nothing to eat? Tea, I think, a box of dried oatmeal, let's have that, wait till I get my land legs. Oh, Jesus, now I've banged my head on the table! Double lumps I'll have, they'll think I'm a camel on the train, they'll put me in the freight car with some straw. I'd best lie here and let you scrounge around. The box is on the shelf, you know, the one with the smiling Quaker

in the black hat. That'll stop the trembling for a while, no
need to cook it, we'll eat it raw. I saw them once on the
Bowery in New York. No, not the Quakers, not on your life,
they're all in Pennsylvania practicing the Golden Rule. The
worthiest of rules, I suppose, except in the mouth of a sadist.
I mean the indigents, the dispossessed, shaking with d.t.'s,
visions of sugarplums danced in their heads. Even that's lost
its charm, they used to be all white and now they're mostly
colored. Now, *that* is prejudice! What I just said is anchored
in prejudice. We even want our tramps and Bowery bums to
be Caucasian. Actually, I've always thought these things
should properly be included in final wills and testaments along
with stocks and bonds, prime land, Granny's diamonds,
Auntie's pearls—that most American of codicils: to my be-
loved son I leave the stinking legacy of slavery.

Ah ha! Lipton's to the rescue. I wonder if I'll make it to the
last drop. Did you let it steep? One time I didn't let it steep
long enough for Winger, oh, that man could make me laugh!
He looked at it there in the cup, tepid and weak, he said,
Laura, I could *pee* a better cup of tea. I'm going to sleep after
this and when I wake I'll bathe, we'll go downtown and buy
a steak, say goodbye to Seth and Elsie, maybe even Nancy
Worth. I could go there now because she's lost him too. He
used to laugh when I was jealous, he'd say, Laura, all she ever
got was crumbs from my table. She's lost them too, the pre-
cious crumbs, I could go there now without wanting to smash
her windows, her Doulton and Spode. I keep trying, in my
addled, whirling, mangled mind I keep trying to define what
it was. I mean the *essence* of the man. This is it, I think. I
shall always remember him lying on my bed with an erection,
lying on his *back*, waiting for me with an erection. You might
not find anything startling in that but I think it takes a man
fundamentally *unsuppressed* to lie on his back with an erection—that is, not to turn sideways and shield it or pull up a
blanket and conceal it or hunker down at the side of the bed,
slouching, to render the urge less explicit. A man unafraid,

as it were, of a shaft of light through the crack in the door or the innocent focus of moonbeams. There's something so blunt and chaste about an unadorned penis, something undeniable about a man without shame. He was at heart artless, he was at love cock sure. I swear to God it's criminal to realize love at forty. I mean the word both ways, Jay. Comprehension and acquisition.

I beg your pardon? What did you say? Are you crazy? What good would a detective do? I already thought of that. Hunt him down and then what? No, Jay, it's over, all over, a flash in my forty-year-old pan. I won't hunt him down, trap him out of the wild like a rabbit, hire Pinkertons. I'll think of him unspoiled in Nova Scotia, Prince Edward Island, walking on an eastern shore, sea spray in his face till he's old and his body gives out. Oh, Christ, you're bawling again, draining away over what? What have you lost? Nothing but childhood. Not innocence. I think you didn't have that to lose. I never had it either, maybe we were born without it, you and I, two freaks contaminated at conception by ulterior motives. You can't feel the loss in your loins the way I can. Do you suppose I'll turn into one of those middle-aged, Middle Western women lusting after young Italians on the Spanish Steps? I know he talked with you, I know he played with you, yes, that's right, I know he loved you too. God in heaven, don't wail like a banshee, don't ask me to console you at a time like this. Lift the cup, I want some tea, I've dribbled again all down my front. Your devotion is admirable, or is it morbid curiosity? I must say you seem oddly disengaged, rather like a movie camera ticking away unlimited footage, recording a can of unspeakable truths for some distant, stout-hearted viewer. That's enough. The discus thrower's got the room in his palm again, everything's whirling.

And now for this sleep I've been talking about. I want to do it in a bed between two sheets, getting from here to there is the problem. The spirit's willing but the body's negative; can you support me, Jay, to the stairs? I'll have the banister there. *I won't sleep in my bedroom, I'll never sleep in that bedroom again, I'd have the dreams of Hieronymus Bosch in that bedroom, remembering the way the nectar flowed. I want to dream Thomson's birches and sumacs, changing seasons, timeless things, take me to the guest room.*

Oh, my baby, you're getting so strong! I haven't paid proper attention to all of your growing phases, savoring each of them as a mother should. This head that tore me fourteen years ago now measures an inch above mine by the yardstick. Forgive me, Jay, my legs are jelly, my brain's been in absentia. Now lay me down, that's a lamb, pull up the cover, I'm cold as the Arctic. I could do with a few strains of Brahms right now to seal my sleep. I expect I'll flail around a bit before dropping off—a suitable sort of death rattle before relinquishing this ache in my loins.

You know what I think, Jay, after all this ruminating in my cups I think the first thing we must do if we're ever to walk abroad with peace in our hearts, the first thing we must do is learn to forgive our parents.

As if God gives a tinker's damn! Goodnight. Goodafternoon. Whatever.

XXVII

At the end of it I had lost all track of time, all sense of season and place. The following morning, after a long bath, I walked out on the back patio, flinched at the light, and saw that an autumnal umber had fallen over Binnie and Elizabeth. I had not been outdoors in four days: I wondered if Rip Van Winkle had felt as I did. It was cold on the patio at ten o'clock; I felt a sudden need for heavy winter clothing. I realized that I needed a haircut, my fingernails needed paring, my summer socks were too lightweight and skimpy in my shoes. I thought of the road gang for a while and wondered who among them would be promoted to supervisor and who, if anyone, could tolerate and manage Calvin Hurd. I sat, shivering and crying, in a chaise until Mother came down at eleven. We must, before we packed, visit the Hilliards. She didn't really feel like going and neither did I, but it seemed important to say a formal goodbye to someone. We noticed that the MacMillans had already closed their house and left for Medicine Hat—really, the only people we were close to were Seth and Elsie and Bob.

We had lunch in town and then drove to their house, parking, for the last time, alongside the prairie schooner.

"She's replaced the geraniums with mums," said Mother. "I wonder when she did that."

There was bitterness in her voice—the implication being that there was business as usual at the Hilliards'. Elsie was not so grieved that she couldn't tend to this mundane seasonal changing of flowerpots.

It was a mistake to go to the Hilliards', one I've regretted all my life, because we ended our friendship on a sour note. Our ease and security with them had disappeared, and theirs with us. We knew within two minutes that Winger had been our catalyst. We stood rather rigidly in their kitchen, trying vainly to fend off the feelings their presence aroused. Elsie was busy canning pickles. There were cucumbers lying about on chopping boards and the place smelled of mustard and vinegar. Again, this activity seemed to denote a certain apathy. It was disrespectful, impertinent, to be canning pickles so soon after the loss of a friend. There was, in our attitude, an urgency to find fault, to insinuate upon them a blame for having exposed us to Winger in the first place, for not sufficiently warning us against involvement, for not somehow preventing his departure and, finally, for not behaving as stoically, at the moment, as we were. For crying and pawing our shoulders and fondling our hands, for emitting the kind of easy pity that comes from people whose lives will continue essentially the same. I envied them their bare-faced abandon. Clearly, their loss was peripheral and superficial. Where Winger had been a physical core, a main artery to our lives, he had been but an appendage to theirs. I looked at Elsie's red, round, tear-stained face, and couldn't imagine her, in any circumstance, lacking the strength to rise in the morning and stoke her stove, and sweep her doorstep, and weed her garden. We showed, additionally, a thinly veiled resentment that people of our background and means could be so reduced, so vulnerable and without resources in the midst of these shuffling, babbling farmers. We could not accept their charity graciously; the more Elsie cried, the more clinging and cloying her sympathy became, the more aloof my mother became, until she pushed the woman away coldly, contemptuous of her familiarity, indignant at her lack of restraint. We inched our way to the door, feeling that we would soon suffocate in the fumes of mustard and vinegar and steam, feeling that they were intent upon pulling us down into the quagmire of their own sweat and tears. We were indeed reduced, reduced immeasurably —all the more reason to leave pragmatically, standing pompously tall at the door of our car. Seth took Mother's hand and whispered:

"You'll see, Laura, it's for the best he's gone. He was the most discontented man I ever knew."

I saw her anger rise as she dropped her hand. Even her tan had disappeared during our four days' hibernation in the lodge. Her complexion was piebald again.

"Dear, dear, Seth. I suppose if he had died you'd tell me it was a blessing."

Seth shook my hand and wished me luck at school. He said, in passing, that he'd spread the word around that Timberline was for sale. We wondered, together, and with embarrassment, who among Seth's acquaintances could afford to live, or would want to live, in such a place as ours. I was glad that Bob had not come out to the car, and as we drove away I saw him, and Elsie, peering from the middle of a tattered lace curtain. Elsie was holding Bob tightly in her arms as if to keep him from bolting into the yard. As if, I thought, to protect him from the contagious malady we carried with us. As they waited for Seth to return to the house, they seemed, just then, more foes than friends. The three of them would band together in their kitchen; in that familial cluster they would blame Mother and me for coming to Buena Vista and carelessly, wantonly causing a rupture in their friendship with Winger. I knew they could not honestly sympathize with us because they believed, at bottom, as Winger did, that we were armed with money, that our lives were impenetrable and that our assured recovery was as near as our bankbook. I have never, since the Hilliards, been comfortable in the bosom of other people's families.

We left the Ford with Mr. McCabe, settled our bill and took a taxi back to Timberline. It was mid-afternoon when we drove through the town. The air was still brisk and people had exchanged their halters, shorts and sandals for woolen sweaters, corduroy pants and heavy oxfords. There was very little activity around the Amberley; indeed, its large staff of schoolgirls had made a mass exodus from Buena Vista on Labor Day. The few remaining cottage owners were out banging hammers, nailing sheets of oilcloth over their windows. The windows in the little clothing shop on the main street announced "one-third to one-half off," and the store that sold camping equipment, golf clubs, fishing tackle, now stocked ammunition, traps and guns, decoys of ducks. Buena Vista in mid-September had returned to the fold of small rural towns. The change was especially startling to me because it happened surreptitiously, sneaking up behind my back during those four inebriated days. It did not occur to me, until we drove past the MacMillans', that I had not said goodbye to Eileen. I found out later, in a letter from her, that she had twice tried to say goodbye to me—once with loud knocking on the front door, to which we did not respond, and once with a tapping on a window. At the latter time she saw both Mother and me lying on the floor, apparently in a stupor of gin and fatigue. She thought that we had poisoned ourselves but she had the good sense not to carry her tale to her mother. I have her letter here, and she closed by saying: "If you are alive *please* answer this letter! If you *don't* answer I sure am glad I held my tongue and let you die in peace. My mother would've squawked the news all over B.V. and then all over M.H. *for years to come.*"

We packed hurriedly, absent-mindedly, badly. Mother's best dresses, none of which had been worn over the summer, had come to Buena Vista carefully folded in white tissue paper. She felt a special disdain for these dresses, throwing them one atop another until the suitcase was full. She then took the numerous dangling arms and crushed them on top of the pile before closing the suitcase. It was the beginning, for me, of a year of desolation and misery. I was so dispirited, every gesture took enormous effort, and I recall that moving one foot in front of the other was a conscious act of will. I simply took the drawers from my bureau and dumped them into the suitcases, crying again as I handled the flute, the jacks, as I broke the spine of my unpackable kite and threw it in the trash. We packed most of the night, finishing around 3 A.M. From three until around five, I helped Mother wash out the refrigerator, scour the sinks and tubs, distribute moth balls among the blankets, mouse poison around the kitchen cupboards. We slept on the living-room couches, with our clothes on, from five till eight, when we called the taxi. Forces seemed to be working against us when, just as we were loading the taxi, a rotund little real estate agent arrived from Calgary. He brought two large "For Sale" signs with him and drove them into the ground—one at the driveway entry and one beside the front door. He wanted to talk business with Mother; he asked her to set a firm asking price and wanted to know the lowest bid she would take. She told him she couldn't discuss it. He was simply to notify her of any offers and she would make the decision from her home in Grosse Pointe. He wanted to tour the lodge, to gain a knowledge of the property he was attempting to sell. It was a reasonable request, but she refused him entry.

"I can't escort you through," she said. "Come back when we're gone and go through by yourself."

The realtor looked disturbed. The contractor had told him that we had particularly fine furniture and paintings in the lodge. Had we no desire to salvage any of it? Mother shook her head, no. He wondered if it wasn't unrealistic to expect to recover the cost of these things on top of the price of the lodge. It would be worth the price of freight, he said, to send the best pieces to Michigan. He winced when Mother laughed. Nothing, she said, was salvageable. But then, as she looked at the worried man, her strength seemed to wilt. His concern over the enormous loss and waste of the proposition touched her, and I was alarmed at her beneficence. She told him to take for himself any objets d'art that appealed to him.

"Don't strip it entirely," she said. "I'll trust you to take only the cream."

She asked him to leave before we did, so that he wouldn't go into the lodge in our presence. And as he went to his car she made a final comment that revealed decisively the maelstrom in her mind.

"A maiden lady would be best, if you can find one. There's the ghost of a splendid man roaming about in the master bedroom."

He took the keys and got into his car, but not without a searching look at me. I showed no visible signs of eccentricity, which pleased him. He passed me a wink and a sorrowful smile as he sped down the driveway.

At the station, we must have looked rather like those photographs of immigrants arriving at Ellis Island. A flannel pajama leg stuck out of one side of a suitcase; I noticed the hooks from one of Mother's bras dangling off another. We had three of Mr. Samson's shopping bags tied with string at the handles, and all of our shoes had been thrown into a monogrammed pillowcase fastened at the top with cord. It was one o'clock in the afternoon, Tuesday, September 20. As the train slowly rolled away, high above the main street, we caught one last glimpse of our totem pole, though we could not see the house itself. Two little town urchins, snaggle-toothed and grimy, played near the tracks at the end of the platform. When they saw us they began blowing phantom kisses, throwing out their arms in unison, like midget robots, tossing and waving their kisses into the air. As we turned the bend, I noticed that the deciduous trees, below the timberline, stuck out like thick yellow brushstrokes against the dark evergreens.

There are so many names for this season—fall, Indian summer, Autumnal Equinox. I've always liked Winger's phrase best. He used it, just once, the day before he left Buena Vista. He called it the shank of the year.

Part Four

XXVIII

We've bought a six-foot Scotch pine this year. We sit our Christmas tree in the same place, in front of the same window, year after year, taking the same pictures off the walls (a bold Vlaminck and two airy Redons), moving the old Sheraton table across the room to the wall near the fireplace. Deborah diplomatically came home yesterday and helped Pat and me decorate the tree last night. We're not very artistic or imaginative, we three: we lay on the doodads heavily, without design or color scheme, and we're generally so tired by the time we get around to the tinsel we stand four feet back and throw it on, helter-skelter. There is one box of ornaments we all get a bang out of every year. It's an old egg carton containing a dozen tiny balls that Deborah made when she was ten. They're walnuts. She sprayed them gold and glued red sparkles on them, finishing them off with hangers of red velvet ribbon. Elise's job—the least interesting but one we like to think she enjoys—is to bring the ornaments from the basement and take the empty boxes back. Today, the twenty-fifth, she rises to the occasion by wearing her extra-special holiday wig. It is light brown, and it has its origins in coal or polymers. It tends to glisten harshly in artificial light and it makes me uncomfortable because it doesn't have a strong hold on her head. By noon her hairline is just above her eyebrows and she resembles something out of the late-TV "Creature Feature." Patricia seems to believe that Christo is really just a passing acquaintance of Deb's, but Elise knows better. Like the cat who swallowed the canary, she walks around with a wide grin, making extra efforts at every turn so that we may impress Deb's young man.

Patricia slept soundly last night, and Deb probably did too, there in her old canopied bed. But I lay awake for hours, thinking of Christo lying awake for hours there in

Deb's apartment. Deception is not my strong suit, and I know I'll have to handle his entrance with kid gloves. I repeat in my mind: remember, you've never met him. Ask him all that stuff about his father and Sofia all over again. I think I can carry it off but I doubt that he can, what with the subtlety of our language and the fluctuation of his moods.

Elise has, this time, a really monstrous Butterball in the oven—twenty-five pounds. The five of us will barely make a dent in it, and I begin to salivate at the thought of the leftovers. Elise does something, some ancient French thing, with leftovers. She puts the meat through the grinder, mixes it with herbs and onions and then wraps up little packages of it in things that look like crêpes. She favors us with these delicacies only twice a year—after Thanksgiving and after Christmas. When I asked her the name she said, bluntly, "leftovairs." They are her version of what is ravioli to the Italians, piroshki to the Poles, chao-tze to the Chinese, and kreplach to the Jews.

Patsy's been nipping at the eggnog already, and I catch her wandering around the house with a can of Glade. There is a pervasive smell of sage in the house, from Elise's turkey dressing, and Pat hopes to cover it up with this scent that reminds me of the men's room at the Detroit Athletic Club. I wrench it from her hand: the sage is vastly preferable. Additionally, today in particular, we don't need Glade. We have all indulged excessively in our Christmas gifts. I am swathed in my new Canoe, Elise is positively swimming in Arpège, Deb's wafting about in a quarter ounce of Joy and Pat's doused herself liberally with Sortilège, which she's liked since the old days when Sherman Billingsley gave it away, free, at the Stork Club. All of this makes for an amalgam that doesn't quite amalgamate. Chez Rutherford reeks today like the proverbial French whorehouse.

The doorbell rings and Patsy lunges for her pack of cigs.

"He's here!" she says. "Deb's Bulgarian is here!" The three of us scramble to the door, noticing Elise's glistening wig as she pokes her head into the hall. I open the door as Christo's cab pulls away and I am greeted with—what's this? A walloping dose of English Leather. "Come in, come in!" I say. Come in, and help us amalgamate.

We are introduced, and in our nervousness all three of us fight for Christo's overcoat. I think Deb has it, she thinks I have it, it falls to the floor, where Pat blushingly retrieves it and slings it on a wooden hanger—onto which are burned the words "Hôtel Pontehartrain." Christo is wearing an ill-fitting navy-blue suit, a starched white shirt (his neck already is chafed at the collar) and a bright-red tie. I am again impressed with the bigness and brownness of his eyes. I stand in the living room, ogling him, pouring out glassfuls of eggnog, thinking the same corny thought that Patricia is thinking. *Bedroom eyes.* Patricia has asked him a question. He replies:

"The principal ports is Varna and Burgas. They is on the Black Sea. We have eight million people in my *con-try* and we is divided into thirty states. We have much agriculture, but more interesting to Americans is our large city, Plovdiv. In Plovdiv there is many old Greek ruins."

Pat and I agree that we must visit Plovdiv sometime. And then Christo reaches into his pocket and takes out a small, square, gift-wrapped box. He has wrapped it himself—it is swaddled in Scotch tape. He walks, ceremoniously, to Pat's chair and bows graciously before it. He hands her the gift while assuring us that it is little, it is really nothing, just a little something from his home—its merits are all contained in the sentiments accompanying it. Actually, it's a green wooden box, a dresser box or a cigarette box. The carving is intricate, with much inlaid satinwood in delicate scrolls. Christo knows the man who made it, and while we all exclaim over its beauty, he tries to tell us about the sad plight of the man, who is a homosexual. In Sofia the man is subject to ridicule from the adults, literal slings and arrows from taunting children who follow him around the old city with mimicking, mincing footsteps. So now, of course, we will always be haunted by the man when we look at the box, and I feel a certain sympathy as I turn its soft exterior in my hands.

Deborah and Christo are hilarious in their attempts to avoid each other. While Christo tells us of his beleaguered wood-carver, Deb's eyes are limpid. Christo's sensitivity, the disturbing frowns which darken his face as he relates these incidents make him vulnerable and appealing. She wants to touch him or pat him to convey that his reactions are compassionate and kind, to convey that she totally agrees that such treatment is barbaric. She wants to do this so badly she removes herself from our midst with some urgency. I watch her walk to the extreme end of the couch, where she pauses and pours her mother another eggnog. But Christo is not as well controlled, and when I take him to the tree and show him the dozen baubles Deb created years ago, he quickly bounds over to the couch. Part of Pat's eggnog spills on the rug as Christo fondles Deborah's hand. He kisses her directly on the lips and explodes with fervent appreciation. "My love, the walnuts is *beautiful!*" The room is fertile with their affection, which is a little unfair to Pat, now on her knees a second time, with a paper napkin, wiping up the mess. Pat's senses are a mite dull at this point, but she looks across the room at me, and she knows. It's not a plate of turkey for a forlorn foreigner, is it? It's not the usual, rather exuberant American holiday invitation extended to some unattended acquaintance. I would prefer anger in her glance, but instead I see a darting, wistful sorrow. As I guide her to the dining room she leans rather heavily on my arm as if this new knowledge is something we must share together—the outcome, whatever that may be, must be borne by the two of

us. I haven't loved Patricia in years—possibly I never did
—but today I like her very much. She will have no more to
drink other than wine with dinner; she will conduct herself
with propriety. It's interesting that, for all of the current new
morality, we cannot take this affection between Deb and
Christo lightly. Nor can Deb and Christo. They watch Pat
as she lists down the hall to the dining room. For a moment,
we are all touched by the seriousness of their alliance.

At the table, Christo is introduced to Elise. We say, as
we always do, that she is our girl Friday, she is Pat's right
arm: she is indispensable to the running of the Rutherford
establishment. Christo cannot conceal his feelings. When
Elise leaves the room he announces, flatly:

"Servitude is slavery. Her generation will be the last to accept it."

Well, what the hell. I am, after all, fifty-five, and for all
of my lack of accomplishment I do know more than Christo.
I know that he's wrong and I know I should tell him he's an
idiot but then we'd get into one of those boring capitalist/
Marxist discussions. He would talk of Lenin, he would tell
me about the czar's diamond-studded Bibles, the various loot
in the Hermitage, the dirty Romanoff laundry that was sent
twice yearly, to Holland, to be washed and ironed by experts,
the awful decadence of mind and body throughout the upper
reaches—the pure, shining nobility of the Bolsheviks. I
would counter, spewing out the Wall Street line, and talk of
Stalin, botched-up, inefficient industry, inadequate housing,
collectivized farms producing runty, inedible *people's pro-
duce*. And then, God bless the free press, he would zoom
in on the Mafia, Appalachia and Harlem. Conveniently, we
skip the first two and move directly to Harlem.

"Forgive me," he says, to Patricia. "But when I come to
this *con-try* I do not know what to make of your Fifth Avenue. I see Mrs. Kennedy-Onassis. She is wearing many thousands dollars' worth of furs on her back. She is look in the

window of this store you call Teefany. I get on the bus and travel north to the other end of Fifth Avenue. This place you call Harlem, I do not know what to make of it. They sit up at night, in shifts, with clubs, by the cribs. Not so far from Teefany, the rats is eating the babies."

He shrugs, and passes a sheepish look around the table.

"Forgive me. I do not know what to make of it."

Shit, man, neither do I, but it's hardly the kind of light banter with which to pass a Christmas dinner. I feel my ire rising. I'll ask him to suggest what Pat and I might do to correct the situation. Put on the right track, we might straighten it out by New Year's. I'll tell him the slaves, unlike the Boy Scouts, weren't prepared. Is that *my* fault? I look at Deb and ask her, silently, if she can take a lifetime diet of this cant. I look at Pat and ask her, silently, to somehow play hostess and turn the table. In a twinkling, Christo laughs his heavy Old World laugh, and thereby rescues us.

"No use to let it ruin the day! We four is helpless: we can't settle it."

He is, in a word, mercurial. But mostly I like him because he's permitting me to take my favorite position, whatever the subject, i.e., helplessness.

"Christo," says Pat, "Deborah says you know all about automobiles. I've lived in Detroit—the Detroit area—for twenty-five years, and I know nothing about automobiles. They've always seemed such a *large* item to manufacture. I come from Massachusetts, where we make small, useful things."

I can't resist. I must confer that bit of information originally given to me a quarter-century ago.

"Mrs. Rutherford's family is in thimbles."

The Boston Bancrofts have had a monopoly on the thimble business since 1880. When her father first told me this I imagined the entire family a bevy of Tom Thumbs, wintering in a thimble, summering on a single lily pad. Patsy doesn't like the dig.

"Needles and pins, hooks and eyes, useful things like that. Deborah says you work part-time at Ford."

"Yes, I do. Is very boring job I have, at Ford."

"Oh, I'm sure it is," I say. "All work is boring after a while."

I try not to notice the startled reaction and arched brows of wife and daughter.

"What do you do at Ford, Christo?"

"I am on the line. I am at the *end* of the line. I am called the 'touch-up man.' If you like, I describe for you the making of a car."

He swallows a mouthful of cranberry sauce and takes a deep breath. Deb looks relieved and pleased. The description, she knows, is lengthy, accurate if somewhat bastardized, and eminently safe. The last point is readily understood by Christo, and he begins:

"First we is having at River Rouge a *boat slip*. Five big boats is bringing *iron ore* down from Labrador. They is also bringing up, from West Virginia, *coal*. From this we is making *steel*. Is very bad place to work, the steel mill. The burning slabs come out, *whoosh*, from the furnace, they is twenty-five hundred degrees hot, *splash* goes onto them the water to cool, *zip*, a big noise is breaking your eardrums, like a cymbals clashing in the symphony. Is *so* hot by the furnace, the first time I visited there I wear rubber shoes, what you call *slinkers*—no, ha, ha—*I* call *slinkers*, *you* call *sneakers*—my rubber shoes they is *melt* on the floor!

"The slabs of steel is cooled now in *soaking pit*—you know soaking pit? Twenty-four big soaking pit at Rouge, six thousand ton of steel we make each day. Then they is *pickled* and *annealed*—you know these terms? Is funny terms, no? You think they is adding *garlic* to the soak, no, they is not. Slabs now is rolled to *sheets* and wound on *spools*, very big spools is cut in lengths what they call *sheared*. Is terrible place to work in rolling mill. Big machinery comes and hauls the spools to area called *stamping*. *Crash*, you got a fender! *Slam*, you got a hood! *Boom* goes the lever, you got four little doors and *such* an earache! Stamping plant is really lousy place to work.

"Big machinery comes again, cradles pieces in its arms, take on a belt to paint shop. They opens up the nozzles and sprays on the paint, very fine, everything is copacetic according to the order on the clipboard, every color of the rainbow into the oven: *bake it till it's done.*

"All the same while they is make the match for the inside. You got a *navy-blue* T-Bird you want the *powder-blue* seat, it's all on the clipboard, some man in Walla Walla, Washington, he write it all down in the first place. You want a tinted glass, electric clock, push-the-button window, white-wall tire, maybe you can afford the AM/FM, maybe you want the little light on the ashtray? Is all prepared for you before it get to *synchronized assembly.*

"Is like magic then, this *synchronized assembly.* High up on the moving belt is hanging for instance the *red* fenders next to the *yellow* fenders next to the *green* fenders because the body is coming down the line like that, red, yellow, green, and from a mile away is coming across the ceiling front seats, back seats—sometimes at the wrong time the right thing arrive, then you hear some pretty good language. Polish and Italian, you get the *international cursing* when the assembly don't synchronize copacetic. The man reach up and unfasten the pieces, like big clothespins they are attached from, with the other hand he pulls down equipment *zap* to make a weld or rivet. Smooth, like the ballet, but underneath you got the poor sonsabitches working in the little hollow pit all day long tightening the same few bolts. How you say what you get when you're locked in the hall closet? Right! They is suffer from claustrophobia in the pit, so bad, sometimes they drink *applejack* down there until they're caught. The black men tell me you get caught by the *brother* you don't catch hell, but this is stupid advice. I see right away the black foreman he catch you he chew you out like a bulldog. I tell them, I say, 'Your black brother, you make him a manager he become a *Cossack!*'

"Don't buy a car assembled on Friday—they is hurrying for the weekend. Don't buy a car assembled on Monday, they is recover from the weekend. I make a little show for you with my description but all in all is a pretty good job we do on the line. Fifty-six cars roll off every hour, a thousand a day just at Rouge, and this is going on all over the world. At end, before wash and testing drive, I am standing with my little pots of paint. They is arranged like the line, red, yellow, green, whatever is coming my way I am ready. Sometimes is a little nick or a chip, a little naked steel, I take my brush, quick with a dab I touch it up. It has to be test, *bingo!* They drive it on the railroad car, the man in Walla Walla, Washington, is drive it home and take a picture.

"The statistic is interesting. I write it home to my family in Sofia to make a big impression. From the Glass House where Mr. Ford number two is in the penthouse, they is paying a million and a half dollars to forty thousand workers every day. In the wide world they is paying fifteen million every day. That, I tell my father, you don't call *chestnuts.* No! Ha, ha! *I* say *chestnuts. You* say *peanuts!*"

Now, over mincemeat pie and coffee, we ask a few questions. Patricia, whose social conscience has been aroused, wants to know if the poor s.o.b.'s in the steel mill are paid anything commensurate with the conditions. I want to know if the men in the pit ever exchange places and work aboveground. Deb wants to know if any women hold responsible jobs in the plant. She wonders if Mr. Ford number two has given any thought to day-care centers. Christo luxuriates in the limelight. He bangs the table, the silverware, the floor: we know before he answers whether or not there is justice in his reply. Elise approves of him and he, in turn, is more than loquacious in his flattery of her culinary skills. However, we're all surprised at the end of the meal when he makes a request:

"Mrs. Rutherford, you have the baby picture of Deborah you could show me?"

This is totally unexpected and Deb is aghast. She tells him we have no loose pictures, they're all on slides, they're all terrible. If he insists on seeing them, she will never forgive him. He insists, telling Pat that he has a very warm place inside Deborah and he wishes to familiarize himself with her childhood. We retire to the living room, I get out the projector, screen, the boxes of slides we haven't looked at in ages. Pat invites Elise to come, too, while Deb shrinks and hunches, dwarf-like, into the corner of the couch.

At the first slide, Deb lets out a wail and cries, "It's obscene!" We view Deb, bare-assed on a blanket, at six months. Drool runs from her mouth and her paltry bit of orange hair has been combed into a wispy question mark. Christo makes small, sensuous grunts. As we proceed, we discover the wide array of nurses we employed through the first six years. Pat remembers them all and tells Christo:

"That one is Agnes. She used to comb her hair over the kitchen range, and we all ended up with abdominal hair balls. That one is Ingrid. She was lovely with Deb but she was, unfortunately, a nymphomaniac, so she had to go. Bridget came to us highly recommended, but she had body odor. When I suggested she buy a deodorant, she bought moth balls instead and crushed them into her clothes. It made our eyes water whenever she was near. So Bridget had to go, too."

I had forgotten Bridget, but with the mention of her name I have a faint remembrance of her presence, before, and after, the moth balls.

Then we have the summer at Newport. My friend Jim Benson (now with *Time*, in New York) leased us his house on the Cliff Walk. Deb is walking now, in front of "The Breakers," amidst white-and-purple morning-glories. Her legs are ringed with fat and her diaper hangs like a G string below her protruding belly. I'm not in any of these pictures, since I took them all, but Pat, or Pat's legs, are in all of them. She looks so young; her dark-brown hair had not a hint of gray, and she wears the "poodle cut" of the fifties. She looks, as they used to say in Deb's old movie magazines, vivacious.

"In these pictures," says Christo, "is so much *spirit* in Mrs. Rutherford's eyes. How you say—the *zest* for the *life*."

"Twenty years ago, Christo," Pat replies. "Twenty years."

He reaches over and pats her hand, as if to soften the blow of passing time. Am I paranoid, or do I feel a suggestion that *I* am to blame for the lost spirit in Patricia's eyes? I'm sorry I'm not in some of these. I was not without my own charisma at thirty-five. I feel the beginnings of tension up my spine. Ridiculous, this urge to show Christo the young Jay Rutherford, the hail-fellow-well-met with his bouncing baby daughter on his knee. They called me Fearless Fosdick on the squash court that summer in Newport. I've made a good impression so far, I think. Why do I want to flash my image across the screen, so to flex my youthful muscle, show my verve, my energy, so to somehow redeem myself? Patricia bestows one of her effortless profundities on the moment.

"We had few regrets in 1950. That is, mutual regrets."

I feel maudlin, until the next selection, at which Deborah screams, "Oh, no! Not *these!*" A whole series, twenty of them, a pictorial rendering of Deborah's two-year association with the orthodontist. One, in particular, makes her recoil into the springs of the couch. She has been eating an orange. The pulpy flesh of the fruit hangs in shreds off the braces as she says cheese for the camera. In another, she's been eating raisins. They stick, in gluey black chunks, all across the expanse of her smile. "Wasn't it worth it, though?" asks Pat. And to Christo. "Doesn't she have a lovely smile?" He is speechless. It's his turn now for the limpid gaze as he nods his head in agreement.

When the clock on the mantle chimes nine, Christo says he must be going. It's snowing. I know he can't really afford a cab back to the city, so I offer to drive him downtown. Deb, slowly recovering from the indignities of the exposé, says that *she* would like to drive Christo home. And Patricia, the wistful sorrow having moved from her face to her voice, says:

"Debbie, it was awfully nice of you to be with us this Christmas, but you really don't have to linger on for our sakes. If you'd like to go tonight, rather than tomorrow, it's fine with us."

When they leave, Christo shakes my hand, and Pat's, thanks us profusely, and hugs Elise. We thank him for the little green box and tell him, awkwardly, that we'd like to see him again soon. They mention that they've been invited to Deb's boss's home for New Year's Eve. Christo links his arm in Deb's and strikes a pose. "We will dance the hora at the Silvers'."

Still, as he stands in his overcoat, I have a mysterious urge to grab him and tell him I'm not the old capitalist codger he thinks I am. I was Gorgeous George at the U. of M., Fearless Fosdick at Bailey's Beach. I was unflappable during the war —after being decorated the word around the barracks was that Audie Murphy had nothing on me. As he climbs into Deb's Mustang he turns and waves.

"Goodnight, Mr. Rutherford. Have a good sleep!"

The whack of the pack, the crackling fire, the wing-back chair. The end of another Yule. Patricia inhales, and smiles.

"Well, old bean, what are you going to do?"

"Oh, I think I'll attack my Christmas Solzhenitsyn. What about you?"

"Oh, all right. I guess I'll feel my Christmas Oates."

Predictably, my pipe, reamer, matches and tobacco are never in the room I happen to be in. I retrieve them from the living room. When I return, Pat is already on her second smoke.

"Jay, they're sleeping together, aren't they?"

"Yes, I think so."

Her face is overcast as she breaks open her new book—

properly, I might add—a few pages at a time, without cracking its back.

"Believe it or not, I'm rather anxious for grandchildren."

"Really? I wouldn't have thought so."

"My granddaughter, you know, will be the fourth generation at Vassar."

There's something presumptuous in the remark, but I don't dispute it. Much as I've always wanted to extend the narrow little boundaries that pinch our world, I must admit that, at middle age, we are what we are. We sit, two old lap dogs, with our books and stimulants, until well after midnight.

XXIX

I think—I certainly hope—that I have come to grips with the summer of '32 and have, through persistent personal scrutiny, realized why the following year was so traumatic for me. The last vestiges of childhood fell away swiftly: I had molted precipitously, without an appropriate passing of time to temper the new underskin which was to see me through my middle teens. In fact, the experience was so brief and so condensed it has been difficult to code and catalogue all the pieces until just recently—somewhere around my fiftieth year. And then, at the first glimmer of understanding, I reacted by getting thoroughly juiced at the bar of the Yacht Club. I had to be forcibly removed from the stool by my friend Ed Humboldt. Crying like a baby, still clutching my bourbon smash as I was hauled across the parking lot, I leaned on Ed's shoulder and divulged my bit of distilled wisdom:

"I didn't fuck 'em up! They were all fucked up before I was born!"

And Ed, who was almost as drunk as I, and who hadn't an inkling of what I was talking about, replied thickly:

"Of *course* you didn't fuck 'em up! As long as old Eddie's around, nobody's going to say anybody fucked 'em up but their fucking selves!"

First and foremost, for fourteen years my mother had allowed the sun to rise and set in my ups and downs, my smiles and frowns. She had lauded my minute successes, triumphed with me over high grades, minimized my failures, stood me in good stead whenever those warm zephyrs of boyhood turned to chill winds. I had come to expect effusive hugs for good report cards, mustard plasters when my chest was congested with cold, hot-water bottles for any one of a multitude of aches and pains, a ten-minute review of my day at bedtime, in my room, with a final assurance that whatever was bothering me would resolve itself in my sleep. Or, if I was giddy and nothing was bothering me, a reminder that life was a serious business and that I must control my essential flightiness and begin to think of the gravity of what lay ahead. Pat insists that I was spoiled and pampered—a difficult thing for me to admit. Actually, if we consider that I was an only child, that the total parental burden fell to Mother and that we were, after all, people who could afford to indulge our desires, I wasn't quite the brat Patricia makes me out to be. Anyway, it was long before her time, so what can she know of it really? And what can she know of the desolation I felt when it stopped, promptly, at fourteen? She, Pat, was aided, comforted, abetted by her family well into her thirties until I finally put a stop to it and sent them all packing back to Boston. And even then, thanks to A.T.&T., Mother Bancroft was but a few digits away. But for me, the aiding and administering ended abruptly on the living-room floor at Timberline, and it came to me on the trip across the Saskatchewan prairie that we had reached a point of no return. On the train, I tried, once, to take Mother's hand in mine, and I was spurned. I was embarrassed, she was angry;

she seemed to be repulsed by my boyish affection and I never tried again. I don't mean to imply that there was never again any warmth between us—quite the reverse. We became the best of friends, but I left it to her, thereafter, to set the scene and initiate the gesture.

My father took an apartment at the Tower House, on the Detroit River, roughly a week after our return. For the first few days all three of us attempted to conduct ourselves normally, meeting each evening at the dinner table. It was impossible. We were totally estranged. Father's eyes were as full of questions as Mother's were blank, and I had to excuse myself every ten minutes in order to relieve my nervous bladder. At the end of the week, Father faced us, in the library, with the news that the time had come for him to move on. Winger Burns had not been mentioned until then, but at that time Father stated that what little we had together in the past was now sullied, that he felt Winger's presence *upon* us and that, in his words, life was too short to live in a vacuum, especially when he, in particular, had other fish to fry. It seemed odd to me that Mother should be condemned for her *one* fish, while Father had access to the whole ocean. Deborah assures me that this double standard no longer exists and, if true, that's all well and good for her generation. But for mine, sad to say, there remains something dissolute and gross about a woman who casts her line and angles about after marriage.

Mother asked Father if he would like a divorce, and he declined the offer. She took a surprisingly firm position on the divorce—I say surprisingly because a divorce would cost, and cost dearly. I understood that, if Winger was the reward, it was worth it. I didn't understand why she pressed for it now. She explained that with a formal, legal rupture, Father would have "visitation rights." This would insure, or actually make compulsory, occasional returns to the house to see me. She feared that, without a set of designated visiting days, my father would quickly forget any obligation to me. It was probably the only instance when she underestimated him. He rarely came to see me, but he made a point of calling me every Monday night, at nine o'clock, until I was eighteen and left for college. So we remained, she and I, in the sprawling Grosse Pointe house, vastly outnumbered by help. She was ill, and unavailable to me, through most of 1933, and my recollection is that of a cold, dank, unheated house. This is one of those unaccountable memories, not based on fact. I distinctly remember continual visits to the thermostat to see if the great, hulking furnace had finally given us its last gasp. I remember my surprise at finding the little red arrow pointing directly at seventy-two degrees. Still, my strongest memory is that of inclement rooms, ceilings that rose to seemingly wintry heights, chairs that bore no human imprint, couches whose pillows were forever plumped, knickknacks arranged like toy soldiers atop surfaces which were never disturbed by personal clutter, shelves displaying a wide array of unused crystal and china: I felt that we lived in a museum-like chill amidst relics from a bygone age. The Monday-night phone call from Father was, I must admit, eagerly anticipated and more than a little reassuring.

For the first few months I fervently hoped that we would hear something of Winger, or possibly even hear from him. I spent many hours alone in my room conjuring up situations wherein he would have no alternative but to call upon us. These situations were usually dependent on dire illness. Many times, in my sleep, I confused him with my grandfather and imagined him calling us from some maritime lumber camp—calling with his one remaining arm. I wrote Bob Hilliard once a month, hoping that Winger would have changed his mind and returned to Buena Vista. Bob's letters were friendly, and newsy, and kind. He put off, as long as he could, the sentence that told me no, they had no word of Winger or his whereabouts. Once, in December, when my life seemed irreclaimable, I called the information operator in Halifax, Nova Scotia, and asked if Winger Burns was listed in her directory. That night, in my dreams, the call went through on a heavenly wire and he promised to meet me in the lobby of the Amberley, on Dominion Day, the following summer. The next morning Mother entered my room to find the receiver dangling off the hook and me, babbling unintelligibly, with a fever of 104. And I prayed. My God, I prayed with the zeal of Rasputin to be reunited with Winger, always ending these prayers with the same dramatic plea: "Please, dear God, if not in this life, *in the next.*"

I have, each year, along with a birthday and an anniversary, a Most Irrational Day, although Pat insists it's difficult to distinguish my most irrational from all the rest. Still, my most irrational does occur every July 1. My heavenly phone call is not recurring: the ghostly appointment is. So sure am I, each Dominion Day, that Winger is roaming the cavernous lobby at the Amberley that I cannot function normally on that day. For years now, forty to be exact, I have postponed or canceled all engagements and left the calendar blank. Sometimes I drive over to Windsor and watch their parade, sometimes I spend the better part of the day at Mother's grave, in communion with the two of them. Ten years ago, I went so far as to call the Amberley on the first, and have Winger paged. Had he been there, he'd have been sixty-eight years old. I had convinced myself that, upon retiring, he would return to Buena Vista to finish out his days. This coming summer, on the first, he will be seventy-eight. Patricia is certain he's dead by now, but I don't think so. When he dies an exorcism will occur; I will be free of him at last. I'll wake up and know that he's gone. I'll call up Ed Humboldt and we'll go sailing on the first. Poor Patricia. Even her gestures denoting madness are dated. She reacts by pointing her index fingers to the sides of her head and whirling them in circles around her ears, while the weed hangs off her lip. She may whirl to her heart's content. I will know it when he leaves the planet.

It could be said that I sank to the lowest depths of that period in the spring of 1933. I left the grounds of Croydon one day to find a pale, withered man standing on the corner handing out pamphlets. The pamphlet depicted a bearded Jesus and proclaimed, "I Am the Way." I read it on the way home, and though I was, even then, suspicious of pamphlets, petitions and other redeemers, be they holy, secular or political, I determined to go that night to a hall on Jefferson where the Reverend Samuel Bouchard promised to point out the Way to the general populace. I told Mother I had to go back to school to do some lab work, and I walked down to the hall. A large metal sign was propped against the building. Across the top it said, "The Church of the Burning Bush." Underneath, there was a photograph of the Reverend Bouchard, holding a staff. I ventured in, feeling corny, and conspicuously under forty, and sat down beside a woman who was afflicted with a large goiter. There followed an hour of evangelistic exhortations, at the end of which the Reverend Bouchard entered into a sort of give-and-take with his audience. He asked that we raise our right hands in answer to a series of questions; he bade us slough off our inhibitions and participate in the dialogue. For a tumultuous, climactic ten minutes, I, and a vociferous throng of two hundred others, admitted to anger, avarice, envy, gluttony, lust, pride, jealousy, corruption, thievery and other, similar transgressions. The woman with the goiter shed copious tears throughout. I was enthralled by the unfettered emotion of it all, and when the Reverend announced that he was available to talk to those with the heaviest hearts, I assured myself that no one in the gathering qualified more than I. I sprinted forward and fell upon him, finding, at last, my shepherd. He had spoken with such authority on such a wide range of passions and foibles I believed that I could talk to the man and find solace. I was impressed by his performance—I was convinced that he embodied a boundless understanding of the *Comédie Humaine.*

What developed, upon his realization that it was my mother's lover for whom I yearned, was a kind of slapstick panic in the mode of the Marx Brothers. He called forth two burly assistants. The three of them surrounded me and sat me on a chair. I would normally have felt threatened by this action but I was, instead, incredulous at their questions and the intensity with which they began to "pump" me. They approached the subject with such unnatural ardor, such orgiastic glee, I immediately felt I was in the clutches of Satan himself. I volunteered an inordinate amount of information, foolishly thinking that their grunts and groans were signs of recognition. Yes, I thought, they've heard similar stories, they've traveled this route before, they'll unravel my thoughts and provide me with a resolution. It was not until they asked me if I had ever seen Winger's penis that I was struck by the incongruity of the scene. I rose like a phoenix and tried to pass them, to the door. They followed me, demanding my name and address. They began to chase me up Jefferson, insisting that they must accompany me home and meet my mother. I threw two garbage cans across their path and, even above the clamor, they ranted of profligacy, venery and violation. When I reached home I fell on my bed and banged my head, furiously, against the headboard. I felt stupid, imbecilic. I had hoped to salvage my life by reaching for God, I had ended by flying down Jefferson like a fugitive, with Groucho, Chico and Harpo, three frenetic, inflamed, overstimulated zealots, in hot pursuit.

I was brought to my knees in prayer only once again, some five years later, when my raven-haired Valerie lay wasting away with leukemia. I went to the chapel every day for over two months, and said silent mini-prayers through I don't know how many hours of history or philosophy lectures. When she died, I vowed that I would never pray again, and never have. I remember, when Deborah was eight years old, she fell out of a tree house and landed on top of her head on a block of flagstone. She was unconscious when we found her, and she then went into a coma at the hospital. Pat stayed in the children's ward and knelt all night by Debbie's bed.

I came home and sat in my wing-back chair and read an issue of *Esquire* cover to cover. I learned something of Truman Capote's nocturnal habits, and I laughed at all those cartoons of portly men in baggy shorts and bulbous-breasted women in diaphanous nightgowns. At 5 A.M. Pat called and said that Deb had regained consciousness. Clearly, I do better with the wing-back chair than worship.

My real staff of life after returning from Buena Vista was Dougie Clark. I could depend on him to listen for hours with total empathy. When I was moody and depressed and, more often than not, preoccupied with the dour predictions that came out of Gilbey's dry cathartic medicine, he made excuses for me with the other boys. He was able to change the subject and detour the conversation with consummate tact, without indicating lack of patience or boredom, without ever deprecating what must have been my monotonous need for reassurance. However, in February of 1934, he was expelled from Croydon. The expulsion was a wrench for me for two reasons. First, he had become my only close friend and I didn't think I could get through the year without his support. Second, I was hurt and annoyed that he hadn't been fit to include me in the acts which led to the expulsion. A group of four seniors, with Douglas as leader, had smuggled a fourteen-year-old Polish girl into the boarders' dorm. They had smuggled her in many times, but in February, Vincent Pellegrini, of all people, squealed on them and they were caught. The scandal was made worse by the insistence of the girl's parents that she had been examined by a doctor and was, technically, a virgin. The girl, Zena, then confessed that continuing virginity was her intent: she had performed fellatio on the four of them, for a fee of five dollars apiece. Douglas was sent home to Flint the following week, the other three tottered between disgrace and notoriety for a time, but were allowed to graduate.

The school was a-dither with the firing, from janitors to faculty to headmaster, so the circumstances of our parting were hasty and inappropriate. We stood in the hall near the library while groups of boys passed us, chortling, blushing, shuffling their feet. I tried, awkwardly, to convey the magnitude of my feelings. I told Douglas that he would be sorely missed, and made him promise to keep in touch with me after his father had found another school. And, since I harbored feelings of indignation, I asked why, as his best friend, I had not been included in the festivities. Both of us were near tears, maudlin, yearning for privacy. We turned our faces toward the wall and Douglas leaned against a locker, and groaned grievously.

"Shit, Red, I love ya like a brother, but we were taking a helluva risk. You're just too goddamn *refined*."

I did not hear from him again until March. He had been accepted at a school in Cleveland, but was being made to repeat his senior year, and was subjected to the indignity of a nightly visit from the school chaplain. Zena, the Polish girl, was Douglas' first sexual experience and I've often wondered if that initial foray laid the foundation for his lifelong vicissitudes with women. He began with an orgy—a plateau many of us never reach—he was jaded at love by the time he was twenty. In Cleveland, he took up with a thirty-year-old Jewish ceramicist and made the headlines when her husband beat him to a pulp and threw him down a fire escape. He has been married four times at this writing and has traveled the length and breadth of these fifty states sampling the bosoms and buttocks of southern belles, blueberry pickers in Maine, pineapple pickers in Hawaii, a lady bush pilot out of Nome, Alaska, and a liberal congresswoman in Bethesda, Maryland. And, of course, an endless stable of starlets at home on his own turf. I run into him once or twice every ten years or so; each time I do he wallows in memories of Zena. I saw him last in London, in 1972. He was there, sporting his Malibu tan, working on a movie script. We went to a restaurant in Soho and, as the evening wore on, we talked at length of politics first, then of the deaths of my parents and his. I waxed eloquent again about Buena Vista, and then we talked, inevitably, about sex in general. He recalled the delightful Zena, and the firing, and, from the vantage point of his mid-fifties, allowed as how it was all worth it. He used, I remember, the current "gang bang," a term I found a little too hip for Douglas. All of them, he said, from the ceramicist through the bush pilot through the wives, were but a backward journey. He laughed and said that he finally understood that he had been on the rebound for thirty-five years, on the rebound, yes, from Zena's marvelous oral facility. I watched him, with his longish gray hair fringing around his bald pate, his suede vest fringing around his ample posterior, his flared pants and his silver P.O.W. bracelet, and I listened to his mellow accounting of the pleasures of that first fellatio. And it occurred to me that Zena was his Buena Vista, and that we were two old fools basking in Courvoisier and diffuse remembrances of things past.

XXX

Mrs. James Rutherford regrets
that she is unable to accept
your invitation to dinner on
October 7th, for reasons of
ill health.

For over a year my mother languished, impaired both physically and mentally, a flimsy shadow of her former self. She summoned the energy for the trip home, and for my belated registration at Croydon, and from then on she was noticeably absent from the house. She rallied for an hour at the end of the first week, in order to watch my father haul away his worldly possessions; she went directly to her rooms that night and left them then only once a day, at four o'clock when I returned from school. She seemed to feel that, to maintain some semblance of normalcy, her appearance was necessary at the end of my day. When she came downstairs she came like an apparition, morose and lethargic. She came for no reason and therefore never settled anywhere. I would find her ambling around the living room, or the solarium, in nightgown, robe and slippers—hair unkempt, traces of cream on her face—at four in the afternoon. The slippers were shabby, old and run-down at the heels; she neglected to button the robe before tying it. It hung open loosely, falling away from her shoulders, and on the hot days in October I would see a line of perspiration on her nightgown, between her breasts. She was withdrawn and vacant; she rarely spoke. She would give me a brief, enervating smile; the trip down and the smile were all she could muster. The slovenly stance and the lassitude of the shuffle back up the stairs made me feel helpless and uncertain. After a while even the servants could not bear the sight of her; she set their teeth on edge to the point where they ran to the basement at the sound of her foot on the stair. To this day, I cannot bear to have anyone on the first floor of the house in robe and slippers after 10 A.M. If they are deathly ill, I don't want to see them. If they're healthy, I want them dressed and active. Otherwise, I feel that we none of us are in control and that these first signs of personal laxity are the beginning of an insidious neglect that will eventually lead us all to ruin.

This gloom and brooding ended climactically on Christmas Day, 1932. I have never quite forgiven Winger for his package (received on December 22, postmarked Halifax), containing two hand-tooled leather bookmarks. He said that he wanted Mother to have a memento, and he could think of nothing else she might use. The bookmarks were decorated with sprigs of laurel. Upon receiving the package Mother's condition worsened and, once Christmas vacation began, she saw no further reason to descend the stairs at four. She then confined herself solely to her rooms. I dreaded the holiday and took the step of asking Douglas if I might spend Christmas with him in Flint. However, he, too, dreaded the ten-day interval and had invited himself to the home of his aunt in Philadelphia. On Christmas morning there was an envelope containing fifty dollars, from my father, but there was no gift from Mother. Cook rather hastily wrapped up a book for me and gave it to me at Christmas dinner. I had hoped to share the meal with Mother, in her rooms, but Cook insisted that I eat in the kitchen with the servants. She had visited my mother that morning and returned to say that my mother had not eaten since the twenty-second, that she was indisposed and that if I wished to preserve my sanity I would take the meal in the kitchen and like it.

I don't recall the exact sequence of events over the next twenty-four hours, but I remember accepting the book from Cook and then going to the phone in the library. It was approximately eight o'clock in the evening. I didn't know precisely whom I would call but I felt very near the end of my tether and needed to talk with someone. I could no longer endure the lack of a tree, the lack of festivity, the absence of my father, the macabre silence pervading the house. Once in the library, I called my father's apartment at the Tower House. I was going to ask him to pick me up and spend two or three days with me. To my surprise, a woman answered the phone. She immediately handed over the receiver to Josh Whitcomb, who told me that Father was spending the holiday in Montreal with Harold Peterson's widow. I hadn't realized that Mrs. Peterson had lost Mr. Peterson. I'd met the family and knew them to be the wealthy owners of a large Quebec brewery. Unaccountably, I asked Josh to pass on my condolences when next he saw the lady, and I hung up. I then tried to call the Peterson residence in Montreal, and was told that theirs was an unlisted number. With mounting frustration, I called the apartment again and asked Josh if my father had left the Montreal number. Josh paused a moment too long, and when he said no, he had no idea of the Petersons' number, I called him a liar and hung up.

Having by then worked myself into a frenzy of nerves and anger, I determined to visit Mother, present an ultimatum and have it out with her. I wanted her to dress, and eat, and function normally as a mother again, or I wanted to move out and board at Croydon for the rest of the year. I burst into her room, fortified with pumping adrenalin, fully prepared to rout her out of bed and engage in a knock-down-drag-out argument. I found her sitting in the middle of the floor, in her nightgown—only her back was visible to me. In one quick scan of the room I saw, spread around her, an aggregation of Winger's gifts. The cheese cutter, meat thermometer, rolling pin, wire whisk, tea caddie and potholders. She was holding the bookmarks in her hands. Her bed was unmade and I saw, strewn over the pillows, the only photographs we had of Winger. They were the ones my father had taken the day the men erected the totem pole.

I walked directly into her line of vision and was horrified when I saw her face. She was deathly pale, but there was a kind of demented concentration in her eyes as she peered down at the bookmarks. But for the deliberation in her eyes, she seemed to be in a catatonic state, unaware of either my presence or the cold draft which blew across the floor and caused goose flesh down her bare arms. There were deep-purple welts on her cheeks and throat—lesions so startling I felt sure they had been produced by her own hand, possibly with one of the utensils. There was a gash, and dried blood, on the calf of her right leg. She looked up at me and asked two questions in a childlike, whimsical way.

"Is there no relief, Jay? Will he plague me to the edge of my grave?"

She then fell back on the floor and began to writhe, twisting her hips and thighs forward and back, undulating against the nap of the rug while holding the bookmarks against her breast. She whimpered weakly but thrust away my hand with enormous force when I tried to raise her to the bed. After a moment she dragged herself up to a sitting position, her spine was erect, and the deliberation in her eyes became all the more purposeful.

"I'll have to go away, Jay. I can see the results of all this in your face. You don't look like a boy any more. I need to go away before I do really irreparable harm. I need medication. A hypodermic. I've lost all will. Call Cook, please, and take me to a hospital."

She spent the months of January and February at a "rest home" called The Oaks, in Macomb County. Cook and I accompanied her there in an ambulance. I visited her, sometimes with my father, every Saturday afternoon. I have no recollection of the drive to The Oaks or, for that matter, of the rest of the Christmas recess. I remember returning to the house about 2 A.M. on the twenty-sixth. I first called Josh Whitcomb, told him what had transpired and asked him to locate my father at the widow Peterson's. Then, passing Mother's rooms on my way to bed, I saw the kitchen utensils still lying about on the rug. I went in and gathered them up and packed them, along with the photographs, in a hatbox. I debated throwing the box in the garbage but decided, rather sagaciously for fourteen, that the gifts were simply effects, rather than causes. It was not in my power to rid the world of all tangible traces of Winger Burns. If she recovered, fully recovered, she would come to terms with the loss. She would learn to smile her enigmatic smile and tolerate the presence of his gifts. If she didn't recover, it didn't matter. The doctor, in conjunction with the hospital psychiatrist, said that she would be committed permanently to The Oaks if there were no signs of improvement within a month. So I put the hatbox on the wardrobe shelf and decided to wait and see.

I'm sure they go about things differently nowadays, but at that time the psychiatric profession, or at least those doctors at The Oaks, believed that Mother should not be aroused from her depression too quickly. She was kept in the intensive-care unit under heavy, immobilizing sedation for the first week. I felt thoroughly cut off from her and attempted, during the week, to send her flowers. I stopped at our florist's, picked a large bouquet of cheery anemones out of the glass cooler and gave the clerk Mother's address at The Oaks. The woman's pencil came to a halt at the name of the hospital. Her eyes widened and she avoided my gaze. It seemed that flowers could not be sent to The Oaks. They were forbidden because patients had been known to break the vases and flowerpots and use the resulting jagged pieces to harm themselves. This information sent shudders through me—I hadn't thought the place an asylum. I could, of course, send straw-flowers in a papier-mâché container, but I declined, and left the shop.

The first Saturday Father picked me up and drove me out to The Oaks, but Mother was sullen and grouchy, still partially drugged. We stayed only half an hour. The following Saturday my father was away in Montreal with the widow Peterson, so Cook drove me out, and let me see Mother alone. Her face had healed and she'd been given a shampoo. Her hair, noticeably grayer since my previous visit, stuck out every which way like a floor mop. She was rather feisty then, complaining that the food was all puréed, and was particularly scornful of the nurses, who denied her the use of her metal curlers, her silver mirror, even her toothpaste. "They think I'll do myself in," she said. A little smile flickered around her mouth and she added, "They don't know I'm saving *that* spectacle for the Foshay Tower." And went on to say that when she *did* do it, she'd do it on a bellyful of sirloin, not prechewed baby mush. The Saturday after, Father was back from Montreal and accompanied me again. I was distressed to see that he, too, had visited the florist's and had succumbed to the strawflowers and the papier-mâché. Mother was out of bed by then, and we were permitted to meet in a sitting room at the end of her ward. We were pleased at her animation, and laughed when she took the strawflowers and examined them.

"Now what, I wonder, can I do with papier-mâché?" She paused, and glanced down the hall to the nurses' station. "I've a mind to shove it up the rear of that head nurse."

She talked for nearly an hour, describing her ward mates at The Oaks. She decidedly did not consider herself at one with their plight, and commented on their behavior rather like an observer at a circus. She noted that the wealthy patients had all rebelled at some time and delighted in fancifying those times when they had groveled along the seamier side of life. The few poor patients had, on the other hand, delusions of grandeur. It was amazing, said Mother, how the poor ones all seemed to have their origins in the Mississippi Delta, having left behind them columned mansions, magnolia, wisteria and a vast assortment of uncles. They were alcoholics mostly, plus a few senior citizens in their dotage, plus, said Mother with awesome candor, the sexually disturbed like herself. There was a sixty-year-old woman who thought she was Cleopatra, and a twenty-year-old girl who thought she was Aimee Semple McPherson. The various descriptions were not derisive. When Aimee Semple passed through the sitting room, wearing a sheet, clutching her Bible, Mother said, "There but for the grace of God go I." And we knew, then, that her will had survived and that she would leave The Oaks after an interval.

When she returned home in March, it was difficult to say which of us had suffered more—which of us bore the deepest scars. I had lost thirteen pounds, which I could not spare. I was tired to my teeth, acrimonious much of the time. My bladder problems continued to worsen and I took dizzy spells at school, which necessitated my walking near walls for support, and waiting at the stairs for a space at the banister. After my bout with the Reverend Bouchard, I developed an itchy rash around my elbows. It subsided for a couple of months and then, after Christmas, flared up in scales. Cook sent me to the doctor, where I learned that I had a chronic case of psoriasis. Together, Mother and I were the gold at the end of the pharmacist's rainbow: fat amber bottles with typed labels were everywhere in the house. We had breakfast together on Mother's first morning home, and I noticed Mother perusing the myriad pills, liquids and salves on the breakfast table. She shook her head and muttered, "We were not cut out for summertime liaisons, you and I."

The psychiatrist at The Oaks had warned me that I must not equate full recovery with Mother's behavior prior to Buena Vista. She would be different now; I must expect the signs of improvement to be gradual. He suggested that I encourage whatever route she chose to take, but encourage honestly. She had, said the doctor, an X-ray vision into people's motives. She would not be cured by flattery or false pretense. At the same time, she mustn't be coddled. He had observed that, when challenged, she was wont to defend herself rather than cringe. This defense mobilized energy, thought, verbosity, all of which rescued her from self-pity and dispersed her inhibitions. It seemed an impossible task to encourage without condescension, to be firm without being obdurate.

When I returned from school at four the following day, there was a written message on the vestibule table:

"I'm not coming down at four any more. Please come and see me."

This seemed to be a sign for the worse, and I was perplexed as to which tack to take. She must not recede and make a warren of her rooms. I envisioned visiting her daily, finding her wan and sickly, thin against a propped pillow, with a strong medicinal smell to the room. I entered her room with trepidation, but found her neatly dressed and smiling. There was a fire in the hearth, and there were bouquets of flowers in both the sitting room and the bedroom. Throughout the spring, every Friday morning, a florist delivered these two bouquets for her rooms, while the rest of the house went bloomless. Cook brought us tea that afternoon and while we waited for it I noticed several books and a jigsaw puzzle spread on one table, scattered recordings on another, and on her desk many sheets of blank foolscap. The radio had been on—in future visits I realized that she always listened to the Canadian station in Windsor. I found these signs of life encouraging, and she noticed my pleasure.

"I'm not going to try and live in the house any longer. Just these rooms. I'm quite comfortable here and I—truthfully— I get quite ill when I come downstairs. The house smacks too much of wasted years—you know—prodigality. For over a decade I had a stiff upper lip, and you know what happens to stiff upper lips. They atrophy from disuse and lose all sense of feeling. I hate the house and I hate the last fifteen years. Quite an admission, you know, for someone who's always avoided the more dramatic passions.

"I'll make a pleasant little shelter here. The flowers help tremendously, don't they? I've also decided to write poetry, try it, for an hour or so every day. I don't think it's very good. I've read it for years, but God, writing it is something else, especially when you've developed a critical eye. I won't show it to anyone but you. I *despise* the poetry of lovelorn ladies—here, read this. Tell me, is it gauche?"

Cook knocked on the door and brought in a tea table. We'd never done this before, this American facsimile of English high tea. Compared with the slovenly smiles of the past six months, it was a wonderful relief. The sitting room had a bay window with an inside seat and velour cushions. I took the paper there, into the light, and read. The piece was titled "Hand."

I
Darkly, your hand lies under mine
Fragrant of thickets and columbine
Stained with earth and pitch of pine
Dark, substantial, under mine.

II

There is, in your hand, the strength that allays
Old scorn, old worn, indelicate ways
Intemperate adjectives, years of malaise.
Your hand is the ballast that steadies my days.

I liked it, even though it was lovelorn. I looked at the scattered albums, the jigsaw—the valiant attempts to cast out the gloom, and I was pleased.

"Well?"

"It's nice. Nice and woodsy. Evocative."

She smiled. Lord, yes, an enigmatic smile.

"Not quite up to 'The Shooting of Dan McGrew,' though, eh, Jay?"

That was a put-down, and this was a test. The insinuation that I was so limited in experience and understanding that I could only comprehend Dan McGrew's shooting, or Sam McGee's cremation, offended me. She seemed to be taking the loss and the pain as solely hers, forgetting that I, too, had been in attendance, that I, too, had held the dark, substantial hand and felt the sticky pitch of pine. And, of course, she couldn't know that I had, just recently, suffered untold humiliation while searching for my own ballast somewhere in the vicinity of the Church of the Burning Bush. I wished, for a moment, that I had herded the Reverend Bouchard and his minions into these rooms, and cast a stone or two, and pointed an accusing finger, and let them see a fallen woman firsthand. The wish was preposterous; I began to giggle. As fallen women go, she would have proved a disappointment.

(Patty is a master at that sort of put-down. She knows I love Thomson's nature paintings, so whenever we're confronted with Monet's field of poppies or van Gogh's sunny Arles, she says, "Not quite up to Thomson's birches, though, eh, Jay?" That one little mistake, now slumbering unseen in our attic, gives her license to make these remarks. Not since my purchase of Lazlo Olzewski's *Sunrise on the Doge's Palace* has she given an inch where my artistic judgment is concerned. Screw it.)

"Now, look. Even though I knew the locale, even though I knew Winger, even though you're my *mother* and even though I prefer Robert W. Service, I still think it's a pretty good little poem. So don't give me that *up to Dan McGrew* stuff because I know what I like."

"Good boy!" she said. "I am, just now, beginning to know what I like. With a little luck, if it's not too late, I shall become your quintessential hedonist."

Strangely, the more she confined herself to her rooms, the more disentangled she became from the old routine, the more she revived. And in May, when one of her poems was accepted by *The Michigan Scrivener*, she experienced her first feelings of accomplishment. She waved the five-dollar check at me and rejoiced.

"I have *earned* this, Jay! I've been *paid* for thinking!"

The small piece was titled "Tattoo." It had, symbolically, to do with the ineradicable marks of youthful escapades. I knew that the inspiration for the poem was Winger's clipper ship, and I learned, only then, that he had always been ashamed of his tattoo. He considered it a particularly mindless thing to have done, and thought that it relegated him, permanently, to the lower class. Mother wrote two or three poems a month for the next twenty years and it is from these poems that I have gleaned some of what I know about Winger Burns. All of them had their origins in Buena Vista in 1932, all of them were an attempt to write Winger out of her system or, at least, to provide an objectivity whose handmaiden would hopefully be sanity. I find it rather insupportable that my own endeavors in this regard are simply a matter of inheritance, and it disturbs me that the effect of the man goes even one generation further. The other day I overheard Deborah giving a thumbnail sketch of my character to

Christo, by way of explanation for my seemingly bizarre existence.

"Contemplative, yes. Washed up out of the mainstream years ago when his mother ran amok. Brooding about it ever since. Maddening, for Mother and me."

The single event which finally brought my mother back into the house, which liberated her from the demons of her youth and the failure of her marriage, was, not surprisingly, the death of Grandmother MacAllister. Grandmother's death occurred while she was visiting us for Christmas in 1934. She rose that December morning, performed her ablutions and prepared for a trip to the beauty salon. She was to have her gray roots bleached the honey-beige color she'd worn for the past twenty years. She suffered a massive coronary at breakfast and died two hours later. Her last request to Mother and me, while we stood, bedside, attending her, was that she wanted an open-casket funeral only if the mortician could arrange to camouflage her last month's growth of gray hair. If he could not engage a beautician willing to work on a corpse, then we must, without question, close the casket. The beautician was found and, for an exorbitant sum, she agreed to go to the funeral home with her bottle of peroxide. The funeral took place in Grosse Pointe on December 19. Grandmother's roots were the familiar honey beige, and she wore a recently purchased rust-colored Chanel suit which complemented, we thought, the ivory-satin interior of the casket. Mother and I took great pains to orchestrate Grandmother's swan song stylishly. Beauty may indeed lie in the eye of the beholder, but Grandmother had always believed that the beholder was a fool, an amorphous mass of undetermined prejudices. She believed you could align and crystallize the opinions of anyone if you were endowed with what she called "economic muscle." This theory has worked fairly well for U.S. world policy; I see it working with great efficacy up and down Lake Shore Road every day. I've used it myself,

I'm ashamed to admit, to remove the social constraints my sloth and my trust-protected days have placed upon me. Mother used it, too, to excuse her eventual erratic, quintessentially hedonistic behavior. Henry Ford, just up the street, flourishes on it, singlehandedly, even against the multitudinous efforts of the U.A.W. I would take this tenet as truth but for Abraham Lincoln and Winger Burns. Some of the time, with some of the people, it just doesn't work. I might today be a simple Buena Vista shit kicker, except that Winger Burns didn't have a price.

Anyway, the Detroit newspapers adhered to the idea wholeheartedly. Their coverage called my grandmother "a famous Detroit beauty" and noted that, at sixty-three (with her camouflaged roots and nifty suit), "she held time at arm's length and looked as young as she did on the day of her marriage."

For the first time in two years, Mother and I went out together that evening. We went all the way down to Woodward and Hancock, to St. Paul's Episcopal Cathedral. We listened to Handel's *Messiah*, and when we returned we sat in the kitchen and drank hot chocolate.

"I think I'm going to be all right now, Jay. What about you?"

"Oh, I'm going to be all right, too. But different."

"Different, certainly. We're both different. But in what fashion will you be different?"

"I'm going to *maximize* for a while. Jump in with all fours."

"Not like Dougie Clark, I hope."

"Not like that at all. I'm going to undertake the maximum at school, rather than my previous minimum. I want to study; I want to learn, get high grades, really *excel*. I'm curious to know if the rewards are real."

She sighed and frowned, and seemed burdened with ominous thoughts.

"Well, that's admirable. My motherly duty, properly,

should be to encourage you. At the risk of being cynical, Jay, I'm not sure it'll be worth your while. I think you'll find your rewards, eventually, in something other than certificates. That is, if you're blessed, and you find them at all."

XXXI

In the fall of 1936 I entered the University of Michigan. I was in fine fettle; the faculty at Croydon knew me as a boy who had overcome significant personal difficulties in order to graduate near the top of the class. I had weathered the storm, and though my teachers had not been apprised of the details, they knew I had withstood dramatic events and they gloated over my accomplishments. Mother was told that I had my head screwed on right; I was smart, competitive, doggedly persistent at those subjects in which I didn't excel (calculus and physics). I was considerate, outgoing, sensitive to the rights of others, well rounded, cognizant of the world around me. And when I declined an acceptance at Harvard, and chose Ann Arbor instead, the Croydon faculty rejoiced. I preferred, they said, to stop the brain drain to the East and keep Michigan's natural resources in Michigan.

No one knew better than I what I'd withstood, and I patted myself on the back for it. I enjoyed recognition; I enjoyed being held as an example for the lower forms. I was appropriately modest and humble when Vinnie Pellegrini stole the I.Q. sheets and announced that Rutherford weighed in at 160; I was appropriately smug and disapproving when the seniors philandered grossly during our class trip to Washington, D.C. It was good to be a scholar, a man of parts, a survivor. It was good to be good.

I got even better in college; in fact, I got so insufferably good I even got political. On the larger campus it wasn't quite so easy to shine. Now there were contenders aplenty for everything I wanted. It wasn't enough to wow the professors—I had to learn how to rally my peers and mount a campaign in order to get elected across the wide board of extracurricular activities. Oddly enough, my success was widely attributed to my "liberated" parents. Mother and Father frequently drove out to visit me together. Everyone knew they had amicably agreed to live apart, without divorcing. Everyone thought all that amicability highly civilized and sophisticated. So many of the other parents outwardly observed the laws of conformity and respectability, but inwardly ranted and raged, thus thwarting the offspring. With parents like mine, I'd grown up without the usual, castrating taboos. I hadn't been tethered with middle-class values: I'd been a free agent, free to investigate and adventure at large. Proof of that theory rested in the people themselves. Mother became known as an eccentric, a woman with outlandish opinions, original wit, a congenital dislike of artifice and an obvious scorn for fashion. Father was singularly distinguished-looking at fifty, still able to attract the stares of coeds. He continued to dress superbly and, since his strength had always lain in first impressions, he came off remarkably well on campus weekends where he could scratch the surface, drop a bon mot and leave the innocent student feeling somehow privileged to have met him. They were not your average Mr. and Mrs. Well-Heeled Bourgeoisie, bringing spongecakes and crew socks to their son away from home, and that, went the theory, was why I made such a spectacular showing. Everyone else was under surveillance—on a leash—but I'd been cut loose and was accountable only to myself.

Of all my friends, only Douglas Clark knew what it meant to be accountable only to yourself. When barely in our teens the two of us learned that, without surveillance, things rapidly deteriorate. Douglas was off raising havoc at Swarthmore by then ("Dear Red: The natives are restless but the Friends are friendly enough"), but we corresponded, and I believe

I drew my lessons from him more than anyone else. True, we were both without watchdogs. There was no fear of repercussion, admonition, no harshly meted-out discipline or denial or punishment. To me, this was an onus. To Douglas it was sublime emancipation. Both of us dreaded inactivity, silence, passivity. Both of us were terrified of solitude. Both were intent on making every minute count, however compulsively or improvidently. I made every moment *matter* with my rabid desire to please. Verbal assurance didn't suffice—I had to be able to tally it up at the end of the year with tangible diplomas, awards and honorable mentions. Douglas accomplished the same recognition by incurring displeasure on every side, and toting it up annually as a brilliant array of "life experiences" which he labeled *encounters, escapades, journeys into the mysteries of the human psyche.* In other words, he sought to expand in the world of the senses, all five of them, where I sought to expand my intellect, the world of the mind. I knew, with corroborated certainty, that if I stopped achieving, the void of Buena Vista would rear up and lay me bare once again. The odds against surviving twice were long and heavy.

The second, most crucial test came with Valerie. I say most crucial because it occurred in my maturity. Winger left us when I was fourteen; henceforth I attempted to explain, excuse and justify the wrench and the pain by reasoning that those were hypersensitive, adolescent years. I was made of stronger stuff by the time Valerie came upon the scene. I was happy, healthy, achieving furiously, and I'd developed a fine facility for gauging the long and the short of the opposite sex. Again, there were several contenders. Valerie had previously been smitten with an athlete—a football player who had played her false. She was looking around for a different sort of fellow and, though I knew from the start that I was precisely the kind of different sort of fellow she had in mind, she remained unconvinced of our destiny for several months. I pursued her with unremitting ardor through cafeterias, lecture halls, bookstalls. I "happened by" Onondaga, Michigan (an unlikely place to happen by in any circumstance), every weekend that she went home. And I wore blue, from head to toe, for six whole months because I knew it was her favorite color. I haunted the jewelry shops and priced engagement rings for weeks before our liaison was consummated because—Douglas Clark's warnings to the contrary—I knew I could search the world over and never again find a girl so categorically *right*.

On the weekend when her parents were called away to Grand Rapids, and she and I lay in her sunny bedroom in the brown bungalow in Onondaga, I knew I had done it again. I'd laid myself spiritually bare before another human being; I'd permitted another person to become indispensable to me. I knew the alarming fear I had known when I sat with Winger on the firebreaks. The pulling away of a hand, a glowering frown, a cold shoulder could once again send me into frightening depths of depression. I so clearly remember the patchwork quilt on her bed, the pink and beige primroses on the wallpaper—I recall them even now with a feeling of dependency, followed by the feeling of ultimate rejection that came, in 1939, when the silent killer surfaced first as acute anemia, then the white cells overtook the red, and we were finally, conclusively, put asunder.

Her brother, mother and father and I were invited to view the deceased in a little anteroom in the Onondaga Funeral Parlor before the service began. I fastened my eyes on the jet-black hair, the lithe twenty-year-old body that I had shared so intimately. And that, specifically, is when I lost my hold on the realm of meaning and achievement, though I went through the motions for several more years. I rose with Valerie's family and sang:

I walk through the garden alone
Where the dew is soft on the roses
And the voice I hear

Falling on my ear
The Son of God discloses
And He walks with me
And He talks with me
And He tells me I am His own
And the thoughts we share
As we linger there
No other has ever known.

I was nauseated, I had to pee, I felt an urge to lunge
forward and tear the blanket of pious yellow roses from the
coffin. The He in the hymn was, in truth, the grim reaper,
and He had dealt me His second, and last, diabolical hand.

I moved out of my fraternity, resigned as captain of the
Debating Team, dropped my column in the newspaper and
became the absolute, reclusive scholar. But in the midst
of all this maniacal achievement, the question of what to
do with my life had me in a quandary. I remember slumping
over a table in the library, and seeing a book someone had
left near my elbow. It was Silas Bent's *Justice Oliver Wendell
Holmes*. I read it, and it had no immediate effect on me. However, a month later, when time was running out, and I was on
the verge of admitting that there was nothing, really, that I
wanted to do with my life, it dawned on me that Harvard
Law was probably within my grasp. I noted, many pages ago,
that I had a talent for minutiae. So, when Justice Holmes
described law as a "rag-bag of details," it sounded right up
my alley. I thought I could combine my investigative talents
with my need for public performance and public appreciation.
My pal Jim Benson applied, too, and then invited me to
spend a month at his home in New York before going up to
Cambridge. We graduated in 1940, and spent August of that
summer raising hell all over Manhattan, while Germany
occupied Belgium, Luxembourg and the Netherlands. Ostensibly, Jim was going to help me drown my sorrows and pick
up the pieces of my sex life. Actually, there were an infinite

number of things he'd been itching to try, but he needed a companion. His parents hadn't approved of any of his previous companions and I seemed the perfect houseguest to present to the senior Bensons. I was, as Douglas had so cruelly put it, refined. I still had my head partially screwed on right; I'd graduated magna cum laude—all of this salved the Bensons' qualms and gave them leave to spend August at their home in Newport, while leaving the 72nd Street apartment to Jim and me. Mr. Benson was a manufacturer of trolley cars and was well known in the city. Jim felt no compunction at using his father's name whenever it could provide us with leverage into preferential places or out of scrapes.

I had fun to the point of dissipation, and I'll always be grateful to Jim for that month because without it I'd have languished in Grosse Pointe and wouldn't have gone to Harvard at all. We dated girls who slept under skylights in Greenwich Village, and we dated girls who went to Harlem in ermine and pearls. Jim managed a connection with Seventh Avenue and got our entire fall wardrobes for forty percent off, and we spent our savings at the Stork and 21. We trucked and praised Allah to the Big Apple, we got drunk on Macdougal Street; fifteen minutes later, rolled on Mott. We went to Coney and ate bologna on a roll, and we finished off several evenings up on 122nd Street, watching the bums piss on Grant's Tomb. I doubt that Oliver Wendell prepared for Harvard Law in the same manner, but for me it was Balm of Gilead. Except—given the fact that it *was* me, I felt rather guilty having all that fun when any genuinely principled person would have been languishing in Grosse Pointe, bereft at the loss of his raven-haired Valerie.

We left for Boston a week early and it was on the train, in the environs of Bridgeport, Connecticut, that Jim pulled out a list of names his mother had given him. At the top were the Boston Bancrofts—what Jim called "needle and thread" people. He had promised his mother to call them but he was unenthused. The Bancroft daughter was, he said, one of those "serious, mental people." I took that to mean a wallflower and was therefore surprised when I accompanied Jim to Sunday dinner at the Bancroft residence. Patricia was not a wallflower. She was attractive and, when not totally reserved, outspoken to the point of rudeness. She was much taken then, as now, with the verses of Edna St. Vincent Millay. She seemed old—nay, ancient—for twenty. Her older brother was infantile beside her, a big, bumbling boy who needed three chairs to sit down in: one for his derriere, one for his basketball arms and one for his Lincolnesque legs. Father Bancroft made no bones that the brains in the family skipped Gregory altogether and went directly to Patricia.

"We're in thimbles, Jay. What're you in?"

"Well, uh, trees, I guess."

"That's right. Michigan." He turned to Patricia. "You remember, Pat, Benson's family's in trams." He turned back to me. "Patricia, you'll find, is rather frequently in *the doldrums.*"

I would have liked Patricia better had she not been quite so glacial toward Jim. He said that we were anxious to "get into the ring" and asked her to help acquaint us with Boston's hot spots before she left for Vassar. She replied that she was *not a pugilist,* and was more familiar with Boston's museums and libraries. Father Bancroft overrode the ensuing chill by recounting his meeting with Paris Singer and Isadora Duncan in 1910. I knew it was an old, cherished story from the way he nursed it along. I hadn't an inkling that I would come to loathe every pause and nuance over the next twenty years.

It suddenly struck me as ironic that Father Bancroft had met Paris Singer. For no reason at all I began to run off at the mouth about a man I'd once known who had purchased an old Singer treadle for a woman named Cheeoh in a seaside shack near Vancouver. She would fritter (I said "fritter") away a month of evenings jabbing away with her thimble, forcing my friend to buy the old machine. He dismantled it and oiled it and brushed each part till it gleamed . . . They all looked askance and wondered what the point was. Was it too much wine causing this passionate harangue, or was it a lack of cultivation? Too long in the forest, this Michigan boy exposed glaringly rough edges. I paused and apologized for the pointlessness of the story and realized, as I have so many times since, that Winger Burns would rear up constantly, unexpectedly, pointlessly, till the end of my days.

In some ways, Patricia is very much like my mother. I recognized the similarity at our first meeting, and it frightened me. I was impressed by her essential isolation, her serious, mental pronouncements. I liked the distance she placed between herself and others. She seemed always to be smoldering, not with anger, certainly not with pent-up gaiety. It was a smoldering born of protest. They both of them vehemently objected to their placement on the planet in the first place, and the insinuation that they must participate in the abounding idiocy or perish. All of those qualities were endearing in my mother; they gave her the originality I so enjoyed. But in a twenty-year-old they were eerie, and I fled the Bancroft residence fully realizing, for the first time, why Mother had been unattached at twenty-three. Patricia came freighted with too many thorns. There was too much undergrowth to wade through. She already had an unfathomable Jang box. In the cab back to Cambridge, Jim turned to me and said:

"They're going to have to *buy* a mate for that one."

The judgment seemed harsh, and certainly precipitous. I reflected upon Miss Bancroft for a moment, but it was hard to pinpoint the problem. She was female without being feminine, too independent, finally, ever to bring your pipe and slippers without fear of bondage, too cynical ever to accept male affection without fear of chicanery. I worried that there might be a "Bancroft Purchase" in her future, and I fervently hoped not. It was unjust to relegate her to a Purchase just because she wasn't a pugilist. I was overcome with pangs of grief for the jovial Valerie as we crossed the bridge, and I thought no more on Patricia until after the war, five years later.

On December 12, 1941, I received a hysterical phone call from Mother:

"If *I* were a man I'd find me some Japs and kill them. What are *you* going to do?"

There was such noise and tumult surrounding me at the time of the call I could barely hear the question. Long lines had already formed at the recruiting office; no one had done an iota of work or talked of anything else since the seventh. If I wanted to wait a bit, strings could probably be pulled over the Christmas vacation and I might obtain a commission. It was Mother's suggestion and I don't know why she made it. Her lack of enthusiasm for the idea was palpable over the phone, so the suggestion was as rhetorical as the question. We were eight years away from Buena Vista then, but the next comment came as no surprise.

"Winger would want you to enlist, I think."

Yes, he would. He'd be proud to have me shinny up rather than wangle a commission. I enlisted in the army that week, went home for Christmas, and directly into basic training at Fort Benning in January. Mother and I spent Christmas alone that year; Father was with Mrs. Peterson in Montreal. He was with her almost constantly in those days; both of her sons were in the R.C.A.F., and she depended on Father's moral support. My father's reaction to F.D.R.'s declaration was at one with Mrs. Peterson's: it was about time the Yanks got in.

In March I entered Officer's Candidate School, and four months later Mother came to Fort Benning to watch me receive my commission. To my chagrin, she brought a photographer with her, from the Emerson Studios in Detroit, in the belief that there weren't any photographers in Georgia. She pinned the two gold bars on my shoulders and then tacked a rose-colored blanket to the wall behind me: a proper backdrop for a proper portrait of Second Lieutenant Rutherford. I was more fortunate than many of my colleagues who spent months waiting for action in London and Iceland. My outfit was sent to Algeria in the fall of '42, landing at Oran after dodging U-boats two-thirds of the way across the Atlantic. It was, I thought, a sensational way to begin. Five hundred troop and supply ships, escorted by some three hundred and fifty warships, made the massive invasion. The enormity of the numbers stirred my blood, and touched every man among us. We were fresh, young, vigorous gladiators and we felt the exhilaration one can only feel at the beginning, before our bodies were deprived and diseased, our bravery questionable, before the reality of Rommel, combat, casualty lists. We fought across North Africa through the spring of '43; it was in May, I think, when I received a letter from Mother. She'd heard from Seth Hilliard that Bob had been killed at Dieppe in August 1942. We had not kept up with the Hilliards beyond Christmas cards, and it seemed strange, after ten years, for them to write with such urgency. Apparently Elsie had found Bob's old books of wildflowers while disposing of his things, and they hurriedly sent off a note to Mother. Seth had closed the letter begging Mother to use every resource at hand to keep me out of the military. He said that Elsie was halfheartedly organizing Victory Gardens around Buena Vista, and she, too, urged Mother to pull whatever strings she could to assure my safety. It wouldn't be seen as lack of patriotism or courage. It was different, he said, for those of us who had only one son to lose.

By January 1944, I was Captain Rutherford, commanding two hundred and forty men. I lost ninety of them at Anzio, where we'd been sent with Mark Clark's Fifth Army. But at Cassino I led the remaining hundred and fifty out of an encirclement and was given a Silver Star.

In my opinion the Silver Stars given at Anzio are among the most tarnished awards of the war. By the end of it we had three thousand dead and eleven thousand wounded. In the middle of it I saw two soldiers crouched down on the beach behind a homemade barrier. All stones, shells, driftwood had long ago been used for this purpose; that part of the beach had been mined and was barren. I lifted my binoculars and was horrified to see that their barricade was a small wall of blown-off limbs. Naked arms and legs piled up without a shred of tattered uniform to tell the viewer where they came from, friend or foe, Allies or Axis.

Our devastated unit was dismantled, assembled again and flown to London to await the invasion of Normandy. We accomplished the "greatest amphibious assault ever attempted" on June 6, when four thousand ships, covered by eleven thousand airplanes, hurled across the Channel. I sailed from Weymouth with the U.S. First Division, landed at Omaha Beach and was introduced to the Normandy *bocage* country—the stiff, obstinate hedgerows, four feet high, centuries old, virtually impenetrable. On July 18 St.-Lô finally fell and we broke out of Normandy, into the Battle of France. At that point someone above—someone with extrasensory perception, perhaps—reasoned that I'd had enough. I was assigned to regimental headquarters with the Twenty-ninth Infantry and essentially shuffled papers until the end of the war.

I must say, in all honesty, the war had little lasting effect on me, adverse or beneficial. I didn't come home feeling that I'd wasted time, so I didn't scurry around doing so many of the things my buddies felt they had to do in order to make up for wasted time. I didn't ponder man's inhumanity to man (except in the heinous treatment of the Jews), because it seemed to me that Aeschylus and Sophocles had done all that before, to no avail. I was ashamed, for a year or two, of Hiroshima and Nagasaki, but even that shame was short-lived and I am reminded of it only sporadically, through photographs. The pictures, the mounds of extracted gold from Jewish teeth, the seared and mutilated Japanese at the first-aid stations are painful reminders, but one can always close the book or magazine and take a nap, if need be. I didn't consider our victory a matter of survival of the fittest, or purest, or even best. War games were just like any other games; success lay as much in chance, luck, speculation and opportunity as with skill. The reaction to the action was, too often, and at all levels, a case of temperament and personality. Decisions and methods were shot from the peculiar hips of Bradley and Patton as often as they were Pentagon-formulated or dictated by cartographers. And suffering, pain, death were just as horrible to witness in the brown bungalow in Onondaga as they were at Anzio, but at Anzio we had a reason for it. When I view today's yen and mark I'm not quite sure what it was.

The rush for stability and permanency in the form of a house and a wife and progeny escaped me, too. I recall flying out of London with men who wept at the thought of the row house in Baltimore, the farm in Wisconsin, while I was strangely rapt in thoughts of returning in some kinder, more civilized time when eggs were plentiful and the Dome of St. Paul's was reassembled. I didn't even feel a continuing rancor toward the Germans. They'd been cursed with Hitler, one of nature's more grotesque mistakes—there was little worse that one could wish them.

In 1864, Captain Oliver Wendell Holmes left the Twentieth Massachusetts Regiment and found his way back to Harvard Law School. I attempted to follow in his footsteps once again, but this time around I had lost all patience for the "rag-bag of details." I did not want to continue with law; I didn't feel like returning to Mother's new, small house; I was too tired to get on the merry-go-round of dating: phoning, teasing, beguiling, and then the bother of ticket reservations, trinkets, posies, perfumes, Barton's chocolates. I was enervated at the very thought of the courting process, though I longed, more than anything else, for a comfortable female companion. Mother put it down to "battle fatigue," but I knew that it was my own intrinsic Rutherford fatigue. It had plagued me, and I had wrestled with it manfully, since Buena Vista. I had feared, for nearly fifteen years, that without will-ful, furious activity I would somehow disintegrate mentally. I would waft through life unattached, like so much goose down on the wind. And, with my brain disconnected from meaningful thought, and my limbs disconnected from pur-poseful employment, I would emerge a blithering fool, a hulking piece of social dross. You would find me, but for the parsimony of my ancestor, deep in the heart of the welfare rolls, a living travesty of the Puritan ethic. What I *did* want is what I've always wanted; I want it to this day. I shall make the infantile, preposterous confession here and now. I wanted to be fourteen again, in the bucolic Rockies, perched atop some ancient boulder, with Winger by my side. Second best, I wanted to be twenty-one again, in the Onon-daga bungalow, slumbering under a patchwork quilt, with Valerie by my side. Insane, implausible desires for a man with an I.Q. of 160, a hero at Anzio, recipient of a Silver Star. Not so implausible, perhaps, for a survivor.

I wandered around Cambridge for weeks, unable to settle down to the routine of study, strangely unable to move my hand and commit the professors' words to the note paper in front of me. I played a bit of billiards, I saw a double feature nearly every day, I drove to Provincetown and walked the shoreline most weekends. On a freezing Sunday afternoon in February 1946, I went to Fenway Court to have a look at Mrs. Gardner's pictures. I felt lost, forlorn, empty-headed, and the blizzard without had left me hunched and quaking. Nature, deploring the vacuum in my mind, led me directly to Rembrandt's *Storm on the Sea of Galilee,* and consequently to Patricia Bancroft, who was studying the master's brush-strokes with a magnifying glass.

"Excuse me. Aren't you—you're Pat Bancroft, aren't you?"

"Yes, I am."

"Jim Benson, five years ago—"

"Yes, I remember. You knew a man who bought a Singer treadle for a Jap."

"That's right."

She looked me over carefully, apparently appalled at what she saw.

"Did you know that Berenson called her The Serpent of the Charles?"

"Who?"

"Isabella Gardner."

"No . . ."

"You look absolutely awful. Where were you?"

"Africa. Anzio. Normandy."

"You must have seen a great deal of dying."

"Well, yes. But it loses its effect after a while, you know. I mean death. Repetitious death is tedious."

"My, my, my. Who actually said that?"

"What?"

"Repetitious death is tedious."

"Jesus, I don't know. I thought I did, just now."

"I'll look it up in Bartlett's, when I get home. Are you back at Harvard Law?"

"Halfheartedly. I seem to be looking for some sort of emancipation. *From* what, or *for* what, I don't seem to know."

"That sounds familiar. I mean, I'm acquainted with that. Why don't you come home with me for a few days and we'll see if we can't straighten it out. *In the bosom of the family,* as they say."

She wanted, I think, to play the Duchess of Alba to somebody's Goya, but instead she got me. I just happened to surface at the right time and place. As a full-fledged art historian, and a Brahmin to boot, she had sought to have her fling with any number of grubby artists along the Eastern seaboard. But it hadn't turned out quite like the Duchess and Goya romping in the Escorial. It had been grubby, and she had been expected to poach up eggs the morning after, scour the grease from the pans at noon, run for wine and cheese at night, pay for all of it herself. And she had felt them ignorant, truly uninformed, most of them, of the world beyond the loft. She found, to my utter amazement, a certain *machismo* attached to my dubious heritage—the sawdust millionaire, the Rape of Michigan, the amputation, the timid mother, the virile Winger, the tragic loss of Valerie, the goddamned Silver Star. She smoked too much, even then, and was able to drink me under the table, even then. She was not quite intact mentally, and when I probed for the reason I was met with "Scrub," a poem by Edna St. Vincent Millay:

If I grow bitterly,
Like a gnarled and stunted tree,
Bearing harshly of my youth
Puckered fruit that sears the mouth;
If I make of my drawn boughs
An inhospitable house,
Out of which I never pry
Towards the water and the sky,
Under which I stand and hide
And hear the day go by outside;
It is that a wind too strong
Bent my back when I was young,
It is that I fear the rain
Lest it blister me again.

The wind was an uncle named Harvey, her mother's brother, who had attempted to seduce Patricia over a three-month period one summer at Wellfleet. She was ten years old, she thought him vile, but nevertheless she fled his advances across the dunes for three months rather than tell her mother. He was clumsy and gauche—mercifully, he did not succeed. At twenty-five, Pat felt more pity for him than blame. However, she had never since been able to look her mother straight in the eye, or to accept from her mother advice on sexual matters, or to find credible her mother's endless boasts about that side of the family, and Harvey in particular. The constant strain between the two was unfair to Mother Bancroft, for she had no inkling of her brother's aberration. They flail about, the two of them, to this very day, with Mother Bancroft confused and perplexed at Pat's distant image, and Pat remorseful and repentant, but the latter, unfortunately, only to me.

"Listen," I said. "I'll match blisters with you any day."

I told her much of what I've told here in these pages. We related to each other, and I was immensely pleased that there was no need for posies and trinkets. With my inheritance from trees, and hers from thimbles, we decided to emancipate ourselves from the world, march to our own drummer, tie the knot to each other and hope for the best. It has turned out, in the matching of blisters, that mine tends to fester.more than Pat's, and I find more solace in Demerol than alcohol. And, rather than playing Alba to my Goya, she has played, all too frequently over the years, nursemaid to my invalid.

XXXII

From the beginning, Grosse Pointe was not quite big enough for these two women, my mother and my wife. I am more than partially to blame, but I shall come to that sequentially.

Though she thought herself a free spirit, Pat could never really abide my mother's ever-growing lack of conformity. She was charmed by my father and she was considerably taken with Mrs. Peterson, who was persistently cheerful and notably unhampered by ancestral ghosts. She even found Josh

Whitcomb to be a rather pleasant old gaffer in his bumbling way. She was wont to admire those historical women who had burned the candle at both ends (Hamilton with Nelson, Sand with Chopin, Alba with Goya), but my mother's affair with Winger was too close to home, too close for comfort. She managed fairly well in crowds, but whenever she was alone with Mother the past reared up like a wedge between them. The continual outpouring of lovelorn poems offended, too; it seemed to Patricia that a woman now in her fifties should leave off with that libidinous propensity. Additionally, Pat did not like my mother's new house. It was the gatehouse of an old Jefferson Avenue estate, a Gothic stone affair which Mother purchased when I first left for Harvard. It was cold and damp, smack up against the road; the rumble of traffic at nine and again at five was unbearable. Worse, the great house had been torn down and there now stood on that property fifteen "Cape Cod Bungalows." Those two- and three-car families had, of course, to pass Mother's gatehouse fifty times a day, with their sheepdogs and mewling children hanging off the back of their station wagons. Mother's room, located in the big, round turret, was called by Pat "the garret."

Pat also deplored my mother's disdain of fashion, and felt special contempt for Mother's choice of shoes. My mother thought women's shoes were designed with singular lack of regard for the shape of the human foot. She began wearing Murray's Space Shoes around 1950, those large, molded, individually cast shoes that made a woman appear to pad about rather than walk. When Mother shopped, rather than carry a shopping bag like everyone else, she strapped on a backpack and, with her load to the stern, hunched down Kercheval to forage for herself—there were no servants at the gatehouse. (Consequently, there was quite a lot of dirt.) Pat would see Mother lunging down the avenue in her molded shoes, slightly stooped under the weight of the backpack, and Pat would turn around and come home rather than risk a public meeting. After one year in Grosse Pointe, Pat's judgment was that Mother lived within an inch of a return, and conclusive, trip to The Oaks.

My mother's poetry found its way to print two or three times a year, which eventually caused her to exchange her Grosse Pointe friends for a small group of Detroit troubadours. They came to the gatehouse most weekends, they were considerably younger than Mother, and they tended to bring along, under their coats, recordings of Lenny Bruce. They were always hungry, and Pat felt that in their voracious gobbling up of whole hams each weekend they were shamefully taking advantage of Mother. However, Mother felt that it was easier to be generous with whole hams than it was with one's time and one's *self*. The old Grosse Pointe friends, of whom Pat approved, had required a great deal of time and self.

Some of Mother's friends had stayed married, and continued to carry in their billfolds photographs of their children and grandchildren, which they displayed at the drop of a hat. But Mother found these women to harbor grievances aplenty: after attending a twenty-fifth-anniversary party for one of them she commented, "Behind every silver anniversary you can find at least *one* martyr." Some women had divorced and then gone to great lengths to prepare themselves for new onslaughts at the Yacht Club. They dieted and exercised, sent to New York for corsets, Gaylord Hauser for creams. One woman's vanity was so great, and her wealth so abundant, that the clerks at Hubbard's actually snipped out the size-12 labels from her clothing and replaced them with size 10. The woman was none the wiser; she preened and, insulted by the offerings of size 12's at other stores, purchased all of her clothing at Hubbard's.

Very often these women used my mother as chaperon—two of them would go to a charity ball or a concert, ostensibly for either social or cultural reasons. But Mother frequently found herself left behind at the end of the evening while

the other woman rendezvoused with some new aging Gala-
had. Mother resented being used, and because she failed to
phone and follow up the outcome of these flirtations, it was
thought that she didn't genuinely care. Indeed, she didn't.
Her Grosse Pointe friends were gradually, firmly, politely put
aside. She tried doing charity work for a period, and attached
herself to one of those agencies that provide remedial-reading
help to adults attending night school. After a year of that
she burst into our living room one evening near hysteria.

"You know what I am? I'm goddamned Lady Bountiful
parading in the slums! *I will not do it!*"

At Christmas, in 1950, I gave Mother a set of oil paints
and she assiduously applied herself to the painting of many,
many Chianti bottles, loaves of French bread, bowls of Con-
cord grapes. She painted outdoors, in her gooseberry garden
in summer, and indoors, in her garret, in winter. She painted
badly; her efforts were a constant embarrassment to Pat. But
Pat is one of those people who know so much about art they
think it presumptuous for ordinary mortals to lift a brush.
The only successful work (deemed so even by Pat) was a
head of Winger, done from memory. It surprised both of
us in its unromantic, unembroidered excellence. I was, quite
honestly, shocked at the perfect execution of the smiling eyes,
the scar, the curly hair, the over-all air of discontent.

Together, Pat and I read Mother's poems, we hypocriti-
cally admired her paintings, we gave her jewelry, books, recordings, soaps, scarves, perfumes, several pieces of Steuben
glass. We encouraged the making of gooseberry jam. We took
her with us on occasional vacations, accompanied her to the
theater, the opera and an endless round of parties whenever
we all went to New York. But now we come to my own
mea culpa. Even after we had presented Mother with Deborah, and were ourselves ensconced in the joys and pains of
child rearing, I couldn't extricate myself from the past. I
excused myself from the family unit and attended Mother
nearly every day. I did this partially because I found the con-

tinual company of an infant more than a little nerve-wracking, partially because Pat changed perceptibly after the birth of Deb. She became rather matronly, and wore unattractive shirtwaist dresses whose pockets bulged with cotton balls. And she dutifully kept a log, recording Deb's urine, stools and ounces of formula. But mostly I scurried to Mother because I was more comfortable with her than I was with anyone else. We could sit in her gatehouse and talk, or not talk. I was fascinated, more and more as I grew older, by her sensitivity, her awareness, the air of staunch *endurance* which clung, rather paradoxically, to her frail being. She had paid her dues, risked everything for that summer with Winger— the full proportions of the risk strike me even now as enormously hazardous. Where would we, we of all people, have turned if disinherited? We hadn't between us a single useful skill. But more to the point, we had paid some dues together; rejoiced together at finding Winger, suffered together at losing him. And in our sharing of that, and all the intimacies it encompassed, Patricia was unfortunately shut out. She stood on the periphery of our mingled memories, apart from the bond of our mutual experience, outside the realm of our loss. She, Pat, came to shudder and cringe at our secret, collaborative affinity for Winger, the past, *what might have been.*

I had not then even noticed my wing-back chair, and when the details of living began to encroach upon my freedom, I went, lickety-split, to the gatehouse. Patricia nagged, Debbie bawled, nurses were hired and fired, the eaves fell off, the bills were due, the gardener thieved, the ceiling leaked—lickety-split to the gatehouse for tea and talk, an unforgettable introduction to Lenny Bruce, a passing acquaintance with Ferlinghetti.

And the Bancrofts came. Mother, father, Gregory. They came bearing large tin boxes of English biscuits from Fortnum and Mason's. It seemed to me they never left. Gregory's rubber limbs dangled off three chairs at a time; it was amazing how many times Father Bancroft initiated a conversation with the story of Singer and Duncan in 1910. Mother Bancroft reported regularly on the doings of Uncle Harvey, whereupon Pat clutched Deb to her bosom and ran to the nursery, as if the mere mention of Harvey's name would taint the air and cause Deb some future traumatic affliction. They wondered why I didn't "go to business"—why I didn't at least *pretend* to go to business. They wondered, with morbid curiosity, why I went to the gatehouse, what it was that drew me so magnetically to the garret. Sometimes it was my affinity for *what might have been,* sometimes it was the thieving gardener; when the Bancrofts were there it was simply them. When they weren't there, they were on the phone. The conversations were ludicrous. A three-minute discussion of what time it was in Boston as opposed to what time it was in Detroit, a three-minute discussion of Deb's urine, stools and formula, a three-minute musing on the part of Father Bancroft:

"That all sounds great, Pat. Now, tell me, what's Jay doing with himself these days?"

As the years passed, my mother's idiosyncrasies and my own lack of meaningful employment removed us from the people we knew, removed us even from Father and Josh Whitcomb. Though those two never attempted anything "meaningful," they seemed always to be engaged in some activity, bustling around the world, busy as ants. The more we felt ostracized, the more insular we became. The reproach from without only served to enforce the rapport between Mother and me. By the time Debbie was two, Patricia had unconsciously aligned herself with my father. They stood off to the side, audibly mumbling, visibly jealous, mutually scornful of Winger Burns, and nauseated at the very mention of the summer of '32.

Mother became alarmed at the obvious schism in my marriage and tried, rather tepidly, to persuade me to spend more time with Pat. But Pat was encumbered with Debbie. And the gamut of my intervals with Debbie ran from A to B. She either peed on my lap or spat up on my shoulder. Patricia's pre-dinner martini first expanded to two, then three. She finally defined my relationship with my mother as "unnatural"—a word whose connotations sent me directly up the wall.

"What the hell do you *do* in that gatehouse?"

"It varies."

"How much can you mine from one measly summer? Surely it's an empty vessel by now. I think you hold hands and wear shrouds and pay homage to that head of Winger."

One day, when I attempted to take Deb with me, Patricia refused to let her go. She cursed the gatehouse, called it a den of iniquity, called Mother the devil incarnate. I responded with a left hook to the jaw. I left Pat whimpering on the floor, retrieved my daughter from the nursery and went to visit my mother. When I returned, Patricia met me with a request for a divorce. Had she been angry, had she showered me with scathing insults, I would have acquiesced immediately, for those were younger years and I was easily ignited. But she sat quietly on her chair at her dressing table, she was quite literally bruised and battered, and her reasoned, weary summation of our state cut me to the core.

"Perhaps we deserve what we've got. We married indecisively, more out of sloth than passion. That sort of dishonesty is never without retribution."

Her words were shattering; I was plunged into despair, overwhelmed with feelings of abject failure. I embraced her, and cried, and begged her not to leave. She was somewhat diverted by my reaction, but we were more diverted, all of us, by the deaths, in October 1958, of my father and Josh Whitcomb.

In 1949 Josh Whitcomb had been instrumental (to the tune of $100,000) in forming the Larrimore Flying Academy in Oakland County. He got such a bang out of the plans, the planes—he was so enamored of the dashing, daring pilots that he himself learned to fly. In 1950 my father shelled out five hundred dollars for lessons, while Josh assured all of us that this sum was a rock-bottom discount price for friends only. The two became proficient in the cockpit, and eventually flew as far as Montreal, where doughty little Mrs. Peterson waited, expectantly, on the runway. When their Piper Cub crashed over Traverse City, Michigan, they were killed instantly. My father's pilot's and driver's licenses showed the address at the Tower House. When the investigators got no answer there, they went back to his billfold and found a receipt from a florist in Detroit. Father had, two weeks earlier, sent a dozen carnations to Mrs. Peterson. So she was the first notified, then Mother, then me. After the funeral several of us, including Mrs. Peterson, went to Mother's gatehouse for coffee, and it was there that I made what I now consider a crucial mistake.

Mrs. Peterson surprised us with the news that my father's sister was living in Toledo, and should be notified. In 1916, when he married Mother, he told her that his sister had fled Toledo shortly before he did, in an effort to escape the stigma of their father's notorious stock swindle. They had not kept contact and Mother could vouch that, for the period 1916–1932, he never once mentioned her. It was not until he was sixty-seven, the year before he died, that he told Mrs. Peterson about his sister. She had never left Toledo; she had married a young Italian boy immediately after graduation from high school. Her name was Bertha Castiglione. When I called I thought her inordinately emotional—more at having found a nephew than at having lost an unknown brother. She wept and wailed and begged me to come to Toledo with my wife and daughter. I promised that I would; I hung up and, inexplicably, went directly to Mother and asked her to accompany me. Pat, who was fonder of my father than either my mother or I, stood idly by while we prepared for the trip. I thought she would find my aunt a bore. The visit was obligatory and bound to be wearing; I wanted to spare her that at the time. She, for her part, thought I did not want to be alone with her for several hours in the car. She had felt herself, for ten years by then, to be a losing competitor in the battle for my affections. The reunion with my Aunt Bertha proved to be Patsy's last straw.

If I have slighted my father thus far in this chronicle, it is because I know very little about him. My Aunt Bertha, at sixty-four, had not seen him in thirty-eight years, yet Toledo is but a two-hour drive from Grosse Pointe. She sat with Mother and me for an afternoon, above the little fruit market that she and her husband still operated, amidst rather garish color portraits of her sixteen grandchildren, and she told us the tale of the stock swindle. I include it here, in hopes that it is not too late to dull the edge of that brazen negotiation on the porch at Mackinac. Much as I would like to digress further, I will only say that it did not dull the edge for me.

They had been wealthy until 1906 and then, without explanation or warning, a bailiff came and took away all of the furniture. The three servants packed and left in a huff; a month later their mother abdicated all responsibility and left for parts unknown. During the following three ignominious years, they continued to live in the vast, ornate house, eventually using only four rooms. The children scrimped and scrounged, and watched their father become an alcoholic. Bertha lingered on this point. He was not a garrulous, starcrossed, carousing alcoholic, but rather a monastic, mendacious, desolate drunk. The two children, with their earnings from after-school jobs, purchased a new icebox. A man came to the door late one night and took the icebox in exchange for a case of whiskey. Their father had a set of antique, nacre-handled pistols. These, too, were silently passed to the shadowy man at the door. There were violent arguments between my father and his father; Bertha watched them struggle once, with a butcher knife hanging in the balance—and watched her bedroom bureau go to the man at the door the same evening. In 1909, when Bertha was sixteen and my father twenty, my father awakened in the middle of the night to the sound of hammering and creaking hinges. The bedroom door was solid walnut, the border decoration was handcarved. The house was barren—there was nothing left to sell. The crazed, sotted man paid no attention to my father's pleas. The man at the door was waiting with a case of whiskey and my father slept, that night, in a doorless room. The following morning he was gone, leaving Bertha to marry the son of her family's greengrocer, Joseph Castiglione.

"Oh," she said, "he was *handsome!* He looked like Douglas Fairbanks."

And she took my mother's hand.

"Was he kind to you? Were you happy?"

My mother smiled at her, not unpleasantly, but could make no reply. I heaved a sigh and waved at the bank of portraits on the piano.

"All in all, Bertha, I think you came off slightly better with your greengrocer."

XXXIII

I returned from Toledo to find this man named Lawrence Motta sitting in my living room with Pat. The period 1958–1960 was a difficult time for us, and I don't wish to go into the details of it here. He was, I thought, even more effete than I am, but that, of course, is my opinion. He ran a large, successful art gallery in the Penobscot Building (the building that is presently called something else). I think of him rarely now—only at Christmas when we move the Vlaminck and the two Redons to make room for the tree. All three pictures were purchased from him. They met somewhere for lunch twice a week; she was generally home by three-thirty when Deb returned from school. She sashayed in, relaxed and unrepentant. I must say, there was a notable lack of guilt surrounding the whole thing. Someone once said, "All animals, but woman, are sad after coitus." Or, "After orgasm all animals are sad, save woman." Or something like that. I'll have to look it up in Bartlett's one of these days.

I continued visiting the gatehouse during that period, but Mother's eccentricity began to get on my nerves. I was gradually coming to value such mundane things as meals at the right time, alarm clocks, a regulated laundry, women who didn't listen to Lenny Bruce, women who stayed home between the hours of twelve and three-thirty. In turn, these new inclinations got on Mother's nerves. She said, a few months before her death, that I had become impossibly finicky—"pristine," I think, is the word she used.

My mother died in 1960, quietly, in her sleep, after a ten-day bout with pneumonia. She was to be buried in the family plot at Acacia Cemetery, on Thirteen Mile Road; however, we soon discovered there was no room in the family plot. We had been told there were two places left, one directly above my Grandmother MacAllister and one above my Grandfather MacAllister. My father's casket was placed, perhaps fittingly, on top of Grandmother, but when the diggers opened the ground they found no available space above Grandfather. So mother was buried a half-mile away, by herself.

LAURA MACALLISTER RUTHERFORD
1892–1960

That is all the headstone says. Each time I visit the cemetery I am struck anew by how little one discerns from gravestones.

Patricia came with me to empty the gatehouse. I was all set to throw out the cheese cutter, meat thermometer, rolling pin, wire whisk, tea caddie, potholders, the two hand-tooled bookmarks. But Patricia, whose Jang box continues unfathomable, lugged it all home and stored it in our attic. This paraphernalia, too, would fit under the label "International

Swindlers I Have Known." I still think it was shitty of him to sneak out like that. Like clockwork, Pat returned to the fold, never to see Lawrence Motta again. Rumor has it that he was heartbroken and moved his gallery, lock, stock, and Brancusi, to Chicago. I like to think the better man won— he really was milquetoast personified, but again, you'll have to take my word for it. Certainly, he had no Silver Star to recommend him. I'm not entirely sure just what it was they found in each other; I do know that, together, they both hated poor old Thomson's birches. He called them "execrable." Indeed, I have a multitude of things for which to forgive him.

So we bumble along, Patsy and me, Saturday night, Sunday morning, seven days a week, fitfully sparring, still occasionally unable to settle for what we got. She is thought to be indispensable down at the Art Institute, and I, of course, have, first, my omnivorous reading. (I like Nabokov very much. I like his enigmatic smile. I don't know what he's up to half the time, but the half of the time that I *do* know, he is *like wow*, as Deb says.) I also have, from year to year, my various projects. We are rather droll about my projects, for good reason. I got off my Yousef Karsh kick and then I went into my hi-fi kick and then I struggled in the garden with tuberous begonias. I messed, in my basement, in January, with sphagnum and vermiculite; I handled the hairy little tubers with kid gloves. I watered, fertilized, supervised their daily drainage. Tubers are very strong-willed. They either will or they won't, and for me they didn't. Then Ed Humboldt got me involved in fund raising. He is expected, down there at G.M., to take a vigorous hand in the United Fund every year. I ran around all the Pointes with my sermon and leaflets, gave parties, even got into the homes of those few mafiosi who live on Lake Shore Road. I raise money for the Detroit Zoo in the same manner, running around the Pointes calling wolf once a year. I've found, much to my dismay, that people are generally inclined to give more to hungry elephants than hungry minorities. (Elephants, by the way, are veritable shit machines. Judy, my favorite, is only half grown but eats a bale of hay, twenty loaves of bread, thirty pounds of fruit and vegetables and a supplemental quart of grain every day.)

I sit on a committee that's been talking about cleaning up Belle Isle for three years now. We discovered, at our last meeting, that none of us had been there in the past three years, and we passed a resolution to go. We went, and were angered at the heaps of litter, but as far as I could see nobody bothered to pick anything up. We keep trying to organize the Detroit high school kids and have them do it, but our telephone negotiations have not proved successful. And we're all afraid to go down to Pershing, Central, MacKenzie, and ask them face to face. We are currently in search of a black committee member in hopes that he wouldn't be afraid to approach the kids. However, in my limited experience with blacks I've found that, once they attain the status of committee member, they don't much care to spend their Saturdays picking up other people's trash. So I think we're going to come a cropper on that one, too, but in the meantime Nellie Humboldt always brings a fine array of French pastries to the meetings, and it gets me out of the chair.

I can't seem to maintain an interest in the Red Wings since Gordie Howe retired. I'm certain I won't see the likes of No. 9 again in my lifetime. I do continue to keep tabs on our old Tigers. Like my mother, I've always admired athletic prowess, and I admire it even more when the team is past its prime. Our old Tigers display an amazing amount of chutzpah. (Deb threw this word at me recently, and was surprised to learn that I picked it up years ago from Lenny Bruce. Which caused my stock to rise a point or two in her estimation.) A couple of years ago I decided to do something for the kids who live down around the Eastern Market. I spent a summer building a fort for them, designed it, bought the wood and shingles, did all the carpentry myself. Ed insisted they'd tear it down—they wouldn't play in whitey's fort. Ed was wrong. They are less willful than the hairy tubers and their gratitude was boundless. I sometimes wish I could look forward to retirement at sixty-five, as Ed does, but, having taken an early one at twenty-eight, I shall miss out on that ceremony. I try to console myself by thinking that I don't really need another watch anyway.

And every four years I lament the people's choice of President.

Pat and I try to go to Holland, Michigan, for the tulip festival every spring. We spend a few days walking around Lake Macatawa and then, usually around the latter part of May, we experience our annual spiritual exhaustion with each other. This phenomenon began to occur about six years ago, when she took a letter opener down the wing of my wingback chair. And I, heeding the Surgeon General's warning, threw a whole carton of her smokes into the incinerator.

"Why don't you fish or cut bait?" said she.

"Why don't you try growing up?" said I.

I went to London for a month (while my chair was being repaired), and have done so regularly each spring since 1967. I love the city; eggs are plentiful, the Dome of St. Paul's is reassembled, and I:

> Go down to Kew in lilac-time,
>   in lilac-time, in lilac-time;
> Go down to Kew in lilac-time (it isn't far from London!)

Patricia stays home. There are not enough cities in all the world to satisfactorily divert her springtime angst. I'm rejuvenated when I come home in June, and I remain so until July 1. Then I have my Most Irrational Day: I visit Mother's grave; I try not to have Winger paged at the Amberley.

I pass the old gatehouse now and then—that part of Jefferson is slowly going to seed. The gatehouse has changed hands several times and is now inhabited by a large commune of young people. Deb and Christo were invited there just last week, and reported that my mother's gooseberry plants have been replaced with clumps of cannabis.

Yesterday, I made my reservations for London. Douglas Clark is there again, working on a movie about Mary, Queen of Scots.

Dear Red,

I am exposing this corrupt, Catholic whore once and for all. I wonder why we continue to dally with her when, clearly, Lizzie was born with some gray matter, and Mary was born with nought but a crotch. The costumes are *magniff*. Let's meet for dinner in Soho and chew the baby fat, as we do.

But, oh, I want to go back to Buena Vista! Time's winged chariot has left me now with bifocals that make me trip and step down when there isn't a stair; I awaken once a week with a muscular cramp in my shoulder to which I apply swabs of hot, pungent Heet, thereby stinking up my pajamas, the sheets, the whole second floor of the house. The great banks of clouds over the Great Lakes cause a dampness which stiffens my joints—my fingers are often rigid till noon. My feasts have become truly immovable. No amount of bran or prunes will dislodge my bowels, and I dread the insertion of glycerin suppositories. They must be kept, these gelatinous bullets, in the refrigerator. The jar is handed to me by Elise, the keeper of the kitchen, who's no spring chicken herself, but still she delights in the humiliating hand-over. She wears her crooked smile; she thrusts the jar forward with that special vengeance reserved for servant and master. Up *yours*, Monsieur Ruzzerford! After something like moussaka or spanakopitta my gastric acids run amok. The ulcer flares up and I must nourish myself with cottage cheese (creamed, small curd) and custard—a diet severely limited to the secreted fluids in the mammary glands of a cow. I am, we agree, the most rapidly deteriorating man in Grosse Pointe. I try not to exaggerate my discomfort because sixty is around the corner and, as everybody knows, it can only get worse.

I want to go back to Buena Vista, not, I think, to link arms with my youth, or to find our old haunts, or to communicate with the dead, but rather to confirm that it is there, that it exists for others as a mere magic resort, rather than a punctured dream or a geographical extremity. I should like to verify that my booby trap of a memory has served me correctly, if indeed painfully. I ache to see just once again Acorn and Pinto, the Seven Sisters, pink Corydalis, Bobby Hilliard's Goose Tansy.

Oh, my God, I want to go back to Buena Vista! I want to take my mother's earthly remains and bury them high in the mountains. I think her bones do not rest peaceably out there on Thirteen Mile Road. She had in her blood lines the Rape of Michigan; I have a nagging suspicion that the earth, like our polluted air, bears a grudge and continually agitates its worst offenders. I wouldn't choose Elizabeth, that belching, dyspeptic old bitch, but rather Binnie, where she laughed, and loved, and went to bed with Winger's laurel in her hair. I would fly this time, Air Canada, across the plains, accompanying her coffin to its final resting place. And I would tell her, as I never could in life, that I've recalled, many times, the observation she made on the floor at Timberline.

"I think the first thing we must do if we're ever to walk abroad with peace in our hearts, the first thing we must do is learn to forgive our parents."

She was wrong to equate the two. I have not succeeded at the former, as the Demerol and cottage cheese (creamed, small curd) will attest. But I forgave her a long, long time ago.

A NOTE ON THE TYPE

The text of this book was set in ELECTRA, a Linotype face designed by W. A. Dwiggins (1880–1956), who was responsible for so much that is good in contemporary book design. Although much of his early work was in advertising and he was the author of the standard volume *Layout in Advertising*, Mr. Dwiggins later devoted his prolific talents to book typography and type design and worked with great distinction in both fields. In addition to his designs for Electra, he created the Metro, Caledonia, and Eldorado series of type faces, as well as a number of experimental cuttings that have never been issued commercially.

Electra cannot be classified as either modern or old-style. It is not based on any historical model, nor does it echo a particular period or style. It avoids the extreme contrast between thick and thin elements that marks most modern faces and attempts to give a feeling of fluidity, power, and speed.

Composed, printed and bound by The Book Press, Brattleboro, Vt.
Typography and binding design by Camilla Filancia